Sl

the Defiler

CELTIC WARRIOR AND son of the Sessair tribe, Sláine Mac Roth, learns the secret murderous scheme of the evil Slough Feg to destroy his tribe. Desperate to thwart these plans and save his people, Sláine must journey to the dangerous Otherworld of the Sidhe on a quest to retrieve a series of powerful magical items including the Cauldron of Rebirth, a gift fit for a High King. Will Sláine and his trusted companion Ukko the dwarf be able to survive the perils of the Otherworld and return victorious to stop Slough Feg before it's too late? Only then can Sláine claim his place at the forefront of his people, redeemed.

More Sláine from Black Flame

SLÁINE THE EXILE

Sláine created by
Pat Mills & Angela Kincaid.

Sláine the Defiler

The Lay of Sláine Mac Roth Book Two

By

Steven Savile

For David Gemmell

Who showed us that there is room in the world for heroes

A Black Flame Publication
www.blackflame.com
blackflame@games-workshop.co.uk

First published in 2007 by BL Publishing, Games Workshop Ltd., Willow Road, Nottingham NG7 2WS, UK.

Distributed in the US by Simon & Schuster, 1230 Avenue of the Americas, New York, NY 10020, USA.

10 9 8 7 6 5 4 3 2 1

Cover illustration by Max Bertolini.

ISBN 13: 978 1 84416 493 6
ISBN 10: 1 84416 493 4

A CIP record for this book is available from the British Library.

One
The Harper of the Storms

"THAT, MY UGLY little friend, is the sweet smell of freedom," Sláine said. Breathing deeply, he let out a contented sigh as he threw his arms wide to embrace the countless fragrances of the Earth Mother.

"Gah! Sláine, my warped friend, only in your bumpkin-like brain does freedom stink of cow turds." Ukko muttered as he made a show of covering his nose with a dirty hand.

"There's nothing wrong with a big steaming pile of dung," Sláine said, "it is Danu at her most natural."

The dwarf shook his head in despair. "If natural means fragrant I won't argue with you, big man."

"I would have thought you, of all people, would love that smell, Ukko," Sláine sniffed. "If my nose doesn't deceive me I'd say it is pure bull dung, not cow turd."

"Oh, please stop talking to me. Pretty please," Ukko wheedled, falling to his knees, hands clasped together in mocking prayer. "I am begging you, Sláine. My head is going to explode. There are too many jokes in there right now. I swear keep talking and it is going to go boom, brains everywhere. You wouldn't want that would you? Oh, no, then where would you be, eh?"

Sláine stopped a moment, appearing to mull it over. "Well, I would still be here, but you on the other hand..." He let his words trail off as he spread his hands wide as though to say he had no idea where Ukko would be but maybe that wouldn't be such a bad thing.

Ukko sniffed. "You are a bad man, Sláine Mac Roth. A bad, bad man." Ukko jumped up to his feet and stomped away, kicking at one of the stones that pocked the old road. It skittered away into the briar hedge disturbing a crow. The bird cawed aggressively as it circled above their heads. Ukko flapped his hands, waving it away.

Ten paces down the road, Ukko turned to look back at him. "Just hurry up would you? The sooner we get to civilisation the sooner I can take my exploding head out on some fat-thighed lovely."

"And you think *I* am a bad man?" Sláine rolled his eyes and followed Ukko.

It was good to be on the open road again, out of the oppressive Forest of Dardun, even if it meant they were a little closer to Murias and the inevitable confrontation that going home promised. After the animals had retreated from Danu's cave the sense of isolation and loss had been almost overpowering. Sláine had remained in the cave's mouth for hours, unmoving as he stared at the denuded branches and the dirt. He couldn't explain the sudden isolation he felt to Ukko. The dwarf wouldn't have understood, or even cared. He left the cave humbled. He left the wood determined.

Dardun loomed like some vile spectre behind them. The great forest was immense, scores of miles deep and wide, twisted roots bulging out of the earth where they had leeched every ounce of nutrient out of the soil and begun to spread in the desperate search for succour. It had taken the pair of them weeks to navigate the perils of Dardun. And Sláine was in no doubt that it was perilous – a forest, a normal, healthy forest was a living thing but with the animals scattered Dardun was no living forest. It had been stripped back to its skeletal frame, revealing its diseased core.

Sláine hurried to catch up with the dwarf.

When he reached him, Ukko was hunched over a small white shrine dedicated to Danu. There was a tiny font in front of the white stone statue and the runt was scooping water greedily into his mouth. He looked up, drooling.

"Aren't you going to drink?"

Sláine shook his head. "Drink from a bird bath? You do know what that white stuff is, don't you?"

"The sweet taste of dung, of course. You take all the fun out of life, Sláine, I hope you know that."

Sláine stretched, working the kinks out of his muscles.

The elongated shadows cast by withered branches reached down the road as though the forest itself was trying to claw them back into its cankerous heart. The road unwinding before the pair of them was not that much more inviting, truth be told. The taint of the Sourlands had crept north during his prolonged exile, reaching out beyond Dardun into what had once been lush fields and farmland. Five years, six, seven, the way the world had changed in that short time those few years might as well have been a lifetime. In the world he had grown up in Cullen of the Wide Mouth had been the biggest evil he could imagine. Cullen. The memory of their innocent loathings made him want to laugh now.

Evil had come into his world.

True evil, bearing skull swords and stinking of sloughed skin. The man Sláine had become had been forged on the steel of those self same swords. He wasn't the boy he had been when Grudnew cast him out, feckless and reckless. He was a survivor. A warrior.

Ukko wiped the water from his mouth. "Come on then, let's see if we can't find a warm bed for the night."

"Finally some sense comes out of those flapping lips."

They trudged on, the makeshift road taking them through a cornfield. The heads were blackened and blighted where they had wasted. He reached out and snapped off one. It was riddled with bloated white maggots. He cast it aside. Deeper into the field there were some golden sheaves of corn, but they were precious few and far between. It struck him as peculiar that with so much sickness around good food had been allowed to spoil.

In all likelihood the villagers were sick themselves, or dead and riddled with maggots like their corn stalks.

"I will heal you," he promised the Earth Mother. Above him, the crow heckled. Sláine railed on it, shouting up at the sky: "Do not doubt me, creature of the Morrigan. This place will be healed. Golden heads of corn will grow, not wilt."

"Oh, they will grow, no doubt," Ukko said. "But will there be anyone left to harvest them? That's a more pertinent question. Given that these have been left to rot, it doesn't take a genius to guess that the farmers were otherwise indisposed. Dead and dying, most likely. That's the new world, Sláine. Honest men rot in the mud, fertilising their crops." Ukko stopped talking as a smear on the horizon caught his eye. "Look," he pointed at the dark smudges where they smeared the sky.

"Smoke," Sláine said.

"Do you think they're burning the chaff?"

"No. And where there's smoke…"

"There's probably a dozen skull swords setting blaze to the place," Ukko finished for him.

"We should–"

"Yes we should, but even if we start running now, we won't hit whatever's burning for a good two hours or more, by which time the skull swords will be long gone."

"But–"

"I know, you're completely right," Ukko cut in smoothly, "a great hero *would* charge in blindly without a care for his safety, swinging his axe like a demon possessed, without the faintest hope of arriving in time to save a single wretched soul, but doing it anyway. I agree whole-heartedly. That's what a great lummox – I mean hero – would do. But the reality is that while the hour gained between running and walking might theoretically make all the difference, they don't leave survivors, do they? The skull swords take them as slaves and anyone left behind is dog meat. So we'd be busting our guts to reach a few villagers who are already dead. We'll bury them, swear some kind of insane pledge about avenging them and liberating the land before breakfast... The thing is we could just as easily do all that *and* walk there, arriving fresh and invigorated instead of exhausted and ready to collapse. So how about we use our heads this once, eh? Go on, Sláine, be reasonable." Ukko was talking to himself; Sláine set off running down the road. "Nice!" Ukko called from behind him, scurrying to catch up. "I *hate* bloody heroes. Give me one good reason why the world needs a flippin' hero?"

Sláine looked back at him. "To fight evil," he said earnestly, no hint of a smile on his rugged features.

Ukko looked up at the heavens in despair. "I could have met up with a coward, but oh, no. I get the idiot hero. You really do believe that nonsense, don't you? You make my brain bleed, Sláine Mac Roth. I hope you are proud of yourself."

Sláine ignored him and carried on running towards the smoke.

Ukko had no choice but to keep chasing him.

As much as Sláine was loathe to admit it, Ukko was right. The chance of there being survivors was non-existent. Slough Feg's butchers were brutally efficient in their culling of the countryside. That didn't stop him from running – it hadn't stopped him when Murias burned. Indeed, it only served to spur him on. Had he been a few minutes quicker that day his mother, Macha, might still be alive. Today, he ran faster.

"Wait… for… me…" Ukko gasped between laboured breaths. Sláine looked back to see the ugly little dwarf on his knees, retching into the withered stalks of corn.

"Meet you at the village," Sláine called back.

"I hate you."

Sláine focussed on the plumes of black smoke, pumping his arms and lengthening his stride until it ate the miles. His chest burned. Fire spread from his calves into his knees. He ran on, ignoring it, never letting his gaze drop from the smoke in the sky.

★ ★ ★

THE VILLAGE HAD been sacked – though it was little more than a cluster of wattle-and-daub huts. The hungry fire had consumed everything, leaving behind ash and black-charred earth.

He walked through the smoking ruins.

There were no survivors.

There were no corpses for them to bury, either.

A mess of hoof prints churned the dirt around each patch of scorched earth. Tracks led off towards the next village. The sun was already low in the sky, day giving way grudgingly to night. There was no way, even if he set off running now, that he could reach them in time to make a blind bit of difference. He fell to his knees, burying his hands in the churned dirt. He leaned forwards, pressing his forehead into the earth. It still simmered with the latent warmth of the flames. He wanted to pray for guidance, to beg for help, but there were no words inside him. Instead he wept until he heard the exhausted shuffle of Ukko's feet behind him. The acrid smell of smoke stung his throat. Sláine wiped away the tears, smearing dirt across his cheeks.

"This is the part where we swear vengeance, right?" Ukko said.

"Yes."

The dwarf looked around at the smouldering ruin that had only hours earlier been a home. "Good. What's the point of hanging around with a hero if the evil bastards get away with stuff like this?" The look of pain in his eyes belied the callous words.

Sláine knew Ukko well enough to see past the bluster. The sight of the skull swords' plunder affected him every bit as much as it did the barbarian.

"So vengeance it is," Ukko said, harshly. "We shall not rest until the bastards responsible for this are worm food." Ukko turned his back on the young Sessair warrior.

"And now it is time for us to liberate the land."

"Before breakfast," Ukko said without turning around.

"I'M NOT BEDDING down in the middle of a slaughterhouse," Ukko insisted, vehemently. "I'm not doing it and you can't make me."

"Suit yourself," Sláine said, shouldering Brain-Biter. "You do know they can't hurt us?"

"Shows how little you know, your warpishness: vengeful spirits, wraiths, the restless dead. Those words ring any bells in your thick head?"

"Come on then, another mile, and then we make camp. We don't want you having nightmares, now do we?"

"Just walk," Ukko grumbled.

"I'm just saying–"

"I know full well what you are *just* saying. Look, don't you find it a little disturbing that there are no corpses? I mean there was plenty of blood soaked into the ground, more than enough to suggest a handful of dead, but there's not a single charred body." Ukko scratched at his scalp.

"No sign that they have been buried either," Sláine agreed.

"I don't like it, Sláine. I don't like it one little bit. It gives me the creeps."

And although Sláine would never admit it, the absence of the dead unnerved him as well. There were no obvious graves, and the bodies could not have been so utterly consumed by the fires as to be reduced to nothing. There was blood and signs of murder aplenty, but no corpses. It didn't sit right with him. The only explanation was that someone had taken the village's dead, denying them their right to peace. There was little that was sacred any more. The skull swords and the vile Slough priests defiled the very land itself, splitting her body open and corrupting all that was healthy and vital. The miles and miles of soured land were all the evidence he needed to know the depravities the enemy was capable of – but the thought of violating the sanctity of death went beyond scorched earth and rotten harvests. It was repulsive.

They walked awhile in silence, each wrapped up in their own thoughts.

The moon as it rose was a perfect circle, its bright-white a knife-edge that cut the black night cleanly. Sláine strode ahead, locked in the turmoil of his doubts and angers. He wanted to run, to fight, to unleash the pent-up frustration trapped within him to dull the despair he felt gnawing away at him. They had Feg's precious book. They would deliver those dire words to the Celtic kings so that they might fight back when the skull swords came. He pictured Niamh, imagined the suppleness of her body beneath him, opening up for him. He tried to remember her face but it had been a long time and images of her beauty merged with the string of uglies and beauties he had rutted with since leaving his home. Though of course in his traitorous memory they were all shades of beautiful; after all, no man would bed an ugly woman, or admit to one as a conquest, especially to himself. What he remembered was an ideal but that did not stop him from thinking about her. Thoughts of Niamh calmed his restless edge. Perfect or not, she healed him and tamed his fears.

He cast a long moon shadow down the gentle hill.

A man knelt by a stone cairn on the roadside up ahead. Sláine slowed his walk. The man reached out and touched one of the rounded stones. He turned and looked their way. The moonlight made him appear ill, his skin impossibly pale, dark crags drawn in by age, and hollows added by grief.

"Can I help you?"

"We have no wish to intrude on your farewell," Sláine called.

The stranger eased himself slowly to his feet. He was a wisp of a man, built like the willow bow at his feet. Even as the shadows shifted it was plain to see that he was an ugly man, his face pitted with the scars of some pox he had survived. His smile was warm, belying the sadness in his eyes.

"Well met," he called out, dusting his hands off on his britches. "Caoilfhionn would not object to you joining our farewell, I am sure."

"Your friend?" Sláine nodded towards the cairn. "I am sorry for your loss."

There was a scattering of trinkets, a jade necklace and a silver brooch fashioned in an endless knot, left as an offering for the dead. Neither piece looked particularly valuable. Beside them were a pack and a small harp. The harp's frame bore the countless chips and dents of constant travel.

"She was murdered this gone night," the stranger said, looking down at the mound of stones. "It seems so little for a life doesn't it? A pile of rocks and a few cheap jewels on a roadside in the middle of nowhere. She was worth so much more in life."

"Keeps the crows off," Ukko said, earning a cuff around the ear from Sláine. The dwarf grumbled, twisting his face. "Well, it does, doesn't it?"

"I'm sure she'd be happy to feed the Morrigan's birds. There are worse fates, especially for a woman like Caoilfhionn. She was a devotee of the three-faced Goddess, though she lived as a Weatherwitch. It was a petty magic, to be able to read the whims of nature and make gewgaws that promised luck in love and healthy harvests, but even such a small gift in these dark days appears to be worth the enmity of the butcher Feg."

"Slough Feg; now that is a name I never tire of hearing, stranger." The irony of his words was not lost on the man.

"You know the Lord Weird then?"

"Who does not? A man of his appetites earns his fame."

"More importantly," said Ukko. "His weirdness knows old Sláine here."

"Indeed? Feg's soldiers sought Caoilfhionn out. Her friends tried to hide her but what can a handful of farmers do against armed soldiers?"

"Precious little," Sláine agreed. "They turned her over to the skull swords?"

"No, they refused, forcing the soldiers' hand. These were simple people. They couldn't have anticipated the wrath their refusal brought down upon their heads. The skull swords went from house to house, setting fire to every homestead in the village and still they would not give her up, so the soldiers dragged one of the women into the village square and cut her tongue out, promising to do it again, every five minutes, until Caoilfhionn gave herself up. She had no choice. She surrendered to save her friends; her life in exchange for theirs. The cowards slit her throat, bleeding her out into the dirt like some fatted calf. And worse, they forced her friends to watch her die."

"And then they killed them," Sláine said, supplying the end of the bloody story.

"And then they killed them," the stranger agreed. "War – because that is exactly what this is, make no mistake – war should be between soldiers, not slaughtering peasants whose only crime is poaching to fill their bellies. Not burning down their homes. Not slitting the throat of a woman who made love potions and told people stories to bring happiness. It is barbaric." There was anguish in his voice, sadness in his eyes.

"These are black times," Sláine agreed.

"That they are, my new friend, that they are. Come, sit with me, raise a jug of pocheen and toast the departed on their way to the Otherworld."

"It would be an honour to stand vigil with you."

The man held out his hand. "Siothrún."

Sláine clasped Siothrún's wrist. "Well met, Siothrún. I am Sláine Mac Roth, and this little weasel is my, and I use the term very loosely, friend, Ukko."

They broke cornbread on the roadside. The thick cakes were dry and needed considerable chewing to digest, but they were food. Sláine hadn't realised how hungry he was until he had swallowed the first dry mouthful and felt his gut revolt. He crammed the rest of the cake into his mouth and ate ravenously.

Siothrún pulled a clay jar of potato wine from his sack and uncorked it. He took a swig and handed it to Sláine. It was a bitter brew, and potent. Sláine drank deeply, feeling the bite of the alcohol even before the first swallow was halfway down his throat.

He smacked his lips and passed the jar on to Ukko.

"They killed everyone, yet you live," Ukko said, stating the obvious. He took a deep swallow and spluttered, nearly coughing up half of his lungs. "That's disgusting! The drink," he said a moment later. Ukko shook his head violently, contorting his face as though trying to scrape the taste of the pocheen from his tongue with the top row of his teeth. "Not the fact that you're alive. You being alive is good, obviously." He broke off into a coughing fit. Sláine slapped him on the back, hard enough to rattle his jaws. "Much better than being dead."

"Ah, thank you for clarifying. Yes, I live. Though I will confess that right now it feels like my curse. I live but I don't weep for the lost. These were my friends too, my people. I should weep for them. I ought to be wracked by grief. Instead Feg's men have planted a black need for vengeance in my soul. I want them to hurt. I want them to fear for their children, their wives. I want them to forget what it feels like to be safe. I want their homes to be ash, their loved ones dead at their feet. And they have done this to me."

Sláine took the jar of potato wine back from Ukko and drank deeply. He felt a moment's light-headedness as he turned too quickly to pass the clay jar back to Siothrún, who stoppered it and stowed it back in his pack. As he did, his sleeve rode up, revealing a small crescent-shaped scar, the skin burned smooth.

"So you didn't run away to save your own skin?"

The stranger chuckled mirthlessly. "No, friend Ukko, I did not run. I arrived at the village too late to save them. Otherwise, if I thought it could have made a difference, I would have been down there with them at the last. As it was I saw the last few fall beneath the bloody swords of Feg's men. There was nothing I could do."

"Well at least you didn't run in like an idiot and get yourself killed," Ukko said encouragingly. "That's something."

"You'll have to excuse my ugly little friend," Sláine said. "He idolises cowards. I think he aspires to be one."

"I already am," Ukko smirked. "And proud of it. The world can never be short of enough cowards, believe you me. The very foundation of any functioning society is built on cowardice."

"I am not sure I understand, and to be honest I am not sure I *want* to understand," Siothrún said.

"Oh, it is. It is," Ukko said enthusiastically. "Cowardice spawns discussion, alliances, treaties, even peace. Imagine a world filled with heroes. Not only would it be excruciatingly dull, dull, dull, it would be brutal. No hero ever solved a dispute by the power of his mighty intellect. He hits things. Cowards make life safe for normal folk like you and me. He who turns and runs away lives to run again another day."

"Well, that's one way of looking at it, I suppose," Siothrún conceded.

"Don't listen to his blather, he'll have you convinced day is night and black is white and somewhere along the way to that revelation he'll have you parting with your purse and thanking him for making off with your money."

"You say that like it is a bad thing," Ukko said, his grin anything but innocent.

They talked some more, Siothrún recounting some of the stories he had heard on the road, Sláine sharing some of the horrors he had seen perpetrated in the name of Feg. They talked of death and sadness; of children being caught and set alight for the amusement of the soldiers, of wives being hunted like game, brought down by arrows in the legs and raped savagely for sport, criminals burnt alive in giant wicker effigies, and of the sickness blighting both crops and villagers across the desolate land.

Siothrún reached across the pack for his harp. Setting it on his knee, he plucked a few stray notes, teasing a melody out of it as he adjusted the tautness of the strings. Like the harpist, his instrument was ugly to look at, but the beauty of both resonated through the music they created together. Siothrún sang a song of sorrow and joy, his voice rich and melancholic. It was a song of keening. A lament. His voice rose, his words bittersweet:

"*Do not look to my pillow in the morning*
Do not reach out to touch my cheek
I am not there.

I do not sleep.
Do not look to my grave and weep
Do not mourn, my love
I am not there.
I know no rest
I am scattered on the thousand winds that blow away my pain
I am the thief that steals from your heart
I am the whisper half-heard in the night
And when you turn
I am not there.
I have no face.
I am melting in the newly fallen snow.
I am the kiss of sunlight on ripened corn.
I am the soft and gentle autumn rain on your face.
I am not gone.
I am here, my love, I am here."

Siothrún laid his harp aside and closed his eyes. His pitted cheeks were stained with the tracks of his tears.

"We will build a fire. You are welcome to join us later if you wish," Sláine said, offering the harper a few moments of solitude.

Siothrún met his eye, and nodded his thanks. "I appreciate your kindness, friend Sláine. As, I am sure, Caoilfhionn would."

"Think nothing of it, the kindness of strangers costs nothing, Siothrún."

"And yet it can be the most precious kindness of all."

"The pair of you have gone soft in the head," Ukko rolled his eyes. "I'm off to find some faggots to feed to the fire."

THEY BEDDED DOWN a short distance from the cairn. The fire burned low, crackling and spitting sparks. Shadow dancers flickered and writhed across their makeshift camp. The wind carried its eulogy across the night.

When it came, Sláine's sleep was restless. He tossed and turned fitfully while Ukko snored, oblivious, his lips rattling against his teeth.

He dreamed a thousand fragments of dream, but one rose up within him, fevered by the edge of prophecy. A woman knelt by his side, her face close to his, her lips leaning in to taste him. He gave himself to the kiss though their lips never touched. He felt the invasive presence of her mind within his, scratching around through all the memories that made him who he was.

Who are you? He gasped but he knew – because just as she touched him, so he touched her, melding with the woman of his dreams.

Caoilfhionn, the name sang through his head. Whether it was Sláine, the voice of his dreamself, or the Weatherwitch naming herself, there was no way of knowing.

Her ethereal fingers slipped inside his skull, pressing deep into his mind. He wanted to scream but this dream-self had no mouth. He bucked and writhed, trying to dislodge the witch but it was as though bonds of iron tied him to the earth. He could not fight her.

Do not struggle, Son of the Sessair. Let me inside you. Deeper. Surrender.

If you weren't already dead, woman, you would taste my axe.

I would taste so much more, warrior. Her icy hand reached down to cup the silver tusk of his boar's head codpiece, tugging it aside. There was no tenderness in her touch when it came. It was hungry. *Such anger in you, such pain. Let me take it away. Let me help you. I can, with just a word.*

GET OUT OF MY HEAD, WITCH!

He concentrated on his hands, even as his body responded to her touch, forcing them to reach out and grasp either side of the witch's head. Her grasp on him tightened. An elemental charge, like lightning, coursed through his body as he pressed and his fingers sank into her insubstantial skull. Sláine screamed out against the charge wracking his body, the agony fierce enough to tear a raw hole where his mouth ought to have been. The pain was visceral, his response to it primal. He struck out, looking to batter the witch until she relinquished her hold on his flesh.

Such sadness consumes you, warrior, the ghost of Caoilfhionn said, feeding off his pain. She licked from his nose to the centre of his brow in a parody of erotic sensuality. The greater his suffering the more substantial she became beneath his hands, the more forceful her grip. She threw her head back, relishing the spasm that shook his body. A sheen of perspiration clung to her too-pale skin. Her lips parted hungrily, eager to devour more of him. Ribbons of mist leaked out between sharpened teeth, coiling lazily down towards his nose and mouth and slipping easily into him. The mist clogged in his throat. Sláine thrashed about wildly, retching and choking on the ethereal ribbons as they delved deeper inside him. He tried desperately to reach out for the Earth Serpent, to harness its power with his mind, to surrender to it, but the witch's fingers drew more exquisite pain from him, and the serpent recoiled, leaving him alone with Caoilfhionn, helpless against her invasion.

What do you want from me? It was more of a plea than a question. The final spasm wracked his body.

And in answer to it she offered him a sunburst of images; places he did not know, names he could not grasp or understand flashed through his mind. Spiralling towers of ivory and bone clawing up into the red sky, a city of wonder and fear populated by the pale ones, burning giants brought low, The Morrigan and Blodeuwedd, black hounds and crows and scaled monstrosities all blurring into one as her final words floated like a ghost beneath, behind and between everything that he saw: *find the Skinless Man.*

Sláine came awake with a start, gasping and sweating in a tangle of fur where he had become embroiled with his cape. The fire was dead, charcoal and ash all that remained. He looked around, trying to focus. Dawn had brought a fine mist with it.

The tenuous fingers of the dream-witch clung to him even as he blinked back the sleep, feeding on his guilt and sorrow. And still the trailing edge of her voice echoed inside his mind: find the Skinless Man.

"Where?" he asked, but there was no one there to answer him – not that he needed an answer. The city he had seen belonged to the pale ones: the Sidhe. Ukko's bedroll was empty and the harper was gone. Sláine rose unsteadily, the dream had drained him more than it had any right to. The mist made it impossible to see more than a few feet in any direction. On the verge of panic he spun left and right, and stared running. "Ukko!" he called out, "Ukko!"

He staggered, turning his ankle in a rut in the dirt, and cursed. The curse was met by childish laughter.

And a moment later he saw the runt with his britches around his ankles relieving himself against the side of a roadside marker.

"Were you worried?" Ukko grinned. "You were, weren't you? Oh, I'm touched, Sláine. I am. I'm touched."

"Just pull your britches up."

There was no sign of Siothrún.

Sláine wandered over to the Weatherwitch's cairn. It was no burial mound. It was nothing more than a pile of chipped and broken stones. He kicked at them, toppling the stones. There was no body buried beneath.

The tang of pocheen was still bitter on his tongue.

The charade bore the hallmarks of the Sidhe.

Ukko came to stand beside him and pointed up at the sky, "Look." A lone black bird watched them from a high branch. "I've got to say I've no liking for the way this day has started. None whatsoever."

Two

The Doorway Between Today and Tomorrow

UKKO HURLED A stone at the bird's head.

"Go on, scat! Get out of here! Shoo!"

The crow burst into flight in an explosive flurry of black wings.

It cawed angrily.

Ukko gestured obscenely at the creature as it flapped in circles around his head. Its beady yellow eyes glared back at him malevolently.

"Bloody creepy birds," Ukko grumbled. "Go on! Hie! Hie!" He bent down and picked up another shard of rock and hurled it at the bird, missing by a good yard and a half. The crow, mocking him, circled lower and lower until its wings beat at his head. Ukko lurched backward spluttering and swatting at the air, nowhere near close enough to threaten it. "I hate the damned things. If I get my hands on it I'll wring its bloody neck!"

Sláine watched the bird as it evaded Ukko's miserable attempts to catch it. It banked low and swept high, its trajectory forming a rough circle around the pile of broken stones once, twice, deosil, and on the third counter-sunwise pass vanished into thin air mid-wingbeat. One moment it was there, the next it wasn't. Sláine stared at the air it had disappeared into. There was nothing remotely peculiar about it. The bird had simply ceased to be.

"Go on, disappear, you damned bird!" Ukko cursed, aggrieved. He sat down on the grass and grabbed his pack, rooting through it until he found a chunk of hard cornbread which he broke off with dirty fingers and started to eat. He threw a nugget of cornbread to Sláine. "I am so tired of this damned bread. I'd kill for a good bit of goat, nicely charred over a fire, still dripping fat and juices."

"That was... unnatural."

"You always did have a way with words, big man. It was peculiar, uncanny, outlandish, extraordinary, bizarre, mysterious, inexplicable, remarkable, you could even say astonishing but let's be honest, it was just plain *wrong*."

"That's what I said," Sláine walked across to the stones, half-expecting to feel something, a charge in the air, a peculiar static, anything that could offer a hint as to how the bird had disappeared. He knelt, touching one of the stones. It was cold beneath his fingers but otherwise utterly unremarkable. He turned it over. There were no markings on it. He tossed it up into the air and caught it, then dropped it back onto the pile along with the other stones. "I had a dream last night."

"Sounds like a confession. I'm not sure I really want to hear about it. It's been a long time since you had a woman. What I don't know won't hurt me and all that," Ukko said. "If you did unspeakable things to me, or a goat, I think you should just keep them to yourself."

"It wasn't that kind of dream," Sláine said, explaining how the Weatherwitch had melded with him and the visions he had had in response to her invasion of his sleep.

"It wasn't natural," he finished, as though that explained everything, the harper, the dream of the dead witch and the disappearing bird. "By that I mean not a dream as much as a prophetic vision. I am not even sure the harper was real."

"Well his drink was real enough. My head is still throbbing, thank you very much."

"If he was, he was not a mortal man. His skin was too pale, face too thin, fingers too long. No, I'd wager he was one of the Sidhe."

At the mention of the fey folk from beyond the veil all colour left the dwarf's face.

"We need to follow the bird."

"You don't really mean that."

"The bird is the key, thrice doesil around the broken stones and it left. We must follow it and find the Skinless Man."

"Have you listened to yourself? Find the Skinless Man, because you had a dream. And now you want to track a vanishing bird. Now I know why I am not a hero," Ukko shook his head. "And the best part is you say that as though disappearing into thin air is the easiest thing in the world. Why is nothing *ever* simple with you?"

"Probably because, as you like to remind me, I am a hero," Sláine said, a hint of mirth reaching his eyes.

"Lug save me from heroes," Ukko muttered. "I just want to mention again, just in case you missed it first time, this whole thing makes me very uncomfortable."

Sláine walked back to the bedrolls and gathered his possessions together. Slough Feg's accursed book lay open on Ukko's cloak. Sláine could not make hide nor hair out of the spidery scrawl of Ogham. "Found anything of interest?" he asked, not that he trusted Ukko to tell the truth even if he could decipher the runes. That was why he had decided to take the book to Tall Iesin. The wanderer would be able to interpret the full implications of Feg's plans and the impact they would have on the Land of the Young if they ever came to fruition.

"Enough to know I don't want to go chasing after some vanishing bird," Ukko said, closing the book and stowing it in his pack. "Ever heard of the word 'trap'? No, didn't think you had," Ukko answered himself before Sláine could. The dwarf had an annoying habit of running off at the mouth when he was nervous – which was more often than not. "Let's just say there is a reason Throt called it Feg's Ragnarok book. You *do* know what Ragnarok is, right? End of the world stuff. The cataclysm. We're talking about epic storms riving the world asunder, oceans rising to swallow the land, wiping out humanity. Feg's spewing his bile onto vellum. It's little more than a monotonous screed denouncing the depravity of the world. After reading a few pages of his book I can see why so much of the south has gone sour; it must have withered beneath his tongue. Feg is one bitter old cuss, believe me."

Sláine had no liking for what he heard. But could the ravings of a lunatic really be the key to regaining his honour amongst his people? It was doubtful, but then it was equally doubtful Ukko had understood one word in ten and was doing anything but fabricating a lot of stuff and nonsense to justify his fear. The bird's disappearance had unnerved Sláine, but coupled with the things he had seen during Caoilfhionn's violation, it only served to pique his curiosity. Who, or what, could the Skinless Man be? No man could live without skin to seal his flesh; surely he would bleed to death. He had seen a burned man die because his skin could not breathe. No, this Skinless Man he sought could not be a literal Skinless Man. An entity, perhaps? A wraith or revenant shade? A statue or even a story? The Sidhe were fond of tales. Perhaps that was it. The notion just confirmed his need to find Tall Iesin; if there was such a being in the stuff of stories the wanderer would know.

"Tell me."

A yellow-jacketed corn fly buzzed from dead head to dead head of corn. Aside from Siothrún it was the first living thing he had seen since leaving Dardun. It was such an unremarkable thing, yet watching it drew a smile from the young warrior. The minutiae of life did not stop. Once more he thrilled at the sheer wonder of creation. Even now, with the reek of Slough Feg's Sourlands spreading, the smallest of Danu's creatures sought to flourish. The fly would lay eggs in the corn, the eggs would hatch into maggots which in turn would bloat on the dead corn and transform into flies themselves – a perfect cycle of life. Even the ash from the victims of the skull swords would nourish the earth, enriching the soil and so feeding the Goddess, just as he himself would one day: from dust to dust returned, as the druid, Cathbad, had liked to say. In time the air would be thick with flies.

"What is there to tell? He uses the word vile a lot and babbles about the need for cleansing the sickness from the carcass of the Danu. No, that's not quite what he said... the pox-crusted carcass, that was it: cleansing the sickness from the pox-crusted carcass of Danu. I get the impression he is none too fond of your Goddess. Then again his weirdness is not overly enamoured with anything," Ukko tapped at his temple with a dirty finger. "He is a raving loon. Some words – even complete sentences – appear over and over. One he fixates on is deluge; I found five separate pleas for tidal waves and lashing storms to savage the land. Like I said, cataclysmic stuff. If wishes were fishes, we'd all be very wet. So how about we forget about the bird and forge on towards your old homestead and surprise that chief of yours with the ravings of this homicidal lunatic?" Ukko said, hopefully.

"I am going after the bird," Sláine said, reasonably. He stretched, working the muscles in his shoulders and then lower back. He made a show of looking left and right slowly, scanning the blighted harvest and lingering on the ruins of the nameless hamlet. "If you wish to remain here, alone, so close to where skull swords burned down a village and put the inhabitants to death, well, by all means. You are right, following the bird, if even possible, could be walking into danger. A friend would not force another to join his folly. So in the name of our friendship, it would be unfair of me to force you into risking your life. You should trust your finely honed self-preservation instinct. Stay here. I'll just take the book off you and we'll make our farewells. I'll go my way, alone, and you will go yours. Alone. I am sure you *will* make it out of here alive just fine without me. You're a resourceful one, hard to kill, right?"

Ukko scratched behind his ear. "Have I told you lately that I hate you, Sláine?"

"And there was me thinking you wanted to be my friend?"

Sláine turned his back on Ukko, shouldered his pack and walked back to the stones. Ukko came scurrying behind him, grunting and grumbling as he tried to wriggle into his pack and fasten his thick wool cloak at the same time. He looked at the sky. It was heavy with thick white cloud, though not unbroken. The sun streamed down in bright unbroken beams through the breaches. Without waiting to see if Ukko was with him, Sláine made the first circuit of the stones counter-sunwise. Halfway through the second a tiny static charge thrilled across the tips of his fingers and through the roots of his hair, barely touching the extremities of his being. He took another step and felt the tingle chase down the nape of his neck and into the core of his spine. Two more and it gripped his heart. "No matter what you feel, keep walking!" Sláine urged, pushing on another step to complete the second circuit of the smashed cairn.

The earth power rose within him, swelling to fill his flesh. No, he felt the difference. It was not the earth power swelling into him. He was not feeding off the world. This was different. He was feeding the world. It was his strength. It was being drawn from his marrow, teased out slowly at first and then with more and more urgency as he made the circle. The sensation of power flooding through his body was almost erotic in its intensity. He felt his body swelling, his heart beating arrhythmatically as the peculiar journey took its toll on his flesh.

A sudden thrill surged through his blood, pulsing through heart and mind with equal fervour.

The Serpent coiled through every fibre of his flesh in answer to the call of the stones.

Sláine walked on. His vision swam and blurred, pulsing black.

He closed his eyes against the erratic strobing of pitch black and bright light but it helped little. Pain flared at the base of his skull and rooted down through the ladder of his spine. He felt his knees buckle but refused to fall until he had completed the final circuit to wherever this doorway between worlds took him. The pain intensified. He felt the flesh of his face strain against the bone beneath, lips peeling back with his grimace, forcing his mouth unnaturally wide in a macabre parody of a smile. The pink of his gums pulled back, stretched until they bled around the white of his teeth. Sláine dug deep, drawing on a well of strength outside his body to make the final step. His eyes rolled up inside his skull rendering him blind and still Sláine forced himself to step into the darkness. It hit him like an axe to the chest, slamming into his body with raw elemental force as he completed the third and final circle.

Sláine pushed through the haze of pain and fell to his knees on the other side of the invisible doorway.

His chest heaved. The journey had cost him far more than a few laps around a pile of stones. His head pounded savagely, the blood pressing against the inside of his skull. He looked up. It was immediately obvious he was nowhere near the Forest of Dardun or the burned village. The sky was black, the clouds reduced to a few wisps in the otherwise clear night. A gibbous moon hung low, silver moonlight shining on an empty plain. He had lost more than a few hours of daylight making the passage – last night the moon had hung full and bright, more than a week must have passed for the moon to have grown. There was something uncanny about it. Indeed, the moon's position in the sky was wrong – for it to be where it was months had to have passed in a single heart beat.

The pain receded slowly. He slumped forwards, retching, and wiped the bile from his lips with the back of his hand.

He tried to absorb the most immediate and obvious changes in his surroundings while at the same time struggling to make sense of the time shift, the sudden return to night, and cope with the agonies the journey had wrought.

The landscape was too much for his mind to translate; it stretched on and on and on, unbroken and featureless. He turned to look behind him and saw more of the same nothingness. The absence of landmarks was disquieting.

The quality of the dark itself was thicker.

There were no stars.

The ground was coarse, ever-shifting to the whims of the wind, like sand but not like any sand he had ever seen.

"I can't see the damned bird."

Sláine looked up to see Ukko standing over him, scanning the horizon. He tried to speak but could not. The little runt seemed utterly unphased by the transition between worlds. Sláine's head lolled on his shoulders and he slumped back to the ground. Fine grains of not-sand pressed into his cheek. They were cold, like tiny chips of ice.

"What's wrong with you?"

"He is stripped of all bonds to the earth," a coarse voice answered. He hadn't seen anyone approach and there was no way they could sneak up unseen in this barren wilderness. Sláine looked up to see a black-cloaked figure standing beside the dwarf. "Not only is there is no power in the earth here, there can be no residual or latent power in anything that resides here. He is, for the first time in his life, bereft." Caught suddenly in the moonlight Sláine saw its face was that of an enormous crow, its cloak fashioned from slick black feathers.

"Ah," said Ukko, his face betraying the fact that he didn't have even the slightest inkling what the cloaked figure was talking about.

Sláine knew: some called her the Great Queen, others the Queen of Phantoms. His mother, Macha, had called her the Spectre Queen; the Crone; Great Mother; Moon Goddess; Great White Goddess; Queen of the Fey. The Goddess of war, fate and death, the Morrigan.

"We are in the el between realms," the crow-faced aspect of the divine cawed.

She stank of death.

"What? We're in hell?"

"No," the Morrigan said, "We are in the space between worlds. You are in a doorway of sorts, a portal between today and tomorrow and yesterday. Or at least your spirit is. Your flesh lies on the floor beside a pile of rocks. When you leave this place you will return to it."

"Er, can't we just go back there now then? I mean, I'm kind of attached to my body. At least I was."

"When it is time, not before. From here you can go anywhere, anywhen. Tir-Nan-Og is not the only place of life. There are other realms. Being between them like this, in this place, means that nothing of Tir-Nan-Og is sustained here. Sláine is suffering because of his link to the Earth Goddess. She completes him just as he completes her."

"Ah," Ukko said again. "Oh." The dwarf's eyes widened in fear as something, a phantom shape, rose up out of the sand at his feet. He backed up a step. "Shoo, get away from me, gah!" It would have been comic but for the fact that his panicked hand passed straight through the formless face of the phantom.

The crow woman laughed callously. "Do my children frighten you, little man?"

Ukko stumbled backwards, tripping over his feet and landing on his backside with a grunt.

The rolling glass sands stirred as one by one, more silhouettes shimmered into dubious life. Sláine stared at them, trying to focus on the ever-shifting shapes but there was no substance or definition to the blurs beyond the most basic outline. It took him a moment to recognise the play of movement but when he did it was unmistakable: they were victims, half-dead, trapped in this place, re-enacting their deaths, or more accurately reliving them: *thrust and parry, savage blows raining down, arms thrown up in defence, bodies crumpling*. Sláine knew what they were – or rather what they represented. Ghosts of sound rang out, just above and just below the register of normal sounds so they came through both dull and blunted while simultaneously being sharp and insistent, clashing swords, screams, death rattles. These were the lost souls trapped between realms, unable to pass on into death as long as they were held here by the Morrigan.

There were thousands of them, hundreds of thousands, more – their number beyond counting. The shadow-shapes stretched as far as the eye could see, coming to life in all directions. They were legion.

Sláine struggled to stand.

"We can go anywhere, Crone?" He fought to get the words out between fresh waves of agony that tore at his flesh.

The crow's beady yellow eyes turned on the warrior, radiating sickness. "Anywhere, anywhen," she said.

"I would travel to the land of the Sidhe, to find the Skinless Man."

The Morrigan's laughter brayed out harshly. "You would, would you? And why should I aid you, son of the Sessair? Why should I not leave your soul here with the rest of my children to live and die through an infinite cycle of suffering?"

Sláine had no answer for that.

"What you would do is impossible – these are not the same things. One does not immediately facilitate the other. You cannot travel into the Sidhe *and* find the Skinless Man. He is not there. I am helping you already, warrior. For more, you must offer me something I desire."

"What do you desire, Crone? What would you have from me?"

"I desire nothing, mortal. I have lived too long to crave things."

"Then why goad me? Why not leave me here to rot?"

"The future is one of infinite possibilities, every action and interaction influencing the play of life. In some you and the dwarf are no doubt great heroes to your people, in others little more than drunken lecherous buffoons. In some, no doubt the very best thing I could do for the Land of the Young would be to leave you here to feed the sands, but in others keeping you here could damn the whole world. I cannot know what will come to pass any more than you, but dare I risk damning creation?"

"You are the aspect of battle and death. How does it hurt you if you deny salvation? Surely it feeds you, no? Gives you more fighting and agony to glut on, to gorge yourself and grow fat."

"I am old, warrior. I have lived a thousand life times. I have come to love the land – because more than it is your land, it is *my* land. Walk with me, Sláine." The crow woman held out a clawed hand, gesturing for him to follow as she set off, walking towards the moon. "Is it better to have a debt owed or a promise fulfilled?"

"Is this idle speculation, witch?"

"There is a purpose to everything in this life, warrior. Everything, every word, every action, be it from spite or kindness."

"So what is your purpose?"

"Ever the aurochs charging in headlong, take your time, think for yourself, Sláine. Do not expect answers on a platter of silver."

"There's no point in beating around the bush, Crone. You want something from me, that much is obvious, and in turn I need something from you, it seems. You have the upper hand. All the rest is bull turd."

The Crone ruffled her feathers.

"Think of it as mutual back scratching, we have *itches* we can help each other with. My purpose is simple. I would have you do something for me. A favour, nothing more."

"What?" Sláine said, suspiciously. He knew enough not to trust the Morrigan. The words that came out of her mouth were always bitter, twisting around from promises to lies, offering hope and delivering despair. She was a traitorous bitch. His doubts reflected in his face.

The Crone craned her head, first to the left, then the right. "Do not be in such a hurry to anger, barbarian. I would merely have your word on something."

"On what? Just spit it out."

"A promise. Promise to obey a single command from my mouth without question and I will grant *you* what you desire. That is my offer, take it or be damned, it matters little to me. How dangerous can a promise be?"

Sláine had no liking for such an anonymous promise. It was ludicrous for the Morrigan to expect him to bind himself unthinkingly to her. "I am not a fool, hag. To the likes of you a promise could be the end of all things as likely as it could be their salvation. What would you have me promise? And speak plainly; I'll have none of your riddles or half-truths."

"Patience, the time will come for you to know. Now is not that time."

"You expect me to pledge myself to an unknown promise – and to keep it? You're a bigger fool than I took you for. Tell me, in those many futures, do I ever actually keep this blind faith pledge?"

"Aye, you do, son of the Sessair. You do indeed."

Sláine grunted his disbelief and shook his head slowly. "I guess I will just have to take your word for that, won't I?" Sláine said, sceptically. "How do I even know if this dream invasion is prophetic? How can I be sure this is the path I must tread? A trick of the Sidhe or a trick of yours, Morrigan? There is nothing that says the hand of fate is playing a role here."

The air stank of mould and rot.

"It is your destiny to make this journey, Sláine Mac Roth. I offer no lies–"

"Only shades of the truth," Sláine finished for her.

"You seek to return to Murias to be reunited with your people. Do you imagine for one moment your cuckolded king will welcome you back with open arms?"

"The world has changed. We have the book."

"The book, yes, the book. Yes, yes, yes. The book. The book of Feg. It changes nothing. You are reviled by your king. You are unworthy of your people." He only needed to look in her eyes to see she was serious. "They revere the Goddess, the divine feminine. You are unworthy of her, you worship whores, you cuckold good men and treat women as though they are little more than chattels. You rut blindly like an animal. You are callous and callow. And yet she favours you which means you have it in you to be great. To be her champion. But not if you remain the youth you were. It is time for you to shed the skin of childhood and emerge from the imago the man my sister-aspect deserves. Cast off these lecherous ways, be not some sot, devote yourself to the Goddess, walk the path and earn the right to return home a champion of the Celts. Become a man. Your destiny awaits through the archway. Are you man enough to claim it?"

"A promise from me and in return you will take us to the Skinless Man?" Sláine said. Her words stung in a way he had not expected. She was right. He thought back to Niamh, to Bedelia and Brianna, even Brighid the Daughter of Danu. He had treated them all like possessions, like dirt, taking from them what he wanted, not caring about the cost of his selfishness. There was no beauty in the taking. No kindness in the owning. It was, if anything, a parallel to the souring of the land at Feg's hand. He used things of beauty, took from them what *he* needed, and discarded them when they were used up. In his case it wasn't land, or the surge of the Earth Serpent, it was the company of women. In his way he was as much of a defiler as the enemy he sought to pull down. The realisation was both humbling and horrifying. He did not want to believe her accusations, but even as he tried to deny them he remembered more and more moments of so-called worship that were little more than drunken rutting and loud-mouthed buffoonery.

He made a silent vow – he was young, there was time yet – he would change his ways.

"I see you understand, warrior," the Crone smiled, curiosity on her crow-face. "I will open the way for you," she waved her hand; the movement formed a curious pattern in the air, the gestures coming together to dispel the lost souls. Their spirit forms lost all consistency, drifting away like smoke to reveal a white marble altar and arch on the plain in front of them.

Sláine licked his parched lips. He had not seen the archway, though now it towered over them all and it was obvious that there was no way the wraiths of the half-dead could have hidden it. It was an amazing construction, standing a full four times their height and three paces deep. The keystone was decorated with elaborate carvings of the creatures representing the wild hunt. The icons were bound together by serpentine knotwork and spirals that simultaneously drew the eye and somehow repelled its focus. It was an impossible arch. The sight of it churned Sláine's stomach.

"Your eye perceives the doorway in the manner your mind most readily understands," the Crone said. "That is the nature of the arch of time. While it requires no physicality, we do. We make of it what we need to see, and no two people see the same thing."

"Neat trick," Ukko said, coming up behind them. He rummaged around in his pockets and pulled out a lump of cornbread – covered in lint – out and began munching on it. "All this travelling works up an appetite. I'm ravenous. Then again, it's probably *months* since I last had anything to eat."

"Through the arch lies Purgadair," the Morrigan said, ignoring Ukko. "A city on the edge of

Nàimhdiel, a harsh and utterly barren desert. The Skinless Man you seek resides there, but beware child of Danu, this is a cruel place, this city."

"I am not afraid," Sláine said, squaring his jaw stubbornly.

"Of course you aren't, axe of the Goddess. You know all the evils of mankind, do you not? You have walked the halls of the hells, battled free of the underworld, traded blows with demons and lived to tell the tale. Oh, wait, you have done no such thing... perhaps you *should* consider fear. It might serve to keep you alive after you enter the arch. Purgadair is not a city for weakness – and make no mistake, humanity is weakness. If you betray yourselves the beings of the mad city will tear your soul apart. And don't believe you can simply open your eyes and return from here as though from a bad dream. Any harm done to your spirit here will be matched on your bodies back on the fields beyond Dardun. A cut here will bleed there. An eye lost here leaves a blind man there. Die here and you die in the Tir-Nan-Og."

"And this is where the Skinless Man is to be found?"

The Morrigan stretched her neck, clacking the hard edges of her beak together excitedly. "It is, it is. I can open the way if I have your promise, warrior. Such a little thing, a promise. So, do I have it?" The crow-woman asked again, her talons clicking on the compacted glass-sand.

How could he deny her? He had felt the truth – or an aspect of it – in her declamation. He was not the man his Goddess deserved. But would walking this path make him that man? It was impossible to know, and if, as the Crone intimated, the permutations of future possibilities were limitless, then in some futures he had walked the road, in others he had turned his back. The question was, in which future did he triumph? He thought he knew – because for all of her half-truths, what did the Morrigan stand to gain if the world she loved were destroyed, the land reduced to soured dirt?

Nothing.

Perhaps it was his destiny.

But did that mean he could trust her?

"What choice do I have, Crone? You do," Sláine said, "you have my promise even if it damns me."

The bird-woman gestured sharply with her feathered arms and something within the very stones of the arch stirred. A low hum resonated from beneath their feet – more a vibration than a sound as it grew in substance until Sláine's bones resonated in sympathy and he felt the solid harmonies coursing through his entire body. As his skin began to crawl the air cracked sharply, a single harsh snap, and an ethereal blue light beamed from one side of the arch to the other, and spread, joining the columns in bonds of blue fire.

Every nerve and fibre within him sang to the harmonic of the mystical gate.

Sláine stepped towards it, feeling the static thrill stir every hair on his body.

"One final caution," the crow woman said, her hand on his shoulder staying him. "All that you see in this place, or rather all that you think you see, is due more to desire than truth. Be careful what you wish for, warrior. Rein in your guilt and your libido unless you want to experience a very different kind of hell. Once through the arch you have but a single purpose. Do not allow yourself to deviate from it. The only way you can return is with the aid of the Skinless Man. Remember that. Now go with your Goddess."

Ukko poked a tentative finger into the blue light and leapt back as though shocked. He stared at the tip of his finger, raised an eyebrow and stepped through the arch of time, pausing beneath the keystone to look up. The scoundrel said something but his words were whipped away by the sudden swell of wind that rose up around Sláine and the Morrigan, churning sand up into his face.

"It is time," the old Crone said – and in the sky around them Sláine saw the first of her harbinger birds fly through the squall, coming out of the darkness. The divinity threw her arms wide in greeting and the birds came to settle on her. The carrion eaters sank their beaks into her flesh, tugging at the oleaginous black feathers until they wrenched them free. The murder of birds took flight with thousands of feathers crammed into their beaks only to scatter them from above.

The feathers caught on the wind and blew every which way, temporarily obscuring the blue heart of the huge arch.

Sláine pushed through the falling feathers until he stood less than a yard from the keystone. The sheet of blue fire was both mesmeric and fearsome. It shimmered with a life all of its own.

Denuded, the Morrigan crumbled, her body collapsing in on itself until a pile of feathers was all that remained of her. One by one the falling feathers began to rise again, each growing as it metamorphosed into one of the Crone's damned birds and was gone, away on the wind.

Sláine stepped into the blue fire.

HE WALKED OUT into tomorrow.

The desert heat hit him like an anvil. Shading his eyes, Sláine looked up at the sky. A red heat-haze shimmered across the horizon, rising up towards the cloudless red-tinged alien sky. And he was in no doubt that it was alien. Two suns hung low on either extreme of the horizon, making it impossible to tell if it was dawn or dusk, or if the concept of night even existed here: one sun rising always as the other set. The twin suns were merciless, both in terms of brightness and baking heat.

Ukko sat cross-legged on a patch of parched bunchgrass, worrying away at a kernel of corn that had lodged in his teeth. He hawked and spat, back-handing his lips dry.

"You took your sweet old time getting here," the dwarf said without looking up. "I've been sat on this damned hillock for five days. I'd just about given up on you and gone in search of grub."

"Five days, without food? You expect me to believe that?" Sláine said, staring down the shallow decline of the hill he had stepped out onto at what was undoubtedly a city – but it was a city quite unlike any he had ever seen before.

"My stomach has stopped grumbling now it's decided my throat has been cut. It isn't funny."

Minarets and bone-fine towers shimmered mirage-like before him. They appeared to rise in tiers, concentric rings of monstrosity building upon each other one ghastly layer at a time: and at the very heart of Purgadair, one tower dwarfed all the other peaks of the city, climbing miles into the heavens. Sláine could barely see the golden crown at its peak, reflecting the suns so brilliantly it could almost have been a third beacon in the sky. It was a staggering piece of architecture – a white finger accusing the gods. Beneath it, it was easy to imagine the earth challenging the dominion of the lords of the air themselves. Sláine could not begin to comprehend its sheer size or the marvel of construction it was. In the glare of both suns there was not a single shadow that fell upon the elaborate carvings worked into its stone. Sláine could make out none of the details but the overall impression was one of a mind gone mad, so intense were they. Sláine struggled to see more, to make out details over general impressions, but all he saw were huge faces, ten and twenty times his height, demonic and devilish gargoyles and tormented men, reaching out, beseeching.

Rooftops slanted in a crooked patchwork of clays, some hard-baked red, others whitewashed.

Compared with the wattle huts of Murias, even the king's roundhouse, the city of Purgadair was a monstrosity of stone that devoured both land and sky. The inhabitants of this mad city must surely live on top of each other, crammed into tiny spaces instead of relishing the freedom of the land.

What was it the Morrigan had said? There is no earth power here... looking at the sprawl of humanity it was easy to see why. In Tir-Nan-Og the land was weakening as the magic was leeched out of it by the Drunes and their huge Weird Stones spread across the land to act as conduits for the great souring. There were no Weird Stones here, only stone, an overwhelming mass of stone. There was nowhere for the land to breathe. The stone of Purgadair had choked the life out of the land. No wonder it stood on the edge of a great barren desert, how could it not? How could the land hope to stand against the parasites crawling across its skin? And when it succumbed, what then?

"This is the future," Sláine said, struck by a sudden premonition. "Huge heartless monstrosities of stone, people crowded in like pigs, rife with disease from the slop of humanity."

"You paint a pretty picture, my friend."

It was as though a goose had walked across his grave – despite the blistering heat a shiver ran down the rungs of his spine. The revelation was not a pleasant one but that did not make it any less true. But what could he do? He was one man. No, he corrected himself, he was Sláine Mac Roth, son of the Sessair, beloved of Danu.

"I understand your pain," Sláine whispered, not to Ukko, nor even the Morrigan, but to the Goddess who could not possibly hear him: Danu, the Earth Mother. Slough Feg's taint was just the beginning of one long future that would destroy her. How could she live with such knowledge? "I will be the champion you need."

"Why thank you, Sláine. I never knew you cared. I've got to admit I'm touched," Ukko grinned and jumped up to his feet, dusting his hands off. "So how about we go fill our bellies, oh great champion of mine?"

"You'll be touched in a minute," Sláine muttered, cuffing Ukko around the back of the head. "Oh, look, I can foretell the future. In fact if I concentrate hard enough I can see a world of hurt waiting for you, runt. Who would have thought being a seer would be so easy?"

"All right, all right, no need to be like that," Ukko grumbled, rubbing at his head. "It's not as though I asked you to be my champion, you volunteered. Let's go find some food, *please*."

"I am not sure I would eat anything from this place. Take a look at it; what do you see? It is dead. There is no spirit here. How can anything offer sustenance when the ground is barren?"

"Well, if it hadn't taken you a month of Sundays to get here, maybe I would be more picky, but as it stands I am willing to risk it."

THEY ENTERED THE city on the edge of the desert.

The heat of the sand burned through the leather of Sláine's boots, scorching his feet. Ukko didn't look much happier with his plight, hopping from one foot to another animatedly as he scurried forwards. Sláine walked slowly, awed by the might of Purgadair. They were not alone on the path. A traveller walked a little way in front of them. He appeared lost in thought. His grubby grey robes marked him as some kind of druid, if this realm still paid heed to the land. As Sláine neared, he heard peculiar half-whispered words tripping off the traveller's lips, oblivious to the world around him.

He wiped sweat from his brow and as he did, his hood slipped and Sláine saw him for what he was: an abomination of the flesh, a fusion of animals, raven, rat, badger, and hound somehow mutated into a man. Worse, he looked at them as though they were the mutants.

The three of them approached the twin columns of the towering city gate that symbolically denoted the entrance into Purgadair. The gates were guarded by lean, tanned warriors in light leather armour. They wore short brutish stabbing swords at their sides, leather kilts and flat sandals. Their faces, like the traveller's, were a repulsive fusion of so many creatures it was almost impossible for Sláine to be sure exactly which poor animals had found themselves melded into these horrific creatures.

"Good morning, warden," one of the gathered guards said as the traveller neared the gates. He offered a slight bow. The traveller, seemingly lost in his prayer, didn't notice the guards until he collided bodily with one of them.

Sláine stepped up beside him, dragging Ukko with him. If all of the inhabitants of this city bore the same ruinous flesh and animalistic features they would need to find themselves cloaks and hoods or they would draw every eye in the damned place.

They reached the gate side by side.

Still mumbling incoherently, the traveller looked up to meet the guard's eye. Sláine read the unquenchable fire of madness blazed behind his dark eyes. The guard backed up a step under the sheer intensity of his stare. A crazed smile spread slowly across the traveller's face, his bloodless lips curling back to bare a mouthful of rotten teeth, many of which had been replaced by small wooden pegs. There was almost no trace of sanity – no trace of humanity – within the little man's gaze. Instead, his dark eyes promised that all the torments of purgatory were locked up tight within his skull.

The traveller reached out, his hand touching the warden's throat as though offering a blessing.

"Balor spare you, boy." He breathed, in a small, raspy voice. It was a ritual greeting, no more portentous or omen-laden than a simple hello, and yet it placed a chill in Sláine's heart. *Balor One-Eye spare you from the plague of man is the full greeting,* Sláine heard the voice of the Crone inside his skull. *The plague of man being evil, if you haven't worked that out yet. The idea is simple enough, before the advent of man there was no evil.* He pressed at his temple, pushing the heel of his hand into his eye. Her words were like steel spikes being driven into his brain.

"Get... out of... my... head," Sláine rasped, earning a puzzled look from Ukko.

"I don't like this place, Sláine. I really don't like it."

"You are not alone, dwarf," Sláine blinked back the sudden flare of pain. His mouth was parched, and his head swam, the ground shifting treacherously beneath his feet as he walked on past the guards, ignoring their stares.

None of them moved to stop him.

The gates of Purgadair were, like the city itself, immense structures more than five times the height of the men guarding it. Each railing in the gigantic framework was thicker than a man's arm and carved with the finest details. The weather-rot had begun to claim some of the finesse from the masonry but as Sláine reached out for the support of an iron handrail, his hand closed around the brooding likeness of a demon that had been woven into the pitted iron. Red tears of rust ran down its anguished face so it was impossible to tell if the demon regretted the rise of Purgadair or thrived on its soullessness. Together, the sand-blasted weathering and corrosion lent the demon the appearance of a desperate captive trapped within an iron prison.

Beside him, Ukko peered down a long and winding street at the array of insanities on display. Sláine followed the direction of his gaze. There were no people, at least none like him, but there were crowds and mad delights. The street was filled with everything from puppet shows and the mimes plying their trade, weasel-faced children looking on in rapt delight; butchers and bakers filling their windows with foods and smells that tantalised the nose and revolted the eye; to the crazy warren of alleyways and curved stairways that wriggled between the buildings and the barrage of colours seemingly strung across every available inch of sky. Brightly coloured silks tied to bone-white tusks formed canopies over part of the street, shielding the bazaar of the bizarre from the worst of the sun.

Seeing them, the children chittered and squawked animatedly, gesturing wildly at the strange intruders. The commotion served to draw even more unwanted attention to them.

"I think we need to move on," Ukko said, pointedly. "Find this Skinless Man, make like a shepherd and get the flock out of here."

"For once, you'll get no argument from me," Sláine rubbed at his chin, feeling the stubble rasp beneath his fingers. He turned too quickly, a wave of nausea welling up inside him. The pain in his head burned. He winced as he backed away into one of the countless cramped byways leading into the belly of the great city. "Come on."

Purgadair was a place of vile wonder.

Distant roars rumbled, chased by a rolling wave of cheers.

Everything was so daunting, every building a behemoth of stone, every street horribly claustrophobic. Worst of all though were the denizens of the strange city. They were all slants on the same demonic fusion of animal and human, a different blend of species dominant in each of the inhabitants they saw. Their perversion was repulsive to look upon – and yet it was impossible to look away. They were everywhere, on street corners, in windows, gathered around stalls, walking. Sláine felt utterly exposed. The city was populated by monsters. Sláine and Ukko walked side by side, trying to take it all in.

The crack of a whip startled Sláine. A slave driver hustled a group of beaten-down prisoners across the street towards the roar of the distant crowd. A familiar face stared hatefully at Sláine – a face he had never thought to see again: Cullen of the Wide Mouth. The wrongness of seeing his childhood nemesis here in these strange streets where he hadn't seen another human being was undeniable. Cullen was dead – killed by his own gae bolga after his jealousy had bettered the tenuous bonds of friendship the young men of the Red Branch shared. Cullen was dead and yet here he was, captive to these diabolic creatures. The slave driver lashed his prisoners on, steering them towards a wider street.

"I can save him," Sláine breathed, unaware that he had actually given voice to the thought. It felt right. He started forwards.

Ukko snagged ahold of his belt and pulled him up short. "Oh, no you don't, big man. Rein in those suicidal instincts."

"I–"

"I said no you don't. Remember what the crow-woman said. Things you see here aren't real."

"She didn't say that," said Sláine, remembering full well what the Crone had said.

"Might as well have. The street's empty, Sláine. There's nothing there except the ghosts inside your head. We need to find the Skinless Man, right? So let's just concentrate on doing that. This place feeds on your guilt, remember?"

"I remember," said Sláine, grudgingly. "But–"

"Why does there always have to be a 'but' with you? Huh? The Morrigan warned you that the city would manifest your guilt if you let it, and now you would go chasing after the ghost of some long-buried shame. Does that not strike you as, I don't know… erm… stupid?"

"But–"

"Crom's hairy gonads! Don't you ever just *listen*? There's nothing there. The street is empty. I can't see anything, so whatever you *are* seeing, it isn't there. It's in your head. Which means it isn't real. Which means it *is* trouble."

Ignoring the dwarf, Sláine set off after Cullen.

The slave driver herded them on mercilessly, his whip biting into the bare backs of his prisoners, the lash drawing weals and blood. No matter how quickly Sláine ran the slaver kept his captives just out of reach. Cullen looked back imploringly at Sláine, blame in his hate-filled eyes. Sláine could hear Ukko grunting and huffing behind him as he struggled to keep up.

The roars of the crowd grew nearer until, finally, they reached a mighty coliseum. The stone here was red with the blood of the fallen who had given their lives for the sport of the beasts of Purgadair. Through the ground-level arches Sláine could see the track, where charioteers lashed their teams into a frenzy, steel wheels eating the dirt of the arena as they raced for glory.

Sláine stopped, frozen in horror at the sight of his mother, running for her life before the pounding hooves of the teams and the wicked steel barbs set into the wheels. She was fast but she couldn't possibly win. The crowd bayed for her blood. The charioteers yelled at their teams, goading them on faster and still faster, until they were bearing down on the terrified Macha, and still she ran, head back, tears streaming down her cheeks, arms pumping desperately.

Sláine stumbled forwards a step, bumping into one of the hungry-eyed onlookers.

Macha turned into the home straight, the chariots on her heels. Fear and determination burned in her face – until she saw her son, on the side of the track. There was a moment, the space between heartbeats, when they looked at each other and the track, Purgadair, the world, ceased to exist. It was only the two of them.

Her lips moved. He could read their accusation: *you could have saved me.*

But he knew he couldn't – that was his guilt talking – and it all came back, the world, the city, the track and the raging stampede of the teams driven by men he knew, men he had left behind in Murias. Men his drunken sot of a father had called friends.

It wasn't real. None of it was real.

Macha went down beneath the wheels and hooves but before they could trample her to death she faded into nothing, her spirit released as Sláine came to terms with his own failure. "I couldn't save you then and I can't save you now," he breathed. A lone tear rolled down his cheek. He felt so utterly alone. Bereft. Losing her once had been hard. Losing her twice was devastating; a loss no son should have to bear.

Sláine turned his back on the ghosts of the coliseum track and walked away.

"We find this skinless one and get out of here."

Beside him, Ukko nodded.

There were no jokes or admonishments this time.

Three
The Skinless Man

UNDERSTANDING CAME TO Sláine.

The city was a reflection of its people.

At the base it was corrupt, like the flesh and blood of the mortal being, craving and obsessive. Vice dominated the claustrophobic lower streets. The sins of need and desire subjugated anything more spiritual. There was no Earth Power because there was no connection to the land. The creatures that lived on these lower tiers were parasites, bloating themselves on the carcass of civilisation. Sláine and Ukko scoured the streets but found no sign of the Skinless Man. None of the denizens of Purgadair deigned to talk with them. The animals turned up their beaks and snouts and made as though they were nothing more than a bad smell to be ignored. But through each tier rising towards the highest level of the city matters of the flesh dwindled until, on the top tiers they encountered no one, the streets dedicated to dreams and souls and men no longer living.

"This place," said Ukko, "is downright creepy. It's like a ghost town."

"That is exactly what it is," Sláine agreed, pushing open a door and stepping into an abandoned house. The room was dark, the table still set for a dinner that was never eaten. The food had rotted on the plate.

Ukko shivered as he crossed the threshold. The house reeked of abandonment.

"It's like they went out and never came home."

Giving voice to their fears didn't make them any less pressing. Sláine moved through the room, looking for significations for its recent desertion. Wooden shades had been shuttered to keep out the worst of the endless day's heat.

Sláine backed out of the room.

The house next door was much the same, though the shutters were open and instead of food on the table there was a single overturned tankard and a dark circle stained into the wood. The next two houses were derelict, empty but for an uncomfortable sulphuric aroma.

"Perhaps they went down below and became those abominations." He stopped talking as he pushed open the door of the next hovel. The table was set, as with the first house, but the centrepiece was a young man, trussed up, naked, flayed and partially carved. The soft meat of his belly glistened redly on the huge platter. The corpse was surrounded by succulent roots slathered in butter. Unlike all the other food they had found, this feast was fresh.

Ukko pushed in past him. "Is that? No, don't tell me. I don't want to know. I mean… urgh. Cannibals?"

"Is it cannibalism when there's no trace of humanity in these predators? By the looks of things we're nothing more than cattle to them, to be bred, slaughtered, gutted and carved up."

"Can't say I really care about definitions right now. Maybe it's because when mummy dearest gets home she'll take one look at me and think: ooh, din dins." Ukko turned away from the feast, his face suddenly a bilious shade of green. "You don't think that is what the witch meant by Skinless Man do you? Find the dead guy on the plate, he's the key? He was flayed before they laid him out to eat… flayed… no skin."

"No," Sláine said, quite certain the meal was not what they had come looking for. They had found a skinless man, not the Skinless Man. "It feels like a title, not an ingredient. Come on."

"You're the hero, I'm just the lackey."

They moved down the row of abandoned houses quickly, pushing doors open, looking for signs of life, secretly grateful every time they found none.

The sun was relentless. Twilight offered no respite, ceding the sky to the second sun long before it had cooled the streets. Sláine felt his headache returning with a vengeance. At the far end of the street lay a series of troughs used for watering the animals. They might as well have been a mirage; they were dried up, as were the barrels beside them. Sláine cracked the lids off all of them, just to be sure. As Brain-Biter splintered the last piece of wood, a second crack echoed somewhere behind him. Sláine lowered the axe to his side and leaned over the cask, fascinated. He strained to listen, to hear anything else out of place. Ukko scuffed about in the dust for a moment, then even he stopped and the silence was complete. He had almost succeeded in convincing himself that they were alone when he heard it again: a slow drawn-out sighing followed by a *crump*.

Sláine rose slowly, and turned.

The street behind him was empty.

"Did you hear it?" he asked the dwarf, his voice barely above a whisper.

"Aye, I did."

"Stay close to me," Sláine said, hefting his axe and resting it lightly on his shoulder.

"I've got no intention of going anywhere," Ukko said. His resolve lasted exactly thirty-nine steps. On the fortieth the sky caved in – or at least that was how it appeared at first as streaks of fire rained down from above. Ukko bolted. Sláine threw his left arm up to shield his face from the flames. Cinders bit into his flesh, searing through the skin all the way to the bone in four places, like fang-marks. He jerked his arm back, barely ducking out of the way of another trailing flare. He looked up to see five huge carapaced insectoid warriors scuttle out into the street before him. Their mandibles dripped ichor as they skittered forwards, pincers clacking on the hard sand of the street.

Sláine stepped forwards to meet them.

It was a mistake.

They were evolved for the climate and conditions, bred to kill. This was their natural habitat. They surged up the narrow street, scaling the walls, and onto the rooftops. More came in behind the initial five, coming over the rooftops and dropping down into the street. Their chittering spiralled into a hungry chorus as still more came pouring out of the cracks in the stonework, through the dark windows and up through the webway of gutter and sewer beneath the streets. As they neared, the full repulsiveness of their physique became apparent: the creatures were huge, twice Sláine's height and more, and four of their arachnoid legs ended in either savage pincers or wicked saw-toothed blades. Their jewel-encrusted carapaces were covered in scraps of rancid flesh worn like trophies. Fetishes of bone and tooth were draped around their throats.

"Far be it from me to interrupt a family gathering," Ukko said, as the insectoids continued to spill out of every nook and cranny until the street was alive with the hellish chittering and clicking of their mandibles, and he took off running.

The black-carapaced hunters swarmed forwards.

Sláine clenched fists around the hilt of Brain-Biter, kissing the axe's blade. "Come to me then, my uglies. Who wants to be the first to bleed for me?"

Sláine rolled his shoulder, slamming the axe down in a shocking display of raw power, splitting the nearest of the giant insects in two right down the length of the carapace. Blue-green viscous ichor leaked out of the rent as he tugged Brain-Biter free. Sláine stood on the back of the insect, crushing it beneath his foot like the bug it was.

"You die too easily, there's no sport in a bug hunt!"

Two of the critters dropped from the roofs on either side of him, pincers and claws clashing and snapping around his legs. Sláine blocked one set of blades as they scythed towards his ankles, but couldn't parry the second set of pincers as they snapped around his arm, cutting viciously into his bicep. He roared, kicking out at the first of the insects, burying his foot into the soft flesh between its crusted underbelly and the plates protecting its ridged head. The creature's death rattle was grotesque. Before it hit the floor two more had replaced it, blades and pincers blurring into a whirling dance of death. Sláine ducked beneath one cut, barely getting Brain-Biter between his gut and the saw-toothed blade, before having to throw himself out of the path of another. The pincers clashed close enough to scrape whiskers from his chin. Sláine launched himself upright, gasping hard, blood streaming from the slash in his arm as he drove the axe through the insect's hard-cased coxa.

He blocked three more blows on the blade of his axe, and countered with raw fury, scything Brain-Biter through the chittering mandibles of the closest foe. The blade sheered through the spindly legs and dripping fangs. The creature cried out in outrage. Sláine shifted his body weight and reversed the momentum of the axe, cleaving it into the insect's head. The blow split the ridge of shell and buried itself deep into the eye, severing the nerves as it sank all the way through to the mash of the dead critter's brain stem.

Sláine yanked Brain-Biter free; the great stone axe was covered with gore.

He cut the legs out from under the next of the hellish spawn, reckless from the scent of his blood, which got too close to Brain-Biter.

He spread death across the sands, leaving them slick with malignant blood.

Still the creatures came at him. There were too many to count. The air *thrummed* with the lethal harmonics of their pincers and blades, as their tarsi chimed off and scraped against stone and flesh.

Sláine cleaved a set of claws from its surprised owner, then stepped forwards, slipping as his foot came down on a ruptured compound eye that had been rent from a cleaved skull. Losing his balance, Sláine fell to one knee and drove Brain-Biter upwards, ramming the axe's point up under the labrium of his monstrous attacker, sinking it deep into the soft flesh of the insect's brain. The creature howled its pain, torn by paroxysms of agony as its body succumbed to the inevitable death rattle and slumped down on top of Sláine. Its weight dragged him to the floor. Even as he tried to thrust the dead shell aside more of the insects surged forwards, overwhelming him.

UKKO STOPPED RUNNING twenty paces down the narrow street and turned. For a moment it looked as though Sláine would fend the giant insects off, but there were simply too many of them. Ukko watched in horror as Sláine went down beneath the weight of insects.

It was a vision fit for the Underworld itself.

"Bloody stupid heroes... going on stupid quests. Dumb idea to listen to the crow. Now look at what's happening... Don't you dare die on me, Sláine!"

He didn't know what he was going to do until he was already doing it. The little man pushed open the nearest door and rushed into the room. Like all the others it reeked of death; he knew why now. He looked around the room frantically but couldn't find what he needed. There was no fire grate, no logs waiting to burn. "But why would there be?" He chided himself, grabbing a stiff-backed chair and slamming it against the wall again and again until it splintered and he was left holding two splintered legs. All he could think of was the body they had found trussed up on the dining table like a side of pig. That wasn't the way he intended to go – not that he actually intended to go *any* way. "What the feth am I supposed to do with these against a ravening horde of man-eating insects?"

He threw them on the floor, dropped to his knees and shucked out of his sack. "A good thief always comes prepared, Ukko, my boy."

He rummaged around inside the sack until he found the grease he had used to loosen the odd lock along the way. He scooped out handfuls of the oily substance and smeared it along the broken chair legs until he was happy they were coated with the stuff. Without thinking, Ukko fetched his tinderbox out of the pack and struck it over and over until it caught, igniting the oil and turning the chair leg into a blazing torch. He stuffed everything back into his pack and shouldered it, lighting the second wooden leg as he charged, screaming like a banshee possessed out of the hovel and down the street, brandishing the flaming spars like weapons.

Ukko ran straight into the chittering and shrieking mass of insects that had swarmed over the fallen barbarian, thrusting the blazing torches into what he hoped were their faces.

They skittered away from the fire, retreating fearfully from Ukko as he brandished the flame like a madman, slashing around in wild arcs, trying to force them back. "Come on, Sláine! Get up!" Ukko didn't dare look back, he just kept on with his wild dance, waving his arms around and jumping up and down. And then he understood why the insects feared the fire so much. One of the broken chair legs slapped into the side of one of the critters and it erupted in a violent fiery ball. The explosion threw Ukko from his feet, but he rolled and came up grinning as it set a chain reaction in motion: the insects too close to the burning insect shrieked as the gases leaking from their slathering mouths ignited and tongues of fire lashed down their throats, detonating within their guts. Faggots of charred flesh clung to the walls and smouldered on the sand. Fragments of burned-out shell steamed where they had slashed like shrapnel into the carapaces of the remaining spawn.

"Their guts are filled with gas!" Ukko yelled triumphantly, laughing manically as he threw himself forwards again, slashing fire into the faces of the retreating insects to send them skittering away down the street. "That's it, go on! Get! Go! That'll teach you to tangle with a coward!"

His laughter rang down the street.

THE SUDDEN HEAT wrenched the breath from his lungs.

Sláine tried to stand. The fires of agony burned through a thousand cuts across his body.

He couldn't understand why they had let him live.

The giant insects had engulfed him, pincers and claws cutting away at his flesh until he lacked the will let alone the strength to fight back, and then, as he had surrendered to the notion of death here in this hellish place, they had fled.

Ukko stood over him, brands burning in either hand, face lit up like a demented demon, eyes burning twice as feverishly as any physical fire could.

"That's it, go on! Get! Go! That'll teach you to tangle with a coward!" Ukko mocked, flourishing the flaming torches. Sláine wanted to laugh but couldn't because it hurt too much to even *think* about it. He didn't want to contemplate the mess his body must have been in back in the mortal realm. It was a miracle he was still alive.

They had cut him badly, one slash wide enough to open his stomach. It ought to have been a mortal blow. Instead it began to fuse and knit beneath his fingers as he tried to feel out the extent of his injuries until it was nothing more than a white line running across the musculature from his groin to his belly. He tried to sit. The world swam, lurching violently beneath him.

"You look like–" the dwarf stopped speaking as Sláine's fingers found another ragged wound and sealed it. "I thought there was no magic here... I mean... how did you?"

"I don't know," Sláine said, and in truth he didn't. There was no thrill of the Earth Serpent surging through him, no connection with Danu or the land. He couldn't begin to explain it. Was his spirit drawing the last dregs of healing from the land his body lay on back on the fringes of Dardun? Was it an illusion, those wounds still bleeding out from his flesh even though they appeared healed here?

The pain itself lingered even if the wounds did not. He felt it inside, beneath the skin, as though he had been cut and cut and cut, each one searing as he made even the slightest move. Getting out of Purgadair was not going to be a simple case of running – he wasn't even sure he'd be up to *walking* out of the hellish city.

"I'm not being funny, but these faggots are going to burn out soon and then the bugs will be back with a vengeance, so how about we don't sit around here contemplating miracles and instead run for it?"

He held up a hand for Ukko to help him to his feet, and had to stifle a scream as he was tugged upright.

"He isn't here, is he?" Ukko said, casting an erratic gaze left and right as though trying to take everything in at once. "It was a trick. The Morrigan wanted us here so she could do whatever she has to do without us around to interfere."

Do you believe that, son of the Sessair? Truly? Do you believe yourself so important I would need *to dispose of you to carry out my schemes? Vanity is the last resort of the fool. Find the Skinless Man for yourself, your people.*

He didn't know if he imagined the Crone's denial, but he found himself believing it. A being of her power would not need to trick them into some foolish quest – there had to be more to it than that.

There always was with the Crone; deceit came as naturally to the ancient one as did any kind of truth. But, he suspected, the promise she had extracted from him was worth too much to her to waste so frivolously. *Good, use your brain, barbarian.*

"He's here," Sláine said, knowing it to be true. "But he isn't *here.* What did the Crone say? What were her exact words?"

"I don't remember," the dwarf admitted.

I do, the voice goaded. *A city on the edge of Nàimhdiel, a harsh and utterly barren desert. The Skinless Man you seek resides there, but beware child of Danu, this is a cruel place, this city.* The Crone's words rose in his memory, the subtlety of the sentence had misdirected their search.

"He is in the desert, not the city."

My clever, clever barbarian, the voice of the Crone mocked. *Learned to listen at last.*

Sláine took one of the burning brands; more than half of it was charred to the breaking point. "We need more, before these burn out."

Ukko nodded and gestured for Sláine to follow him into the nearest house. "Go crazy," he waved towards the wooden chairs and began rifling through his pack for the flammable grease. Sláine shattered three of the chairs, wrenching the legs away from the rest of the frames and passing them to the dwarf. Ukko liberally applied the grease and stuffed two into his belt, making sure he didn't hold the naked flame too close. Sláine took the remaining staves, lit one on the burned-out torch Ukko had used to save him and stowed the rest.

They went back out into the street.

The vile insectoid creatures lined the rooftops, antennae twitching as their multi-faceted eyes caught and reflected and refracted the light from the twin suns.

"We're going to walk out of here nice and slow," said Sláine, wincing as he shouldered Brain-Biter. "No sudden movements. We don't want to set them off."

Ukko nodded without saying a word.

They walked slowly side by side down the narrow street. His skin crawled, prickling with goosebumps. The hair on the nape of his neck rose like hackles as they passed the first of the lurking insects. The creature's antennac began to twitch furiously, its mandibles grinding together coarsely.

"Just keep walking," said Sláine, advice that was easier said than followed. His eyes roved from high to low, left to right, trying to keep all of the angles covered in case of sudden ambush, but it was impossible.

One of the monstrosities leaned low, distended jaws crunching towards them. Thick yellowish saliva drooled from the fangs, sizzling as it hit the floor. Sláine realised then what had caused the pinhole wounds that had burned into his arm. The knowledge sent a sick shiver down his spine. He walked on, his foot grinding the blistering sand beneath it.

Sláine thrust the blazing torch towards its nose, forcing the creature to skitter back. It gave him a grim sort of satisfaction to frighten the insect even as more loomed over them, crouching on the rooftops, only held back by the flame.

"You do realise when we get out of here I am going to be merciless with the next earwig I see," said Ukko. "And daddy long legs, forget it, those legs are coming off. Ants, flies, cockroaches. If I never see another living insect it'll be too soon."

They followed the curve of the street down to the next level, the insects swelling and surging around them, following their passage back down to the lower tiers of Purgadair.

"We could just torch the place," Ukko said, hopefully. "The way the buildings are cramped so close together the whole place would go up in smoke in no time." The little runt looked delighted at the prospect.

"The buildings are made of stone," Sláine pointed out, fending off another curious insect with a thrust of the brand in his hand.

"Doesn't matter, the roofs are made of wood, in this heat it'd be an inferno in no time."

Sláine shook his head, "No, we'll just make our way out nice and slowly. We don't need to bring the whole place down around our ears, as appealing as it might be. We aren't here as destroyers. Besides, I don't fancy having to fight every insect *and* all of those demonic man-animal guards down there just to get out into the desert and have the Goddess alone knows what looking to skewer us."

They continued to work their way slowly down the twists and turns of Purgadair's streets, each declination offering tantalising glimpses of the whitewashed walls and rooftops of the lower hovels, and the desert beyond the city walls. Many of the hovels were two and three storeys high, or rather deep, these upper levels opening out on the tier below. The lower they went the more the sharp turns began to resemble the staggered steps of a huge ziggurat, descending a few hundred feet every turn of the street.

All around them the insects crowded in, drawn by the scent of their flesh. Sláine lit a fresh brand and handed it to Ukko, then lit another for himself. He resisted the impulse to toss the almost-spent torch up into the middle of the encroaching insects. Barely. His instinct as a warrior was to drive them away, to cleave and crush and smear their viscera across the ichor-slicked streets and stand amid their broken carapaces, victorious, blood pumping, Earth Power firing his veins. Sláine's fist clenched and unclenched around the splintered chair leg as it burned down in his hand. He felt its heat on his face and hand as the flames licked both ways, consuming the wood.

There were hundreds, thousands of the huge insects swarming across the low rooftops.

Ukko let his torch drop for a split second, reaching down to scratch his armpit with his spare hand

– and almost paid for the momentary lapse of concentration. Two of the creatures reacted instantaneously, launching themselves from the rooftop at the dwarf. Sláine lunged forwards, thrusting his own firebrand into the giant insect's labrum, forcing the creature to eat the fire. Grabbing Ukko by the collar Sláine shoved the dwarf, sending him sprawling indignantly across the sand. Sláine ducked and rolled away from the creature barely a fraction of a second before it was engulfed in flame as its own gases erupted and the explosion pasted its guts all across the street. The second insect skittered away and up onto the roof on the other side of the street, barely escaping the explosion.

"So much for no sudden movements," Sláine said, smearing a charred strip of intestinal tract across his brow.

"I had an itch," Ukko mumbled defensively. "What was I supposed to do?"

A SWARM OF angry insects blocked their path; their bodies were crushed together en-masse so that they formed an impenetrable living wall.

Sláine stopped, pushing the burning stave in front of them and waiting for the fire to open up a path through the insects. They were packed too close together to allow for retreat. It was impossible to tell how deep the black-carapaced wall was. Their only chance of getting to the other side of the wall of insects was to burn their way through, but looking at the endless wave of antennae and mandibles Sláine doubted the practicality of charging the wall, fire or no fire. Which meant there was no chance they could leave the way they had come – meaning, in turn, there was no route back to the hillside where the Morrigan had opened the door between yesterday and today for them.

There was no way out.

They were trapped.

"What now?"

The wall of chittering and shrieking insects surged towards them.

"We're not dying here, not to some flaming bug."

"Flaming bug, that's almost funny."

"Just give me your torch."

Sláine hurled the centre of the living wall, triggering a series of deafening explosions as first one and then dozens of the gaseous insects burst into flame. He didn't wait to see the extent of the damage. The harsh series of detonations and the desperate shrieks of the insects was enough to tell him too many had survived. Without thinking, Sláine shouldered open the nearest door and bundled Ukko through it. He planted his own firebrand in the doorway, praying it would keep the creatures at bay long enough for them to find a way out of this hell hole.

The room was barren, the walls smeared with what looked like dried blood. There was no sign of the hovel's previous inhabitants, either here or in the lower rooms, as they descended the rickety wooden stair set into the corner of the corridor leading off the main living quarters.

"We should burn it," Ukko said, looking back over his shoulder at the stairs, "so they can't follow us."

"No point, they'd just cover over the rooftops," Sláine grunted, kicking down the door. "Come on, before they realise where we've gone."

The pair of them ran out into the street, looked left, saw the huge wall of seething insects pressing into the narrow street, multi-faceted eyes blazing, saw-toothed blades dragging a *screeee-scraaaaw* against the baked stone, and ran right, arms and legs pumping furiously.

The air burned in Sláine's lungs. The incessant *screeee-scraaaaw* rasping swelled to fill his head until it was all he heard; a death sentence scratched out on the very fabric of the nightmarish city.

The street ahead divided into three branches, left, right and straight on. Sláine took the sinister path. Beside him, Ukko gasped and panted, his short legs struggling to match Sláine's powerful stride. Sláine stooped low and scooped the dwarf up, hoisting him over his shoulder. The dwarf wriggled around like a lizard, struggling to break free of Sláine's iron grip. "Just lie still and tell me if you see them coming!"

Thirty yards down the left-hand path the shadows of the huge insects returned, crushing down on them from the high rooftops of the hovels. Sláine didn't waste energy or momentum looking at them, he ran for his life, Brain-Biter in one hand, Ukko in the other.

This time there was no fire to keep the insects back.

THE STREET OPENED up into a vast square, outside of the city walls and yet not a part of the desert proper. The centre of the square was dominated by a towering leafless tree. It was a remarkable sight, soaring into the blazing sky, a thousand skeletal branches reaching out over every inch of the square. Their emaciated shadows crept into every crack and crevice, worming into the hard-baked ground, between the stones of the walls of the hovels.

"They're gaining!" Ukko gasped into his ear, kicking Sláine in the chest frantically as though trying to spur him on.

Sláine grunted, and looked around, trying to decide which way to run.

The choices were rapidly disappearing as, street by street, the wall of insects became a noose, tightening around the square until no avenue of escape remained. His heart hammered in his chest. He tried desperately to draw upon the Earth Serpent, but was answered by the sucking emptiness of the void where the Goddess ought to have been.

They had been corralled in this direction, herded into the square.

He lowered Ukko to the ground and grasped his axe, ready to fight.

Beside him, the dwarf pulled out a short pig-sticker of a blade. He looked utterly terrified. Sláine had no words to comfort him.

"Stupid bloody quest," Ukko mumbled, looking despairingly at each and every one of the blocked streets and then at the floor, hoping against hope that it might open up and swallow him before the creatures of Purgadair could. His face curled up into a bitter sneer. "Just so you know, I've got no intention of dying here, so you'd better work something out."

They edged back, step by precious step until their backs were pressed against the mighty tree, and still the creatures poured out into the square.

"Can you get another one of those torches lit? Maybe we can burn the tree or something?"

"Urm, Sláine, you might want to look at this."

Sláine twisted, trying to see where the dwarf was pointing: but all he saw was the trunk of the great tree.

The sea of writhing black bodies parted, and through the centre walked a monstrous regiment of deformed and perverted creatures, blades drawn, feral faces hungry for blood.

"What?"

"I think we found him."

It took a moment for the dwarf's words to register. When they finally did, they made no sense whatsoever. "What?"

"The Skinless Man, I think we found him."

Sláine risked another backwards glance, trying to see what the dwarf was going on about. This time he saw it: in the folds of the bark, the silhouette of a man's anguished face. Fingers of wood reached out of the knotted bole, clawing at the life that had been stolen from the man as he was locked within the wood.

This was their saviour? A man trapped within a dead tree in the middle of some hellish desert?

Sláine laughed bitterly. "You stupid bloody fool, this is what you get for listening to the Morrigan."

"What are we supposed to do now?"

"Die," Sláine said.

"How about we don't?"

Sláine thought about it for a moment, and made his choice. "Burn the damned tree down. Let's go out fighting. The music of their hunger excites me," Sláine roared, a terrible boiling anger surging through him. "I will teach them a thing or two about death."

"Spoken like a true hero," Ukko grimaced.

UKKO HAD NO idea how long Sláine could hold the animal guard off without the *riastrad*, his fierce berserker warp-spasm, roaring through his veins, swelling his musculature to transform him into the juggernaut he was.

Minutes, no more, surely. Less.

Every instinct cried out: run! But there was nowhere to run to.

Ukko couldn't let himself think about it.

He needed to burn the tree: Sláine was counting on him. He wouldn't let him down – at least not deliberately.

Shaking, fear coursing through his limbs, the scoundrel emptied his pack out across the sand, pawing through the pile of junk until he found the tin of grease. He unscrewed the lid. It was all but empty. He scooped out the last smears of grease and rubbed them into the gnarled face trapped within the bark. He looked around desperately for anything else that might burn. There was nothing.

He fumbled with his tinder, trying to strike a light but he was shaking too much. He dropped the flint and straw and scrambled around in the sand trying to find it.

"Crap, crap, crap, ah *there* it is!" His quick-bitten fingernails snagged the jagged splinter of rock.

He looked up. There was a shadow over the sun, a black winged shape. For a moment Ukko imagined it was some hideous Other Realm winged daemon come to add insult to his injuries, the way it flitted against the burning sphere, and then it gained more solidity and definition: one of the Morrigan's birds coming out of the sun.

He never thought for a moment he would ever be glad to see one of those damned crows. He was wrong.

"Sláine! Sláine! Look!"

And then the battle was joined with a hellish chorus of animalistic growls and roars as Sláine launched himself at the advancing beasts.

There was a dark need in the barbarian to cause pain; that was the true Sláine, not the surly companion he walked with. Sláine was a warrior to the core. Fifty beasts, one hundred, a field of fiends, he did not think it too many. Ukko looked from the bird to the warrior and back to the huge circling bird.

Brain-Biter dripped with the gore of the dead.

"Kiss my axe, dog breath!" Sláine raged; his battle cry drowned out the screams of the animal-men as they threw themselves at the lone axeman. There was no compassion, no humanity, only naked savagery as the Sessair drove his axe in a glorious dance of death as he charged to meet his foe head-on. Even without the blazing power of Danu surging through him, the barbarian in battle rage was an awesome sight. The front ranks of the dog-faced guards broke, howling their frustration as Brain-Biter tore into their flesh and fur. Their cries ululated over the chitinous taunts of the insects. Their death-rattles punctuated the chorus.

In moments the sun-blasted square reeked of slaughter and Sláine was in the thick of it.

A dog soldier's arm fell at Ukko's feet, blood gouting from the ragged stump where it had been severed. The blood stained the sand a dark red.

Ukko shuddered and kicked it aside.

He struck the tinder, desperately trying to cause a lethal spark, but his trembling hands betrayed him. "Come on, come on, come on," he urged himself, almost dropping the damned flint again. He swallowed, mouth raw. He couldn't stop the shakes now that they had taken hold. "I've been in worse messes than this, just concentrate, you can do this with your bloody eyes closed." He fixated on his grubby fingers fumbling with the flint and steel, striking them again and again, begging the grease to catch one of the sparks and burn.

He couldn't bring himself to look at the face trapped within the ancient tree, fearing what he might see in its ancient eyes.

And then one of the sparks caught and the grease smeared into the tree smouldered. Ukko blew on it gently, encouraging the flame to feed on the tree. A moment later grease and bark crackled, the spark spreading. Ukko fanned the tiny flame, desperately trying to get it to bite...

And the bark-covered eyes flared open, the face trapped within the tree wracked with pain and sudden fear as the flames caught, searing into it. The bark withered and blistered, splitting beneath the sudden intense bloat of heat. And as it cracked and flaked away, the flesh beneath emerged like a snake shedding its skin.

The fire did not touch the Skinless Man as his distorted face pressed out from the charring bark, stretching the wood hideously until almost the entire head had breached the wooden prison. The bark across the Skinless Man's mouth splintered in a silent scream as the tormented soul tried desperately to vent his pain and anger. Ukko reached up with the smouldering tinder, touching it to the wood around the Skinless Man's screaming mouth. It caught and burned, shrivelling away to char and crumbling beneath the ferocity of his sudden cry as the grip of his prison finally relented and he tasted the acrid air of freedom.

Ukko was torn between watching the destruction of the tree and the slaughter of the monstrous man-animals as Sláine hacked and slashed into their soft bodies, gutting them, splitting their carcasses in two, severing limbs, opening grotesque full-face smiles as Brain-Biter carved from bloody grins that split the heads from cheek to jowel.

The air stank of blood and burning.

The screams of the wounded spiralled, choking off abruptly, silenced by Brain-Biter's hungry edge.

Ukko wiped the sweat from his forehead and tried to calm his racing heart. The trembling had become full-blown shaking. He straightened slowly, drawing a deep breath. Smelling the dank wood of the tree's ruptured soul, the scoundrel felt the ground beneath his feet shiver, small tremors in the sand churning up earthworms and insects and the foetid stench of death. Fingertips broached the bark, pressing out towards his face. The wood blackened and charred beneath the bite of fire, flaking away until all that remained were the questing fingers covered in a swirl of blue-inked tattoos. The fingers clawed at the air as the Skinless Man emerged from the tree inch by agonising inch. The hands tore free of their prison then turned on the jagged splinters of wood, shredding the pulp as the conflagration swelled to engulf the entire tree.

The Skinless Man's arms were free; the tattoos continued up the hands in amazingly intricate detail. As more and more of the bark and blackened pulp fell away Ukko saw that there wasn't an inch of skin uncovered.

The flames parted around the Skinless Man's arms; they didn't touch them.

The flat bone of his fontanele breached the bark, breaking through in a perverse re-enactment of birth.

Ukko stared at the Skinless Man's head as it pushed out through the wound in the tree.

Like his arms, every inch of the Skinless Man's head was inked with intricate images.

"Thank you," the man rasped, spitting splinters from his mouth. His arms straightened and started to press down against the burning trunk of the tree, the sheer strength alone pushing his body gradually free of its prison. Half in and half out of the flaming tree, the man reached out for Ukko. "Help me, please..."

Ukko reached up and grabbed the tattooed hand. It felt peculiar, cold as though no blood pumped beneath the inked skin. He tried not to think about it. Instead he heaved with all of his might, throwing his bodyweight behind one massive wrench. The wood splintered all around the Skinless Man as he threw his head back and screamed, dragging the remainder of his body from the burning tree.

Even as he fell free Ukko saw, with horror, that his eyes retained a wooden veneer; as though part of him had failed to escape.

He collapsed into Ukko's arms, barely clinging to consciousness. The resurrection had been brutal.

As he lay sprawled in the sand at the foot of the ruined tree Ukko saw that the endless knot of tattoos formed a single grand design.

The flames roared up the ruptured trunk of the lone tree, consuming everything they touched, every inch of bark and wood, spreading voraciously along every branch, crackling and snapping as the wood blistered, charred and died. A series of sharp cracks resonated through the heart of the old tree. A withered branch fell, still burning. Then another, and another, falling on the upturned face of one of the repulsive gaseous insectoids. It opened its mouth as though to scream, and fire blazed out ripping into the hide of a wolfen man-animal rearing up to strike a savage blow into Sláine's unprotected side. The beast went down, the skin scorched on its back, leaving it raw and bloody and black, blisters and welts oozing as it writhed on the ground in agony.

Sláine put the wolf-man out of its misery, crushing its skull beneath his boot as he decapitated another of its kin with ruthless efficiency. He was covered in a score of shallow cuts, the worst of which ran from his temple to his nipple, bleeding into his eye. Another wound opened across the barbarian's chest as he parried a leonine warrior's claws on the head of Brain-Biter. The slash hadn't touched him, yet the wound bled as freely as any of the others on his body. Ukko understood instinctively what the impossible wound signified.

"Sláine!" he yelled in warning as another fell beast launched itself at the young Sessair's unprotected back.

The Morrigan's crow cawed harshly, its wings beating down on the rising flames as it circled the burning tree. The heat from the fire was overpowering, the stink of burnt flesh joining the heady melange of stinks. Ukko shielded himself from the worst of it, feeling his skin beginning to blister as the bird settled in a shimmer of heat-haze. Its black feathers moulted from its back and wings as the huge crow blurred out of focus, losing all shape and form as it slowly transformed into the hunched spectre of the Morrigan herself. The Crone hobbled towards the unlikely trio of Sláine, Ukko and the tattooed man, throwing her arms wide: "You must hurry, Sessair! This way, this way! Your mortal forms are under attack!"

She wove a pattern in the air, stirring the sand up from the ground like a spinning devil. The sand danced to the Crone's gesticulations, the vortex at its core quickening. The sudden surge of wind was fierce. Ukko looked into the heart of the devil and saw himself, Sláine, the pile of broken stones and dark shapes moving towards them threateningly.

The Skinless Man stared in sick horror at the wretched crow-faced hag as she opened the portal back to Tir-Nan-Og. "Morrigu!" He spat, lurching back as though struck.

"Save your hatred until you are safe, Myrrdin Emrys."

"You will pay for what you did to me, Crone," the man rasped.

"Yes, yes, yes, pay. But first, you must flee. Run mortal, run for your eternal soul. Run for your humanity. Run for your life!"

The churning devil of sand flew apart into a million tiny fragments, cutting into the ranks of Purgadair's grotesqueries, scything them down like row upon row of rag dolls.

The doorway between today and tomorrow and nevermore flew open.

"Come! Now! I cannot hold the way open for long." Judging by the strain in the Crone's voice the toll opening the portal had extracted was immense, and holding it open even for a moment was as much as the Goddess could endure.

A ribbon of blood ran down the side of Sláine's face. The battle rage was hot in his eyes. Brain-Biter lashed into another misshapen foe, spilling its guts on the sand. The man-animal's intestines unravelled in slick grey loops. Sláine swept the axe around in a savage arc, pushing the creatures back beyond its reach.

Without a second's hesitation the warrior turned, ran five paces and dived forwards, hurling himself through the shimmering portal. The Skinless Man followed him a moment later, his tattoos writhing with a life of their own as they came into contact with the immense power of the gateway.

Ukko stood on the edge of the portal and, against every screaming instinct, turned to look back. The mass of grotesqueries swarmed after him but the Morrigan stood between them, holding the monsters at bay. It hurt her, diminished her, and yet she did not falter even for a heartbeat.

"Why are you helping us?"

The Crone cackled madly, "My sister seems fond of this one. It would be a shame for him to die just yet. Go now, dwarf, or stay forever. I am closing the gate either way."

Ukko did not need telling a second time.

He stepped into the unknown.

Ukko's vision swam as the world swam, his balance betraying him.

He fell.

Four
Running the Stags

SLÁINE OPENED HIS eyes as the skull sword's blade thrust towards his throat.

A heartbeat later and he would have been dead.

He lunged to the right instinctively, sweeping his legs around and dumping the swordsman on his backside. It was enough to save his life but not enough to win his freedom. Two more filthy blades stabbed down, one hovering an inch above his heart, the other over his balls, effectively pinning him to the ground.

The skull sword he had tripped loomed over him a moment later.

"Well, well, well, what do we have here?" He removed his helm. Beneath the hair mask he looked utterly unremarkable. There was nothing that marked the man as evil. Nothing that betrayed his dark master. That was, perhaps, the most frightening aspect of Slough Feg's insidious evil: it tainted otherwise good men.

Sláine said nothing.

"Found this one hiding in the woods," another faceless skull sword said, two more brutes dragging the Skinless Man between them. He was battered and bruised, livid blue-black marks swelling beneath his skin. The unconscious man had taken a severe beating; reward for his resistance, no doubt, Sláine thought bitterly. As they dragged him closer, Sláine saw that rather than bruises much of the colouration was down to his wildly tattooed skin.

Ukko lay beside him, on his stomach, trussed up with his hands tied behind his back. The little runt squirmed around until a booted foot crunched into his side. "Don't be getting no ideas, ugly."

Sláine twisted his head and sneered: "Hey, big man, why don't you try kicking me instead?"

The skull sword standing over him grinned. "Mighty stupid of you to insult Taranis while you're indisposed, neighbour."

"Just because you asked nicely." The skull sword called Taranis walked up to stand beside Sláine's head, scuffed his boot in the dirt and then delivered a thunderous kick to Sláine's temple, snapping his head back. Blood and pain smeared across his vision as the force of the kick rattled his brains. He grunted and turned the other cheek, offering it to the Drunes' soldier. Moving his head caused the blood to run into his eyes. It turned the world crimson. He blinked but that only made it worse. He couldn't reach up to wipe his eyes. "Better?"

"Was that the best you've got, lassie?" Sláine goaded, spitting blood. "My dead grandmother's got a better kick on her than you."

"That is because you keep trying to *mount* it." Taranis laughed at his own lame innuendo. He nudged Sláine's face with his boot, getting the toe under his chin. "Come on, Murrough, best get donkey boy and his lovers back to Cor Havas; Slough Maug will want to have some fun with the big one, no doubt."

"On your back, hero," Murrough, the unremarkable skull sword, said, gesturing for him to roll over. Sláine looked rather pointedly at the two blades still levelled at him. Murrough nodded and the two skull swords withdrew their blades another foot, giving him room to roll over. "If he tries to escape, kill him."

Once he was on his stomach the skull swords wrenched his arms behind his back to the point of dislocation, and bound them securely with a cord of rope, lashed it around his feet and drew his ankles together tightly.

"My man, Kilbain here, is a deviant so and so by nature, enjoys hurting people a little too much for my taste, and luckily for him and me, one of the things he excels at is knots. His speciality is a peculiar little puzzler, for sure. The way it works is like this, the more you struggle the tighter it will draw itself until it becomes really unbearable. So it really is a case of how uncomfortable you want to make the next few days for yourself. If I were you, I'd just lie very, very still and think of some big-titted wench caressing me. Might as well enjoy being trussed up."

Sláine grunted as strong hands hauled him to his feet. They dragged him to the waiting flat-bed cart and bundled him in. He wriggled around until he was on his back. Even those small movements tightened the knots by a degree, the coarse fibre chafing against his wrists. Blood puddled in the socket of his right eye, filling it over the course of the next hour as the cart jounced and juddered along the rutted track back towards the Drune fortress of Cor Havas.

It was another hour before the Skinless Man regained consciousness.

Another five before Taranis stuffed a rotten apple into his mouth, forcing him to swallow the bruised fruit. It was sour, like the land that had nurtured it.

Another nine before the cart rolled beneath the shadow of an evening tree and the skull swords threw a tarpaulin over them. They spent an uncomfortable evening on the back of the flat-bed cart, sleeping fitfully. The Skinless Man tossed and turned, trapped in his dreams. And they were not, by any stretch of the imagination, sweet ones. He mumbled pleas, begging, whispering and screaming. And woven through all the rest, one word was repeated over and over: Morrigu.

It took no great wisdom to know the Skinless Man and the Crone shared a history.

Sláine occupied himself during the dark hours by wondering what this Myrrdin Emrys' story was.

By dawn he had decided that the Crone had lured the druid into that hellish place and sealed him within the one tree. It made no sense – but since when could a mere man fathom the schemes of the immortals? So he asked himself a simple question: what did the witch stand to gain by freeing him now? He had no answer.

The Forest of Dardun was vast, and made more so for the circuitous route travellers were forced to take around bogland and chasms that sliced right through Dardun's withered heart.

Ukko had been curiously subdued during the first day's travel, barely trading an insult with Sláine and not so much as a word with their captors. Truth be told, that worried Sláine more than their predicament. The little rogue was not one for brooding. Scheming, yes, conniving, yes, double-dealing, two-timing, back-stabbing, self-serving and swindling, yes, yes, and thrice yes to all of those, but not brooding. Ukko was not given to introspection. It didn't suit him. Sláine kept expecting to see the weasel-faced thief roll over and wink at him a moment before hatching whatever cunning plan he had tucked away up his sleeve. But even as night became day Ukko still hadn't moved. No wink, no smile, no plan.

They moved out as the sun breached the treeline. A brittle frost still clung to the ground. As the day wore on Sláine grew to hate the sluggish *clop-clop* of the horses walking along beside the cart, their hooves dragging on the road, and the rattle and *slop* of the steel-rimmed wheels sludging through the mud and grinding over the cracked and broken stones that fell beneath them. The rhythm of the road offered no lulling peace. Every judder only served to remind him where they were going and how close they had been to freedom before the cloud curragh had crashed back down to earth.

The trees grew thicker the deeper they went back into the heart of the wretched wood until there was no sun. The claustrophobic track necessitated they move in single file. Skeletal limbs dragged low over the narrow track, snagging at horse and rider as they passed. The skull swords grunted, their complaints growing louder the deeper into Dardun they went. The prisoners fared no better; their bonds grew evermore uncomfortable as the road took its toll.

Fetishes and gibbets dangled down from the branches above the narrow track. Either side of the path death masks had been carved into the lightning-blasted trees.

Midway through the second day Sláine was cursing Kilbain's passion for knots; his back arched like a bow, the rope burns around his wrists were livid red and bloody from the constant chafing.

Ukko still hadn't said a word to him.

As the day wore on he began to worry that Taranis' boot had scrambled the dwarf's brains – even for Ukko two days was a long time to sulk.

Then again, the Skinless Man was not exactly garrulous, and when he did speak Murrough was quick to silence him under threat of violence, so perhaps the dwarf had decided to rein in his tongue and save the sarcasm until they were in a position to make a break for it.

They spent another night on the road, though not beneath the stars. The withered trees obscured the sky. Murrough had two of his men haul Sláine off the cart and prop him up against one of the trees so that he could share their fire. The skull sword wanted to talk, Sláine didn't. Murrough cut his ropes; it was no great bravery or foolishness on his captor's part. With twenty swords at his disposal Sláine wasn't going anywhere.

"So, warrior, it comes to this. Come the morrow we will arrive at Cor Havas and you will be handed over to the Drune priests for interrogation. We are both men of war, there should be no bullshit between us. We know how this will go. They will torture you, you will talk, then they will either kill you, or your big brave heart will give out from the agony of their branding irons and their tongs and whatever other implements of pain they choose to use on your body. It won't be pleasant. There is no nobility in the suffering. To be frank it is quite unnecessary."

Sláine gently rubbed the circulation back into his wrists while he listened. The corpse of a great stag had rotted down to brittle bone and lay tangled beneath the huge roots of the ancient tree at his back. It was impossible to tell if the stag had died and the tree claimed its bones or if the tree had strangled the life out of the majestic creature.

"So you would have me spill my secrets out of gratitude for a warm fire on a brisk winter's night? Should I value them so cheaply, do you think? If they are worth torture, surely they are worth a good meal and an hour with a pretty maid?"

The skull sword chuckled. "Quite. Though Taranis is the closest I have to a pretty maid."

The longer he spent in Murrough's company the more difficult it became to demonise him. The man was not the pure evil Sláine needed him to be; not obviously corrupt, not tainted by the vile magic of the Drunes, he was not, in fact, unlike Sláine himself. It was a disturbing revelation.

"I should hate you and all you stand for," Sláine said, "but it would be like hating myself."

Murrough nodded, understanding. "That is ever the way of war, isn't it? Good people pitted against one another in the name of faith or for the lack of faith or some other reason they cannot fathom. And make no mistake, this is war. A slow, creeping war but war nonetheless. My masters and your mistress are opposed and we are in the middle. But for the place of our birth we could easily have found ourselves fighting on the same side of this conflict."

"And yet, for all that you say, you serve a master who would drain the land dry of the very goodness it needs to feed its people, and who solves starvation by murder."

"Tough times demand a sure and firm rule."

"A terrible swift sword to decapitate the rebellion, you mean."

"No, no, no, far from it."

"Then how do you justify the culling of the villages? The murder of innocents?"

"In Nemere, my own home, everyone was starving. Everyone. It broke my heart to see those I loved slowly withering away, knowing they were doomed through no fault of their own. They were all eating, but none enough, so they were only prolonging the inevitable. The famine is hard on everyone, warrior, but it takes a brave leader to find a way through to a solution."

"Murder is not a solution," said Sláine.

"And yet the survivors of Nemere would contradict your stubborn refusal to see reason. Twenty were culled in the first month, the elderly and the infirm who offered little in terms of usefulness and still consumed a full portion. With twenty less mouths to feed the survivors filled their bellies."

"That does not justify slaughter."

"Really? Sixty live where eighty would surely have died without our intervention. The land still gets worked, the young are tended to. There is hope where there was despair."

"Until you are too old to be considered useful."

"What?"

"There is hope until you are too old to be considered useful. There is despair when you think of the fate of fathers, grandfathers."

"It is a harsh world, warrior. You can see the truth of that if you just look around yourself."

"But it need not be, where I come from there is plenty. And yet you come and feed the land with blood, tainting it. Your master does not care for the Land of the Young. He defiles it with his very presence."

"And yet through his justice many who would be dead, live."

"And many who should live are dead," he said, meaning: like my mother. "You cannot blind yourself to the truth."

"The same could be said of your philosophy, warrior. In your mind it seems my sister, my son, my mother, my entire clan should be dead by rights, and why? Because you decry the sacrifice of a few for the many."

"I did not say–"

"Ah, but you did. You said that very thing. You see the crime but you do not see the greater good it does. Can something that feeds the good of many even be a crime? It is beyond my simple knowledge to argue properly, but when we reach Cor Havas I am certain Slough Maug will be eager to broaden your understanding."

"Will that be before or after he tortures me?" Sláine said, picking subconsciously at one of the weals burnt into his wrist.

"Very good," Murrough grinned; the smile reached his eyes. It made him look five years younger. "Shall we cut to the chase, then? You have something in your possession that I am reasonably sure will fascinate my master."

"The book."

"The book," Murrough agreed. "A curiosity, to be sure. One wonders how it came to be in your possession?"

"I killed the man who had it," said Sláine.

"Really? Fascinating. You are a thief and yet you lecture on morality. What a complicated soul you are."

"He was evil. He deserved to die."

Murrough shook his head slowly, his lips pursed. "Can your world really be so black and white? So absolute?"

"If you mean: do I condemn all evil, greater and lesser? Then yes, I do. And yes, it is that simple. There is wrong and there is right."

The skull sword pushed himself to his feet, dusting the arse of his britches off. "Cor Havas will be tough on you, I fear, warrior."

"So be it," said Sláine. "But in turn I will make this promise: I will teach Cor Havas the truth of what it means to be Sessair. I will be a blight on your people. A canker in the dark hearts of the priests of Carnun that shelter within the so-called safety of the fortress. I will bring death to their pet swords. I will be justice incarnate. I will be a plague, bringing blood and pain to their petty regime. I will be deliverance and damnation. I will be the liberator, overthrowing the yoke of oppression that chokes the very life out of the land. I will be a pox upon their flesh just as they are a pox upon the flesh of my Goddess. The evil of Cor Havas will dwell in narrow houses when I am through. That is my promise."

"And in that hatred you will become all that you despise. I pity you, warrior."

THE FOREST FORTRESS of Cor Havas was little better than a cluster of wattle shanties behind a crumbling limestone wall. It was not the impressive, daunting, citadel he had imagined. The sight of it did not strike fear into his heart. Cor Havas verged on ruin – which was strangely fitting for a Drune stronghold dedicated to the ruin of this once great land. But mother earth was no helpless maiden ripe for the plucking. Her pretty darling buds had thorns. Indeed, Dardun had already begun reclaiming the land, its twisted roots undermining the foundations of the stone wall, growing between the crevices where the stones did not quite mate perfectly. In a few years nature would have done her work and it would be as though Cor Havas had never existed.

"I would walk to my doom like a man, not be dragged like a child," Sláine said as they neared the gate.

"I am sure you would," Murrough agreed, conversationally. "But if so, then the young cadets of the fortress would see the proud warrior, undaunted, walking under the gateway into his enemy's stronghold. You would rise to be this colossus in their superstitious minds. After all, who but the greatest of the enemy would willingly walk into the den of his would-be killers? No, I think not, warrior. This way you are humbled, a prisoner wheeled in on a ramshackle cart. The message it gives is one of defeat. There is no fight left in this enemy. It is a good lesson to give our young men: even the so-called mighty bow down before the strength of our swords."

"Do not make the mistake of thinking I am beaten."

"Oh, but you are, warrior. You most assuredly are. There is no great hero coming to your aid. Victory will not be snatched from the jaws of defeat by some archer's arrow, thief's pick or champion's sword. There will be no miracles from your precious Goddess. You are dead to her, now. How does that feel? The cold certainty that you are utterly alone?"

"I am not alone," said Sláine.

"No, you have that ugly dwarf and the painted man, companions who strike fear into the heart of every evil man in the world."

"Do not mock me, Murrough. You are a decent man. It will hurt to kill you."

The skull sword chuckled. "As I imagine it will hurt to die."

On Murrough's signal four riders spurred their mounts and cantered ahead. The procession rolled slowly down the shallow hill, into a wide glade. It took two men to open the heavy timber gates. They groaned inwards. Ukko prodded him in the side with a stiff kick. "Idiots built this place." They were the first words he had said in days. A cunning smile spread slowly across his face. "Who builds the gate of a fortress gate to swing *inwards*? It doesn't take a genius to know that a crew with battering ram would make light work of those gates."

"Stupidity or supreme arrogance," Myrrdin Emrys offered, struggling to rise. A backhanded cuff from Taranis's gauntlet dumped the tattooed man on his back. He groaned, wincing. The blow had split his lip. "Thank you for demonstrating my point with such brutal efficiency."

"You talk too much, old man," Taranis said, shaking his head. "Perhaps Maug will pull out your tongue."

The irony that those four words were all that the tattooed man had said in hours was not lost on Sláine. Taranis was a bully and easy to despise for it. He lacked the empathy of Murrough; he didn't care about what Murrough had called the "greater good", he enjoyed hurting things. People.

It had begun to rain – or it had been raining all along with only the dense trees sheltering them and now they were gone, either way. The first fat drops spattered on Sláine's upturned face. He closed his eyes.

"It is not unreasonable to suppose that they fear no one," Myrrdin continued. "Because there is no one here to fear. Who, after all, would – could – come this far into their forest to bring the fight to their door?"

And that was the truth; it wasn't stupidity, or even arrogance, it was a message to every captive brought to Cor Havas: you are ours. No one can help you once you pass beneath the portal.

With the message ringing joyful and triumphant at the front of their minds, they entered the stockade.

It was no more impressive inside, but then it did not need to be. Sláine rolled onto his shoulder, enduring the increased discomfort of the fresh knots for the chance to take in the layout of the fortress. A little pain in advance could inevitably save considerably more later.

To the left of the gates were all the necessities of life; the bakery, the oast house, the smithy, the kitchens and the smoke house, and to the right the reasons for the fortress: the barrack buildings, the stables, the training ground and drill hall, and the hovels the cadets shared and the latrine trenches. No doubt the goal house would be there as well. Sláine studied his surroundings as they passed, seeing the young cadets twelve and thirteen summers old, sparring on the training grounds to the bark of a harsh instructor. He could just as easily have been watching Murdo put the Red Branch through their paces. He remembered all too well the relentless drilling; the driving rain only served to make the image more vivid. The boys struggled in the quickening mud, stumbling and slipping. The instructor slapped a wooden sword out of the hand of a wide-eyed boy soldier, yelling furiously in his face. His words carried to them: "No, no, no. You left yourself wide open, Braifar! Why can't you be more like Gannon?" The admonishment took him back ten years. He saw again Cullen's open loathing, Wide Mouth mimicking: *why can't you be more like Sláine?* The memory sent a cold shiver through Sláine as he realised: but for the grace of Danu, that could be me.

There was no sense of permanence to the settlement. The buildings appeared on the verge of collapse. The construction was slipshod – as though it wasn't expected, or needed, to last. There was no pride in any of the workmanship. The daub had cracked and flaked away from the wattle, exposing the dried reeds on some of the chattel houses. He couldn't imagine his own people living so close to squalor. But for all its ugliness there was order to it, and logic. The builders exhibited far more foresight in that department than the founders of Murias had.

The fortress was divided into five unequal parts, four quarters separated by the path of the sun and the seasons and the central core where the Drune priests themselves resided in a domed temple adorned with more of the vile fetishes they'd seen coming through the forest. It reflected the arrogance of the priests, placing themselves at the heart of all things. For all his vanities Cathbad at least had the humility to understand his role as teacher; he was set apart from the people, a guide, a source of knowledge, a repository of history and tradition. He was not king, he did not marry the Goddess. He lived to serve. And like the druid himself, the nemeton was set outside the realm of everyday life.

It was not the only difference he saw within Cor Havas.

The quarters themselves were physically divided by low interior walls, making the fortress feel like an elaborate labyrinth; the Drunes at its centre, and Sláine nothing more a mouse let loose to run in it – only "loose" was of course an illusion, his tormentor had him by the tail and was gleefully about to snap a metal trap shut on his skull while he scrambled about madly.

Sláine slumped back into the cart. He had seen enough.

The rain continued to fall.

THE VILE STENCH preceeded Maug by a dozen paces.

The rancid aroma told Sláine all he needed to know about the Drune: he had attained the rank of Slough, shedding his mortal skin. His body now was a corruption of the flesh held together only by the strength of the priest's dark magic. The strength needed to defy nature so boldly was immense. For all the slaughter of the Sourlands Sláine and Ukko had encountered only two others who had accomplished the same shedding of mortality – Slough Throt, the thief of Feg's Ragnarok book, and the Lord Weird himself.

Taranis grabbed hold of the rope binding Sláine's feet together and dragged him bodily off the cart. Without his hands to break the fall, Sláine fell hard, cracking his skull off the side of the wagon and landing on his shoulder and face at the foot of the wretched priest. Without the skin to bind his bones and muscle Maug moved with a clumsy lopsided gait, his joints bending too far in one direction and overcompensating in the other. He relied upon a staff of bone for balance. The staff itself was carved with some quite sophisticated renditions of tribal art not dissimilar to the countless fetishes that adorned the branches of Dardun. The effect would have been comical if the young Sessair warrior did not know what he was – and what he was capable of.

But it was not Sláine that interested the Drune.

Maug stood over Myrrdin, a curious look of contempt on his rotten lips. A fat-bellied maggot wriggled out through the Drune's gum, crawled down what remained of his neck and disappeared beneath the rotten strip of flesh behind his clavicle.

The Slough priest poked and prodded the tattooed man with his staff as though inspecting a piece of meat. "Turn him over," Maug rasped a moment later, continuing the inspection after two skull swords had manhandled Myrrdin onto his stomach. The Drune circled the tattooed man three times sunwise, shaking his head and muttering to himself. The rain streamed down his ruined features. "My, my, my. What do we have here, Murrough? Visitors? And such a motley rabble. A barbarian, a dwarf and this painted freak." He circled Myrrdin, cackling at some unheard mirth. "Could it be? Do you think? No. No. This wretched creature cannot be the druid. Can it?" He peered down at Myrrdin, the flayed muscle of his lip curling in a sneer. "Tell me, are you the druid? No, don't tell me. You are. You are. But I must admit you are not what I expected, druid. I am quite disappointed, Myrrdin Emrys, the fabled Lord of the Trees. To hear talk of you one would think a god walked among the mortals. Three hundred years of superstition and prattle and *this* is the great Myrrdin?" The Slough priest shook his head though it did not so much shake as loll on his neck.

Myrrdin opened his eyes. "I am the druid, Myrrdin," the Skinless Man said, his voice devoid of emotion. The sight of the wooden orbs caused the Drune to step back involuntarily, then take four more forwards and lean in close, fascinated by the fusion of nature and humanity. "A living embodiment of the great wood... now *that* is more interesting. Perhaps there is something to your legend after all. Perhaps. Trust me, your suffering shall be every bit as legendary as your life warrants."

Maug limped away from the tattooed man, talking animatedly to himself.

Sláine could not make out a word that dripped off the priest's tongue.

The rain intensified, quickly turning the ground to wet sucking mud.

The Drune's bare feet sank into the ground, leaving maggots of flesh behind as he moved. The sloughed flesh writhed with a repulsive life all of its own.

Maug walked the line, inspecting Murrough's captives. The skull swords had formed up in two ranks. As Maug moved so too did they, dividing again to form the final two sides of a cordon around the prisoners. Maug turned his attention to Sláine, and even then, his withered eyes barely registered the Sessair.

"So, what do we have here? A wretched footslogger in the company of the great druid?" The priest of Carnun toed Sláine's side with a scabrous foot, seemed about to turn away and then stooped, sniffing. The ragged wounds of the Drune's nostrils flared open. "Oh, no. So much more than that, aren't you, soldier boy? Yes, yes, yes. I can smell her on you." Maug's pustulant tongue laved along a ridge of black teeth that made Sláine's stomach churn. One of the yellow sores eating into the muscle ruptured, leaking pus down the Drune's chin. "Yes, yes I can. You're *her* creature aren't you? Mother, maiden and Crone, the bitch has her talons in you."

"It is amazing you can smell anything," said Sláine, earning himself a jab in the throat from the bone staff. He gagged, gasping as he tried desperately to suck in a lungful of air.

"The body is such a frail thing, warrior. For all the rippling muscle and supposed strength of your carcass, a single well-placed blow could snuff out your life like a tallow candle. Do not make the mistake of thinking you are immortal just because you are Blodeuwedd's lapdog. Never forget that her sister-self, Ceridwen, is mother of death."

"Lord Maug?"

"What is it, soldier?"

Murrough shuffled, obviously uncomfortable, drawing attention to himself. He clutched Feg's book to his chest. "There is something you should see. It was found in their possession." He held out the book.

"Well, what is it?" Maug said, impatiently.

"A book, my lord."

The Slough priest sighed, "I can *see* that it is a book, soldier. So what, pray tell, makes you think it is important enough that I should want to see it? Is it the druid's grimoire perhaps?"

"No, my lord," Murrough backed up a step.

Sláine watched the exchange curiously; for all that the skull sword had pretended respect for the slough-skinned ones it was plain that fear of his master was what motivated the soldier.

"Well, do not keep me waiting, Murrough. I am not at my most patient in the pouring rain."

"Of course, my apologies, Slough Maug. The book appears to have belonged to the Lord Weird, himself."

"I am not sure I understand, soldier. Your lips are moving and I am hearing words, but all they seem to say is: *blah blah blah*. Explain for me how this rabble might have come across a book that belonged to Lord Feg, and of what possible significance it is to the situation before us now. You are a soldier, Murrough: report!"

The skull sword stiffened as though physically slapped. "It is my belief that they stole it from the Lord Weird, Slough Maug."

"That is conjecture, soldier, assumption not fact."

"With respect, my lord, I disagree. If you were to examine the book itself you would see it is not some obscure Tale of the Sidhe, but rather a more sensitive artefact. I have not read the work in its entirety, but there was no need. I saw enough to know the Lord Weird would not surrender this tome willingly. As to how it came into the possession of these three, I believe they are just the final link in a longer chain."

"Meaning?"

"The men talk, my lord. Word has come from Drunemeton that Slough Throt turned renegade and was, ah, *dealt with* by the Lord Weird."

"And you have decided all by yourself that these three somehow recovered the book from the hapless Throt? That is a lot of thinking for a man of the sword, Murrough."

The skull sword looked down at his feet.

"So," Maug turned to Sláine. "Is it true? Has Murrough deduced the riddle of your possession – and better yet, the conundrum of my brother priest's failing? Tell me, I am curious."

Sláine looked up at the wretched maggot-riddled face of the priest. "I'm sorry, I can see your lips moving but all I can think is: *by Carnun's left nut, you stink worse than a shepherd after a busy night of offering devotions to his flock.* And just to be clear I do mean the fleecy ones, not some metaphor or anything clever like that. Now, did you actually say something or was it that skin-thing you've got causing your lip to tremble?"

The priest lashed out again with his staff, cracking it off the side of Sláine's cheek.

"I shall enjoy hurting you, northman. I shall send your bones home to your mother in an oilskin."

"My mother is dead," said Sláine.

"Then I shall just leave your corpse out to feed the Morrigan's crows. Perhaps it will please the witch. I do not care one way or the other. I just thought you might want to be buried at home."

The Slough priest turned his back on them and walked with that curious, awkward lope back towards the doors of the temple. His stench lingered. "The book, soldier. Bring it to me."

With that, the Drune disappeared into the temple, ignoring Ukko completely.

★ ★ ★

TRUE TO HIS word, Maug delighted in inflicting pain on both Sláine and Myrrdin Emrys.

The priest took the iron poker from the brazier of hot coals and walked across the dungeon floor to where Sláine was chained. Devices of pain littered the chamber. Its vile purpose contaminated the very stones of the walls and ceiling; the blood of the nameless prisoners stained deep and dark, desperation-worn grooves cut into them where those same nameless ones had ground their manacles in hopes of weakening the iron binding them.

Ukko had swooned and fainted at the first poker plunging into the coals. The shackles around his wrists prevented the dwarf from slumping to the floor, indeed his toes barely reached the straw spread out beneath them.

"You are a simpleton, warrior. You think I actually care about the dung that streams out of both of your orifices? I don't. Sincerely, with all of my heart, I hope you do not talk for a long, long time. Hurting you is fast becoming my only pleasure in this wretched forest. So I beg you, bite your tongue."

Maug pressed the red-hot poker up against the sole of his left foot and rolled it slowly from heel to toe as Sláine screamed out his pain. The skin sizzled and blistered, the stench of burning flesh joining the odour of rancid meat in the airless room. Sláine writhed against his bonds, tears burning red in his eyes that was more than a match for the blistering poker as Maug lanced it back into the coals, stirring them up violently in a shower of sparks.

"Nice, thank you. So tell me – by which of course I mean please do not breathe a word – how did you come across Feg's precious book?"

Sláine hawked up a wad of phlegm and spat in the Drune's corrupt face. "I have nothing to say to you."

"Oh, how delicious. Thank you, warrior. I was beginning to worry you would prove to be a big disappointment. I am glad to see I was wrong. Now, before I ask again, I am going to paint you a mental picture, please try and concentrate. Are you with me?" Hatred blazed in Sláine's pain-fuelled eyes. "Oh, you *are*, aren't you? You are feeling everything. How utterly marvellous. Now," Maug withdrew the poker from the coals, "imagine, if you would, the sensation of this instrument entering your flesh; not your mouth, or your eyes, both are far too banal for a man of your *guts*. Imagine it slipping inside your arse, and up, cauterising the wounds even as it ripped you open. Now, tell me again that you have nothing to say to me."

Sláine's head came up. He looked at the dwarf and the druid chained either side of him, and then back at his eager-faced torturer and the glowing red tip of the poker in his hand. He tried to touch the Earth Serpent, but the Souring of the land here was too thorough, the forest dead to the Goddess. "I have something to say to you, Maug."

"Ah, such a bittersweet moment, on the one hand the joy of victory, however inevitable it might be, and on the other, disappointment that my fun is at an end so soon. So?"

Sláine told him, speaking clearly and enunciating every word: "I shall enjoy killing you."

The sudden flare of fury in Maug's eyes was worth the agony of the poker searing into his side and being dragged up across his chest.

This time he did not scream.

He refused to give the Drune the satisfaction.

THE TORTURE LASTED days.

Sláine did not break.

Maug utilised all of his instruments of pain. At first he had enjoyed the game, pressing the searing pincers against Sláine's earlobe, squeezing down on them until both fiery tips met inside the skin, describing the more hideous delights the coming days held in store, reminding the young Sessair warrior again and again that there was no hope of rescue. But the fun quickly went out of it. Sláine did not scream as the pincers pierced his skin, did not beg or plead as Maug lovingly described the effect of the pear, how its barbed petals would open like a flower inside his arse and rip him apart as it was extracted, did not whimper as the Drune snuffed out any dreams of salvation. He simply took it, surrendering his body to the pain. It was as though the physicality of it did not reach his mind, that somehow he dislocated the pain from his flesh.

Under other circumstances Slough Maug would have enjoyed the challenge of breaking the arrogant son of a bitch. As it was, he just wanted the job done.

If he had to kill the warrior, so be it.

He retreated to his chamber, lit a solitary tallow candle and pored over Slough Feg's uncontrolled scrawl. The Lord Weird's innermost hopes were laid bare. It was a fool who recorded the truth of his secret self on parchment, Maug decided. Reading Feg's words gave Maug an unprecedented insight into his soul. He *understood* the Lord Weird. Who else could claim that? The realisation excited the priest.

He called for Ballinus, his man-servant. "I hunger, bring me meat and ale."

The servant returned a few moments later with a silver platter laden with honey-soaked vegetables arranged around a succulent meaty thigh. Juices gathered beneath the parsnips and turnips. It smelled of the boy, Hadren, who had fled the compound earlier in the week. The foolish boy had thought to run. The hunters had brought him back and Maug had executed him on the training ground. It was occasionally necessary to make an example of their failures, to instil fear and assure unquestioning loyalty. Deserters were not tolerated among the ranks of the skull swords, no matter how young. Hadren had provided the most recent lesson and now, thanks to the boy's sacrifice, Maug ate good fresh meat.

Ballinus set the platter down and began carving.

The boy was delicious.

He wondered, idly, what the Lord Weird would give for the return of his words?

Murrough's unique find promised to be quite fortunate.

His mind returned to the prisoners. The warrior was fascinating – but not entertaining. Bringing fresh pain was a challenge, but it grew wearisome. For all that his ability to withstand the manifold pains Maug wrought upon his flesh was impressive, it would end. If he would not break, he would die, as all flesh died.

He called for Ballinus once more.

The man-servant appeared in the doorway.

"See that the hounds are prepared. Come dawn the young Sessair and his friends will run like stags."

"Yes, my lord. Will that be all?"

"For now," Maug said.

"Very well."

Alone, Maug sat back in his chair, enjoying the heat of the fire and the thoughts of Sláine being torn apart by his wolfhounds. The warrior's death would be slow and deliciously cruel. Maug idly wondered if the man would scream as his flesh was consumed by the hungry dogs. From that delightful thought his mind wandered to thoughts of Slough Feg's generosity. What would the Lord Weird give him for the return of his precious book?

Everything his withered heart desired, Maug decided, savouring the thought.

AND SO, IN the darkness, when they were alone, the prisoners talked.

"Tell me," Sláine said into the darkness. "The priest knows you, Myrrdin. Who are you that he talks of legends? He called you the Lord of the Trees?"

Myrrdin Emrys told them his story:

"As I was, once, but that was a long time ago. You would not believe me if I told you it is three hundred years since I last looked upon Tir-Nan-Og, Sláine, and yet that is the truth."

"I found you trapped within a tree on another plane of existence peopled by man-animals and giant insects, druid. You would be surprised what I am capable of believing."

Myrrdin chuckled, a genuinely warm sound despite their harsh surroundings. "I was someone, or so I foolishly believed, my friend. I dedicated my life to the gathering of wisdom. I served the maiden, Blodeuwedd, with all of my heart. I tended her forests, shepherded her flock of creatures. She loved me, warrior. She could not live without me, or so I believed. I saw her suffering and believed I alone had the power to save her from the rot that seeped into her core. I saw the birth of the Sourlands, the coming of great evil, the rise of the wyrm, Crom-Cruach, and the enmity of Slough Feg. I believed I could stop the inevitable, warrior. I believed I had the power to end the threat of this evil that now grips so much of her land. It is not new, this sickness that sours the world. It has taken centuries to grow so strong. Its taint is insidious. Its corruption irresistible."

"Nothing is irresistible," said Sláine.

"Except a big-titted wench with that hungry look in her eyes that says she's game for a bit of Ukko-loving," Ukko chimed in helpfully from the other side of the room. It was the first thing he had said in a long time, and so typical of the runt that Sláine could not help but smile despite their circumstances.

"Hubris is an unfortunate trait that so often comes with power, warrior. Like you, I was strong, or so I believed. I felt Danu's love flowing through my veins whenever I came into contact with the earth. I believed myself strong enough to make a pact with the Crone. I would have done anything to save the Goddess, Sláine. She owned my heart. I know you understand what I mean when I say that."

"I do," said Sláine.

"She betrayed me, of course. That is her way. You take her at her word, but everything you say she twists to her advantage, everything she says has multiple meanings, none of which are ever clear. Her word is treacherous. Morrigu is a devious being. I begged her help against the evil that I saw coming from the south. She said she has walked many futures and in many of them has seen the Goddess, Danu, emerge victorious from the souring of her body – and in all of these futures, she said, I, Myrrdin Emrys, had a vital part to play. Her assurances fed my inflated sense of self; flattery has a way of undermining common sense. She had seen my transcendence, my becoming one with the woods I protected. I should have known, but her words were sweet to my ears. I imagined the mastery of my world, she delivered centuries of imprisonment, trapped within the living wood I had chosen to serve. It was my destiny, she promised, to become the Skinless Man. I thought for a moment she meant that I would become like Feg and the others, and slough my skin. I despaired that I might be weak enough to betray all that I loved but Morrigu herself removed my skin as it was, painting the past of the forests on my flesh, the history of those great domains. She said it was the first stage in becoming the maiden's champion, that I must *be* what my enemies most feared, a living embodiment of the great forests."

"Sounds to me like you just weren't listening," Ukko said.

"I heard what I wanted to hear, good dwarf, there is a subtle difference."

"You still wound up trapped in a tree, so it isn't much of a difference if you ask me."

"How did you end up in that place?" Sláine asked, meaning Purgadair, not the one tree of Nàimhdiel.

"I answered her call. The Crone bade me travel the El Worlds in search of the hero my beloved needed to save her. That was my role, she said. I was not a fighter, for all that I had mastered the sacred knowledge and had the strength to open the very mists of time to enter the Annfwyn. Danu had need of axe and sword over wisdom and learning. My role in this play of life was to be a guide, not the champion. It was difficult for a prideful man to swallow, but I put my arrogance aside and accepted my part. Morrigu claimed to have seen me find her hero through the mists in a distant hell she called Purgadair. I took her on her word and opened the way. It took all of my power to breach the dimensions, and then once I made the transition I was impotent. The sudden absence of the Earth Serpent, the abandonment of the Goddess, undermined my resolve. I believed myself beaten before I had taken ten paces in that blighted place. What I did not understand was that it was a trap. That realisation came too late to save me from my conceit. Instead, I walked into it, like a fool, with my eyes closed. Without the power to draw upon, the power that had been my life, that had fuelled my quest to save the land and the woman I loved and so much more, I was humbled beyond my own arrogant ability to believe. I was weak for the first time since childhood. Believe me, it was a bitter lesson for a proud man to swallow. I followed her like one of her damnable crows following a trail of breadcrumbs. The last words the Crone said as the jaws of her trap slammed shut sealing me in the tree were that she loved me."

"That's harsh," Ukko said.

"She is a harsh mistress, this Goddess of ours, dwarf. Make no mistake. She was true to her word, I was at one with the forest I served, and I did indeed meet my axe-wielding champion in the desert beyond the walls of Purgadair. Everything she promised came to fruition, just not in the manner my hubris had chosen to believe it would happen."

"Do you regret your pact?" asked Sláine, thinking of his own unspoken promise to obey the crow-aspect of the warrior Goddess in a single deed of her choosing. The notion that the Crone had already walked the paths of various futures and knew both the promise and the outcome and would not give voice to the actual deed did not sit well with Sláine, but there was nothing he could do now but live with the promise he had made, whatever it might be.

"Three centuries have been stolen from me – by rights I should be feeding the worms of my forest now. Instead I am here, forced to look upon the ruination of all I swore to nurture. This, around you, was my home. I was 'lord' of this place. Dardun was my home, Sláine. You ask me if I regret my bargain? When I look at the twisted roots and the rot that has eaten into *my* trees, I do. This canker has spread far beyond what it was when I stood as guardian to the great forest of Dardun. The roots of its evil have had three hundred years to spread unchecked. That is a long time by anyone's reckoning. But, having paid Morrigu's forfeit, now I would collect on her promise."

"It does not end here, druid," Sláine promised the darkness. "You shall have your forest back, and it shall flourish again. Mark this promise between us now. As you said, the Morrigan has walked the path of futures and has seen it. And so it shall be. With your wisdom we shall bring deliverance from the menace of Slough Feg and restore this once great land to her former glory. We shall root out Feg's weeds and let the garden grow anew."

"See," said Ukko, "that's why he's a hero. You ask for help and he promises the earth in return. I just hope you won't care if he delivers it soaked in blood."

THEY WERE WOKEN by their gaolers an hour before dawn.

It was the brute, Taranis that loosened their shackles. Sláine collapsed as the chains were undone, falling at the foot of the skull sword.

"That's right, *warrior*," Taranis mocked. "Beg for your miserable little life like the maggot you are."

Sláine pushed himself to his feet. The pain standing on his burned soles brought was exquisite. It fired his blood. For the first time in what felt like months he felt the faintest touch of Danu there answering the agony with just the trace of her tender salve. He embraced the pain and forced himself to his full height. He refused to show Taranis his weakness.

Ukko had no such qualms; he hit the floor whimpering and lay there as they unchained Myrrdin Emrys.

The tattooed druid stepped away from the wall. He did not stagger or fall. He stood. He did not rub at his wrists or give the slightest sign of discomfort from his imprisonment. He fixed his wooden eyes on the men who had let him down. In the flickering oil lamp light his eyes appeared uncannily alive, as though responding to the nearness of Dardun and her sickened trees. Taranis stepped back from the druid, licking his lips nervously.

Myrrdin helped Ukko stand. There were twelve soldiers come to escort the three of them; a sure sign of how much the skull swords feared their prisoners.

"Maug has plans for you three," Taranis said, unable to hide the hint of excitement completely. "You are to run the stones. I have ten tin bits on the ugly little one being the first one to fall to the dogs," the skull sword chuckled mirthlessly. "Ballinus tells me the dogs haven't been fed since last night, though he did stir them up a bit by dangling part of a boy's rotting carcass over their cages for an hour this morning to fire their blood up. They should be ready for quite the feast by the time Maug lets them loose. Best not keep them waiting."

The skull swords pushed them forwards, out of the dungeon and into the first light of morning. Sláine breathed deeply as he stepped through the door. He regretted it immediately. The air was rancid. He saw the repugnant Slough priest shuffling towards them. Maug's eyes blazed with feverish delight.

"Good, good, good," the Drune crooned, rubbing his wretched hands together like some miser over a pot of silver, relishing the prospect of their renewed pain – as momentary as he hoped it would be. "Has Taranis explained the morning's trial? No?" he said, without waiting for any of them to acknowledge his rhetorical question. "Then indulge me. We few shall go for a short walk. I would show you one of the wonders of this old forest, the huge dolmens that mark the ancient ley dissecting Dardun. Within this temple," he waved a rotting hand at the building, "stands the first of the great megaliths. Or lies, to be more accurate, as it serves as altar to the Wyrm God,

Crom-Cruach. The stones are evenly spaced along the ley line and run exactly one league. Your trial will be one of strength, cunning and speed. Survive it, and you will be absolved of your crimes against the Lord Weird. To fail is to be found guilty. Guilt is punishable by death, but fear not, my friends, it will be a rather abrupt happening. I cannot imagine you will have much time to hurt."

"You expect us to run for our lives?" Sláine said.

"Yes, I do," Maug said, insufferably smug as he walked the line. He barely acknowledged them to look at, making it plain they were no better than bugs to be crushed beneath his deformed feet.

"His smelliness knows us so well," Ukko said, rubbing briskly at his wrists to get the circulation going. "If there's one thing a coward knows how to do well it is the subtle art of running for his life."

"The running of the stags is one of the ancient justices of the forests, is it not, Myrrdin?"

The druid, hearing his name, came back from wherever his mind had wandered. He turned his wooden eyes on the Slough priest. "It was a barbaric practice from the dark age of man, if that is what you mean, Drune?"

"Interesting that you should say that, druid, but I cannot pretend your words don't confuse me. After all, was your great sacrifice not for the conservation of the self-same 'barbaric' rituals of your beloved Earth Mother? That was my understanding of the old stories about the great Myrrdin Emrys, that you gave everything to safeguard the sanctity of a few trees and meadows, trees made strong by the ritual sacrifices to the land your Goddess demanded."

"Not all of the old ways are worthy of preservation," the druid said.

"That is where we differ, old man. I believe all of the old ways are worthy of nurturing. Be contented by the knowledge that your blood shall feed the land, the energies carried far and wide by the great stones. Your deaths will mean something to someone, somewhere. There is a wonderful irony wrapped up in this predicament, I am sure. "

The spear-tips of their guards kept them moving. The barks of the hounds intensified as they approached their handlers. Eight men struggled with the leashes of forty hounds. The strain of holding them back was telling: their faces were set with stubborn grimaces, their arms locked and trembling as the dogs pulled relentlessly. They were in a relatively small glade, unique only for the single standing stone in its centre. The monolith was carved with a simplistic device: an endless knot tied by the heads of two horned men, renditions on Carnun, the Horned God. The presence of the likeness placed a chill in Sláine's heart. The stone was a smaller version of the same stones they had found at Carnac, the same stones that crackled with life the length and breadth of the Sourlands, draining the very essence of the Earth Serpent and channelling it to Slough Feg's foul domain for whatever purpose the Lord Weird plotted.

Sláine felt the sick pull of the standing stone as he neared. It lacked the overwhelming power of Carnac but there was no doubting its grip on his soul. Where the dolmens of Carnac had left him a wretched mess grubbing in the dirt, barely clinging to lucidity, this single stone was akin to an angry wasp buzzing in his face constantly; a distraction, an irritation, nothing more.

The dogs were hungry – it was in their eyes.

"Be so kind as to introduce yourselves to the dogs," Slough Maug said, salivating at the prospect of a quick and messy kill. "And be sure they get a good sniff so they recognise your scent."

Taranis shoved Ukko in the back. Ukko stumbled forwards, landing on his knees inches from the frothing muzzle of the nearest hound. The dog strained on its leash, jowls bared on slick gums and yellowed canines. It jaws snapped less than an inch from the dwarf's nose. Ukko flinched, reeling back. He turned to look up at the Slough priest, and then across at Sláine and Myrrdin. He winked, very slowly and very deliberately, making sure everyone saw it. "We better get very close then, your smelliness, given as your *sacred stink* is, ahh, rather overpowering, don't you think? It has to be very confusing for the poor dogs, doesn't it? You being the smelliest thing in the whole forest and all, everything reeks of your *divine putrescence.* I mean, we wouldn't want them coming after you by mistake, now would we?"

"Laugh now, dwarf," said Maug, lumbering towards Ukko, his bone-white staff sinking deep into the near-black loam of the top soil. "Let the sweetness of it roll off your tongue while it is still in your head. Enjoy the salve it spreads across your soul. It is called gallows humour; in the blackest moments the psyche finds ways of protecting itself, finding mirth in the danger it faces. I will forgive you this once simply because I won't have to forgive you ever again. In a few minutes my beauties will be grinding your bones and laughter will seem a long, long way away. Now, though, I tire of this prattle. It is time for you and your friends to run."

Sláine's feet were raw, the soil and the spoils of the forest a fire beneath them. Thorns and dead brambles dug into his soles, cutting into the seared flesh, bleeding him. Each step brought more pain. The skull swords had brought Brain-Biter and the rest of their belongings along. They lay in a pile close to Maug, the intimation being that they were just waiting there to be collected after this silly little ritual had been completed. He looked along the line of stones. There was no way he would be able to outrun forty hounds for over three miles, even with a head start on the beasts – and a stand here, against a dozen skull swords, the dogs and their handlers and the Drune lord himself, was out of the question.

A flutter of black caught his eye.

A crow settled in one of the higher branches. It could have been an ordinary creature of the forest, of course, only there were no creatures in Dardun. The bird watched them with a curious intelligence in its yellow eyes. It was the Morrigan's creature. Myrrdin Emrys had seen it but their captives seemed oblivious of the crow's presence. Not for the first time Sláine drew strength from the presence of a bird; if an emissary of the Crone could broach a dark place like Dardun then so too could Danu's other aspects. Unlike Purgadair, this time he was not alone.

"I am feeling generous," Maug said, rapping the end of his staff off the carved stone, "I will give you five minutes' start on the dogs. If you run, and run hard, those five minutes could mean covering as much as a mile, a third of the way. It is conceivable you might outrun them. But before you get too excited, I feel a burden to be truthful: no one has ever made it to the end of the stones and won their freedom. That does not mean you cannot be the first. I just did not want you entertaining unreasonable hope. Now, my dear fellows, I suggest very strongly that you run."

Maug clapped his hands together sharply, and the human stags bolted.

* * *

SLÁINE HEARD THE dogs.

They were less than four hundred paces distant and gaining fast.

Myrrdin moved gracefully between the withered trees. Sláine kept pace with him easily. For a moment he had thought there was a chance that they might make it, reach the end of the stones and claim their freedom – but he knew Maug would never let them go. It was all a ruse, a game to delight the Drune. He didn't care if the dogs caught them or if they fell to swords or a damned pox. The means was irrelevant. All that Maug cared about was the end – that Sláine, Ukko and the druid, Myrrdin, were riddled with earthworms.

The dogs came on, their hungry gait devouring the distance between them and their quarry. They pursued Sláine and the others with rabid insistency, nostrils flared, following the scent of sweat and fear stinking on the stale forest air. Their barks transformed to ragged howls as they grew closer.

They ran hard.

The end of the stones was still a mile distant and the trees were thickening, making it difficult to keep any kind of momentum for more than a few paces.

Ukko struggled to keep up, his shorter legs needing three paces to cover what Sláine and Myrrdin managed in one. It didn't matter that his arms pumped furiously, strings of hair matted to his scalp, or that the grimace pasted across his ugly face was one of pure pain and bloody determination, he wasn't going to make it. And he knew it.

Sláine shortened his stride to run alongside the dwarf. Utter despair consumed Ukko's eyes. He stopped running, sank to his knees and looked up imploringly at the barbarian. "I can't..."

Sláine stopped running and turned to face the dogs as they came on.

"We will stand together, dwarf. And Danu help the dogs. We will send them back to Maug in hessian sacks."

"You don't have to–" Ukko began.

"I do," Sláine finished for him.

Then the first hound launched itself, hitting the young Sessair hard in the chest and barrelling him off his feet. Sláine rolled over onto his stomach, hands inside the snapping jaws of the huge dog. He pulled the teeth apart with all of his strength, not stopping as the tendon snapped and the bone dislocated, tearing the lower jaw from the shrieking hound's head even as he felt the fangs of the second hound sink into his calf and the claws of a third rake down his spine. He threw the dead animal aside and reached out for the beast feasting on his leg. The pain was unbearable – and these were just the first, there were so many more that had his scent and would be on him in moments. Howls rent the dawn, the animals baying, spurred on by the scent of his newly spilled blood on the grass.

Sláine twisted his neck to avoid the savage snapping teeth of another huge hound, and saw the druid standing over him, his wooden eyes smouldering. Myrrdin reached out and touched him and a sudden explosion of power – agony and raw and blazing rage – tore through him, firing every nerve and fibre of his flesh. He tore the hound in his arms in two, splitting it open like a game hen on the feasting table. The animal's ribcage cracked open one bone at a time as Sláine opened it up and its guts and organs spilled out in a bloody lesson in anatomy.

Sláine felt the heady rush of the *riastrad*, his warp spasm, burning within his bones, driving through his musculature, the fire of its heat swelling him beyond the bounds of flesh into a fearsome giant slayer – but this was different, even as the anger within him raged a part of Sláine realised that this wasn't the power of the earth feeding him, it was the druid himself acting as a conduit to Danu. He could taste the druid's thoughts, and fears, and beneath them, his bitterness at his entrapment and his failure.

Sláine devoured the druid's strength greedily, feeding on the Earth Power and so much more, surrendering to a pure scarlet rage.

His roars drowned out the savage barks and the frightened whimpers both.

The barbarian tore into the dogs with his bare and bloody hands, stripping flesh from bone, blinding his enemy, grinding its teeth until they were reduced to a pile of ruined flesh and hair at his feet. Forty dogs dead, and he did not think it too many.

Gore clinging to his hands, Sláine set off at a run back towards the encampment and Maug.

The killing was not done.

He saw Ukko kneeling over the druid. Anger refused to allow worry to enter his mind. He would find Slough Maug and strip his rancid flesh from his bones. He would recover Feg's book and he would return home – even if he had to kill every last stinking wretched sack of shit skull sword in the process, it would not be too many.

UKKO CROUCHED OVER the druid.

The whimpering of the dogs had stopped, which meant the dying was done. The surge of relief was short lived.

Shudders wracked the old man's body.

There were no marks on his flesh. None of the dogs had come near him. No, Ukko reasoned, this attack was spiritual – some dark magic of the Drune's. He spat three times in rapid succession to ward against the black arts before he checked the druid's throat for an erratic pulse. At the contact Myrrdin's face twisted, pain rooting through his body. The sudden and violent seizure mirrored the spasms of Sláine as the warrior raged in battle frenzy – only where the *riastrad* empowered the

Sessair these spasms weakened Myrrdin Emrys to the point of collapse. Myrrdin's eyes flared open. His jaw clenched, teeth grinding as he bit back on the sudden surge of agony. He was trying to speak but no words could escape between his locked jaws.

Ukko didn't understand what was happening.

He took the druid's hand in his.

It was cold and lifeless.

And Ukko knew then that the druid was dying. He could feel it in his skin. The Earth Power was literally stripping the strength from his flesh. It was a miracle he was still alive – but it was no mercy.

"Sláine!" Ukko yelled, twisting to see the warped warrior charging back towards the Drune stronghold. "Sláine!" but the warrior was deaf in his battle rage.

"Lug's balls, don't you dare die on me, old man. I am fed up of having to save people," Ukko muttered bitterly.

ABSOLUTE TERROR BLAZED in Drune's eyes as Sláine, brutally warped and growing with every step, strode out to meet him in the centre of the clearing.

The slough-skinned Drune priest's hand closed around the bone-handled dagger at his hip. A slow cunning smile spread across his face.

"You are running the wrong way, brute."

A ring of skull swords moved to protect their leader, gathering around Maug, their swords quivering before the sheer physical enormity of the warped one.

Sláine ignored their anxious blades. "Now you die, Maug, just like your dogs died. And I promise it will be agonising. What was it you promised the druid? A death befitting his legend? Add this to my promise, Drune. Your death will be wretched and inglorious, bloody and cruel. There is no salvation for failed ambition. No glorious seat in the Otherworld. It ends here, in piss, shit and blood. Now you die. Your death will be worthy of your malevolence."

"I don't think so," Slough Maug rasped, drawing and throwing the wickedly curved blade in a single smooth motion. The silver and bone spun through the air and slammed into Sláine's chest.

Sláine looked down at the elaborately carved bone handle protruding from his chest, then reached up and drew it slowly free of the warped muscle. He tossed it to the floor, ignoring the gaping wound as though it were little more than a wasp's sting. "Hubris, Drune," the giant warrior said, shaking his head. A heartbeat later he surged forwards, tearing out the throat of the first skull sword careless enough to get in his way. The sword clattered to the floor an instant after the dead warrior.

Sláine stepped over the corpse.

A rusted blade hacked into his forearm. He batted it away, thundering a right cross into his attacker's face, rupturing bone and cartilage, driving the man's nose back into his brain. The man fell, convulsing before his nerves ceased their desperate screaming for the life that had left them. Three more skull swords lay dead before the twitching stopped completely, their chests open to the world, their guts spilled out around their ankles in slick grey loops of unravelled intestine. The raging Sessair grabbed a man by the hair of his helmet and another by the throat, slamming their skulls together with such ferocity the bone shattered inwards and the blood and brains spilled down over his hands as he discarded them.

"I'm coming for you, Maug!" Sláine roared, hurling a severed arm at the priest. A warrior lay at his feet, screaming and clutching at the stump gouting out his lifeblood. Sláine crushed him beneath his feet like a bug. The skull sword's face caved in, his eye rupturing, the viscous liquid dribbling down his cheek. He didn't scream. He was already dead.

The priest was a coward to the core: seeing the corpses of his men lying in pools of blood at Sláine's feet, he turned and ran, clutching Feg's precious book to his chest.

The rage within Sláine consumed him. He reached down, his huge fist tangling in the hair of one of the dead, and hauled the corpse up until its feet hung inches above the ground. Hooking his fingers inside its slack jaw he forced it apart, past the natural limits of the bone, until something beneath the skin snapped and the dead man's skull hung slackly on a broken neck. The jawbone came away in his hands. Grunting, Sláine yanked back on the top row of teeth, forcing the bones back until the skin split and the muscle tore and what remained of the head came away in his hands. He dropped the rest of the corpse.

Sláine hurled the skull at Maug's back. The Drune had staggered and stumbled fifty feet through the deadfall littering the glade. The dead man's skull exploded against the back of Maug's head in a spray of blood and brain and bone. The priest staggered on two more steps before his legs betrayed him and he fell. His arms didn't reach out to break his fall.

Earth Power thrashing through his system, Sláine stood over the priest. The back of his head was a mess. It was impossible to tell if any of the gore and grey matter was the priest's. He did not care either way. Sláine knelt, and thrust his hand down through the Drune's back, tearing out his spine to get at his heart. Vile magic sustained the withered organ. Roaring his triumph, Sláine plucked out the still-beating heart and crushed it in his bare hands.

Maug's death satisfied his rage.

With the blood of the heart spilling out through his clenched fist Sláine felt the mighty warp spasm begin to leave him.

He opened his hand and stared at Maug's ruined heart until the last vestiges of anger had left him and he felt diminished.

UKKO HEARD SLÁINE'S primal scream of triumph.

The druid stirred in his arms, opening his eyes. His smile was tired but already the colour was returning to his face.

"He has triumphed," Myrrdin managed before his head fell back and his eyes rolled up into his skull.

"He always does," Ukko said to the unconscious man, "He's Sláine."

Ard Ri.

Ukko didn't know if he had even heard the words or if they were even words. They could easily have been a susurrus stirring amongst the dead trees. The words hadn't come from the druid's mouth; that much he knew. Ukko scanned the blackened branches looking for one of the Morrigan's damned crows but they were alone. He drew no comfort from the knowledge.

"You're hearing things, you damned fool." He peered back along the line of huge stones and then through the rows of twisted tree trunks, imagining an army of ghosts circling, closing in.

Deciding to keep the voices in the air to himself, Ukko reached out for a thick stub of a branch that had fallen near him, and sat with it in his lap, waiting for Sláine to return with their things.

Five

The Ragnarok Book

THE DRUID'S STRENGTH returned during their flight from the forest, as though each step away from the dark heart of Dardun was a step on the road to recovery. The correlation did not pass unnoticed by the three travellers, though of course it was only Ukko who dared mention it and his understanding was woefully wrong. Sláine had no wish to burden him with the truth – that it was his own warp spasm that had so brutally injured their companion.

Likewise, Myrrdin was disinclined to talk.

Guilt simmered away inside Sláine. He had known that it was different, that the power he was drawing on was not purely of the earth herself, and yet he had devoured it, sucking the very life out of the man who acted as a conduit between the distant Goddess and her champion. His greed had almost killed the man as effectively as his rage had done away with Slough Maug.

Worse though, by far, were the visions that had come to him through the merging – the memories of the druid, of his life before as guardian and

Lord of the Trees, and then his flesh trapped within the wood, feeling the very stuff of the tree growing into him, dampening his thoughts until there was nothing within his mind but a decades-long scream.

It was horrific in the simplicity of its torture – and amazing that the druid had held on to any shred of sanity during it. The fact was that he had marked Myrrdin Emrys as a man of uncanny power and staggering will. But Sláine had felt it, there, a great formless shadow in the darkness lurking behind the druid's memories. He had recognised it as it touched him: hatred. Pure and dark and festering. It was that hatred that had warped so powerfully through his flesh, driving him to such extremes of naked savagery with his bare hands. And he knew, in some fundamental way, it had changed him. Even as it coiled back into the druid its taint remained, the shadow of anger worming its way beneath, behind and between his conscious and subconscious thoughts.

He walked a while in silence, brooding over the strange sensation that slowly crept beneath his skin. He was not comfortable with the invasion, with his unwitting violation of the druid's pain. Worse though was the sure and certain knowledge that the druid had experienced his life in return, the pain, heartbreak and betrayal that had made him what he was – if not who he was.

Sláine couldn't bring himself to look at the druid.

Instead, he looked at the dirt and the bracken, at the withered thorns and the calcified wooden tree trunks, at the gossamer threads of a huge web strung from branch to branch above their heads and at the insects trapped within it, cocooned in pupae to keep their meat fresh for the spider that ruled the beautiful web. The spider moved, scuttling forwards on its spindly legs, barbs clicking over the fine filaments of web, playing it like an exquisite instrument. Light caught and refracted in the dew as it spilled down, scattering a rainbow across the detritus of the forest floor. It would have been enchanting if not for the sudden fury of the kill, as the spider sank its fangs into its trapped prey and feasted, pulling away at the cocoon until it could gorge itself on the meat it preserved.

Sláine crunched through the deadfall. He wanted to put as much distance between them and the dead as he could. Dardun was no place to spend the night with the deaths of so many on your hands.

"Come on," he called over his shoulder, urging the others to hurry up. He wanted to be free and clear of the damned forest before sundown.

THEY FINALLY ESCAPED the oppressive clutches of the dead trees an hour before dusk.

Before they were even one hundred feet clear Ukko flopped down onto his backside and crossed his arms. "All right, that's it, I am done. Feed me. My stomach feels like my throat has been cut again. A dwarf was not made to go on fumes alone, as powerful as my farts are."

"We can't stop here," Sláine said, impatience creeping into his voice. He was tired, hungry and irritable, but he wasn't stupid enough to think that they were home free. He looked at the druid for support. Myrrdin nodded. "Come on, you miserable little runt, get off your arse. We don't stop until it's too dark to put one foot in front of another."

Ukko grumbled – loudly – but he did what he was told, dragging his feet, kicking up stones and tearing off a stream of profanities as he trudged along five paces behind them.

Myrrdin didn't say a word.

Sláine found himself obsessing over the druid's silence – convincing himself it was down to something Myrrdin had seen inside his memories. After all, he had found the druid's darkness – what presence had Myrrdin Emrys found within him? What darkness lurked within him? What taint did he nurture?

In the hour they walked it went from a nagging doubt to the size of a cow within Sláine's mind. The druid had seen something within him, something that had silenced him.

He clutched Feg's book to his chest as though it were salvation itself.

THEY STRUCK CAMP on the lea of a hill, using its incline for shelter against the rising wind.

Sláine struggled with the fire, trying to strike a spark and fan it into a stuttering flame. The kindling was damp and refused to ignite. He gave up and sank back against the cold stone of the rockface their camp huddled up beneath.

Myrrdin leaned forwards, whispering a word that Sláine didn't catch but knew was one of power – a thin wisp of smoke coiled up from the kindling. The druid breathed on it gently, encouraging it to fan out across the wood and truly burn. Sláine watched in mute fascination as the druid brought the small fire to life.

Ukko hunched forwards and rubbed his hands briskly over the flame as though right up until that moment he had been freezing. He grinned at Sláine. "So, what are we going to eat?"

"Whatever you catch," Sláine said, holding out Brain-Biter.

"You cannot be serious..."

"I don't see an inn nearby, do you? Or perhaps you have some of that dry cornbread left?"

Ukko huffed as he pushed himself to his feet. "Fine, you just sit here; leave it to me to feed us. I thought the brutes were meant to be the hunters!" Grumbling, the dwarf disappeared into the darkness beyond the ring of firelight. In seconds the dwarf had blended in perfectly with the night. Sláine closed his eyes and leaned back against the rock, listening to Ukko's receding footsteps. Within a few minutes he was asleep.

The sweet aroma of dripping fat and the sizzle of crisping hare woke him. He kept his eyes closed, recalling a fragment of the dream he had been having – he had been watching a woman weave through the blackened trunks of Dardun, a bundle of blankets cradled in her arms. Within the blankets was a dead child. He knew it was dead, he could smell the decay in his dream. She looked at him, beckoning him through the trees, but as he moved to join her she faded. All that remained by the time he reached where she had been was thc tattered shreds of the blanket her child had been swaddled in. She had simply disappeared before his eyes leaving him alone in the forest.

Sláine had no idea what the peculiar, haunting dream signified. Who was the fading woman? Who was the child? How had it died? What did they want from him?

He opened his eyes, the last remnants of the dream slipping away. Ukko had returned with a brace of hares, skinned them and was licking his lips as he blackened them over the fire. Myrrdin sat across the fire from the dwarf, Feg's book in his lap, lost in its pages. Whether it was a trick of the shadows and the erratic firelight or not was impossible to tell, but the druid looked every one of his three hundred and fifty-something years. Dark shadows hollowed out his cheeks and sunk his wooden eyes, bringing out every harsh angle of the skull beneath his face. Even the texture of his tattoos had taken on a disturbing bark-like quality, the heavy lines of age carving deep scores down his cheeks. The druid looked up from the book, somehow aware of Sláine's scrutiny.

"I can see why the Lord Weird would fear you, warrior," Myrrdin said, laying the book aside. For a moment Sláine thought the druid was hinting at the thing he had seen within their merging, but then the druid continued: "This book is more than merely the ramblings of some madman. It is his soul laid bare. Admittedly a lot of it is incoherent but that is not a sign of the author's madness, more a clue to his true nature – so much is going on inside his head and he is clearly determined to capture it all, but it is impossible to pour it all out onto vellum at once, and even as he struggles to do so his own thoughts and fears distract him from that singular purpose. Instead his words chase clarity but lose themselves in incoherence."

"Can you make anything of it?"

"More than Slough Feg would ever want," the druid said, smiling for the first time in days. It was not a pleasant smile. The terpsichorean shadows made him look quite mad beneath their erratic play.

"Will it help us?" asked Ukko, as he finished burning the hare. He tore off a hind leg and bit into it. Fatty juices squirted down his chin. He smeared them across his stubble with a grubby hand and then licked the grease off his fingers appreciatively.

"He is the enemy of our lady, Danu. How could his soul laid bare before us fail to serve our cause?"

"Then we have a chance," said Sláine, choosing to ignore the many and varied failures he could imagine even just off the top of his head.

"We always had a chance," the druid countered. "The difference is now, with this, we have what we need to craft a plan."

"We do?" asked Ukko between mouthfuls of meat. He ripped a second leg from the burned hare and tore into it with his teeth.

"We do, my little friend, we most assuredly do," Myrrdin said, his wooden eyes burning in the firelight.

Sláine raised a quizzical eyebrow towards the dwarf. "I thought you said you could read the book?"

"I didn't say that exactly," Ukko evaded, masticating a mouthful of piping-hot hare rump. He looked everywhere except at Sláine. "I might have intimated that I ahh *understood* it a little more clearly than I actually did... to add a little colour to our dreary lives... but I most certainly never claimed that I could read the madness of Lord Weirdo's beyond a few choice words, like deluge, if you remember? It's not hard to work out what it is all about when you keep reading *great flood, elemental disaster, cataclysm, Ragnarok,* and *deluge* a few times every dozen or so pages of rambling."

Sláine shook his head in disgust. He shuffled forwards, moving closer to the fire. "So what *does* it say?" he asked Myrrdin.

The druid scratched his chin. "Well the dwarf isn't wrong when he says Feg is obsessed with bringing on the deluge–"

"See!" Ukko interrupted, stabbing a greasy finger in Sláine's direction. "I said so, didn't I? Great flood, I said."

"But this book holds so much more than that. It is a confessional. The need to unburden is a common weakness of powerful men, especially ones as dangerous as Feg. He mentions more than once the treasures of Tir-Nan-Og. Are you familiar with the legends?"

"A little," Sláine admitted.

"Well, there were four great artefacts of legend that were divided amongst the tribes of the Goddess: the Cauldron of Rebirth, the Spear of Lug, the Stone of Destiny and the Sword of the Moon. These were no mere trinkets, far from it, together they symbolised the Land of the Young united. One was given to each tribe of Danu, in part to prevent their theft, but mainly to reduce the chance of corruption amongst the brother kings. The fear was that if one man held all of the treasures he would become the invincible king – and few invincibles possessed the strength to remain pure. Power on that scale can only serve as a breeding ground for greed, selfishness, covetousness, and ultimately self-aggrandisement, treachery and betrayal. How could it not? After all who can stop them? They are invincible. There is wisdom in the separation of the treasures. The Sessair were given stewardship of the Cauldron – but even before my imprisonment it was lost to them, shattered into four pieces and scattered on each of the four winds."

"Then what hope is there in these stupid stories?" Sláine said bitterly, a sudden sense of helplessness welling up inside him. They were chasing children's sagas. Great treasures scattered to the four winds. Myrrdin might as well have said they needed to pluck a single hair from the Morrigan's crusty lips for all the hopes they had of reclaiming the Cauldron. He knew all about the failure of his people. The Cauldron had many names, and purposes. They called it the Cauldron of Plenty, for any pure warrior who reached into the steaming pot would be fed. Others knew it as the Cauldron of Rebirth for its links with the kingdom of the dead and its restorative powers. It was also the home of the freak Avagddu, the Morrigan's foul child. Its sundering had trapped the monstrous child within whatever hellish El World the beast had been banished to. They had cost the Crone her child; was it any wonder the Morrigan hated his people?

"They are far from stupid, champion. They are our histories. These treasures are not some child's fantasy. They are our heritage. Do not be so quick to dismiss them. Feg refers to them repeatedly for a reason, I am sure."

"And what reason would that be?" said Sláine, more harshly than he intended. The smell of the hare reminded him of just how hungry he actually was. He took the second animal from the fire and tore out its breast. The meat was stringy. The hare had obviously died running, muscles bunched taut with fear – he could taste it in the cooked meat.

"The very best one – he fears them."

"What is there to fear from a few trinkets long since lost?"

"Not the treasures, precisely, but what they represent to the people of Tir-Nan-Og. They are iconic. They remind us of who we are. Where we come from. They are focal points of our history, wielded by Lug himself. They bring hope because they signify the tribes united. Never underestimate the simplest of powers – hope is a mighty weapon against the oncoming storm. The treasures epitomise the power of the Goddess herself. To wield the sword, to hurl the spear, to feast from the Cauldron, to stand upon the holy stone of destiny and be proclaimed high king by right – all of that is ours! That is to be Danu's champion, to be her chosen one, her warrior! That is what Feg fears! He fears the very heart of our beautiful land. That is why he sours it so. He seeks to suck the marrow out of the very stuff of life, to drain the Earth Serpent so its power cannot thwart his dark master, the Wyrm God itself, Crom-Cruach. Only by killing the very land itself can he hope to prevail."

"There is no Ard Ri," said Sláine. "There is no unity between the tribes. What you speak of does not exist outside fireside tales."

"Indeed," said Myrrdin. "Like the Cauldron itself, they are fractured. But, in that similarity lies the genesis of our plan. To stand against Feg we – *you* – must reunite the tribes of Danu, and to do that you must reforge the Cauldron itself," the druid looked at Sláine across the fire. "It is a gift fit for a king." And Sláine knew then, with a cold certainty, that the Lord of the Trees had seen his shaming and understood the nature of his exile, and more tellingly, his desire to return home despite the risks such a homecoming promised. "And one that might well bring forgiveness with it."

And suddenly he understood. Realisation crystallised with his mind. It was not about Feg, or Danu, the Sessair, not even Tir-Nan-Og. No, it came down to something as simple as a mother's love.

He had known from the start that he was being manipulated, finally he understood by whom; at the root of everything that had happened since he had first set eyes upon her back in the forest glade so close to home, the Morrigan. His mother's death, his exile, his journey south into the Sourlands, the Crone was behind it all, even, no doubt, the Weatherwitch's visitation. The Sidhe had foretold his return, directing him to find the Skinless Man, and even as he awoke from the dream the Morrigan had been there to steer his feet to the very tree where she herself had bound the Lord of the Trees centuries before, the same Skinless Man Sláine sought.

Coincidence?

Hardly, the Crone was playing the long game.

Her pieces had been in motion for centuries working towards this moment, on the fringe of the dead forest where once Myrrdin ruled, and why?

The answer was as obvious as it was simple: so that the druid returned could set another subtle chain of events into motion. And that chain of events? The reforging of the four fragments of the lost Cauldron – the same Cauldron that served as prison for the Morrigan's only child. The manipulations of the Crone were far-reaching but their purpose was the most natural of all, a mother's love.

Despite the fire, a cold chill touched his heart, put there by a sudden thought.

With the Crone's machinations laid bare another possibility arose, one that Sláine could not afford to discount: had the Morrigan somehow fed the madness of Slough Feg? Had *she* created the monster that she would ultimately need to provide the threat to the Land of the Young knowing that would in turn prove to be the impetus for the liberation of her son?

It made a perverse kind of sense, one that adhered to all he had ever heard of the Crone from Cathbad.

It was like seeing the strands of a huge and elaborate spider's web picked out by the morning frost; suddenly it was all too clear.

"You know where these pieces lie hidden." It wasn't a question. The druid gave no sign that he had caught the subtle difference in Sláine's intonation. He nodded.

"One is in the possession of the Sidhe king, Finvarra, on the Isle of Glass. Another was claimed by Weyland the Smith. The third is in the saddle bags of the fabled Huntress."

"And the final piece?"

"That is held by the Morrigan herself," the druid said.

"So what am I supposed to do, Myrrdin? Appeal to the better nature of these fabled folk and hope they take pity on my fool's quest? Or steal the pieces and invoke their supernatural wrath and earn their immortal enmity?"

"It will be no easy thing," the druid admitted. "Indeed, the reforging of the Cauldron is a hero feat worthy of a true king. With such a treasure a man could return home without fear of his fate – not just as the voice of doom but as a beacon of hope. That, champion, is what Feg fears the most. That is why she brought us together. We both know it. It is our destiny. You are the champion I was promised, Sláine Mac Roth. This one act was what you were born for. All aspects of the Goddess have marked you; Mother, Maiden and Crone, you are their chosen one, their warrior. You are the light."

And there it was, the bait spoken.

It hung in the air between them.

Sláine took another bite from the hare's charred carcass and swallowed the greasy meat without taking his eyes off the druid for a moment.

Sláine grunted, tossing the stripped bones into the fire. The fat caused the flames to crackle and spit, leaping high enough to obscure the druid's wooden eyes for a moment. The elemental dance of the orange flame was hypnotic, seductive. A part of him yearned to enter the fire and be forged like iron by the flame. He watched the bone shrivel and crack open, the marrow scorched by the intense heat until it was all but consumed. He was the bone within the Morrigan's fire. Her quest would consume him.

He knew that. But he had no choice. If he refused her all the Crone had to do was ask it of him and he would be forced to play the part she had scripted for him. One promise eroded his freewill. In this, and in so much else, he knew, he was the Morrigan's plaything. When the flames diminished, he said "What would you have me do?" across the top of them.

The druid told him: "We must travel north, into the heart of Emania and reach the Moon-Torn before the Night of the Questing Moon. The Night Bringer is a legend, like the great smith. To find any of these immortals one must understand their nature. The Huntress and her wild hunt are tied to the stories people tell about them. She is the sum of the stories, trapped in a cycle of repetition, cursed to live again and again the sagas mortals spin about her myth."

Sláine nodded his understanding. "And one such story promises that the Great Hunt will ride through the hill fortress of Navan on the night of the Questing Moon."

"Exactly," Myrrdin said.

"What do you know of this Huntress? You called her the Night Bringer?"

"Before you boys get all wrapped up in hatching your schemes and forget about me, let me just remind you that a little misdirection and sleight of hand goes a long way. Or put more plainly, if there's any stealing to be done, I'm your dwarf," Ukko smirked, licking the last of the hare's juices off his fingers. "Now, what were you saying about this Night Bringer? Doesn't sound like a particularly pleasant individual if you ask me. How come we never go hunting for the Smiling Goat or the Gentle Giant? It's always the Night Bringer, the Dark Mistress, and the Raging Banshee that you heroes are obsessed with." Ukko shook his head in mock despair.

Six
The Night Bringer

ACTING AS THEIR guide and teacher, Myrrdin told them what he knew of the Huntress and her wild hunt as they journeyed on. The stories did little to soothe the doubts nagging away at the back of the young warrior's mind.

She had two names: the Huntress and the Night Bringer. The duality reflected both aspects of her legend. As the Huntress she led the spectral hunt of the dead and damned, refused the peace of eternity. To join her hunt was to earn immortality of a sort.

"The Huntress is not a woman," Myrrdin said, the dwindling sun at his back. "She is an essential being."

"What?"

"An energy, a spectre drawn from the land herself. She is not as powerful as a true aspect of the Goddess, but more like a shade fuelled by Danu's essence, if you would. She is a part of the Goddess – Danu is the land, but in the sky above her there is an uneasy truce between the sun and moon. The Goddess is at the mercy of these things and thus she channels part of herself into the Night Bringer, a warrior aspect mighty enough to rail against the very heavens above and bring on the night in answer to her summons."

"Are you really sure we want to find her?" Ukko said, his short legs struggling to match their longer strides.

"If there was another way," Myrrdin said, "believe me, I would choose it."

"Well, that's even more comforting, I must say."

The further north the companions travelled the closer winter drew around them, until, almost in the shadow of the Great Cairn itself, the first flakes of snow began to fall. The landscape was harsh – outsiders often called it the savage frontier. There was a wild beauty to it. Fields rolled out, blanketed by lavender and lilac heathers. Gorse and bramble filled in the patches between the purples. Jagged spars of rock rose like broken teeth, the chalk-white hills and the iron-rich ores adding grey, white and red hues to the countryside. The vista was hauntingly familiar – so similar to the land he had grown up in – but that was unsurprising. They had travelled deep into the territories of Emania. They were less than a day's walk from Ard Macha, two from the Great Cairn and the fortress of Navan. The fortress demarked the northernmost edge of the lands of Emania – or as Sláine thought of the geography – the southernmost fringes of Sessair territory. If they were to walk north by north-east they would arrive in Murias before the week was out. The proximity of his childhood unnerved him.

"How do we find the Moon-Torn? I have lived most of my life in the shadow of these white-capped mountains and I have never heard talk of them. What are they, more ghosts?"

"They are not ghosts," the druid said, without meeting his eye. "Not truly."

"I don't like the sound of *that*," said Ukko. "Funny how this almost ghost thing never came up over the last few weeks of walking to find them, isn't it?"

"They are people, just like you or I. It is their curse that makes them… different."

"Oh, a curse, this just keeps getting better every time he opens his mouth."

"Hush, dwarf," Sláine said, brushing aside Ukko's snide remark. He stirred the fire with a stick, causing a shower of sparks to punctuate his rising anger. "Explain, druid. I am in no mood for surprises," Myrrdin looked decidedly uncomfortable under Sláine's scrutiny. "If you won't talk, it ends here, Myrrdin. Don't make the mistake of thinking you know my mind just because you shared a few memories. Murias is close enough that the duty to warn my people burns inside my chest. It is called loyalty. Now it is time to lay your cards on the table. You know something of these Moon-Torn and whatever it is, it concerns you enough that you are uncomfortable talking about it. That in itself tells me enough to know I should be wary."

"There is not much to tell."

"Let me be the judge of that."

"Very well. Their curse is an old one. In many ways they are just like your people... or rather, they *were* your people once, long before the sundering of the Cauldron and the diaspora of the Goddess's tribes."

"Speak plainly, man. I am no fan of your fancy words. They were Sessair, yes or no?"

"Not Sessair, no, but children of Emania, brothers and sisters of your tribe. They turned their back on the Goddess, offering benediction to the heavens. They believed that the skies surpassed the wonder of the earth, and moreover, that the stars themselves sheltered ancient deities worthy of their worship. They paid lip service to Danu, but even as they did, they betrayed themselves with ceremonies of star worship. The Morrigan blessed them with what they believed was their heart's desire: she drew the strands of her dark self from deep within her being, conjuring or creating the Night Bringer, the Huntress who rode the land for eternity, claiming all those who looked upon her in her aspect to join her savage hunt."

"Looked?" Sláine said sceptically, not for a moment believing that the sight of something, no matter how hideous, could be enough to still a human heart.

"To see her was to embrace death, warrior. Make no mistake, the essence of the Goddess is mighty, her dark side far worse than anything Carnun could inspire. Carnun is a parasite on her flesh, the Night Bringer *is* her flesh – an apparition of it. What in the world could hold more power? Or more threat? The onlookers perished, their souls drawn to join the hunt for eternity."

"Until people stop recounting stories of the wild hunt?"

"Exactly. Until that day, they are bound to the endless winter night, running at her side in search of other souls to join the chase. The Morrigan's blessing was two-fold; on the one hand, she gave them the Night Bringer, on the other she gave them to the Night Bringer."

"I am not sure I follow."

"They worshipped the essence of the night. The Night Bringer became their precious deity, the moon her symbol. In return, the Morrigan gave *them* to the night and the moon. That was the duality of her gift, the curse that nestled in beside it. When the moon rides full in the sky the Moon-Torn children of the Night Bringer fade to nothing. They become invisible, save by the light of the moon itself when they are transformed, like the ghosts of the hunt they worship, appearing ethereal, insubstantial."

"That's... that's..."

"Barbaric? Evil? Hateful? Vile? Inhumane? Yes, it is all of these, and more, for the curse is handed down from generation to generation, the children suffering for the failings of the fathers with no way to break the cycle save for their story to stop being told. And in telling you this I merely prolong their suffering. As long as there are lips to blather they will suffer the torment of the moon."

Sláine put his head in his hands, scratching at his scalp as he tried to think. "How could a spirit being whose visage brings death come into possession of a piece of the Cauldron of Rebirth?" But he knew the answer even before he had finished the question: the Morrigan. Her fingers were all over this latest facet of the quest. He was being bullied into a course of action he had no control over; they all knew it but none of them mentioned the way seemingly random events were actually intertwined if you scratched beneath the thin patina of chance.

Was it any coincidence that the Crone was responsible for the curse that created one of the guardians of the fragments of her monstrous offspring's gaol?

Almost certainly not.

He was beginning to believe that there was no such thing as happenstance. There was a purpose to everything, no matter how innocuous it appeared to be; a guiding hand that shaped events to its need, want and desire. The Morrigan herself had confessed that she had walked paths of various futures – how could anyone with such knowledge not manipulate the here and now to their best interests, having seen how they would play out? The temptation to meddle would be too great, surely? Which all served to confirm his suspicion; they were being manipulated by the Crone. It was all part of that complex web of hers.

He didn't give the druid a chance to answer: "The Moon-Torn... their curse makes them invisible every full moon?"

"That is the nature of the curse, yes."

Sláine nodded, thinking it through. "And the Night Bringer comes when? Every month? Samain? Beltane? Once a year? A decade?"

"According to the saga of the Moon-Torn, the Huntress rides through Navan on the Night of the Questing Moon."

"Only once a year?"

Myrrdin nodded.

"Does it not disturb you that *chance* has delivered us to this very spot in time for us to witness the wild hunt as it rides through? It feels too convenient."

"Morrigu lead us to this place, this time. She pledged to aid me, to deliver to me the champion Danu needed for her salvation. You are that champion. These events transpiring now will temper you, not break you. I have faith."

"You just spent three hundred years inside a tree," Ukko mumbled, "so you won't mind if I don't share your optimism, will you?"

THE NIGHT OF the Questing Moon was the holiest of holy nights for the Moon-Torn.

The heather leant the night its rich fragrance. The three travellers walked side by side, following the moon-shadows towards the wooden wall of the hill-side fortification. The air was brisk, with the chill of winter to it. The serrated edge of the spiked wall sheared across the top of the mountain; with the moon at its back, it looked as though the rocky pinnacle had been sliced clean through, exposing Navan as its stony heart. Behind the wall, the stone buildings of the fortress proper looked tiny set against nature's might. Sláine needed no such reminder of the fleeting quality of life against the permanence of the mountain. He had sworn an oath to be the mountain, to be the river. That was what it meant to be Sessair. One life was brief, a mote in the eye of the time. The sum of lives, of generations added upon generations, of wisdom learned and shared; that was to be the mountain, that was what it meant to endure, to make a mark upon the world. To live. There was a durability to that succession that the man-made fort could never hope to emulate.

Even so, beneath the fortress they were little more than ants marching across the fields of heather and gorse.

The moon was a silver-white orb that owned the sky. Wraiths of breath coiled in front of his face. They curled lazily into the air above his head, climbing high before they finally dissipated, becoming one with the night.

A storm was brewing in the western skies.

Sláine studied the cloud formations: a warrior of the Red Branch learned to understand the skies, to read the mood of the weather. It was a poor battle king who led his men into combat with the elements against him. Mortal foes were enough. This was no ordinary storm front. The heavens roiled with angry life, thunderheads rolling in, and yet where he stood there was not so much as the faintest breeze to stir the air.

Myrrdin had noted the peculiar weather patterns as well. The druid looked pensive.

"The Night Bringer's doing?" Sláine asked, instinctively reaching for the familiar weight of Brain-Biter. The axe was slung on a leather thong across his back. He began loosening the leather ties.

"Possibly, or it is just a storm. Not everything that happens is down to some sinister purpose, champion. The world moves no matter what we do, what we plan; the sun rises, the rains fall."

"You don't believe that for a moment, do you? This is all a part of the Morrigan's scheming, Myrrdin. The more I see the more I know for sure and certain that nothing happens by accident in this realm."

"Well, there was the time I knocked up that barmaid back in Lundin," Ukko grinned, winking lasciviously at Sláine. "That *was* an accident, believe me."

"No, that was a miracle," said Sláine. "A miracle in that she let your scabby little backside anywhere *near* her in the first place."

"Hey! I'll have you know that plenty of women come looking for some Ukko-loving. They don't all swoon at the sight of your rippling muscles and your rugged jawline. Some of them like a little–"

"Runt?"

"That's *not* what I was going to say," Ukko grumbled, folding his arms and turning his back on Sláine.

"Oh I know, how about throbbing dwarfhood?" Sláine offered helpfully.

"Now you arc just being stupid, I'm not talking to you."

"Suit yourself," said Sláine. "So, druid," Sláine turned back to Myrrdin, "how are we going to find these cursed tribesmen?"

"I think the Moon-Torn have found us," Myrrdin said. Sláine followed the direction of his gaze. At first he could see nothing; then, as the cloud that had obscured the moon passed, the shimmering naked silhouettes of six ethereal figures slowly solidified enough for him to distinguish their sex. The moon's silver radiated within them, making the six women luminous. Sláine stared – and knew he was staring. Their curves were beautiful, subtle and rounded, fulsome and lithe, their breasts proud and sagging, small and pendulous, their hair close-cropped, long and luxuriant, braided and cascading in loose curls; between them the six women were everything a red-blooded man could have possibly desired. He felt his blood stir, fired by their grace as they moved – they didn't walk, they ghosted over the ground, glided as though floating a few inches above the heather – down the hillside away from them.

The Morrigan's taunt returned to him, mocking him for being a carnal being, for worshipping the flesh and the desire and need of meat, and his promise to himself to change, but be pure in his devotion to the Goddess.

Ukko's face lit up when he saw them. He rubbed his hands together gleefully and started to follow them but before he could manage five eager steps the druid's hand clamped down on his shoulder to restrain him. He turned to look at Sláine for support but getting none seemed to shrink in on himself, crestfallen.

"Not so fast, little one. By your master's admission nothing in this realm happens by chance. These comely creatures appear to guide us, not some goat-like old man with a withered staff beckoning us to follow. Let us think, and not blunder into some ill-conceived trap like lusty lads driven by our cocks. Let your big head do the thinking for once."

"I was," Ukko's grin spread as he cupped his crotch with a grubby hand. "You're worse than Sláine, do you know that? You take all the fun out of life, old man." He screwed his face up distastefully. "Whatever happened to sucking the marrow out of life, eh? Six naked lovelies on a hill, breathe it in, man. You could smell their lust on the wind."

"Exactly, my hormonal little friend, and how better to bait a trap than with some honey?"

"Well, fine, but don't pretend you've never let your animal out to play. Everyone needs a little honey every now and again."

"Look," the druid commanded, his voice taking on an edge of authority Sláine had never heard before. That one word gave a hint to the enormous well of power that lay within thc man. Hc turned in time to see the Moon-Torn women fade to nothing as another cloud obscured the moon. "That is what we face, dwarf, the cursed women of the wild hunt, not some naked lovelies on a hill as you so colourfully put it. What possible use could they have for your flesh? Think. No, I will tell you, they would feed you to the Night Bringer's black dogs. Is your lust worth *that* fate?"

"Well, I'd enter eternity with a smile on my face, which is more than can be said for a lot of deaths I can imagine," Ukko said, "but I get your point, no need to belabour it. Naked women bad. I understand. Let's do what we have to do and get out of here, shall we? It's getting bloody cold and to be brutally honest I'd rather be tucked up in my bedroll than standing out here in the middle of this blasted moor."

It was getting considerably colder, Sláine realised. The temperature of the night air had dropped considerably in the few minutes since the Moon-Torn women had appeared to them. The falling temperature presaged the stirring of the breeze, which quickly became a more insistent, bludgeoning wind that swept across the fields of heather.

The sounds came next, tribal drums pounding out mystic rhythms.

Sláine gestured for the others to follow, and loped towards the sound of the drums. The heather came up around his ankles, masking the treacherous ground. He stumbled several times, barely keeping his balance. He was not a graceful hunter, but he was a swift one. On the crest of the hill he dropped into a tight crouch, aware even as he did so, that he presented the bright moon with enough to betray himself to the Moon-Torn in the valley below.

He needn't have concerned himself. They were not scouring the hillside for the interlopers.

For the heartbeats it took to exhale a slow shallow breath, he thought the valley was empty. Then the first jag of lightning forked, three spears lancing down into the earth, turning night momentarily into day. The lightning revealed hundreds of glittering spectres all across the field. They moved with a haunting rhythm, men and women locked in a wild sexual dance that pounded with a base, raw, animalistic passion. Scores of men spun and twisted, their sex rigid, their movements oddly beautiful as they succumbed to the primal cadences of the drums, throwing their hands above their heads then stooping moments later into a tight stalking crouch before launching themselves again, over and over in this mimicry of the hunt.

It was a breathtaking sight.

The moonlight brought them to life – as the storm gathered and the thunderheads ghosted across the moon they slipped into insubstantiality and blended with the night, simply gone.

Myrrdin and Ukko joined him on the hill.

"The dance is a celebration of the moon herself, a benediction to the Night Bringer, and, more than anything, a eulogy for the lives they have lost in her service," the druid whispered. "They ingest a distillation of ipomoea alba seeds, or as they are more commonly called, moonflowers. The seeds are mildly hallucinogenic, inducing a trance state that the celebrants believe brings them closer to the Huntress, allowing them to call her – that is the dance they are doing."

As though in response to the frantic gyrations of the Moon-Torn the gathering storm strengthened, the wind swirling around them until a few minutes later it was fearsome, battering at them as though by sheer elemental might it could bully them down the slope.

Lightning crashed, searing the sky with ozone. Thunder rolled over the hills, folding in on itself until it gathered into the sky's own primal scream.

Sláine watched the Moon-Torn's ritual, this time struck by the humanity of it: the dance encapsulated all that it meant to be human, from birth to death re-enacted with sheer frenetic joy. Around the circle women waited, watching their men. One by one they reached out, drawing a lover from the dance. Their coupling was every bit as wild and desperate as their dance had been. Sláine felt an uncomfortable arousal at their base display of sensuality and sexuality. Beside him Ukko's face brimmed over with lust. Even the druid seemed touched by the wild dance's euphoria.

The celebrants were untouched by the weather, even as the storm broke and the rain came down in driving torrents, they danced on, they thrust towards satisfaction and release, they whooped and cried out and lost themselves in the pure physicality of the self and the small deaths of the spirit that came with release. The rain did not soak them. The cold did not freeze them. They were living between worlds.

Another fork of lightning rent the sky asunder. The thunder when it came was deafening.

The Moon-Torn froze mid-motion, captured in the moment, bodies locked, limbs sheened with lust, eyes turned to the sky in adoration.

The entire scene was both haunting and voyeuristic, as though they were somehow spying upon ghosts trapped in those last precious memories of love.

But here, now, Sláine was left with the distinct impression that it was the land that had died, and the ghosts themselves that were more alive, more vital where the land was a spectre of itself. He wondered which the Night Bringer would be drawn to; the ghosts or the wounded land? Was that what the ritual was truly about, the joyous defilement of Danu's flesh?

He turned to Myrrdin, but before he could share his thoughts, he felt the hunt nearing, the earth herself trembling at its approach. He pressed his hands flat against the dirt, feeling it shiver at the approach of the Night Bringer. "They are coming."

The druid nodded, once, looking beyond the young warrior. Sláine turned to follow the direction of his gaze and saw the huge hounds leading the charge. They were enormous, their powerful muscles bunched beneath slick ebon coats of fur, eyes the smouldering red of coals, glowing with all the hate of the underworld's damned fires. Their coats were impossibly black against the night, deeper and richer than the darkness. They came out of the black at a frightening pace. In their wake came the others, great shoggy beasts, lupine and feline, fanged, horned, boar-headed, but all of them spectral – these were the outriders of the hunt. There were hundreds of the beasts, thousands. The hunt came on and on and on, the macabre procession never-ending.

Seeing them, Sláine felt panic rise inside him and tasted bile in his throat. It was replaced a heartbeat later by a surge of absolute and compelling hatred that swept over him. He recognised the taste of fear.

The roars of the Moon-Torn swelled behind them, drowning out the thunder.

And then he saw her, the Night Bringer. He knew it was the Huntress immediately.

She was beautiful. He hadn't expected that.

She was not some vile wizened witch with warts and weals and thick sprigs of wiry grey hair sprouting from her chin. She was glorious, majestic, mighty. She radiated death – not the cold blackness of eternity but a *vital* death. Silver hair cascaded halfway down her back and streamed out behind her. The hair framed an elegant sepulchral face of harsh angles and deep shadows augmented by sulphurous eyes. She was a beautiful demon astride a power Night-Mare. The Night Bringer wore skin-tight black leather armour trimmed with thin silver. In it, Sláine knew instinctively that the newly dead could see their own lives – what they had been, those they had loved, others they had wronged – played out within the immaculately lacquered plates of the

Night Bringer's armour as she passed judgement on them.

He shuddered to think what she would see in them.

Her mount was at least eighteen hands high, bigger, more powerful than any roan or stallion. Its nostrils flared, steaming smoke and licks of sulphurous flame gathered around its night-black hooves as they struck flint and stone beneath the heather.

The fire singed the gorse, steaming, but the huge downpour prevented wildfire from consuming the meadow.

The sight of the Night Bringer drove the Moon-Torn into ecstasies, their cries charged with the raw sexual energy of their coupling. Waves of passion emanated from them like some massive psychic charge. Sláine felt his own lusts stirring in response. It took all his willpower not to shed his cloak and tear aside his boar's head codpiece and step out of his trews and charge down the hillside to join them as they rutted in mindless ecstasy.

He looked up at the moon, delighting in its radiance.

He wanted so desperately to feel its pull as he felt the earth within him, firing his blood, making him whole, but there was nothing. He pressed his hands to the earth, relishing the sensation of the rain as it slapped his face and squirmed beneath the trim of his cloak, spilling down his back. He breathed deeply, savouring the storm as it dampened his lust.

Down below, Sláine watched as the Moon-Torn pressed themselves into the dirt so that they could not see the mad procession of creatures. And he understood the full extent of the druid's words and the Morrigan's curse; to look upon the hunt was to invite death.

Through the dance the Moon-Torn embraced their mortality. They worshipped not from love but from fear of the Huntress. They summoned the Night Bringer so that more of them might be put out of their displaced misery, but they were the few, not the many. When it came down to it the Moon-Torn feared the ultimate surrender of life. They rutted in the dirt like animals to remind themselves what it meant to be alive, revelling in the physicality of the flesh, losing themselves in the passion of living because a moment later, if they had the strength to break their curse, they intended to join the hunt.

A lone black crow circled above, riding the worst of the storm with ease.

The bird did not fall from the sky, did not turn to stone, did not die. Sláine watched its erratic flight with grim fascination, immediately sure it wasn't a part of the hunt. Sláine watched the Morrigan's creature swoop low, weaving between the ranks of shoggy beasts, too fleet of wing for them to snag it and feast. The bird stirred strife through the beasts of the hunt. They scented its vitality. The bird taunted them with its mortality; they thirsted for its blood.

"How are we supposed to stop *that*?" Ukko breathed, all the usual bluster gone from his voice.

"We aren't," the druid said. "No mortal can stop the hunt. It is a danse macabre, a huge funeral procession that never ceases. It roams the land in torment. It, like the Goddess, is eternal. Whatever the hunt captures, it kills."

"Well, excuse my stupidity, but what in the blue hells are we doing here, then?"

"We've come to steal the Night Bringer's fragment of the Cauldron," said Sláine.

"*Finally* you are speaking my language," said Ukko with a malicious grin. "What do you want me to do, big man?"

"Nothing," said Sláine flatly as the moon broke free of the clouds, bringing the ghosts of the Moon-Torn back to vivid life before them. "This is my task. The Night Bringer keeps the relic near?"

"It is tied like a fetish to the saddle of her Night-Mare," the druid confirmed.

Sláine nodded. "Do you have a plan, then, druid?" Myrrdin's wooden eyes didn't meet his gaze. "Good," Sláine said. "You said it yourself, druid, to look upon the hunt is to die. I know what I must do."

* * *

UKKO WATCHED IN mute horror as Sláine charged, sky-clad, down the hill, brandishing Brain-Biter over his head.

Lightning crashed, illuminating the full horror of the hunt's mutated pack. Muzzles dripped saliva and blood, eyes blazed with madness, muscles contorted, flexed, bunched, heads thrown back, mouths roared. And the Night Bringer rode in their midst, Queen of the Hunt.

A spear of lightning forked into four spars, each one hanging in the sky even as they arced into the earth. Ukko felt his heart beat wildly against his ribcage; he lost count of how many times. The lightning refused to relinquish its hold on the Goddess's flesh.

The thunder when it came was immense – but it was no match for Sláine's savage battle cry as he threw himself bodily into the writhing mass of the hunt, swinging Brain-Biter madly left and right. The Sessair warrior hewed through the insubstantial spectres of the damned creatures, cleaving a path towards the Huntress. The beasts shrank back from the axe's bite, but even from his vantage high on the hill Ukko could see that it wasn't actually wounding them.

The crow cawed excitedly, swooping low enough for its wings to graze the heather before it rose high into the night sky.

"By Crom's hairy gonads, what the hell does he think he's doing?" Ukko breathed. He put his hands over his eyes because he couldn't bear to look, but as another jag of lightning split the sky he peeked through his fingers, unable not to. "Why isn't he warping? They're going to kill him."

"That's his plan," the druid said sickly, finally grasping Sláine's foolhardy scheme. "He isn't trying to draw on the Earth Power, he's sacrificing himself! We've got to run! We've got to get down there before he kills himself!"

The next fork of lightning highlighted the slaughter: the unearthly hounds hit Sláine, fangs and claws raking at his flesh. Brain-Biter spun from his hands. "*Taaaake me, witch!*" Sláine bellowed. "*End it noooooow!*" At the centre came a huge albino shoggy beast bounding forwards. The creature, part man, part wolf, launched itself, slamming into Sláine's unprotected chest.

Ukko screamed as the warrior fell back, buckling beneath the weight of the beast's assault. He disappeared beneath the savagely snapping fangs.

Without a thought for his own safety, Ukko set off running after the druid.

Myrrdin was already halfway down the hill, slipping and sliding in the mud as he raced to Sláine's aid, but it was too late.

Even before he was halfway across the mired field Ukko saw the spectre of the warrior's essence rise from his corpse to join the hunt.

* * *

Even in death Sláine felt the bond with Danu burning within him – it went beyond flesh, Danu was joined with his spirit, his soul, his very being. They were bound by ties stronger than death.

"Thank you," he breathed, surging up from beneath the press of hell hounds.

Only his body remained on the floor, trampled by the thundering hooves and the stampeding feet of the hunt's lost souls. He looked to the right, up the hill to where Ukko and the druid were screaming, and knew they saw him, now, like this, and knew they understood and could make good his sacrifice. He thought about Brain-Biter, and suddenly the axe manifested in his hands, cold and deathly. He kissed the twin heads of the axe and turned to face the Huntress as she bore down on him on her furious Night-Mare.

The Night Bringer's steed scorched the heather and gorse, burning a black scar through the heart of the meadow.

Sláine rocked back on his heels, then sprang forwards, one, two, three huge strides, before he brought the axe whistling around in a brutal arc, slamming it into the Night-Mare's thick neck and burying it deep. The blow would have decapitated a mortal beast – the Night-Mare didn't falter so much as a single step in its powerful gallop. Sláine maintained his grip on the axe and swung around so that he was clinging on, being dragged by the grotesque horse.

The Night Bringer looked down at her uninvited passenger with distaste on her aquiline face.

Sláine met her hate-filled gaze for a moment, then broke eye contact to follow the line of leather traces dangling from her saddle. A score of fetishes and other gewgaws dangled on the silver chains, obscuring the one thing of value that hung from the thirteenth chain – the rust-corroded fragment of the Cauldron of Rebirth. Sláine smiled coldly and pulled himself hand over hand up the length of the axe's shaft until he could reach out and grab the chain securing the metal shard.

He reached out and snatched the chain, shocked at the sudden cold that thrilled down through his fingers into his heart. The Night-Mare reared, trying to dislodge him. The Huntress sneered, drawing a wickedly curved blade from the sheath at her side. "How many times do you wish to die, manling?" She thrust down, the blade piercing the hollow between his neck and shoulder and plunging down through his heart and lungs. The cold seared his body, the pain enormous until he remembered his corpse was lying in the dirt fifty yards away and it was only the ghost of agony that pierced him. It took every ounce of strength the young Celt had to relinquish his hold on Brain-Biter and grasp the freezing chain that held the fragment of the Cauldron.

The Huntress threw back her head and shrieked, the cry whipping her creatures into a frenzy of tooth and claw.

The Night-Mare shied, kicking the air, its smouldering hooves cracking the earth and stone beneath them as they came down.

And still Sláine clung to the chain.

His feet dragged on the ground.

The Huntress's blade pierced his throat, sliced into his arm, sank deep into his gut, and still he refused to relinquish his hold.

And then the chain broke and he fell, clutching the fragment of the Cauldron.

He hit the floor hard, his spirit form sliced in a score of places, each blow fatal for mortal flesh, and started running.

OVERHEAD, THE Morrigan's huge black-winged bird seemed to grow in size, its mocking caws melding with the raging thunder until it became impossible to distinguish one from the other.

The Huntress wheeled her Night-Mare around, spurring the beast on, her silver blade vicious in the moonlight. In that instant all thoughts of the Moon-Torn were forgotten. The hunt would claim more souls, but this one, this warrior was the prize. She would claim his head and the impetuous fool could run at her side without it for eternity. She would feast on his eyes and string the empty head from one of her saddle chains.

He was hers, forever. Her creature.

The Huntress loosed a war cry that matched the crow's, rending the night in two.

And then she rode for the warrior, savouring the invigorating moment as the thrill of the hunt surged through her cold, cold flesh.

"He's dead," Ukko moaned, disbelieving as he cradled Sláine's head in his hands.

He felt... empty.

"Heroes die," Myrrdin said, kneeling beside the dwarf. "It is what they do, but do not weep yet, friend Ukko. Spirit and flesh are still close and may yet be reunited, Danu be willing."

Ukko sniffed, a ribbon of snot dribbling down over his upper lip. He wiped the back of his hand across his mouth and sniffed again. He didn't want to hope. Hope hurt. He looked up at the druid, hurt in his eyes.

The hunt galloped on away from them, Sláine lost somewhere in the middle of it.

The druid planted his staff in the dirt, forcing it deep into the belly of the earth, and began a slowly rising chant, the words indistinguishable from one another until Myrrdin was shouting a single one over and over again: Annfwyn.

The first lick of mist rose like smoke from the heather ten feet beyond the staff, coiling lazily into the night air. A second and a third quickly joined it, tangling in the air. All around the staff wisps of mist rose from the field, fusing into a single spectral wall that shimmered beneath the moon.

Across the field the Moon-Torn celebrants screamed as the hunt took them.

"The path is open," Myrrdin said, grabbing hold of Sláine's wrists. "Help me. Take his feet."

"To where?" Ukko asked, sniffing back more snot.

"Through the mists, the path is open between life and death, darkness and light, the path between the El Worlds."

"And this will save him?"

"I don't know," the druid admitted. "But to remain here will damn him; that much I am sure of."

Together they dragged Sláine's corpse into the mist.

SLÁINE STOOD ROOTED to the ground as the Huntress bore down on him, her silver blade parting the moonlight like fine silk.

Brain-Biter was still buried deep in the Night-Mare's neck.

Thinking about the axe was enough; he felt its weight in his right hand and smiled. He held the fragment of the Cauldron in his left. He could grow used to being one of the dead and the damned.

The thought sent a shiver through his soul.

He looked beyond the Huntress to his corpse, and saw his friends dragging it into a shimmering wall of mist. One moment they were there, the next they were gone, swallowed by the swirling wall of white.

A moment later a black smear swooped low across the open face of the moon, and banked, disappearing into the mists: the Morrigan's bird had followed them.

Already, he saw, the mists were beginning to recede, the edges fraying as the enchantment binding them together lost its hold and they came undone.

And then the huntress was on top of him, her blade scything low to claim his head.

Sláine threw himself to the ground, rolling on his left shoulder and coming out of the tumble in a run.

The Huntress shrieked, wheeling her beast around, spurring it on wildly. The Night-Mare answered, surging forwards, its huge gait devouring the ground between the Huntress and her quarry.

The mist was failing quickly now, dissolution eating into it. *Run, my beautiful boy, run!* The Maiden's voice echoed inside his mind, and hearing it, Sláine knew that to be stranded on this side, separated from his mortal flesh, would doom his spirit to eternity with the hunt. He did as the Goddess begged. He ran.

The Huntress's blade pierced his back, lifting him off his feet. He fell hard, bleeding, then looked at the blood with confusion and it ceased to flow. He scrambled back on his arse, hands and feet digging at the dirt – he could feel the earth screaming at the Night-Bringer's violation as she stepped down off her huge mount to bring an end to his wretched existence – and into the mists as the Night Bringer loomed over him.

Seven
The Annfwyn

UKKO STEPPED OUT of the mists into a world bereft of any colour.

It was not that it had been leeched of hues, of subtlety and beauty.

The beauty was there, austere and unforgiving, but it was the beauty of a grey world.

The grass, the moon, the rocks, the trees, even the rolling breakers of the water on the nearby shoreline were all shades and layers of grey between black and white.

It was a grim, alien place, utterly unlike the land it mirrored on the otherside. The dwarf struggled to orientate himself. The landmarks were familiar but wrong, and their wrongness made it difficult for his mind to hold on to any sense of place.

They were on a road – a proper stone laid road, better than anything in Tir-Nan-Og. Each stone was an octagonal disc, worn flat by the passage of countless feet over millennia. The road was wide enough for ten men to walk abreast comfortably, even in full armour, shields interlocked. Ukko knelt to brush his fingers across the surface of the stones.

The causeway was ancient, built, perhaps by the gods and goddesses themselves. No mortal hand had fashioned the road, of that he felt uncomfortably sure.

The road led two ways, the righteous path into the high hills, the sinister route dropped away quickly, down towards a stony beach and dead-calm waters.

And, more disturbing that all the rest, was the silence. Despite the fact that they had travelled barely fifty paces from the celebrants and the wild hunt there was complete and utter silence. There was no storm, no thunderheads, no lightning, no whoops and cries from the Moon-Torn, no rabid baying from the hunt's shoggy creatures.

They were under a different sky.

Everything was different here, even the taste of the air in his lungs. It was older, less alive.

"Where are we?"

"We have crossed into the Annfwyn, friend Ukko." The druid pronounced it *an-noon,* drawing the syllables out. "As I promised, we are between the land of the living and the dead. Here nothing can live and nothing can die."

"But we–"

"Will not age while we walk these grey paths, my friend. Time has no sway here. We could walk these roads a thousand thousand years and not age a day."

"So Sláine… ?"

"If there is a breath in his body, it is trapped and he shall live once more; if the death rattle has passed his lips, then he is dead."

"But his spirit? I mean… it rose, didn't it? From his flesh? He was a ghost so surely he had to be dead?" said Ukko, not understanding.

"It is out of our hand now, all we can do is move his flesh towards safety and pray that Danu preserves his spirit long enough for the two to become one again. Help me carry him. We must reach the water."

And so they took the sinister path.

It felt as though the road would never end. It cut through the fields of grey and the graphite hills, sloping gradually down towards the charcoal waters. Together the pair of them struggled with Sláine's dead weight, manhandling him down the causeway until the discs began to separate, forming a steep and uneven stair down the side of the hill to the beach five hundred feet below.

To make matters worse, behind them came the first chilling sounds of the wild hunt; its mistress having crossed over onto this side of the mists, its prisoners had no choice but to follow.

Ukko looked up at the druid, only to see that Myrrdin had not expected the Night Bringer to pursue them between worlds.

"This wasn't in her story," the druid whispered.

"Why don't you add some bit about her being defeated by some fearless dwarf… no better make that a bloody terrified dwarf. What am I thinking? Have her fall off her damned horse and bash her head in on a nice sharp rock. That'd do it."

Ukko peered down the giant's stair. It didn't so much as lead down to the pebbled beach as it did lurch down. Each step fell away two feet or more before it reached the next; only a huge man – a half-giant – would have negotiated the stairway with any ease. Ukko was looking at five hundred feet of bone-jarring agony.

"The moon," the druid said. "We have to get him out of the moon's domain," Myrrdin said, energised by their plight. "We go down, it's our only chance."

The first step was easy, as were the second and third, and for a moment Ukko fooled himself into thinking the tenth, eleventh and twelfth would be just as painless. By the thirteenth, the impact of dropping the two feet to the next plateau had a knot in the base of his spine burning. By the thirtieth step the fire had spread out through the trunk of his spine and out along the branches of his ribs. Sláine was heavy in his arms. Twice a misstep cracked the warrior's skull off a jagged spur of rock – but there was no blood.

Because there's no heartbeat to pump it out, Ukko thought, struggling to adjust his grip and maintain his precarious balance at the same time.

He shuffled back an inch, trying to feel out the edge of the step with his heel. The octagonal stone crumbled beneath his weight, overbalancing him, and suddenly Ukko started to fall. A scream tore from his flapping lips. He wrapped desperate arms around Sláine's leg and clung on for dear life, praying feverishly that Myrrdin was doing the same thing two steps above him.

"Hold on!"

"Damn stupid thing to say," Ukko grunted, his face pressed into the dead warrior's thigh. "I'm hardly going to let go, am I?"

His words didn't carry up to the druid.

Mercifully there was no wind to bully him off the cliff face, only the weight of gravity urging him eagerly to fall.

Ukko scrambled to get his feet under him before the added weight of his momentum pulled all three of them off the stair. He tried to look down. His toe scraped against the rough stone. It was six inches above the next step, which meant he had to work himself slowly down Sláine's leg or risk the short fall. He closed his eyes, mumbling a litany of prayers to every god, goddess, demon and nether-troll he had ever heard of, and more he made up just to be on the safe side, as he edged agonisingly down until the tip of his toe touched the next step.

"We could just drop him you know, being as he can't die, right?" Ukko called up. "It'd make things a damned sight easier." Ukko twisted to look down over his shoulder. They were still two hundred feet from the beach, at least. Impact from a fall like that would make a mess of a body even if it couldn't technically kill it *again;* there wouldn't be a lot left for Sláine's soul to clamber back into. He imagined trying to explain all the broken bones to Sláine including – if he bounced off the giant's stair and landed face-down instead of on his back – the flat face. "Perhaps not," Ukko conceded.

Ukko lost count of the stairs as the pain transmuted from a fire to a raging inferno that consumed his entire body.

He leaned out, clinging on to Sláine's boots, and looked up at the moon impossibly far above them. He felt as though they had descended into the burning pits of the netherworld and that at any second the tiny light of the moon would be snuffed out, taking all hope of escape with it. It was a treacherous notion – the moon was their enemy, but darkness, true, utter darkness, scared seven shades of shit out of him. *And none of them are grey,* Ukko thought, bitterly.

THE HUNT REACHED the giant's stair, but there was no way down.

The Night Bringer sniffed the air. She could smell the warrior's spirit on it. He was running scared. They all were. The stench of cowardice was overpowering. It filled her nostrils. The Night-Mare shied beneath her. She reached down with a gentling hand to steady the noble beast.

"So much fear," she said. "Are we truly that terrifying, my beauty?" the Huntress whispered into the Night-Mare's ear, knowing that they were and relishing that truth. She wheeled around to see a half-man half-dog loping towards her. "We will find another way down, my sweet. Our quarry will not elude us."

"It never does, mistress," the tortured spirit of the man-dog crooned.

UKKO SAW THE spectre of the Night Bringer looming on the clifftop.

He didn't see her face properly; her eyes were sunken pits that transformed her visage into a Samain mask. The moonlight shone on the black plates of her armour, and showed him all he needed to see to know that everything Myrrdin had said about her was true. His head swam with fragments and half-remembered (or -forgotten) memories, midnight promises to whores and doxies pledging love in return for loving, grifts milking money from fools eager to be parted with their coin, buildings and faces, people, places, and then he was falling.

I looked upon the hunt! This is it, I'm dying! Oh you stupid, stupid dwarf! To look upon the hunt is to die. He told you that plain and simple and what did you go and do? You had to look! You couldn't just run. And this is it now, probably dead already and that was it, the sum total of your life flashing before your eyes. What a miserable bloody life it wa-urgh!

He hit the ground, hard, hundreds of unforgiving stones pressing into every inch and angle of his body.

Myrrdin was less than ten feet above him, still holding a dangling Sláine by the arms. The moonlight revealed every crack and crevice in the rock face all the way up to the summit.

The Night Bringer was gone.

Ukko started to laugh uncontrollably. The laughter was manic, a wave that crashed from the sea of dread that drowned his mind and finally spilled out of his mouth.

The laughter died in his throat when he rolled over to see a phalanx of fighting men crossing the stony beach – six abreast in a never-ending line that melted into the grey skies. They were heavily armoured, carrying shield and sword and spear, following the banner of a great rearing bull. Beneath the steel plates of their armour they wore flame-red tunics. They were the first smear of colour in this infernal place – and they were coming directly towards him, their leather-sandalled feet grinding the stones of the beach together. He counted heads, reaching thirty rows before they blurred into one. Beside the bull standard marched their leader; his plumed helmet marked him as different to his fellows.

Ukko couldn't move.

He lay on his belly staring at them.

Sláine's corpse hit the stones beside him in a whorish sprawl. A moment later Myrrdin was tugging at his collar: "Up dwarf."

"This can't be good."

"Just keep your mouth shut. If you get the urge to say something, bite your tongue off."

Ukko glowered at the druid, and then kicked Sláine's shoulder, taking his frustration and fear out on the body just because he could. Sláine had hit him often enough over the course of their travels. Thinking about it, Ukko jabbed two more quick boots in, hoping they left bloody great bruises.

"You, there! Hold!" The warrior's voice was rich and resonant and filled with the familiarity of command.

"Well so much for hoping they wouldn't see us."

"Not another word, friend Ukko, I am serious," said Myrrdin.

Ukko curled his lip disdainfully and shuffled back a few paces so he could sneer behind the druid's back.

"And don't think I can't see you just because you are behind me."

Ukko didn't have time to respond; the leading soldiers marched in step until they were ten paces away, then the warrior in the plumed helmet barked: "Legionnaires! Halt!" and as one the relentless crunch of marching feet on shifting stones ceased and silence swept across the grey beach.

The leader came forwards, removing his helmet. His hair was close-cropped, framing a sharp, almost avian face dominated by a nose that had been badly broken. His eyes were blue, bright and alert and not at all friendly.

Myrrdin walked forwards, meeting him halfway.

"HOW COME YOU here, to this forlorn place?"

"Through the mists," Myrrdin said, careful with his choice of words.

The soldier couldn't keep the sudden flare of hope from bringing colour to his face – in a place of greys any and every other hue was grossly amplified. Myrrdin looked beyond him, at the line of men so far from home. Above them he saw a single black bird circling and felt the presence of the Morrigan's crooked hand in this, too. He knew the armour from his own time. These legionnaires were not only out of place, they were out of time. They had been lured into the Annfwyn and stranded, left to wander the paths between death and life, knowing no freedom, not even that most precious one, mortality.

"Do they remain, these mists?" the soldier leaned forwards, bringing his face close to Myrrdin's, drawn in by the druid's peculiar eyes.

"No, neighbour, they will have succumbed to the wind by now."

"But there is a chance?"

Myrrdin shook his head slowly. "There is not, I am afraid."

"Pity," the soldier said, seeming to shrink as he gave voice to that single word, his powerful frame diminished. He looked past the druid, first at Ukko, then at Sláine's bedraggled corpse sprawled across the grey pebbles. "It feels as though we have been looking for a way out of this hell for eternity, so many rivers and seas have we crossed, always looking and yet never finding a way home." He held a hand to his face, feeling the smoothness of his cheek, cradling his jaw. "My body insists it was only yesterday we were driven from the field, the raving Finians on our heels."

"Is that how you entered this place?"

"We fled, that is our shame. The primitive barbarians came at us, and we broke. The Legions of Pax Romana do not flee, they conquer. The night before the battle an old woman walked amongst us, one of you, a Briton, telling stories and healing wounds with poultices and tisanes. When she foretold it as my last night walking the earth I thought she meant I was to die. I never imagined a hell like this awaited. She predicted similar fates for all the men she tended, her words like a canker in our spirits. We entered the field sure we were fated to lose, to shame the Emperor. Carrion birds circled overhead, mocking us with their impatience. Until that day I had never been a coward but that day changed me. It stole my heart. The battle went badly from the outset. Their leader Oswalk, was a canny tactician, luring us in to a double feint that played on our vanity. We were Pax Romana, the finest fighting force known to man, empire builders. Immortals.

Until the night before, when the Crone showed us death. All I remember of the fighting itself, and that, not clearly at all, was the sheer mass of blue-daubed warriors streaming naked down every hill like demons from the Underworld itself. We panicked. And then we were stumbling through a bank of fog, the rage of battle still in our blood, the fear, the sweat, the tears, the screams of the dead and dying ringing in our ears along with the maddening chorus of carrion birds, into this place. I have christened it Tartarus; a fitting name, no? We have been banished here for our cowardice, after all. This is our punishment."

"Who are you, friend? Perhaps I know your name," the druid asked, but he already did. These men had been missing a century before he himself stumbled into a similar trap. The Morrigan's stench was all over their supposed "fate".

"I am Gwalchmai, and these men of the Eighth Legion of the Bull followed me into this place and share my shame."

"I am Myrrdin. Well met, Gwalchmai of the Eighth." They clasped wrists. The soldier's grip was iron. "I would that we had time to share tales of the old woman's treachery, for believe me there are many, but time is against us, even in this place where the sun does not rise. Moreso here, even, for the moon holds eternal sway. The Crone's meddling hand is in our arrival also. Indeed, I believe you were brought here four hundred years ago precisely for this moment... There is a way for you to regain your heart."

"Speak then," Gwalchmai said. "If there is a way I would hear it."

"My friend is on a hero quest to restore an ancient artefact of his people, and in doing so save the land itself from a creeping death. It is a quest worthy of only the greatest heroes – and you, Gwalchmai, are no coward, your fate is to become a part of that quest."

"Enough flattery old man, what would you have the Eighth do?"

"Our people believe in the tripartite Goddess, Mother, Maiden and Crone. You have met the Crone already upon that battlefield. He is the Maiden's champion. A creature of ultimate evil stalks the cliff tops even now looking for a way down to this beach. She is the Night Bringer, daughter of the moon. Her essence is the spirit of the old woman who lured you here, soldier."

"A woman is no match for the might of the Eighth," Gwalchmai said, his voice flat, obviously remembering how one old woman had undone the might of three and a half thousand men.

"She is not alone, she leads the wild hunt." Myrrdin scanned the cliffs but saw no sign of the Night Bringer or the spectral hunt at her command. "Do you know the legends of the hunt?"

"I have heard stories of the ghost hunt, if it is the same thing. To look upon it is to invite death into your life; it rides for eternity drawing souls to it, though I thought it was led by some pale-faced queen; Bouddica, perhaps, having been humbled by the might of Pax Romana. It is the same thing, no?"

Myrrdin nodded. "It is."

"So it is not just some silly story then, interesting."

"There are grains of truth in even the most fabulous of stories, Gwalchmai, it is how they survive."

"True. So, your friend is being chased by the ghost hunt? Is he already a Ghost Walker? A thing of the spirits?"

"He gave his life to join the hunt so that he might reclaim a part of the artefact the Crone had given the Night Bringer. We must take his body to a place where the moon has no dominion so that it can be reunited with his spirit."

"And he is a part of this hunt? You would have the Eighth battle the ghosts for his soul?" Gwalchmai said. "Will this earn our freedom?"

"I believe so," the druid said, hating himself for planting the seeds of false hope in the soldier's heart. There was no way home for them, even if they returned to Albion, it was not the home they had known. Their civilisation had collapsed. They were relics of a bygone civilisation. They were, in truth, little more than ghosts themselves. They would face the hunt and in those final moments would regain the honour the Morrigan had stolen from them, helping Sláine fight the host of the damned. Victory or failure, the outcome promised to be the same, with the Eighth Legion being consumed by the wild hunt. They would return to Albion with the Night Bringer, one of the dead and the damned running in her wake.

"I have your word?" Gwalchmai held out his hand.

Myrrdin grasped it once more. "You have my word. You will be free of this place, and your sacrifice will not be forgotten." Myrrdin's word in this case was nothing more than a flake off the great unbending brute that was the truth.

"They will sing our names in the ballads of this great hero of yours?"

"They will, Gwalchmai, they will indeed."

"That is enough for me, friend Myrrdin. To be remembered not as a coward but as a man, that is worth a thousand deaths. Peace be with you."

"And you, Gwalchmai."

"Gather your friend and head down to the water's edge. There is a jetty a half-mile back." Gwalchmai inclined his head. "There is a single flat bottomed coracle moored there. Take it, perhaps this hunt cannot cross deep water."

"That is a good thought, soldier, you have my thanks again, it seems."

Gwalchmai's smile was honest, open, "No, it is you who have my thanks, Myrrdin. Through you the Eighth has renewed purpose. We will not fail you, that I promise. Tell me, what is the name of this champion? It would be good to know what legends our band of sword brothers will grace."

"His name is Sláine Mac Roth and he is a son of the Sessair," said the druid.

"Ah, ruthless fighters, the Celts. We fought one who when he raged grew in might and size until he was giant-like. An awesome warrior. It was a pity to humble him but that is what death does, is it not, it humbles all of us." And then: "I hear the hounds, you'd best make haste."

Gwalchmai returned to his men. He drew his short sword as he met the gaze of every warrior lined up before him. "Tonight we dine in the halls of our fathers!" Gwalchmai roared, thrusting the blade into the heart of the grey sky.

They answered him as one.

The ground under Myrrdin's feet trembled beneath the voice of the Eighth Legion of the Bull. Their challenge would reach the ears of the Night Bringer, of that the druid had no doubt.

SLÁINE HAD FALLEN through the mists, cracking his head off a jagged uprising of rock on the skirt of the octagonal causeway, and rolled over to the side of the road into a deep drainage ditch. A huge oak grew between the stone and the earthen ditch, its roots forming a cradle over the side of the causeway. Sláine had rolled into it, eyes closed, breathing hard, all the while expecting the Night Bringer's blade to claim his head – but it didn't.

He lay in the grey cleft in the grey dirt beneath the grey roots and the grey sky, the ghost of his heart thundering wildly in his chest.

And then he heard her coming out of the mist and didn't dare make a sound.

He huddled deep in the charcoal shadows beneath the roots of the evening tree, listening to the Night-Mare's hooves sparking off the hard stones and to the slow mellifluous inhalations of the Huntress as she sniffed him out on the still air.

She had moved on, down the road, the beasts of her hunt following in her wake.

Still Sláine did not move. Not until he saw her riding along the cliff edge, back and forth, frustrated that the causeway had simply ceased, falling away to the utterly flat sea. He did not allow himself to dwell on the weirdness of the place. He could feel his body growing more and more distant, the ties that bound his spirit to it all but unravelled. He cradled the fragment of the Cauldron of Rebirth to his chest. There was a peculiar heat to it now that he hadn't felt on the other side of the mist, as though the metal itself knew that it did not belong in this place and radiated its difference.

He crawled deeper into the cradle of the twisted roots, watching the Night Bringer.

She turned her head and Sláine felt her black eyes sear into him but she did not come galloping back up the causeway, nor did she denounce him to the hounds of her vile hunt. The Night-Mare shied as she brought the huge beast around, its hooves striking the angles of the octagonal stones harshly, and a moment later was galloping along the line of the cliff in search of another way down to the beach below.

She had no interest in his spirit; the realisation sank to the pit of his stomach like a smooth-sided stone. She intended to destroy his flesh. Instead of feeling comforting, the cradling roots felt suddenly constricting.

For the sake of his soul he had to beat her down to the beach.

THE DRUID AND the dwarf manhandled Sláine's corpse onto the flat bottom of the small wooden boat.

Myrrdin held the boat steady for Ukko to scramble into, then pushed it out to sea and splashed into the dead calm, following it. He launched himself into the boat, almost capsizing it as he kicked frantically, trying to haul himself over the side. Ukko grabbed him by the shoulders and dragged him into the small boat.

The coracle lay low in the water, concentric rings rippling away from the oars as they dipped them into the grey sea.

Rowing was back-breaking work. It was as though the water itself didn't want them to cross and was battling them every inch of the way.

The druid began mumbling just beneath his breath and the skin on the water shifted, the reflection of the moon disappearing. The ripples froze in place, never diminishing, as the coracle cut through them, gliding ethereally across the impossibly placid surface.

He heard Gwalchmai's cry from the shore, and craned his neck to see the soldier thrusting his short blade into the throat of a huge hound, even as the front ranks of the Eighth clashed with the ghosts of the hunt.

"Row," Myrrdin rasped, forcing the oar back through the grey water. Beside him, Ukko matched him stroke for stroke.

Steel clashed with bone, fangs sank into flesh, spears cut through fur and ruptured organs, but none of it slowed the beasts of the hunt. They surged on relentlessly, hurling themselves at the soldiers of the Eighth, tearing through their shield walls and their slashing blades.

And the Night Bringer rode through the heart of their defence, her wickedly curved sword paring flesh from bone and head from shoulders remorselessly. Gouts of blood fountained around her as men fell, clutching bloody stumps of flesh where they could, heads rolling where they couldn't. And then they rose, drawn into the hunt, swords still in hand, bodies mutilated in spirit exactly as they had been in life, and turned on their fellow men, cutting them down mercilessly.

Myrrdin looked on in horror as Gwalchmai threw himself in front of the Night-Mare, barely deflecting the first careless cut she aimed for his head.

"For the honour of the Eighth!" his cry echoed all around the beach. It was matched by a roar from the hillside as Sláine's spectre launched itself from the giant's stair into the thick of the fighting. It was too late for Gwalchmai; in damnation he found the freedom Myrrdin had promised them. The Huntress's blade cleaved into his plumed helmet, driving deep into his skull. His body spasmed viciously, the short sword tumbling from his fingers, only for his blazing spirit to grasp it as it hit the grey stones, and rise, bellowing his battle cry once more: "For the honour of the Eighth!"

Only now it was the spirits of the dead that rallied to him, joining with the living to cull the monstrous creatures of the wild hunt. Shoggy beasts roared their pain as the ghostly blades pierced where mortal blades could not, opening wounds their spirits could never heal. As more and more of the Eighth fell to swell the ranks of the dead, the more invincible they became. They rediscovered their hearts, won back their courage. They died men.

The battle turned to slaughter, Sláine at its heart, fighting side by side with the ghost of Gwalchmai. The pair were mirrors of each other; Sláine wild, brutal, strong and deadly whereas Gwalchmai was driven by a controlled fury. He was every bit as lethal as the barbarian, though, delivering true death to the beasts of the hunt with precision. Axe and blade joined to release the animals from the

Huntress's thrall, as willingly, the men of the Eighth rose to take their place in the eternal hunt.

Furious, the Huntress broke their ranks, driving the Night-Mare all the way down to the shoreline. The steed snorted licks of flame that matched its mistress's foul temper.

Myrrdin stared at the serene, frozen perfection of her face as she in turn stared at him.

For a moment he thought they were free, and then she kicked the Night-Mare's flanks and urged the beast into the water.

Eight
The Glass House

THE CORACLE CUT through the water, but it was back-breaking work. For every stroke it moved an inch or two across the placid surface. Panic forced their strokes, making them erratic and unbalanced. The Night Bringer's hideous mount kicked up the spume, splashing deeper into the water.

"We'll never make it," Ukko grunted, struggling with his oar.

Myrrdin looked at him, then at the moon, then back at the ethereal Huntress. "We don't have to," he said, shipping his oar.

"What are you doing? Come on, row!"

"We don't have to," Myrrdin said again. The boat moved on even though he had ceased rowing. Ukko stared down at his own oar, lifting it out of the water. The boat glided on.

"Oh, well that's just bloody marvellous," the dwarf muttered.

Myrrdin gripped the side and struggled to stand, his balance shifting with the bottom of the small boat. He reached down for Sláine's corpse, trying to lift it. It was a dead weight.

"What in the name of Crom's hairy left nut are you doing?"

"We have to get out of here, where the moon holds no dominion."

"And where in the seven els is that?"

The druid pointed a withered finger at the water itself. "Down there," he said and Myrrdin pitched himself over the side, taking Sláine's body with him. The sudden shift in weight unbalanced the coracle, pitching it sideways. Ukko clutched at the sides, staring at the ever-decreasing ripples that swallowed the druid and his friend.

"Why is everyone around me abso-friggin-lutely mad?" Ukko despaired, looking up from the water to see the Night Bringer less than thirty paces away, her beast somehow treading the surface of the still water. The moon shone down on her spectral features, seeping deep beneath her silvered skin to lend her a pearly opalescence. She saw him, her grin curving like a blade across the angles of her face. She spurred the Night-Mare on, the hunger in her dark eyes placing a chill in his heart. "Water, hard place," Ukko said, and closing his eyes, threw himself over the side.

The moment he hit the water he remembered he could not swim. He screamed out in panic and thrashed desperately at the surface, trying to propel himself back to the boat, and then he was sinking and the world above the water disappeared.

The water closed around him like an icy gauntlet, surging into his open mouth as he gasped for breath, forcing the scream back down his throat, robbing his senses. The was no light, no smell, though other senses were enhanced inordinately; he felt his heart hammering against the inside of his chest, his blood drumming in his ears, and tasted the salt-tang of the water as it rushed in to drown his lungs. He fought the water desperately as the undertow wrapped itself around his legs and dragged him down. He kicked and splashed, lashing out desperately but the more he thrashed the more insistent its grip grew, relentlessly pulling him deeper and deeper under the surface.

The crushing sensation of the dark waters clenching around his body intensified the deeper the undertow dragged him below the surface. He kicked and thrashed about, swallowing more and more water as he tried to break free of its pull. The darkness was absolute. He kicked out in sheer terror as he felt something grasp his ankle. It took him a moment to realise what it was, and in that moment it was every nightmare from the deep his imagination could conjure, before his mind could interpret it as it truly was: a hand. And then the images swarming through his drowning mind were worse, frenzied, panicked, of monsters from the deep reaching up to drag him down and feast on his scrawny carcass.

Ukko felt dizziness surging through his head, the drumming of his blood deafening, the hammering of his heart like thunder tearing through the bones of his chest.

There was no time beneath the surface; he could have been under for seconds or hours. There was no way of knowing.

The darkness burned.

There was no hope of return. He would not die in the air, with the sun or the moon on his face. His last taste would be salt, his last sight a lie, his mind playing tricks.

And then there was silence, cold and implacable, and he knew he was drowning; that was what the hand in the deep was, his mind's way of rationalising the pull of death, dragging him down and down relentlessly. It was a curiously comforting notion, his mind protecting him from the numbing fear of oblivion – for a heartbeat at least.

Even then his mind refused to believe; there was no familiar face, no salvation.

His lungs burned, demanding air. He tried to open his mouth but the druid kept his hand clamped firmly over it as they rose up from the darkest part of the water.

Then he felt the presence of the moon and knew they were just below the surface, breath tantalisingly close – but the druid would not let him rise and Ukko knew it was one last mocking trick of his drowned mind, taunting him with light where there was no light, with hope where there was none. He was dead, the light the air-starved part of his mind misinterpreting the blood vessels rupturing behind his eyes.

So this is death? he thought, not liking it one little bit. It hurt. It wasn't supposed to hurt. His lungs burned, his throat felt as though a huge hand crushed down on his windpipe, and starved of air his brain refused to quiet. He had always imagined it would be peaceful. *Fool of a dwarf, this is your punishment... an eternity of noise and hallucination, the madness of death.* And then he remembered the gift of the Annfwyn, no life and no death. He could not drown beneath these waters, no matter how much they pained him. There was no comfort to be had in that thought, only the sure and certain knowledge that this pain would never end.

His lungs cramped, violent convulsions wracking his body, and still they did not breach the surface until the shadow of the Night-Mare retreated, the Night Bringer giving up the hunt.

Only then did the druid allow them to rise again, reborn.

UKKO CAME UP gasping and coughing up lungfuls of turgid black water, Myrrdin's arm around his waist. The druid's grip was the only thing that prevented him from being swallowed back beneath the water. It was a brutal return to the world of the flesh.

The tidal pull of the currents had dragged them far away from the coracle, and further from the shore where Sláine's spirit still battled side by side with Gwalchmai and the Eighth, buying their freedom from this hellish place. The Huntress had relinquished her claim on Sláine's flesh and returned to the shore, content to consume his spirit. The coracle glided over the still waters, continuing its journey to landfall. They trod water, waiting for the boat, then lay inside it, feeling the waning moonlight give way to a colourless sun, as the coracle sailed on towards its destination.

"Ynys Afallach," the druid said, as they came within sight of the sands of the beach and the green-grassed tops of the dunes as they ceded to the land. "The Isle of Apples, some call it, though in truth it is the Isle of Glass, home of the Wounded King. He was brought here after the Battle of Camdon Fields, where he was brought low by a mortal blow from his own son's blade. In this place his wounds cannot whiten, though neither can they end his life. He bleeds still but there is no death for him, no ageing, no release. In his pain he is tended by the White Sisters of Preiddeu, the mistresses of the Glass House."

"You know a lot about him," Ukko said, grimacing as a wave of nausea clenched his guts.

"I should, little man. I brought him here at the behest of the Crone."

"Her again, meddling. When was this? No don't tell me, hundreds of years ago, right? How long is her reach? No, don't tell me. I don't want to know. I like to kid myself my life is my own."

"Ninety-two years before I entered the tree," Myrrdin said, answering anyway. "She came to me the night before the battle, knowing which blow would prove fatal and bidding me open the way to the mists for Finvarra's passage to this place of the ever-living. It is funny, I remember her words clearly as though she spoke them only a moment ago: 'He must not die, druid. Not in this place. He has one last battle to ride out to, you will open the way for his return at the time of the kingdom's greatest need, giving hope to the hopeless. We will ride beside your champion, bringing freedom to the Isle of the Mighty.'"

"She does that a lot, doesn't she? Make a few nonsensical predictions and vague promises while she's really manipulating everyone to her own sinister purposes. You think you'd learn."

"I have, believe me, dwarf, I have; three centuries as her prisoner have a way of peeling the veneer from ones naïveté. She's treacherous, make no mistake. Her words twist around themselves in layers like an endless knot, the truth buried somewhere at their core, indecipherable. But for all that, never make the mistake of doubting her love of the land. She is older than all of us, as old as Tir-Nan-Og itself. It is the flesh of her sister-self. She will do anything to preserve it."

"I still don't trust her."

"And you are wise not to, my friend."

A woman waited on the sands. She wore a simple white shift and stood barefoot, her toenails painted a shade of purple with some kind of lacquer. It was a remarkable splash of colour after the drabness of the other shore. Her hair was fair, the yellow of flax, part-braided, part-falling loose, cascading down the curve of her back and across her delicate shoulders. Her eyes lit up like the dawn as she saw Sláine lying between the druid and the dwarf. She was hauntingly beautiful, too beautiful to be a mortal woman, Ukko knew instantly. Her looks had more than his hackles rising.

The bottom of the coracle ground against the sand, the wave receding so that it was beached.

She held out a hand to them as they disembarked. "Finvarra bids you welcome to his home. He has instructed me to tend to you and your companions' every need. I am Leanan, Sister of Preiddeu, servant of the Wounded King. It is good to see you, Myrrdin. It has been too long since you walked among us. Modron has missed you, as have we all." Her smile was undeniably flirtatious until her eyes returned to Sláine's corpse. "I see you have brought the dead to our shores, Lord of the Trees, and yet you know there can be no death here."

"It was necessary, Leanan."

"I will have him taken to the hospice where his wounds will be tended by my sisters."

"Oh no, I'm not going to let him out of my sight," Ukko said, moving to stand between the woman and Sláine. "Not until he's wide awake and slapping me around the lughole for letting him die in the first place. That's how it works, it is always my fault when he goes and does something heroic."

"Well that's a pity, we had prepared food for you: a succulent brisket, with golden vegetables and roots, braised to perfection in their own juices. Baths are being drawn, even as we dally here, and your beds are being warmed."

"Well," Ukko mused dubiously, "it *would* be a shame to waste such good hospitality. I suppose he's dead already so it isn't like anything worse can happen to him if I take you up on your kindness, is there? He'll still be dead to the world tomorrow morning, I can look in on him then. There, that's settled then. Good food, a hot soak and a warmed bed. I think I've died and gone to a much better place."

Three more women came walking down the sands towards them, each as beautiful as Leanan, each startlingly different in their own way, opposites: hair dark as midnight, silver as the moon and fiery as the sun, lush, fulsome and curvaceous, lithe to the point of boyishness, tall, elfin, delicate, dark-skinned and pale, and yet each was undeniably beautiful for all those differences. They moved with grace on the shifting sands, their smiles as warm as Leanan's as they neared. Each wore the same simple white shift though their toenails were lacquered with different shades, as were their lips. There was something about the women that craved the eye, demanding attention Ukko was more than happy to lavish on them. His smile ran from ear to ear with lascivious glee. "A man could get drunk looking at this lot," he mumbled, rubbing his grubby little hands together like a miser eyeing a pile of coins.

"Sisters," greeted Leanan, "our visitors have brought the dead to our door. They would have us tend to him."

"The dead?" the red-headed woman said, cherry red rising beneath her porcelain skin. Ukko wasn't so wrapped up in her beauty that her tone was lost on him. He looked at Myrrdin to see if the druid knew what had her flustered. "What of the geas?"

"All is as it should be, sister," the ebony-skinned woman said, bowing deeply to the druid. "Well met, Lord of the Trees."

"Well met, Sister Luna," Myrrdin matched her bow. He bowed in turn to the remaining women. "Sister Helios, Sister Solis, you are, as ever, a pleasure for my eyes."

"Save your flattery, friend Myrrdin. We will tend to your friend."

"My thanks, sisters."

"And mine," Ukko piped up, pushing forwards to wrap Sister Luna in a suffocating embrace. He buried his face in the folds of her shift, sniffing deeply and savouring the fragrance of her femininity before he leaned back and looked up at her warm smile. His grin grew wider still. "Now, someone mentioned something about food? I don't mind telling you, I am starving. All this heroing works up an appetite."

A FEW MINUTES later, Sister Helios returned with a makeshift stretcher.

The women carried Sláine between them.

"Tell me, Myrrdin," Leanan said, "his spirit, is it in this place, or in the realm of the living?"

"He is on the far shore battling with the beasts of the Night Bringer's hunt."

The woman inclined her head, "There is a story here, I sense."

"A ballad, perhaps. The Lay of Sláine Mac Roth, son of the Sessair, champion of Danu."

"He is touched by the Goddess?" She broke away from him, resentment robbing beauty from her eyes.

"He is, but that does not change anything, sister. He needs the healing of your house. He has made the ultimate sacrifice for his people, his life in return for nothing more than a glimmer of hope for the women and children of his home."

"It changes everything, druid, do not be so naïve. Finvarra will not welcome the intrusion of her aspects upon his prison."

"He will bear it though, and we will leave. There is no need of conflict."

"Would you take her mocking you so, Myrrdin? He is trapped here, in this no life, and it is her doing. By any reckoning he is an old man. He is tired. He harbours a deep and abiding hatred for those who robbed him of his destiny."

"He would have died on that field if it wasn't for me, Leanan. You know that."

"And so does he, Myrrdin. That was his destiny, to die and earn immortality. He is a proud man. You robbed him of it, always so eager to please that damned Goddess of yours. Now he knows no death, true, but he knows no life either. The wounds inside his mind fester even though wounds in his flesh don't. That is more punishment than you could ever imagine. One day perhaps he will repay that gift. Perhaps then you can judge him, but not before. Think on this, Lord of the Trees: centuries of hatred burn within the Wounded King, Myrrdin, and you are the focus of all that anger. Tread softly around him."

"The events of the world gather momentum, Leanan. Destinies shaped centuries before are being fulfilled even as we walk along this beach. There is much I know, more I do not, but I suspect Finvarra's exile nears an end."

"You mean to end his life? Is that why you brought death to our door?"

"He is safe from me, my lady. You have my word."

"What good is that? We trusted you once, and the Glass House was our reward. You cannot pretend you do not know the extent of the geas the Morrigan placed upon our sanctuary, to exist outside the boundaries of life and death, and yet you bring to us the one thing that could bring mortality here and simply expect us to heal your precious champion, no matter what the cost to us?"

"I did not think..."

"No, Myrrdin, you did not, not then, and not now. I was wrong when I said this place was our curse. You are our curse, my pretty one. It was always you."

"The Land of the Young is dying, Leanan. Day by day, acre by acre. Sláine is her only hope. The hopes of centuries are converging around him; it is not about me, not about what I want."

"That excuses nothing, druid. All things have their season, you of all people should know that. It is the way of life. If it is her time to die, so be it, the things we call gods die. We will tend him, even though doing so may damn us, Myrrdin. Perhaps then we will finally be free of this paradise."

THE GLASS HOUSE perched like some giant predator atop the summit of the island's solitary mountain crag, its shadow leering down over Ynys Afallach.

At first it seemed as though a second sun hung low in the sky; the facets of the huge crystalline construction caught and reflected and refracted so much light it ached to look at it. The Glass House blinded the pilgrims to the island – but that had always been its intent, to inspire reverence and awe, humbling the mendicants that had the temerity to approach.

Even in the shadow of the great structure, Ukko was forced to shield his eyes when he looked upon the sheer majesty of the Wounded King's palace. It was a brilliant trick of the long sweeping arched construction that allowed the Glass House to be between the anvil of the sun and the eye of the beholder no matter when they approached it.

Ukko counted seventeen spires, each, despite the bleached nature of the sun and the moon, suffused with a subtle variant of the visible spectrum, rose and lavender bleeding into topaz and azure. Each spire resembled either talon or fang; there were no smooth edges or polished curves. They were jagged spikes driven into – or rising out of – the crag. Each angle amplified the intensity of the light, in turn serving to mask some other facet of the incredible building.

Still, the nearer they were the more details of the Glass House became apparent, the coronets and embrasures and hanging gables that leant the façade its predatory mien taking shape within the glare reflecting off its hundreds of angled surfaces. The windows were like wounds in its glass skin, raw shadows that marred the perfection of its face, the huge doors a gaping maw into its glass heart.

To the left of the main house was a lake, to the right an orchard fruiting with rich ruby-red apples. The path to the house wound between the two, a tongue of well-trodden dirt. Thorns and ivy grew on either side of the path, though closer to the house they were trimmed back and shaped into topiaries and hedges. The topiaries resembled creatures, giants rooted to the landscape. The hedges themselves had been cultivated to grow along the lines of an elaborate maze. White flowers grew within the variegated green walls, flaunting their imperfection with a splash of light here and there. Wherever the tendrils of reflection from the Glass House failed to reach the landscape they returned to the drab greys and shades of black of the Annfwyn. It was as though the house itself breathed life into the island, setting it apart from everything else on this side of the mists.

To Ukko it felt as though every one of the maze monsters scrutinised their approach.

He did not like it, not one bit.

THERE WAS NO air within the Glass House; that was the first thing Ukko noticed, even though it wasn't exactly true. There was air, but it was dead air, stale, breathed. It lent the place the eerie quality of a mausoleum.

He shivered as he crossed the threshold, chewing on his lip.

"Nice place," he muttered. For all its majesty he couldn't have meant it less.

They entered a wide reception hall with passageways leading off to the left, right and straight ahead, as well as two staircases cut into the glass wall on either side of the passage ahead of them, and a huge broad stairway to the left. Leanan ushered them towards the stairway. They followed her up onto one of the countless galleries within the Glass House, while the sisters bore Sláine's stretcher towards the hospice, hidden away somewhere else within the huge edifice. Her shadow stretched out behind her. Ukko touched the wall, trailing his curious fingers along the glass: it felt cold, like ice. There were no torches or oil lamps or other sources of light that he could see, and yet it was as bright within the Glass House as it was without – brighter even, suffused with the amplified light of the sun. He was left with the unnerving impression that it never grew dark within the Wounded King's palace – rather that Finvarra had somehow suspended the no-time of this place even more thoroughly than it already was, leaving them in the middle of one unending day.

"Sister Urian will see to your needs, friend Ukko," Leanan said, snapping him out of his reverie. Ukko looked up from his fingers to see a big-titted vision of beauty smiling at him, the gentling touch of her hand on his arm banishing all doubts he had. He followed her down the passage to an opulent bed chamber, not even noticing that Myrrdin had been led away by Leanan in the opposite direction. Even the most primitive of his instincts were quelled by the sensation of Urian's hand lingering on his cheek, drawing him into the chamber.

The centre of the room was dominated by an enormous crystal bathtub overflowing with soapy suds and steam. The heat coming off the water leant the room an almost lethargic feel. Ukko followed the Sister of Preiddeu into the chamber, enjoying the gentle sashay of her hips beneath the thin white shift, and the way certain creases clung to her body. It was mesmeric. Condensation from the heat peppered the walls. Sweat dripped from his brow into his eyes.

Urian took his hand and guided him towards the tub, then as she pressed him up against it, let her fingers pick over the strings tying his shirt and unravel them slowly. He stared at her fingers, then beneath her fingers at the swell of her breasts pressing against him. She followed the direction of his eyes and smiled; it was a smile that was every bit as predatory as that of the Night Bringer's hell-hounds. She lifted his arms and drew the shirt up over his head. A distant alarm went off in the back of Ukko's mind but her lips suckling at the warmth of the vein in his throat stifled it into silence almost as soon as it was chimed. He sighed, lost in the heat of her nearness. Urian reached down for the string cinching his filthy britches. His breath hitched in his throat as she untied the string and loosened the button. His britches fell around his ankles.

"I thought it was food, bath, bed, not that I am complaining or anything, I've walked on three different worlds since I last had me some lovin', I'm just saying the woman on the beach promised food."

Urian smiled and pulled her simple white shift up over her head, standing naked before him.

"All right, forget food, I think I died and went to a far, far better place," and a moment later, as she took him in her hand, bringing him back to life with her swift sure strokes, "I think I love you."

Without a word, Urian pushed his shoulders back, unbalancing Ukko and gently guiding him into the water. He lost himself in the heat and the wet beneath the confidence of her touch as she enveloped him more completely than the water ever could.

The water sloshed around his chest. He tasted the soap as her movement splashed the suds up into his mouth. He didn't fight it. He luxuriated in the experience. Ukko closed his eyes, savouring the rush of sensations, all thoughts of Sláine and Myrrdin banished from his mind as her lips closed on his and her breasts pressed up against him, the suds squirming between them. He felt the heat of her sex, more intense than the water, on his legs, then up, on his stomach. Between hungry wet kisses, her hands clutching either side of his head, legs wrapped around his waist, Ukko broke away, threw his head back and laughed:

"You know, I wasn't kidding when I said I was starving before."

Nine
The Moon Turn

LEANAN SIDHE LED Myrrdin to a second door, two storeys above Ukko's.

They didn't speak despite the fact that both harboured a hundred questions close to their breast. Indeed, the Glass House was silent bar the shuffle of their soft footsteps. Myrrdin had no liking for the place, nor, truth be told, its fey inhabitants. For all their undeniable beauty, and their uncanny resemblance to his people, their strange ways betrayed them: the Sidhe were far from human.

Where humans were driven by immeasurable instincts, both rational and irrational, as often likely to succumb to some long-buried primal urge as they were to rise above it, the Sidhe were by contrast a simple people. They were capable of great kindness when it suited, and the most calculating of treacheries when kindness fell short.

There was no concept of friendship, only fealty.

Power rested in a cradle open only to a few chosen ones, and those around it, drawn to it, craved it and killed for it. The game of kings was brutal in the extreme. Only the most ruthless survived to rule, those that failed in their ambitions were cut down, their threat removed. That was the price of disloyalty. And yet the Sidhe fell into one of two patterns of existence; they served their lord or schemed to betray him. There was no middle ground. Strength was admired, feared and worshipped, even envied, weakness despised.

A male child of the Sidhe faced a life of conflict, treachery and betrayal from the moment it drew its first breath. There was no room for a mother's love, no room for games and the fripperies of life. There was no easy camaraderie of youth. But then the life they were being prepared for had no such luxury. It was a life of strength and weakness: the extremes. Those who failed to live up to the demands of the Sidhe were culled, keeping the clans strong. Many of their young died before their thirteenth birthday, many more died after it, when they were sent out to complete the Isolation. It was a vision quest, a survivalist rite of passage: twelve lunar cycles alone in the harshest of landscapes, forced to fend for themselves until their true name came to them, hunted by the youngest hunters of the clans. To survive the Isolation was to be welcomed into the familial home of the clan, returned with an adult name, forged by the worst of the world. To be captured meant death and shame, not only for the child but for the mother and father who raised it, because it was their seed that failed the clan.

It was strength that mattered, nothing more.

The females of the species were no less twisted by the demands of their society; they were bred to serve their men, to seduce and destroy, weeding out other kinds of weakness to maintain the purity of the bloodline.

And Finvarra had been their king, the greatest of them, before the wound that brought him low, before his imprisonment here in this limbo, denied the noble death his reign demanded, and instead forced to live with the knowledge of his own failure – constantly reminded of his weakness, the wound refusing to whiten – because of Myrrdin's meddling. The Wounded King had had centuries for his grief to fester into a deep and abiding despair, the despair into hatred. The druid didn't bother trying to fool himself; there would be no warm welcome for an old friend here.

"Modron will see to your needs, Lord of the Trees," said Leanan, lifting him out of his reverie. Her voice was soft, its quality almost pitying, as though she were somehow party to his thoughts. "I will return soon with news of your companion. Until then, the freedom of his house is yours."

"My thanks, Leanan Sidhe. Though I have no need of a handmaiden, a warm bath and a warmer meal will sate all the needs my body has. I would see Finvarra and have this charade over with."

"As you wish, Myrrdin. You always were your own man when you weren't playing the Crone's sycophant. Sometimes I miss the colours of the world, and the smells and tastes. This place is beautiful, but it is no replacement for a world of so many rich experiences. I wonder, too, if it misses me and my kind, or if we have become a distant memory. Such thoughts are not easy to bear, druid. Once, I truly believed we were the light of the world; that our light would shine forever, illuminating everything around us. Now we hide in this place, the darkness pressing in all around us. This is no kind of life. Have you come to return us to our home? Home," she said, before he could answer. "I forget what it is, in truth. Dim memories lost inside me of places I am not even sure exist today. Perhaps they have all turned to grey, like this no-world around us? Perhaps that is all that is left? The colourless, the blandness. Ah, seeing you again, unchanged after all this time, has turned me melancholy. I shall leave you now in Modron's care. As I said on the beach, my sister has missed you. I think perhaps you owe her the courtesy of at least pretending you have also missed her. I will tell my king of your arrival. No doubt he will be eager to see you again."

"I am sorry, Leanan Sidhe."

"Do not be sorry, Myrrdin. Be strong. That is the man you are. There is no room for compassion or guilt in your world. I know you are not here to set me free, not now, not ever, just as I know you have not returned for my sister, Modron. We do not lie to ourselves here, neither should you. The sisters will care for your friend, and when he is returned to health, we shall return him to you so that you may go about your business. We have come to accept our life, so should you. Now go to her, and for a while allow her to fool herself into believing she has a place in your heart." She gestured down to the end of the glass passage where Modron Sidhe waited for him, the ambient orange glow of the walls lending her a halo of fire.

Myrrdin bade farewell to Leanan, inclining his head slightly in acknowledgement of her words. The shadows here had substance; they were thick enough, rich enough, for pain to hide within them, its grinning mask hidden for the moment.

"I will not lie," he said, more to himself than the woman.

"Because your kind never does," Leanan said, leaving him.

Modron was unchanged. He could have stepped through a portal in time as well as in space. Seeing her again, waiting at the end of the passageway, stirred things within the druid that he had not been prepared for.

"You came back," she said, as he neared.

"I said I would," Myrrdin said, hating himself for saying it, for pretending he had even remembered the young Sidhe and what she believed she meant to him.

"Because your kind never lies," Modron said, not unkindly, not like Leanan Sidhe had said it, in condemnation.

She did not embrace him, and for that lack of intimacy he was grateful.

"Indeed," said Myrrdin.

"So why have you returned? Truthfully? And before you think of whispering sweet lies to appease my sister Leanan, remember I know you, Lord of the Trees."

Myrrdin could not help but smile, the ghost of old familiarities haunted her words bringing with them memories of other lies he had told when they were younger. "There never was any use lying to you, was there?"

"No." She led him into a large chamber, not unlike the one Urian had brought Ukko to, with walls of an amethyst hue and a central bath, like everything else in the Wounded King's palace, fashioned from glass. Plain white towels were neatly folded and set atop a small table, and beside the table were four large crystal jugs filled with steaming water. There was a huge fireplace, as tall as the druid and wide enough for six men to walk abreast into the burning pit. A glass cauldron was suspended over the flames, warming more water. There was a bed, the frame of which appeared to have been carved from ice, covered in white furs. She looked at him, studying his face as though trying to match it with the one in her memory. "It's been a long time," Modron Sidhe said, adding another jug of steaming water to the tub and stirring it in with her entire arm. She dried the soap bubbles off with one of the towels.

"Over six lifetimes by the count of man," Myrrdin said, moving over to the window.

"So long? Time loses sense here. Sometimes it feels like eternity, other times just an age." She tried to smile, then turned away so that he could not see her face. "Now you make me feel like an old woman. Come, while the water is hot. Maybe then you can tell me why you have returned after so much time?"

The druid shed his clothes and stood naked before a woman for the first time in centuries. He felt uncomfortable under Modron's scrutiny, more so as he matched her gaze, looking at her for the first time since entering the room and remembering the woman beneath the gown, and his body began to stir. Seeing his discomfort, she chuckled softly and turned her back, going over to the fireplace. She pinched some fragrant herbs between her fingers and powdered them into the simmering water. A moment later the sweet aroma of lavender and something else, vanilla perhaps, filled the room.

Myrrdin sank into the water, grateful for the thick suds that hid his erection.

He inhaled deeply, closing his eyes, felt Modron's hands on his skin, working the lather in. There was nothing sexual about her touch and yet everything about her touch was purely sexual.

"Talk to me."

"What would you have me say?"

"No lovers' promises, no sweet words, tell me about the world I left behind for you. I am sure much has changed in the time I have been gone. I think of it sometimes and it pains me that I do not know if my brothers live still, if my people still abide or if we have become a thing of the past. Do they speak of the sacrifice of Finvarra?"

"No," Myrrdin said, honestly. "The memories of humans are short, like their lives. Memories of Finvarra are all but gone. Your people no longer dwell within the realms of Tir-Nan-Og, you have your own place within the El Worlds."

"So my people are exiled just as we are exiled?"

The druid winced at the frankness of the comparison. "Not truthfully, no. After the fall of Finvarra, the Morrigan opened a way for survivors to flee, a doorway beneath the hill of the chalk man. It was that or death at the hands of the short-lived ones. Whether you choose to believe it or not, she saved your people."

"I am sure the Crone wept for us as she closed the door, banishing the Sidhe from her realm," Modron said, her hands lingering.

"It was that or extinction, Modron. I brought the sisters here at her behest, to serve Finvarra until his return. She is many things, but she is not evil. What she does, she does for her land."

"Would that we were all that selfish, Myrrdin. Would that we could all justify our wickedness with promises of the greater good. It is easy to justify slaughter that way, winning a dream, though everything to those that don't share that dream is lost."

He breathed deeply again, savouring the aroma, feeling the water and Modron's hands relaxing the tension in his muscles. He felt almost light-headed with the release.

"Tell me, my sweet, why are you here?"

She took a jar of unguent from the table beside the bath, smeared her fingers through the oily substance and spread it across his chest, over his lungs and up, working it into his flesh. She talked to him but the words lost substance, running into images and memories as they swam around inside his head, blurring into one another. He felt himself slipping lower in the tub, the water rising up around his throat, the soap matting in his hair. The heat was soothing, the smell intoxicating. He felt his faculties beginning to drift, his reasoning failing. She entered the water, reaching down to take him inside her. He felt her heat, felt the rush of her heart against his, felt the salve sinking into his skin, everything suddenly tactile. He inhaled again, dimly aware that something in the air had undone him, something that didn't seem to affect the Sidhe woman even as she coupled with him, her movements matching the roll of the water in the cramped tub. But awareness was no defence. The words came out of his mouth, words he never should have said:

"I have brought her champion, he gave his life to the Huntress and this was the only way I could think to save him so that he might fulfil his destiny."

"The Defiler?"

"I do not like that title." His words blurred, his tongue thick in his mouth, too large to wrap around the words he wanted to say. He closed his eyes again, surrendering. "His name is Sláine." He didn't know if he said it or merely thought it.

"Names do not matter, you old fool. You brought him here. How could you?"

"HE IS DEAD."

"Then best leave him that way, sister," Leanan Sidhe said, sweeping into the cold room.

It was a grim chamber deep beneath the glass of the house, buried deep into the stone of the hillside, close to the essences of the earth, lit by six oil burners, each filling the air with its own soothing fragrance.

In the centre of the room Sláine lay on a table like a sacrifice on a glass altar. He was naked, his flesh immaculate. Not one of the wounds that had brought him down marred his flesh. There was a bluish-grey tinge beneath the skin that betrayed death's malignant presence.

Four Sisters of Preiddeu stood around him.

"You know what he is?" Sister Luna said, turning to Leanan. A curious mix of dread and excitement lit her eyes.

"I know he bears her mark," Leanan said, looking down at the corpse. "Modron is with the druid now, learning his secrets."

"But what do you think, sister? Do you believe he is her chosen one?" Sister Helios asked. Unlike Luna her face was not torn, there was no excitement. She was scared. "There is something about him, I can feel it, can't you? It's like a furnace raging beneath his skin, even now."

The door opened behind them, creaking back slowly on tired hinges.

"He bears the weight of destiny," Leanan said, "that much is clear."

"More than that," Modron said, coming through the door. "He carries death with him. He is the Death Walker."

"The Defiler?" Leanan said. "Can it be possible?" and then, more tellingly: "Why would the druid bring him here?"

"Unless to destroy us, you mean?" Modron said.

"So if we save him we seal our doom?"

"Not necessarily," Leanan mused, looking down at Sláine's wide, almost innocent face. She touched his cheek, lingering over the harsh beginnings of stubble prickling his chin, feeling the ghost of the man in each bristle. "The geas on Afallach could conceivably negate the threat he poses... Hear me out, now. If our sister is correct, the druid has brought the Death Walker into our hallowed halls. And where he walks, slaughter follows in his shadow. That is his curse, he is the Butcher of Worlds, the Death of Humanity, the Lord of Ruin, he is all of these things and more, but tell me, sisters, what is the nature of geas that holds us here, out of time?"

"Death cannot abide, there is no place for mortality, time does not flow, we are beneath, behind and between the worlds, outside of everything," Luna said, following her gaze if not her train of thought.

"And what is protected here cannot leave lest it withers and fall, that is the nature of the geas that binds Ynys Afallach. If we use our gifts to reunite the warrior's soul with his flesh the ensorcellment itself will only serve to make him a part of the magic of the island. He will be less than human, or more if you prefer; a creature of sorcery as much as of flesh and blood."

"And the geas will not allow him to leave," Sister Helios said softly, understanding.

"And the geas will not allow him to leave," Leanan agreed, her fingers tracing the line of Sláine's jaw and moving down, lingering over his throat. "So we can do the druid's bidding in good conscience and without condemning our kin."

"It is a risk, sister. What is to say the geas will hold him and we won't be ushering in the end of times in our naïveté?"

"Look at him and tell me, does he look like the death of us?"

"Death comes in many guises, sister, sometimes it is in a pretty package, other times it is dressed in robes of lies and ugliness. Do not allow lusts to cloud your thoughts."

"He is a man, sister," Leanan said, smiling softly. "I harbour no illusions as to his length or girth, nor his prowess, I need only reach down here," she moved her hand lower, "to know he is all that and more. I will not lie to you, I do miss the companionship of a man, the feel of him inside me. I will not deny the pleasure of the flesh appeals now temptation is placed before me."

"There is something wrong with looking at a corpse and feeling arousal, sister," Luna said.

"Would you not want to share him if he were awake, sister mine?" Leanan answered. She turned to Modron, "What did the Lord of the Trees say once his tongue was loosened?"

"Stupid words of love, in the main," Modron said with distaste, "as though he expected me to still yearn for him after all this time. The vanity of the man is immense. I almost pitied him. Almost."

"And of the Defiler?"

"Precious little that I understood; a lot of nightmares and incoherent ramblings, though I pieced together some few things."

"I would hear them, sister."

"He is of the Sessair tribe, to the north, in the Land of the Young. A follower of the tripartite Goddess, Danu, Earth Mother, Maiden and Crone, he is touched by her strength, a Warped One."

"A Warped One?" Leanan said, savouring the thought of the power caged within the mortal flesh beneath her fingertips, imagining it unleashed, unfettered, imagining the life-force the man possessed.

"The first of his kind born in a century, if Myrrdin speaks the truth. Sláine son of Roth seeks to save his people from the threat of one called Feg. I did not understand all of the druid's words, so much has changed within the world we used to know, sister. From what I could follow, this Feg is a slough-skinned one devoted to the Wyrm God. Under his tyranny the lands to the south have soured; the priest has erected standing stones that draw the life from the earth to power flying ships and other monstrosities. Crops no longer grow. It is a place of rot. The son of Roth possesses the secrets of the priest and would return them to his people though it seems his people despise him, and to return is sure and certain death. He hopes to buy his life back with a gift: he seeks the fragments of a relic broken and scattered to the four corners of the world and beyond. That is how he fell to the Night Bringer's hunt. He stole a part of this relic from her possession, giving his life so that he might lift it from her."

"So he truly has the heart of a champion," Leanan said, almost wistfully. She laid her hand flat on his chest, above his heart as though trying to feel its latent power. She looked at the other women, meeting their eyes one at a time, "Are we decided, sisters?"

"It is our duty," Helios said simply, laying her hand on top of Leanan's.

"His sacrifice makes him worthy of our love," Sister Solis said, adding hers to the others, sharing its gentle warmth. "The Lord of the Trees would not betray us."

"Our dedication is to the healing of the flesh," Luna said, and even as she did she laid her hand on top of Solis's. "He has fallen that others may live. His sacrifice makes him precious."

"He is not our concern, sisters. He is not our ward. He is a man with countless names, countless destinies. He is the Eater of Souls, the Death of Worlds," Modron said, staring at her sisters' hands. "He is the Defiler. To save him is to damn ourselves." She laid her hand down atop Sister Luna's delicate hand. "The gods have mercy on us all."

Leanan began to sing softly, her voice barely audible above the breathing of her kin. One by one the others joined with her song, adding their own sweet voices to the chorus of life Leanan wove. Above them, behind them, a bell chimed, a single voice, joyful, triumphant. The warmth spread through their hands, down into Sláine's chest, enfolding his heart tenderly, drawing the life back to it. Her voice rose, her words merging into one long lamentable song, a lover refusing to say farewell. The words of her sisters coiled around her song, snakes of passion and pain adding their power to the enchantment. Leanan leaned in close, parting the dead man's lips with her own so that she might breathe a little of her essence into him, sharing the life that was hers.

There was nothing.

No answering heat in his skin.

No lurch or trip of his heart.

No wisp of breath between his parted lips.

And then the bell tolled again, and it was answered by another, and another, until the glass walls of the palace resonated with the voices of a thousand thousand bells, deep and booming, shrill and screeching, in all of the harmonies that together formed the song of the everliving. An impossible breeze stirred, bringing with it a deep and abiding chill and the redolent musk of the departed. The breeze wove around each one of them, its gentle hand touching their hearts, drawing strength and purpose from the truth of them. The chill deepened, sinking bone-deep, leeching every ounce of warmth from them. The ghost of a voice, a war cry that became a scream, primal, basc and desperate, pierced the ethereal bell chorus, as the spirit of the fallen warrior was drawn across the turgid black water, back towards his flesh.

Leanan touched his lips with hers, offering the kiss of life.

And a sudden, shockingly violent spasm tore through the body beneath her, that first desperate breath catching in Sláine's throat, the born-again warrior choking on it.

Sláine's eyes flared open, his head coming up off the table as body and soul were reunited.

"Shhh," she said gently. "Shh, be at peace, warrior. You are safe here."

He looked about wildly, trying to take it all in at once, to understand what had happened to him, and then, an afterthought, he looked down at his hands and saw the insubstantial shape of the fragment of the Cauldron of Rebirth clutched in them. The women flinched, Sláine's life-force repelling their touch. They stepped away from the man, their eyes following the direction of his gaze, and retreated another step, stunned to see the relic solidifying in his grasp.

Sláine closed his eyes and sank back onto the table.

SLÁINE WASN'T DEAD.

He did not know why – or how – but he breathed. The toll living exerted on his flesh was huge.

The ghosts of Gwalchmai and the Eighth had faded but he wasn't alone. He slipped between consciousness and sleep, dreaming of devils. He felt hands touching his face as he struggled back to consciousness. He didn't have the strength to fight. His spirit was exhausted. Oblivion offered rest, peace. If the Night Bringer's beasts wanted to play with him before they killed him, so be it. He was too weak to argue.

"Kill... me then," he managed to say. The words were barely voiced. He groaned. "Just get it over with because I *hurt*."

He opened his eyes expecting to see the shoggy beasts or the Huntress's hell-hounds, or even

Myrrdin's tattooed face and Ukko's ugly mug leering over him. Instead he opened his eyes on beauty. The woman's face was exquisite, sculptured, delicate bones and porcelain-pale skin, but it was her eyes, older than time and filled with sadnesses he could not conceive, that truly made the beautiful exquisite.

Sláine reacted instinctively, his hand going for the axe that was no longer by his side, dropping the fragment of the Cauldron in his haste. It clattered on the floor. The movement left his head spinning.

"Be still," the beauty soothed, her voice velvet around him.

"Ceridwen?" Sláine breathed, invoking the name of the Goddess's deathly aspect. Surely the mother of death was a hag, not a vision of loveliness. The beautiful woman laughed, a sound every bit as enchanting as her features.

"I must look worse than I remember. No, my pretty one, you are a long way from death."

"Then who?" Sláine struggled to sit up. The effort was dizzying. He sank back to the warm mattress, beaten and breathless.

"A shadow of the woman I used to be, I fear."

"That's no answer, *lady*."

"No," she admitted. "But then, you asked the wrong question. In the pursuit of the truth the secrets most often lie in the why; the who is usually misleading."

Despite himself, Sláine smiled. It hurt. The pain in his shoulder flared as he tried to move. "But there are so many whys."

"So start with the simplest one."

"Why aren't I dead?"

"Because it wasn't your time to be," she said. "You will know when it is."

Sláine laughed; it was a short harsh sound. "That didn't exactly make things any clearer, did it? All right, tell me, where am I?"

"Where isn't a why, but you are in the Glass House, last sanctuary of the lord of the fey, Finvarra. *Why* you are here is a more interesting question, so indulge me as I ask a question now. Tell me, why are you here?"

Sláine closed his eyes, not wanting to see those eyes stripping away his words for truth and honesty, measuring his worth the way the eyes of beautiful women always did. "I do not know. I was dead, fighting beside brave men against the revenant shades of the damned, and then I was pulled back to my flesh. As to why here, this is where my body was. Now, why are *you* here?"

"Ah, a better question. You learn quickly, warrior. I was brought here a long time ago, centuries even, as a young girl to serve the Wounded King. My other life is like a dream now..."

THEY TALKED DAY and night over the days and weeks it took Sláine to regain his strength and his wounds to heal properly.

The darkness of night never came to the Glass House; even the moon's lambent glow brought the crystalline walls to life so the only clue as to the passage of time was the quality of the colours as they changed.

The woman, Leanan, told him she was a Sister of Prieddeu, one of the faithful Sidhe who served at the right hand of Finvarra, the Wounded King. She would sit with him at night, sharing a little food and more conversation, teaching him the ways of the Glass House. He was anxious to be on his way but as weak as a day-old calf, so the demands of the flesh superseded those of his stubbornness. Like it or not, Sláine was forced to rest.

At first he asked frequently about his companions, trying to glean some small hint as to their whereabouts, but all Leanan Sidhe would say was that they had moved on, leaving him on the island to heal. He found his memories of them slipping, almost as though his mind was wilfully trying to forget the scurrilous runt and the Skinless Man. Some nights, in the hours where his pain was most insistent, he would feel Leanan slip into the bed beside him, her naked skin warm against his. She caressed his wounded flesh, tenderly tracing the lines cut into his skin. She pressed her lips against his throat, suckling at the pulsing veins there.

And they made love.

And he forgot himself.

It was not the frantic coupling of youth, the lecherous rutting of the boy he had been, eager to sample the differences of the flesh, the old, the young, the supple, the stiff, but a more mature yearning, a need to be close, to feel alive, and yet even as he surrendered to it he knew it was wrong. It violated the pledge he had made to his Goddess. It betrayed the man he had sworn to be. But he could not help himself. She whispered in his ear, she touched his throat, smeared unguents into his sore flesh, and looked into his eyes, and he lost the will to resist.

Later they walked out into the garden. The moon was high in the sky, a disc of silver watching over the white hills. The ground around the Glass House appeared frozen, a layer of glittering white clinging to the contours of the earth.

"There are so many ghosts here. Can you feel them around you?" she said, as they walked down towards the water's edge.

It seemed like an odd thing for her to say.

The voices of the garden's birds joined in song as he reached down to trail his fingers through the black water. Something prevented him from touching the water. He lifted his fingers to his nose, as though trying to smell some ephemeral residue that might yet linger on them, a trace of the afterlife that prevented him from interacting with the world around him. There was nothing. He tried again, feeling the resistance of the air closing around his hand to hold it still, inches above the surface. He pushed against it but it refused to give.

"You cannot leave," Leanan said softly, kneeling down beside him. Her skin smelled of fragrant oils, subtle, inviting. He stared down at his fingers, trying to force them into the water. "That is the geas the druid and godless Crone placed upon this place. They promised eternity and fashioned nothing short of hell. Life and death have no dominion here, but anything preserved by enchantments of Ynys Afallach cannot cross the water. I cannot leave; I have been here so long to do so would be the death of me, my flesh would crumble to dust as the ravages of time caught up with it. You were reborn here – the geas is all that keeps you alive, it will not allow you to break it. To touch the water would undo all that we have done."

"I am trapped?"

"You are alive. Everything comes at a cost, warrior."

THE HEALING PROCESS was frustratingly slow.

Her words haunted him. The Glass House was a prison, claustrophobic, confining. He yearned to be free of the place. Every morning Sláine would wake from disturbing dreams and explore his wounds with tentative fingers, feeling out the areas of tenderness around the scarred skin, and for the first few weeks even own his light touch was enough to make him wince.

But gradually the pain faded.

He worked on building his strength, running laps around the island to add muscle to his legs, lifting rocks to regain power in his arms. The laps grew faster, the rocks heavier until he began to feel alive again.

Not once in the weeks did he see Ukko or the druid, nor did he see the fabled king or any of his entourage. Resentment fuelled his need to heal. They had abandoned him in this strange place with Leanan Sidhe. Indeed, he had not seen another soul since waking from death. That in itself was enough to frighten him. Again and again he walked down to the water's edge, testing the limits of his captivity, looking for a weakness in the geas that would allow him to escape this wretched place. At night he would dream himself back across the water, fighting once more side by side with Gwalchmai against the Night Bringer's horde, or would come surging up from beneath the press of man-animals with their grotesque feral faces, Brain-Biter tasting malignant blood.

And in some of those dreams he remembered dying – and why he had. He recalled the Morrigan and the Weatherwitch and Feg and the skull swords, and his own people, and his Goddess, helpless against the souring of her body.

And he remembered the Cauldron and what it represented, the hope it promised.

"Where is it?" he asked Leanan when she came to him that night.

"Where is what, my love?"

"The relic I brought here; a shard from the Cauldron of Rebirth. Where is it?"

She hesitated, her breathing shallow against the nape of his neck. Her arm encircled him, fingers lingering over his heart. "That slab of rusted iron you were clutching when you came back to us? Your friends took it with them when they left."

He did not believe her. Something about her words, breathed into his ear, did not ring true, but the more he tried to focus on *what* it was about them that felt wrong the harder it became to concentrate on it. She was lying, but why? His thoughts grew muggy, and his ability to recall even the simplest things about his life before coming to the Glass House faded.

She kissed his throat and the touch of her lips was enough to put the worry out of his mind for as long as they were joined.

He clung to the image of his mother, Macha, dying twice, once on the sword of the vile soldier of Feg, and again beneath the crushing chariot wheels in the hell of Purgadair's coliseum. He fixated on her pain, refusing to let it wash away beneath whatever enchantment the Sidhe wove around him. And seeing Macha he remembered another mother, and the toll her love for Avagddu, her only son, had taken upon the lives of so many people. And recalling the Crone brought with it memories of the Cauldron.

"Where is it?" he said again, determined not to forget this time.

"Gone," she whispered. "Far away. Do not dwell on it, thinking about your life before only hurts and makes it harder for you to accept being here. Oh, my beautiful boy, until you let go, you won't truly heal."

And there was a heady euphoria wrapped within her words and her touch.

He so desperately wanted to succumb to them, to just forget, but his mother's face would not let him.

"Leave me," he said, closing his eyes.

"But, my love–"

"Leave me," he said again.

"No."

"Then I will leave you." He pushed himself out of the seductive comfort of the bed and walked naked across the room. The peculiar subdued light glanced off the edges of his musculature, rippling over the shapes and lines so they made in a shadow play of phantom forms.

"Come back to bed, my pretty one. I have such delicious pleasures to share with you, such violent delights."

"Find yourself a new plaything, woman. I have no need of your flesh."

The woman leaned on one elbow, the single sheet slipping from her shoulder to reveal the gentle curves of side and breast and her body's own shadow play as the light touched her ribs. Her hair fell across part of her face, its gentle waves almost undoing his resolve. She smiled at him and patted his empty side of the huge bed.

"You need me, Sláine," Leanan said, "And I need you. You give me so much, I would not throw this thing away so lightly. We are all we have here. This can be such a lonely place."

"That is a lie, Leanan Sidhe. We both know it is. Do me the decency of letting the truth touch your lips for a moment: you serve your king, I am his prisoner, that makes you my gaoler. This thing between us is nothing more than a distraction, a means to keep me docile, is it not?"

Her smile was anything but warm; she leaned forwards, on all fours like some animal on the prowl, the predatory cunning of her kind burned behind her eyes. "Aren't you the clever little man? Would you rather the cuffs and chains came out? Are you not sufficiently imprisoned by the wetness of my flesh?"

Sláine turned his back on the woman. Whatever hold she had over him was gone. There was no enticement in her words. He saw her for what she was.

"Take me to Finvarra."

"Why would I want to do that, my pretty little manling?"

Sláine fastened the leather belt and adjusted his kilt so that it sat comfortably on his hips. He picked up the boar's head codpiece with its vicious tusks and turned to the supine Sidhe in his bed. "Because," he said, toying with the sharpened teeth of the boar's head, "the next 'tusk' of mine to impale you will almost certainly do a lot more damage to your insides." He made sure she saw the brutal tusks as he secured the codpiece over his groin. "From what I hear about this island such a wound would never heal, but at least it wouldn't kill you. Where is he?"

"He is by the lake, fishing. It is how he spends his days."

"And my friends?"

"They are enjoying the ample charms of my sisters, much as you were until a few moments ago."

"What did you do to me? What kind of enchantment was it that you spun around me so that I could not resist?"

Leanan Sidhe laughed, genuinely amused by the notion that she had somehow seduced the warrior with witchcraft. "Is my beauty not enough for you now? Believe me, it is no magic, my pretty one, no more than any seduction is. You want to lose yourself, to forget. We merely offer you what your heart desires. We know you better than you know yourselves. You came to me broken, I healed you. Sex is vital, vibrant, holy even. It is good for the flesh and the spirit. With my body I gave you yours back. The joy of the coupling was enough to hold back any doubts you had upon awaking, the rush of sensations that came with your release enough to dampen down any guilt or interest in your companions or your quest. You could call it witchcraft, just as you could call it love or lust. In truth the only magic of it is within your own chemistry. You wanted this, you wanted to lose yourself."

And there was truth in her words; truth he did not want to acknowledge.

He hadn't tried to leave. He had allowed his strength to return, had exercised hard, pushing himself, but he had only allowed himself to think about *how* he had come to Ynys Afallach in his dreams. He hadn't been willing to confront his own mortality in his waking hours. He hadn't allowed himself to remember the Night Bringer or the bravery of Gwalchmai and his men. Instead he had been a willing accomplice to his imprisonment. He had convinced himself the geas that somehow prevented him from entering the water also prevented him from remembering, dwelling on the past. It had been easier to cope with the guilt that way, his mind mirroring his own predicament and making a prisoner out of it, consigning it to the deepest parts of his subconscious.

It had taken the most natural of things, a son's love for his mother, to undo his mind's charade.

"I don't believe you," he said.

"That is your prerogative, my beautiful boy, but it doesn't stop it from being the truth."

"You mean to say that we are all willing prisoners here, captive to our own lusts?"

"There was no enchantment that made your ugly little dwarf friend crawl into Sister Urian's bed," Leanan assured him, not bothering to hide her nakedness. "And the only *magic* that kept him there blissfully forgetting all about you was her pillow skills. You overestimate your friend's resolve."

"Hardly, the runt is driven by his lusts, for food, for gold, and for ample breasts and warm thighs. I know him only too well. Myrrdin on the other hand, does not strike me as a man at all."

"The Lord of the Trees is a willing prisoner, just as you are, my pretty boy. It was his own guilts he would hide from just as you hide from yours. To him, Ynys Afallach is a sanctuary, a place free of the burdens of destiny and fate and the manipulations of your world. That is the only enchantment. The Glass House is a place of tranquillity," she explained, and he almost believed her. Almost. He could not ignore the predatory nature of Leanan Sidhe's eyes. There was more to their captivity than the woman admitted.

"Believe me, woman. If I find you are lying you will beg to leave this place so that you *can* die. Your pain will be that great. I know some violent delights of my own."

"I believe you, Defiler."

"YOU TAKE ALL the fun out of life, Sláine," Ukko grumbled, pulling his filthy britches up. "I was just getting familiar with this young lady."

Urian lay on the bed, watching the pair of them with feigned uninterest. She was every bit as exotic as Leanan, her lean, supple nakedness craving the eye. Sláine stood at the window, looking out over the black water. He could not see the far shore because a grey empty mist clung to the still lake.

"Just hurry up and put your clothes on, Ukko. We are leaving this place."

"And from your tone," said Ukko, pulling his food-smeared tunic over his head, "I am assuming you plan on hitting a few things on the way."

"People preferably," said Sláine. "Thieving dwarfs ideally."

"Oh you've got a sharp tongue, Sláine Mac Roth."

"And I've got a sharper axe. Now get a move on."

"Speaking of which, where is the aptly named Brain-Biter? I didn't lug the damned thing all this way just for you to lose it."

"Our hosts have it, along with the shard of the Cauldron. Finvarra, it seems, is rather like a magpie, he accumulates things that are not his."

"Then we'd better get them back, I suppose," said Ukko, stamping his foot and wriggling around, almost falling over, as he forced it into his boot.

"Which is why I am stood here waiting for you," said Sláine, patiently.

"Ah, I see, said the blind man. Well, I suppose we best be off then, can't sit around here all day. Just let me go give Urian a parting gift, wouldn't want to disappoint the wee girl, then I'll be right with you." The dwarf raised a lecherous eyebrow and grinned back at the woman waiting in his bed.

"Don't even think about it, runt."

"It'll only take ten minutes."

"No."

"Five, come on, Sláine. Look at her, she's lovely. You owe me five minutes, the amount of times I have put my neck on the line for you. What harm could five minutes do? It isn't as if we don't have the time. Five minutes in a place where time doesn't even exist. It'd be like it never happened."

"No."

"Remember what I was saying about life and fun?"

"No."

"You're a hateful man, Sláine."

"Are you finished?"

"Haven't even bloody started, thank you very much."

"You can come back and play when we have what we need; if time doesn't exist it isn't as though you'll actually have to wait very long is it?"

Ukko screwed his face up. "I hate you."

"I think you might have mentioned that before."

"And I'm sure I will mention it again." He turned to Urian, a rueful smile on his faced and shrugged. "Hmm, just, you know, hold that thought. I'll be back as soon as Mister Muscle here has got his toys back and we can say goodbye properly."

"I look forwards to it," Urian said, stretching out luxuriously. The white sheet slipped down to reveal the secrets of her anatomy.

"Oh believe me, so do I, so do I."

Sláine turned away from the window, took two steps to come up behind the dwarf, and cuffed Ukko across the back of the head with the flat of his hand.

"What was that for?" Ukko grumbled, rubbing at his head.

"Just reminding you which head you're supposed to do your thinking with."

"Hmm. Don't expect me to say thank you."

"WHERE ARE THEY keeping Myrrdin?"

"How should I know?" Ukko grunted, walking three steps behind Sláine in a sulk. "I'm not his keeper."

"No, but you were *alive* when you came here *with* him, so I think the chance of you knowing is a damned sight better than mine."

"Leanan left me with Urian. I didn't see him after that."

"This place is huge. How are we supposed to find him?"

"Maybe if we put our ears to the walls and listen for the grunts?" Ukko said, helpfully. "That's assuming he wants to be found," Ukko mumbled, falling back another step beneath Sláine's withering stare. "Well, they are attractive and he has been imprisoned in a tree for hundreds of years. It doesn't take a genius to work out he might be enjoying himself. You could try shouting, I suppose, maybe he'll come running."

An unseen hand came down on Ukko's shoulder, long white fingers digging in to the fabric of his dirty tunic. His bones nearly climbed out of his skin in fright. "By the Crone's withered tit, woman! Sneaking up on people like that... damn near gave me a bloody heart attack."

"My apologies, little man," Leanan Sidhe said, smiling. The ruby glass of the crystal passage suffused the folds of her dress, making it come alive with light. Despite the absence of a breeze her skirts billowed out behind her legs as she moved. She moved like a ghost, gliding across the floor. "I did not mean to scare you. I assumed you would be looking for the Lord of the Trees and thought to make your task easier. My sister, Modron, is taking your friend down to the lakeside even as we speak. Finvarra would see the three of you. I can escort you." She inclined her head, bidding them follow, as she turned and walked away.

They followed the Sidhe woman through the labyrinthine twists and turns of the Glass House, always heading down. Despite the fact that Ukko had walked these corridors for weeks – to and from the kitchens – there were many passages he did not recognise. The hues imbuing the walls shifted, the colours deepening and becoming thicker and more substantial the lower they went. In the distance they heard the chime of bells – it took Ukko a moment realise what the sounds actually were: women walking about the Glass House, their footsteps resonating through the palace like music. After a few moments he began to distinguish the sounds, how each of the Sidhe women had their own unique harmony determined by weight and grace. He wondered how they sounded to the sisters: Sláine dull and heavy most likely, a bass profundo, while his lighter, quicker steps as he hurried to keep up would be more akin to a falsetto warble.

Leanan rounded a corner that opened onto a teal stairway leading down towards the huge foyer and the imposing doors that led back outside to the maze monsters and the lake. The stairs themselves had been worn smooth by the endless shuffle of tired feet coming and going. They added a sense of perspective to the sheer size of the Glass House, rising six times Sláine's height as they curved and curved again around the fringe of the foyer.

They did not leave through the massive double doors, but instead through a small side door cut between the facets of the crystal wall so as to appear invisible from the stairs.

The air outside was fresh, invigorating after the stale air of the palace. Ukko breathed deeply, swallowing a lungful of the cold and savouring its chill inside. He shivered involuntarily. Leanan led them down a narrow path towards the jetty. The stones crunched beneath their feet. Ribbons of stratus clouds filled the sky.

Ukko looked up, a flicker of movement catching his eye.

For a moment his mind refused to believe what his eyes showed him, then the dull *whump whump whump* of huge leathery wingbeats filled the air above him. The shadow cast by the beast momentarily blocked out the light of the sun as it banked low, angling towards the water. It opened its huge maw wide, a shriek like the scream of a thousand dying men spilling out as its massive wings trailed through the water, stirring up a spume in the otherwise flat and rippleless surface. Wickedly sharp talons raked at the skin, powerful legs running across the water before the immense wyrm submerged. A moment later it rose, exploding out of the black water in a shower of spray, and arrowed back up into the wisps of stratus. The beast's scales dripped black water like rain.

Ukko clutched at Sláine's arm. He stared at the creature, unable to take his eyes from its elongated, serpent-like head and its yellow eyes as the beast swooped low again, almost close enough to touch. "Well knock me over with an menhir. Is that a... ?" he couldn't say the word.

Leanan chuckled. "It is the Knucker, Finvarra's war mount, though now the beast is more of a pet. I doubt it even remembers how to hunt."

"I don't," said Ukko, remembering the creature's teeth and the feral hunger in its eyes. "Makes you feel like a rat staring at a cat."

The Knucker landed with surprising grace, settling beside the water's edge. Two figures stood beside the huge wyrm, while a third sat on the jetty, engrossed in the hidden secrets of the black water. Myrrdin was recognisable even from a distance, the tattoos marring his flesh seeming to shift to the whim of the wind, becoming dark smears. He approached the beast, laying a hand on its ridged brow. Beside him was the Sidhe woman, Modron. Like her sisters, the woman's beauty was unnerving, though there was a sadness about her that was missing in the other Sidhe, her skin more luminous and more waxen at the same time, as though she harboured a sickness within her limbs, Ukko thought. He could not help but wonder if they kept their ugly sister locked away in some dark room inside the Glass House. The third figure, he assumed, was the Wounded King, himself, although Finvarra did not look particularly regal, sat cross-legged on the wooden jetty, a fishing pole braced beside him.

Sláine strode purposefully towards the jetty. Rather than struggle to match his pace, Ukko gave up trying. He kicked stones, dragging his feet, none too eager to get too close to the enormous Knucker.

Ten
The Knucker

"So THIS IS the fabled Defiler?" the Wounded King mused. "I must admit after all this time I was expecting something more."

"More what?" Sláine said, obviously irritated by the crippled king's condescending tone.

"Just *more*," Finvarra said.

Ukko watched his friend. Sláine was looking at the man, gauging him as he would any foe on the battlefield. Ukko could read his face as easily as he could read Feg's Ragnarok book, meaning he knew well enough when to duck, when to shut his mouth and when to run.

Finvarra favoured his left side; it caused his spine to curve slightly to the right to reduce pressure on whatever wounds he bore beneath his simple homespun tunic. A small stain had already begun to seep through the bandages. His hair was close-cropped, snow-white, his face gaunt, the bones emphasised beneath loose-fitting skin. His cheek bones were proud, angular, his nose aquiline. A scar sliced through the white of his thin beard, from high on the cheek into the cleft of his chin. In the dark shadows, his eyes were cruel, the only real clue to the Wounded King's resolve and a testament to his immortal suffering. Despite his slight frame, Ukko did not doubt for a moment that Finvarra would make a formidable opponent.

Seeing his scrutiny, Finvarra said: "It ought to have been a fatal wound – but for the druid it would have been, I suspect. But in this place it will not whiten, just as my flesh will not succumb to death. So I bleed, but that is a small cost for living. I trust you have found my house to your liking, little man?"

"You have something of mine, old man," Sláine interrupted, cutting across the pleasantries. "I would have it back so that I might be on my way."

The Wounded King turned a disapproving eye on the warrior. His lip curled into sneer "Would you indeed? First I suggest you remember that pleasantries cost nothing. I asked your companion if he had enjoyed the hospitality of my house. Do the little fellow the decency of allowing him the chance to reply." He turned back to Ukko, brushing off Sláine's obvious anger. "So tell me, good dwarf, has my house lived up to your every desire? And remember, it is customary for the guest to at least lie and pretend their host has been gracious even if he has been little more than a gaoler."

"Would that every gaol I've been thrown in was as comfortable, and the guards so, ahh, accommodating, your kingness."

"Very good, very good, now on to less pleasant things." Finvarra turned back to Sláine. "Now, young man, what is it you believe I have that belongs to you? And while we are talking about impossible things, what brings you to believe you can ever leave this place? Did Sister Leanan not tell you that you are bound here now, just as I am, alive at the whim of a geas placed on this island, Ynys Afallach, by the great Myrrdin himself? With that in mind I would say you want much that you cannot have." The old man studied Sláine's face much as he had just been studied himself, weighing the warrior's worth. A slow smile spread across his thin bloodless lips. "Ah, I see you are aware of the geas. Perhaps you have even tested its limits?" he raised a curious eyebrow. "Frustrating, is it not? To be able to see freedom and not be able to reach it? Such is your life now. Still, I am sure you will learn to love it here. The sisters offer many distractions, as I am sure you have already realised. Imprisonment need not be iron masks and manacles, sometimes a captivating smile and a warm bed is enough."

"Where is my axe, old man?" Sláine said, ignoring the taunt in Finvarra's words. Ukko watched Sláine's face contort as he struggled to rein in his temper. In another place the earth itself would have responded to his anger, firing his blood, and the Wounded King would have been confronted by a monster. Here at least it was just anger.

"You have no need of it here, I assure you. No one on the island means you harm."

"Still I would have it at my side – it was my father's. Now tell me, where is it?"

Finvarra turned to the druid. "Did you teach your boy no manners, Myrrdin? Not even a please when he makes demands of his betters."

"He isn't my boy, Finvarra," Myrrdin told him. "You would do well to remember that there is a reason your people named him the Defiler."

"A threat from you? After all this time? And I thought we were friends, Lord of the Trees," the Wounded King chuckled.

"Rulers have no friends; they have allies and subjects, Finvarra. Do not be coy with your word games. You have taken things that are ours; a fragment of the Cauldron of Rebirth, the warrior's stone axe. We would have them returned."

"Would you now? That is a shame, to be honest. You took something from me, druid, something I too would have returned. Perhaps when I get that back you can have your precious things... but then again, perhaps not. This is my kingdom, druid. You would do well to remember that. The whims of your Goddess mean nothing here, and even less to me. Now, enough of this bickering. The truth is your trinkets are a part of my collection now. You remember how much I love beautiful things? Believe me, the Defiler's axe is a relic to rival even Cúchulainn's Gae Bolga and Gwyddbwyll Gweddoleu's miraculous chess board. It is a true treasure of Albion if ever there was one. And, thanks to you, I have in my possession two shards of the Cauldron of Rebirth. I would not give it up for the world. Indeed, I need only the final fragments and I can have my life restored. With it I can live again, a real life, not this half-life, trapped on this damned Isle of Glass. So as I said, I will have back what you took from me before I even entertain the thought of returning a few trinkets to you. I suggest you put all thoughts of these treasures from your mind now. Consider them the cost of your stay, if you like. Payment for the Defiler's life. The price is fair, I believe."

"Well I do not," Sláine said.

"Then that is a pity and you are a damned fool, warrior," the Wounded King said, his words heavy with malice.

Ukko had no liking for the turn the conversation was taking.

"Perhaps, but I have already decided that this place is a blessing – I can tear you limb from limb and still you won't die. I can reach in and rip out your heart, and despite all the blood and all the screaming, you won't escape the pain."

"You think to intimidate me?" Finvarra said, shaking his head in mocking disbelief.

"I don't waste my time thinking, old man."

"I can vouch for that," Ukko said, helpfully, earning withering glowers from the young Sessair, the druid and the king.

"Tell me, which would you like broken first, arm or leg? I can't promise I will make it clean. Perhaps tonight I will claw your eyes out and leave them on the stones as food for the Morrigan's crows. There are so many ways pain can be brought to a body if you take the time to be inventive."

"Indeed. Did your mother never tell you that threats are the last refuge of the coward and the blusterer?" the Wounded King asked, unconcerned by Sláine's anger. "If you want to hurt me, warrior, I suggest you get on with it before I decide to hurt you."

"Don't tempt me, old man." Sláine turned on his heel and stalked away back towards the coruscating façade of the Glass House, clearly struggling to master his temper.

Beside Finvarra the fishing pole jerked as a fish took the bait and drew the line taut in its panic. He reached over and began reeling it in. The sleek silver fish came up, hook piercing its gaping mouth and flapping gills as it sucked desperately at the air, drowning out of the water. It wriggled in Finvarra's hands as he freed it. A moment later he dropped it back into the black water.

"What is the point if you are not going to eat it?" Ukko said, nonplussed. He walked over to the edge of the jetty and peered over the side, watching the silver shadow disappear.

"Sometimes the hunt is more rewarding than the kill. When you have eternity to waste what good is an empty lake? There is a life lesson in the answer to that, dwarf. I will let you fathom it out for yourself," said Finvarra, baiting the hook once more before casting the line back into the water to begin the cycle again.

"And the fish never learn to fear your hook?"

The thought genuinely amused the old man. "Do any species? And in that damning assessment I happily include humans."

He thought of Sláine, so easily manipulated into rising to take the Wounded King's bait, and saw the truth in the old man's words. "So are you hunting us now? Is that the game you are playing?"

Finvarra brought up a handful of maggots from his bait box and crushed them in his hand until their innards oozed out between his fingers. Then he opened his hand and showed the dwarf its contents. Despite the crushing and ruination every maggot still writhed, full of life. "I think you'd make poor sport, don't you, little man? Unless it was to see how far I could toss you..."

"Oh, I think you'd be surprised."

"Very little in life surprises me now, dwarf."

"Then it is a good thing that I am very little, wouldn't you say?"

SOMETHING THAT THE Wounded King had said stuck with Ukko: *your trinkets are a part of my collection now. You remember how much I love beautiful things.*

And the important thing here wasn't that few of Sláine's things were missing, not even the shard of the broken Cauldron. Oh no, far more interesting was the fact that hidden somewhere inside the Glass House was a collection of beautiful things worth liberating. *That* was the important thing. The dwarf rubbed his hands together in gleeful anticipation. The old man hadn't even realised he had said it, Ukko was sure. He had been so busy baiting Sláine that he hadn't for one minute considered the predilections of his audience.

Ukko smiled. "Once a thief," he said to himself. He had left Urian asleep in bed, worn out from his lusty excesses. The Sidhe was pliable, flexible and a whole lot of other "bles". He had drunk his fill, rolled over, farted and begun to snore loudly, faking unconsciousness until Urian's breathing had changed in quality to the regularly shallow rhythm of sleep, then he had snuck out of their shared room. Finvarra hadn't lied; for all its sensory delights, the place was no more than a gaol – and there hadn't been a gaol built that could hold the resourceful dwarf. She hadn't even stirred as he carefully laid the sheet back over her legs, padded across the room to his pile of clothes by the crackling fire, and dressed.

The passageways were deserted, the Glass House in the grip of what passed for night in this peculiar place.

He walked slowly along the narrow corridor, listening at every step for signs of life, but the Glass House was in deep sleep. Even the hues imbuing the walls seemed more subdued, somnambulant.

Now if I were a senile old man locked away on my own for four hundred years, where would I hide my precious knickknacks?

Think.

You've got this whole place to yourself, where would you hide the goodies?

Think.

It's not as though you'd be expecting guests, so there's no need to squirrel them away in a vault, even supposing this place has dungeons, no, you'd want them close at hand, somewhere you could visit them whenever the mood struck. So, where in this endless sprawling palace, would that be? Near your bed chamber? In a chest at the bottom of your bed? You're a king, how about near your throne room? Or up in one of the towers, where the light is always perfect?

It's about splendour, he reasoned, following the curve of the passage to one of the many servants' stairs, and climbing them, *You possess these glorious things, these things of beauty, so you want to revel in them. That means you keep them somewhere that enhances their perfection. Somewhere the light is perfect, somewhere spectacular.*

The chamber at the top of the very highest spire, with wide open windows to capture all the natural light sun and moon have to offer.

Pleased with his logic, Ukko set off looking for more stairways, always rising, higher and higher through the labyrinthine corridors of the Glass House, pausing at corners, breath caught in his throat, to listen. He felt like a character in some dumb fairy tale, disappearing into the woodland without a trail of breadcrumbs to find his way home.

More than once he found himself walking down a passageway identical to one he thought he had left behind two stairways earlier. Then he would walk to the far end of the corridor and peer out through the glass trying to get his bearings in relation to the highest tower and its crooked spire. It was an unnerving experience. Before long he was sure he was utterly lost. And still he headed upwards, following the never-ending twists and turns of the Glass House as though he were in the belly of a huge beast.

Ukko rested his hand flat against the wall, feeling the frequency of the light resonate through his fingers like a pulse, tripping as the hue shifted, racing as it deepened.

And like a body, there was an internal logic to the construction of the Glass House. The rooms fed off the corridors like vital organs, each serving a purpose, feeding the vitality of the place; the corridors, stairs and passageways the veins and arteries that kept life pumping through the Wounded King's home, the servants' stairs the capillaries that made certain life reached the furthest extremities.

Twice he heard the harmonics of movement, the chimes that accompanied one of the Sisters going about her business, and both times he almost blundered into them before he realised that they were closer than the elegiac melody that their footfalls suggested. He ducked down, heart hammering against his chest, and clung to the dark places, watching them until they disappeared before he scuttled off. He wished he had a way of telling the time – or that there was at least some rationality to its passage in the Glass House that he might judge how long he had. The notion that the whole place might wake up at any moment, with no obvious hint as to when or how distant that moment might be, was a deeply uncomfortable one.

Ukko counted all manner and number of doors before he found the one he wanted, tucked away in a far corner of the seventh storey, around the seventh corner in the seventh room. He knew it immediately, even without opening it. Ukko paused, his hand on the door, allowing his spatial awareness to adjust as he mated the image of the Glass House in his mind to the reality of his location. It was a useful skill, one that had served the little dwarf well over the years of petty larceny, especially when it came to hoofing it away on his heels before a disgruntled "donator" could collar him.

The stairwell beyond the door was different, a tight right-hand spiral cut into a cone of solid glass. As with every other staircase in the Glass House, the stairs were worn smooth in the centre. There was no balustrade for support despite the fact that the stairs coiled up and up and up and up, over one thousand steps that burned every muscle in his body as he ascended, until it opened into what was obviously Finvarra's museum of curiosities. It was nothing like he had imagined – or dared to imagine. The tower room was easily fifty paces across, circular in dimensions, with windows cut into the thick glass walls at each of the cardinals. It was unnerving, being so high up, encased in glass and yet able to see not only through the windows but through the tinted walls and the floor. Ukko stood at the threshold, wrestling with the sensation of being suspended over a terrifying drop. It was exacerbated by the floor, which appeared no more substantial than a thin patina of ice crusting over a fathom-deep sea. Ukko breathed deeply, inhaled, held the breath for the count of eleven, then exhaled, and again, regulating his heart and the dizziness that threatened to overwhelm his mind. He reached out with his foot, tapping the floor. He half-expected a crack to splinter through it but of course it bore his little added weight with ease.

"Stupid dwarf," he muttered, cursing his idiocy. Various display cabinets were arranged around the walls and lined up in a concentric ring near the centre of the room. Dubious treasures including pieces of dented armour, blunted weapons, marbled statuary, jade figurines with likenesses to every manner of shoggy beast imaginable, rarities of hunts stuffed and mounted, tablets etched with Ogham and stranger runes, more like pictograms than letters, were proudly displayed. And there in pride of place at the heart of the curiosities, Slough Feg's Ragnarok book on a lectern, open on one of the many pages that promised the end of the world as humanity knew it.

Ukko took the first step into the room. He couldn't help himself – he looked down and through the glass floor at the hundreds of feet of nothing between him and the rocks below. The huge twisted spire rose up from out of the escarpment itself, entirely separate to the Glass House which seemed to have been fashioned around it. The rocks were a black death waiting below his feet. It was impossible to tell how thick the glass was. The fact that the tower had stood for at least four centuries was no comfort – that just made it old and ready to crumble as far as he was concerned.

Ukko closed his eyes and ventured a second step expecting the glass to groan beneath his feet at any second, dreading the sharp crack that would precede the fall.

After a fifth step without the floor opening up to swallow him, Ukko opened his eyes.

Brain-Biter hung on the wall betwixt and between an imperious Gae Bolga and the vestiges of what appeared to be a warrior's grave shroud. On a table beneath it was an exquisite chess set, each piece six inches tall, one army fashioned from pure gold the other appeared to be obsidian or another black rock. Ukko moved closer to examine the pieces. They truly were exquisite, each rendered with the precision of a master craftsman, flawlessly detailed, the features so life-like it was creepy. A game was in progress. Ukko studied the board for a moment, realising with a wry grin that mate was only one move away. He reached out to touch the black knight astride his obsidian destrier only for the horse to glide across the board, answering his instinct to move around the cardinal, and mate the enemy king in the pincer its advance fashioned.

The miniature gold king bowed his head in surrender.

Ukko grinned, forgetting for a moment the thousand-foot drop beneath his feet.

Despite the urgency he felt, he was sorely tempted to rearrange the pieces for another game, but the sudden flare of warmth within the tower room and the brightening of the walls as the sun breached the horizon was enough to deter him.

He collected the book, stuffing it into his pack, and lifted down the heavy double-headed axe, putting it down in the middle of the floor, then stuffed his pockets with a few of the smaller pieces of jewellery he thought would fetch a decent price from one of the more disreputable fences of his acquaintance.

Almost as an afterthought, Ukko pocketed the gold king as a souvenir. *After all,* he thought to himself, *I did win it fair and square.*

He had no idea what the gold figurine was worth, but judging from its weight in his pocket, it'd pay for more than a few nights of indulgence in wine, women and well, more women, which made it worth far more than its weight as the old adage went.

Still, it would be a shame to ruin such fine craftsmanship, but it would be so much easier to spend melted down.

It took the dwarf a few minutes to locate the two shards of the Cauldron of Rebirth; he had expected them to be out among the other treasures but they weren't. Finvarra had locked them away behind glass in one of the many display cabinets that formed the concentric rings around the very heart of the chamber.

Refusing to be rushed by his own impatience, Ukko studied the lock.

It was made of brass, the aperture wide, the mechanism disturbingly simple to pick for anyone who understood even the most basic rudiments of the mechanics going on beneath the hasp. Indeed, it was an insult to a decent thief. Ukko could have opened it with a fingernail, it was that pathetic.

Which in itself felt wrong to the dwarf. It was like a thief's sixth sense, the fine hairs at the nape of his neck bristled and his fingertips itched as he turned the lock over in his hands.

He resisted the temptation to simply pop the lock.

He studied the mechanism again, this time with a more suspicious eye, expecting to see some kind of subtle trap secreted away within the tumblers – a poison-tipped needle perhaps or a trip for something more explosive. The last thing he wanted to do was make a mistake and leave what passed for his brains smeared across the wall, still fully conscious even in his liquefied state thanks to the damned geas on Ynys Afallach.

The dwarf scratched his head thoughtfully. A second layer of protection made sense, considering the elementary nature of the lock itself. Added to that the fact that the two pieces of the Cauldron were among the only treasures locked down in the entire collection (and that was including the gold, diamonds and other gemstones) underlined their value to the Wounded King. And knowing that, only a fool would assume they were going to be easy pickings.

It irritated him that the lock was so crude; a wiser trap would have been to employ a considerably more sophisticated lock with a well-disguised trigger to mask the fact that there was a second failsafe on the mechanism. The would-be thief would find the first, reward for their skill, and vanity would see to it that they triggered the second. There was a finesse to a good trap, a cunning that a thief couldn't help but admire. There was no such finesse to the lock in his hand.

He squinted, peering in through the aperture, identifying not one but two black metal teeth, almost indistinguishable from the teeth of the cogs and tumblers of the mechanism itself, and the spring-loads behind them, poised to drive first one and then the other into clumsy fingers.

He smiled wryly to himself, enjoying the game at last. The trap itself was relatively well disguised, not flawlessly but at least with a little subtlety. There was nothing more disappointing than just being able to *take* what you wanted. Any thief worth his salt wanted to *earn* his spoils.

And like any good thief, he came prepared. Ukko dug around in the lining of his grubby tunic for one of the fine needle-like picks worked into its lining. He teased it out slowly. It was a thin piece of metal, two inches long with a slight hook at the tip. Ukko put it between his teeth while he worked a second, slightly more substantial pick out of the lining, this one half an inch longer than the first and a little thicker, with a blunted tip.

He eased the first hooked pick into the lock, teasing it across the tumblers one at a time, daring them to click out of place and fire the pin, until it rested just beneath the coil of the first sprung tooth. Ukko held his breath, biting his tongue as he slid the second pick in alongside the first, easing it slightly deeper so it negated the second treacherous tooth.

Then slowly and very deliberately he sprung the first mechanism.

The needle, dripping thick poison, stung the air less than a quarter of an inch from his calloused finger.

The second mechanism didn't launch a dart; it cracked a phial within the lock itself, releasing a noxious vapour and corrosive liquid which ate into the metal, quickly fusing the metal tumblers into one solid lump while Ukko coughed his lungs up. Cursing his arrogance, Ukko lurched away from the still-rising vapours and grabbed Brain-Biter from where it lay. Covering his mouth and nose with one hand, he stepped forwards and slammed the axe into the glass front of the display cabinet and reached in through the jagged shards of glass to retrieve the two pieces of the Cauldron from inside. Each fragment of black iron was as heavy as Ukko himself. He struggled to get them into his pack, wrestling with the drawstring and then the shoulder straps as he struggled to lift it. With the pack slung over one shoulder and Brain-Biter over the other, Ukko staggered and lurched down the thousand stairs, his feet running away beneath him as the weight of the Cauldron bullied him forwards quicker and quicker with each spiral of the stairs until he was running, tripping on the lips of the steps as he desperately tried to keep his balance. He hit the wall again and again, lurching and staggering and stumbling, barely maintaining his precarious balance as his momentum threatened to send him arse over tit rolling down the glass stairs.

Then he burst through the door at the bottom of the tower, tripped over his own feet and went sprawling into the room head first. He threw his arms out in front of his face to brace his fall as the floor rushed up to hit him. Ukko's cry of pain was muffled by the press of the glass up against his face. He tried to catch his breath, the wind driven out of his lungs by the savage pummelling of the iron weight on his back driving him into the floor. He lay there for a moment, unable to move, waiting for the inevitable cry of alarm.

When it didn't come he grunted, wincing against the sudden flare of pain as he pushed himself back to his feet. Looking around once more, to be sure the Wounded King wasn't about to complete his own subtle checkmate, Ukko set off at a lurching run to find Sláine and Myrrdin, not caring that his footsteps rang like a mad chorus throughout the Glass House.

"I DON'T PRETEND to understand, druid," Sláine said, worrying away at the dilemma relentlessly. His frustration was, yet again, close to boiling over into outright anger. Sitting, essentially doing nothing, was anathema to him. "Surely if you were responsible for laying the geas on this place, you can lift it also? Can this magic be so convoluted that even you cannot unmake it?"

They were sat in the small secluded courtyard within the centre of the Glass House, surrounded on all sides by towering walls of crystal. All of the colours blended into one. They had taken to sitting in the courtyard and discussing the riddle of their captivity, fruitless though the cyclical argument was. Sláine shunned Leanan's attempts at companionship, choosing instead to retreat from their chamber to the water's edge where he knelt in prayer to the Goddess his heart could no longer reach. He craved her presence within his flesh once more, yearned for the certainty her presence gave his life. Piety and restraint did not come naturally to the young Sessair warrior, but he found strength within it. Myrrdin had grown equally introspective, obsessed with the bonds necessity had forged between Ynys Afallach and Sláine.

"Alas, my friend, life is never as simple as we would wish it. I was not alone in binding the geas to these shores, the strength of the Morrigan's magic supplemented my will, and it is her touch that remains, not mine. I can sense none of my own signature upon the earth here. I do not expect you to understand, but whatever I achieved has long since faded, only the will of the immortal remains. Even if that was not so, the very foundation of the Isle of Glass is bound up within the enchantment. To break it would shatter the place into a thousand thousand tiny pieces and scatter them to the four winds."

Sláine ground his teeth in frustration, scratching at his scalp. "Then what can be done? I will not sit here idly fishing for the rest of my days."

"Finvarra will have his life back, and the only way he can achieve this is through the same Cauldron that we seek for the Morrigan, the gift that will supposedly return you to your people. Perhaps this was the Crone's ultimate intention, to bind the three of us together. She prophesied his return at the time of the land's greatest need. Initially I did not believe our fates were interlinked but now I am seeing it all as part of an elaborate weave, each life of possibilities a thread that the Crone has laid into the pattern. With that in mind it is not unreasonable to believe that Finvarra's return is dependent upon our actions."

"What is your meaning, druid? Speak plainly for once, my head tires of trying to fathom the logic you and the dwarf seem to delight in."

Myrrdin smiled, his peculiar wooden eyes coming to life in the dawn's early light. "I have been thinking about this a lot, my young friend. We are little more than puppets in her shadow play."

"I said plainly, Myrrdin."

"Plainly, yes. As with so much of what has happened, I sense the meddling fingers of the Crone at play here. Can you not feel her work? Consider what little we know: like you, Finvarra cannot leave this place because to do so would shatter the very geas that keeps him breathing despite the mortal wound that ought to have ended his life centuries ago. It is no coincidence that he now has two of the four pieces of the Morrigan's Cauldron in his possession, he sees it as his salvation. To enter the Cauldron is to be born again, that is the magic of the artefact. It is not merely legend. Finvarra has not forgotten the Morrigan's words, he bides his time, gathering treasures to him, but all the while his interest is in the Cauldron because without it he can never leave this place to fulfil his destiny. He cannot be reborn. He cannot return to serve the land once more. He cannot die his hero's death."

"I understand this," Sláine said.

"Good, now consider: both the dwarf and I can come and go as we please, we are not snared here in the same way that you are. The magic is not what keeps us alive. If we were to return with the reforged Cauldron of Rebirth both you and the Wounded King would be saved, born again, and the enchantment could be willingly torn asunder."

Sláine mulled the druid's words over for a moment, considering the implications of them. "So you propose to abandon me?"

"You cannot come with us," Myrrdin said, unable to look him in the eye.

"Which amounts to the same thing, does it not?"

Before the druid could answer a clarion bell clamoured, its shrill harmonic shattering the serenity of the courtyard, and a moment later Ukko slammed through the door, his stunted legs buckling beneath the weight of the pack slung over his shoulder. The miserable little scoundrel had a ferocious grin pasted on his face. He clutched Sláine's huge axe in his hands.

"Time," Ukko gasped between breath, "to make a sharp exit." He dumped the pack at Sláine's feet and thrust Brain-Biter into the barbarian's hands. "Before someone notices their precious collection's been plundered. I've got everything, the book, both pieces of the Cauldron, and ahh, a few trinkets to cover the inconvenience. So come on."

The shrill harmonic gradually subsided, fading to nothing, a ghost in the glass, a memory.

"Not that I don't appreciate your thieving, stumpy, because believe me I do, I do. But there's one slight problem you seem to have overlooked in your opportunism," Sláine muttered. He looked up at the row of windows that overlooked the courtyard and saw the sharp features of Leanan Sidhe looking down at them. It was impossible to read her expression. She didn't move from the glass. "You know, the whole 'one of us can't leave the island without dying' kind of puts a dampener on things."

"Oh ye of little faith, Sláine. I've got a plan," said Ukko, flashing the warrior an annoyingly smug grin. "Trust Ukko, eh, just this once? I mean, when have I ever let you down?"

"You really want me to list them now? I mean, I can, but surely we ought to be running for our lives?" The sarcasm dripped off Sláine's words. "Oh, wait, we can't die here can we, so actually we ought to be running to save our hides from an eternity of torture, that's *so* much better, isn't it?"

Ukko ignored him. "Just carry the gear down to the jetty, I'll meet you there in five minutes," and before either of them could argue, Ukko took off, racing back into the Glass House and the shrill harmonic rose again, as the voice of the building itself cried out: *intruder!*

"I DREAD TO think what the little runt is up to now," said Sláine, dropping the sack on the rotting boards of the old jetty. He had expected Finvarra himself to be sat on the dock, fishing pole in hand, waiting for another silver fish to bite. He shielded his eyes against the glare of the sun. The monsters of the maze looked on impassively, the breeze rustling through the topiaries giving the impression of movement as the leaves stirred. "This is pointless, you said yourself, I cannot leave this place so why run now and risk the wrath of the king of this twisted domain?"

"You are quick to judge ill, friend Sláine," the druid said, "Size and muscle are no measure of the heart. Ukko has stood side by side with you through more than most would, standing resolute despite his fear. Occasionally it would not hurt to just trust the little man."

"Now that's a sentiment to strike fear into the heart of the hardiest warrior," Sláine said. He sat cross-legged on the boards, digging at the splinters with his fingers. The jetty was riddled with woodworm, and crumbled like powder beneath his picking. "Do you have any idea what he is up to? Have you pair been hatching mad schemes behind my back? I wouldn't put it past either of you..."

"Rest easy, my suspicious friend, I am as in the dark as you are, but perhaps I choose to see young Ukko as the spark of light we need."

"To burn the whole bloody barn down, maybe."

They felt the wingbeats, like the dull pounding of a leather drum resonating through the air, before they heard them.

A shadow of movement caught his eye; a blurred smudge of black on soot grey. "*What in all the els... ?*" Sláine gasped, staring over the druid's shoulder at the great black shadow of the Knucker cresting the spires of the Glass House, filling the sky with the filthy promise of fire and pain.

The immense fell beast banked, wings stretched taut, talons clawing at the thermals, and swooped down low.

Sláine pushed himself to his feet, grabbing Brain-Biter from the wooden planking. The weight of the axe in his hands was reassuring, familiar – not that the stone head could do any significant damage to the great winged wyrm.

"This is where trust gets you with the dwarf, druid. Fire-breathing drakes turning your bones to bloody charcoal! Come on then, beastie," he yelled at the sky, "let's see which of us can cause the most pain!"

Beside him, the druid gasped, pointing: "Well I'll be damned… seems our little friend is even more resourceful than I thought."

Sláine followed the direction of his finger. It took him a moment to distinguish the smudge of colour on its spine, and a moment more to realise that it was actually the dwarf clinging desperately to the ridge of the Knucker's saddle horn for dear life. He almost dropped the axe.

"Now he's trying to steal the fething dragon!"

The Knucker hit the ground, hard, claws churning up sod and black loam and then the weathered stones of the beach as the great beast battled the momentum of its wild descent. Ukko tumbled out of the saddle, hitting the ground in a whorish sprawl. The impact failed to jar the idiot grin from his face. The Knucker's serpentine head snaked forwards, the ridges of its brow knuckling up feet from the Sessair's face. It sniffed the air, scenting meat, threw its head back and roared its hunger, a second tongue of flame lashing out to scorch the moisture from the air. Ukko rolled over and out from beneath the wyrm's enormous clawed foot even as the Knucker's forked tongue laved across razor-sharp incisors. A fatty string of meat from the beast's last meal still clung to a crack between its teeth, with blood-matted fur still tangled around the rope of gristle. It looked like part of a lamb's carcass. The tip of the Knucker's split tongue caught the edge of the meat, worrying it back into its mouth. The beast chewed on the flesh for a moment, its ancient eyes falling on Sláine. Cruelty smouldered within the great wyrm's scrutiny. The young Sessair was left in no doubt that the beast could smell the spice of blood pumping through his body, the sweat salting his flesh; to the Knucker he was a meal like any other.

"Your chariot awaits, m'lud," Ukko grinned, spreading his arms wide.

"You have got to be joking," Sláine said, struggling to come to terms with the sheer audacity of the dwarf's theft. Finvarra's own mount! The Sidhe king's wrath would be monumental. "I'm not mounting anything that looks like it wants to eat me."

Ukko turned to the druid. "You see what he does to me, Myrrdin? I try. I *really* try but he has to keep saying things like mounting and eating." The dwarf clutched at his temples theatrically, spinning on his heel as though going into a swoon. "Too many jokes. Head going to explode."

"I'm still not getting on the damned thing," Sláine grumbled, matching the Knucker's hungry stare with one of his own.

He almost missed the druid's low chant; if the dwarf hadn't drawn his attention to him the subvocalised invocation would have bled forever into the susurrus of the breeze. "Oh, no," Sláine said, stepping back half a step. "No, no, no. You're not abandoning me here to clean up your bloody mess."

His foot hit the hessian pack, causing the metal plates of the Cauldron to clang against each other.

"Then maybe you want to get on the *damned thing*, your warpedness?"

In a trance now, the insistent rush of the words spilling from his tongue, Myrrdin raised his hands, drawing the first coil of vapour from the water, and began to open the mists.

MODRON SAW THE smoke on the water first, then the sudden flare of fire in the sky as the Knucker belched a tongue of flame that licked across the low-lying clouds. The great wyrm's powerful wings lifted it high into the grey sky, carrying it out over the water.

Finvarra's prisoners rode its back.

Her hand went instinctively to her stomach. "What is the fool doing? He cannot leave... the geas will be broken."

She had to warn the others but there was no time.

The betrayal would kill Finvarra.

It would kill all of them.

The air rippled around the Knucker, as though gathering shape and substance to stop the beast from penetrating the mist, but the great wyrm's powerful wings tore its resistance to shreds. The mist thickened and then seemed to blow away on the wind as the drake banked and drove, angling for the very heart of it, and then the smoke engulfed the beast and the Knucker was gone.

"He is our doom, sister," Leanan said, beside her. Together, they watched through the hospice's single window, aware of the bitter irony that their last breaths would be drawn in the chamber where the Defiler drew his first. "He always was. He cannot help but kill, it is his destiny."

"The Defiler? He is nothing but a child in a man's body."

"And a pretty body it is." Leanan laid a hand on her sister's shoulder. "But no, your beloved druid, sister. Our pain began with him, and now it ends with him."

"No," Modron said. It was a weak denial. "I cannot believe he would harm his own flesh and blood, Leanan Sidhe, he is not that kind of monster."

"Perhaps not, sister, but you have not told him, have you?"

Modron shook her head. The floor shifted beneath her feet, a sharp crack reporting as the first fissure opened up between the amber of the glass wall and the suddenly crimson floor.

"Then how can you expect him to save your child, sister?"

"We cannot stay here, Leanan. We cannot simply cease to be!"

"There is nowhere to go, Modron."

"But there is." The Sidhe woman pointed out through the window to the smoke on the water and the ghosts of fire in the sky. "Out there."

"We cannot leave – you cannot… your child was given life in here."

"The geas is broken, sister. The world is falling down," and as though to emphasise her point a second detonation resounded, the retort tearing through the very heart of the chamber. A huge slab of the ceiling tore loose under the sudden strain as the building's weight shifted. It shattered on the floor in thousands of shards and viciously sharp splinters. "There is nothing to keep us here now. We need not perish with the Wounded King."

"Finvarra! We have to go to him now, Modron. We have to be with him!" Leanan Sidhe gasped as understanding hit, with the geas broken the wound would bleed out. The king would die.

"No, sister-mine, I am done with servitude, now I claim my freedom. My son's freedom. Mabon will be born in the land of his father. He will live and breathe and grow knowing the ecstasy of love and life and death as it should be."

"Then go, Sister Modron, before the druid closes the mists and you are trapped here to die with us. Think of me, lying beside our king one last time, his life bleeding out beneath us. Think of it as duty, think of it as devotion, think of it as our curse or think of it as our love. Just think of it, do us that kindness. Now go."

LEANAN SIDHE RAN through the swirling dust and falling debris as the Glass House came down all around her. She slipped on a polished smooth sheet of glass and fell, sprawling. She pushed herself to her feet even as the wicked slivers of glass dug into her palms, opening her flesh. Leanan Sidhe bled, the red staining the perfect white of her dress. The Sidhe held her bleeding palms up to her face, her mind swimming with the horror of dissolution as her world came apart at the seams. She had forgotten what her own blood looked like, the viscosity, the rich ruby red of it. All around her colour leaked back into the world – real colour. For too long she had forgotten what it was like to see such a vibrant world.

Now, in death, she remembered.

She did not know if it was a trick of her mind, or the truth, it did not matter.

She ran on, fighting through the detritus and the choking veil of glass-dust in the air. Minute fragments cut at her lungs as she inhaled them, shredding through the soft flesh of her insides. She stumbled into the wall again, a fire burning inside her, reaching out blindly as somewhere above the entire weight of the Glass House shifted. Leanan came away from the wall, spinning blindly, calling out into the chaos of the collapse, but there was no answer. She staggered on as the groans became cries and then, with malicious glee the passageway transformed into a tomb, the Glass House reduced to a tomb of tombs. Leanan shielded her head from the debris, coughing and lurching from side to side as the lights in the walls dimmed and finally went out, the facets of the glass suddenly opaque with all of the fractures. She turned her ankle on a spar of blood-red glass that jutted from the wall of the passage, and hit the floor hard, barely avoiding another lethal spear of crystal that thrust out through the brittle wall precisely where her head had been a moment before. Leanan lay there for a second, struggling for breath, all of her four hundred years weighing on her bones now, returned. She felt beyond old: ancient. All around her the Glass House collapsed in on itself one floor at a time, one spire twisting and crumbling, crashing down to the grey earth, a billion shards of glass blowing out over the maze monsters, shearing away the sides of their leafy forms with savage cruelty, out across the lake and into the mist itself, shredding the wisps of white.

And somewhere in the heart of this chaos her king, Finvarra, lay dying.

The collapse had torn a hole in the centre of the passage, the stresses of destruction peeling the roof away. Through it, Leanan could see one of the great spires buckling, huge facets of its construction breaking away and falling free, end over end on its way down. The spire turned with hideous grace as the inevitable momentum of the fall gripped it, tearing the hole in the ceiling wider even as huge slabs of glass came down like deadly rain. She felt the force of the collapsed building, the weight of death pressing down as time wormed its way between every crack and crevice, working them wider until it appeared as though the black cracks were the talons of some crazy bird tearing into the flesh of the building.

Leanan found the Wounded King in the corridor outside his chamber. He had tried to flee but had been snared by his home, the Glass House refusing to surrender its master as it died. And now they were inextricably joined. Finvarra lay unmoving on the floor. The door behind him had buckled and splintered, tearing free of its hinges. A part of it had broken free and pierced Finvarra's side, spearing him to the floor even as his life leaked out across it, his blood feeding the glass. The old king's legs were crushed beneath great chunks of masonry, smashed beyond repair. For all the horror of the sight, the worst was to come as Leanan knelt beside him. He was still awake, fear plain in his eyes. There was nothing noble in this death. Nothing heroic. He saw her, but didn't recognise her, blind with pain. For a moment she thought she saw the ghost of hope flicker across his eyes, but it was nothing more than a brittle illusion crushed beneath the debris.

The old man was dying.

She cradled his head in her lap, stroking back his hair, soothing him into the long dark night of death.

"He unmade us…" Finvarra managed, his words barely a whisper, falling away beneath the chorus of collapse all around them.

"Shhh, my sweet king, save your breath," Leanan said gently, placing a kiss on each of the blind king's eyelids.

"He broke... the... geas," wheezed Finvarra. "He has brought death into this realm and now everything is undone. Our sanctuary is collapsing. I am lost, sister. I cannot feel... anything. My body is gone. It is only what little residue of power remains that tethers me to this life. I am undone... is this death?"

"Speak not so, my king."

"I will not lie in the face of my mortality, sweet child. I am many things but I am not afraid. I have waited a long time to die. I have had longer than most to come to terms with my death," the bitterness in the old man's voice was harsh, "but I would not perish in this place, beneath the weight of the stones. I would die with the sun on my face, free."

"I don't know if I can move you," Leanan confessed, her hand lingering on Finvarra's cheek.

"Do it, sister. Once, so long ago now, the druid appeared to rob me of my glorious death, promising a greater destiny, and now he has returned to steal that destiny. This anonymous death, crushed beneath the weight of my prison, is all that remains. I will not die here. I would taste the air on my face one last time. Do that for me, sister. Take me down to the water. Let me die on my own terms."

Tears streaked the soot and glass-dust on her cheeks as she dug frantically through the rubble trying to free Finvarra's legs.

Above her and all around her, the Glass House succumbed to the stresses of entropy, every sound amplified now to the point of a scream within the crystalline structure. She cut her hand badly, slicing it on an edge of glass, deep to the bone, and barely noticed as she discarded it, reaching in again for the heaviest of the debris. She couldn't lift it off him. Sobbing, she did all she could, dragging Finvarra out from beneath the crush. He didn't make a sound despite the agony it must have been.

She couldn't see through her tears, and didn't *want* to see. Everything she had known for years beyond counting was collapsing in on itself; even her own body. The weakness permeated her bones, making them brittle. She felt her heart in her chest, straining, her lungs withering with each diminished breath.

She was dying the death she should have died so long ago.

"Not yet," she pleaded, making a bargain with her bones, her heart.

Leanan gathered the Wounded King into her arms and carried him out through the collapse. She wept, blind through the tears, as she staggered out into the light. The doorframe splintered, the arch supporting it shearing in two.

"Soon," she promised, though whether it was to herself, death, or to the old man in her arms even she didn't know. She carried Finvarra down to the water's edge. "We're here," she told him, but it was too late, the life had left the old man. She looked down at him, knowing she had failed him at the last, at his blood on her hands, mingling with hers, at his ruined legs and crushed chest, and knew he had been dead even before she had dragged him out of the rubble.

Leanan looked over her shoulder, for one last look at the Glass House before it became unrecognisable, then towards the last vestiges of the mist Myrrdin had opened into the Annfwyn, and took the first step into the water, and a second, until it came up to her waist. She cradled Finvarra close to her chest as the water rose up over his head to swallow him.

And still she walked deeper, until the water rose up over her breast, to her throat.

She took another step so that the water came up over her mouth and nose, giving herself and the body of her king to the black water.

MODRON WAS LOST in the mist.

She had fled the destruction of the Glass House, reaching the water before the gateway between today, tomorrow and yesterday had closed, and followed the Defiler and her beloved into the Annfwyn. For a moment she had seen the light of life blazing on the other side, and moved towards it only for it to flicker and fail, the light burning out and leaving her in grey darkness. She stumbled blindly through it, knowing even as she did that Myrrdin had closed the gateway, that she was trapped in this limbo between the El Worlds.

She told herself she could bear it, trading one eternity for another, one curse for another. But it was a lie. She was not alone now. Their child grew inside her, little Mabon.

For him she had to find a way out of the mists. She would not condemn the child to being born inside this hell.

If that happened, Modron swore, she would never forgive Myrrdin.

Eleven
Weyland the Smith

THE KNUCKER STREAKED through the sky, the Land of the Young laid out like a blanket of patchwork colours stitched together and thrown over the hills and valleys. The great drake cast its shadow over the villages below, banking, huge wings unfurled, savouring the vitality of the world, revelling in the vibrancy of its colours, its pulse. The Knucker roared, a red lick of flame tonguing out of its snout as it swooped low enough for its talons to rake through the treetops.

"CRONE!" Sláine bellowed from the back of the dragon, "CRONE!"

But the witch did not manifest. Not one of her ever-present black birds joined them in the sky, even as they tried to shake them from the trees.

"CRONE!"

The air streamed through their hair buffeting and bullying the three riders as they clung to the back of the giant winged wyrm.

Ukko hung on to Sláine's waist for grim life, his ugly little face contorting to the whims of the wind as the dynamics of the air pressure shifted around them, remaking it into a hundred different masks as they rose and plummeted from the sky.

"I really don't like this!" the dwarf shouted over the wind as another barrage nearly lifted him out of the saddle. He dug his heels in.

"CRONE!"

The power of the earth flowed through Sláine with a heady vengeance, driving rationality from his mind. It sang in his veins. It surged through his heart. He was alive. He was one with the earth and sky, after so long cut off from it he was rapidly growing drunk on the love of his Goddess. This was his land. His home.

"SHOW YOURSELF, CRONE!"

The Knucker rose again, carrying them higher. Sláine saw the familiar outline of Murias, the amazing physicality of the town and its surrounds laid out on the green. The fast-flowing River Dôn was little more than a slash through the perfect emerald.

Sláine was assailed by memories of Fionn and Dian and Núada and Niall and Cullen and Cormac, childhood lost.

He could just make out the conical shaped tor and the rise of Lugh's Spike looming imperiously, a steely grey finger accusing the heavens, and found himself remembering the day of the Choosing. Now, with the gift of hindsight, it seemed as though all their fates had been cast that day despite the fact that they were only thirteen years old. He thought of Cullen. He didn't like remembering Wide

Mouth. Guilt made him uncomfortable. No matter how fierce their rivalry had seemed, it had been little more than the petty jealousies of children in reality. It should never have been allowed to spiral out of control, to cost Wide Mouth his life. That forfeit was a harsh one for a child to pay, no matter that it had been meted out by another child. And it didn't matter that they had enacted some rite of passage, they had been children.

The memory was a bitter one; friendship torn through lost innocence. It had never mattered who claimed the Daughter of Danu's devotion first, or who threw the javelin farthest, who ran the fastest or leapt highest, but it had felt so important back then when all it had ever been was just another way of goading Wide Mouth. No more, no less.

Sláine could smell the mountains, the sudden rush of fragrances, the lavender and the oak, the pollen and the oast. He could hear the dead voices of his parents, Macha and Roth, ghosts on the wind.

His gaze followed the dark slash of the river through the tufts of long grasses and brambles, drovers' paths and dry-stone walls, the barrows and the cromlechs, hints of grey stone exposed by the savage slashes in the wild turf, past the nemeton to the straw roof and wattle walls of Grudnew's roundhouse. Sláine had forgotten just how truly breathtaking his home was. Before he could dwell upon memories of Niamh, the Knucker soared, the thermals carrying the beast away from the comfort of the home hearth, banking towards the forest where Sláine had first encountered the Crone, where he had chased the Maiden so full of lust and hope, and where ultimately he had learned the hardest lesson of his young life, watching the women of Murias put to the sword.

For the first time in years he allowed himself to miss his friends, such was the weight of his homecoming. He took no joy from the memories. Remembering got in the way of what he had to do.

"CRONE!" he called again, summoning the Morrigan. The wind ripped away his words. She did not answer him, not that he had expected her to come running at his beck and call. Sláine pounded the saddle horn in frustration. "YOU OWE ME, WOMAN!"

"There is a place," Myrrdin said, his words strained as he struggled to maintain his grip in the saddle. The druid's face was troubled, and not merely by the wild flight of the drake. Something weighed heavily on his mind. "It is not far from here. They call it Magh Tuiredh, the plain of pillars."

"I do not know it," Sláine said, knuckles a bloodless white as he clutched the saddle horn.

"I will guide you, if you wish a confrontation with the Crone. She cannot resist you there. The power of the Earth Mother is at its strongest within the circle of stones. Blood was spilled there. Heroes's blood stains the earth there still, soaked deep. The blood is a mortal tie between you and the heroes of another age, Sláine. It is where Llew Silverhand lost his hand in battle against the creatures of the Fir Bolg, and near where Weyland the Smith forged its replacement. Like you, Llew was a champion of Danu. The Morrigan will come when you call. She will have no choice; she will be answering the blood call. Blood magic is strong. As champion of her sister you have a right of redress, she cannot ignore that."

"Take me there."

FROM ABOVE MAGH Tuiredh looked like a field of teeth chomping out of the belly of the earth; diseased yellow and brown teeth.

Sláine was struck by how similar it was to the dolmen of Carnac – but so much closer to home. He felt the draw of the stones in his blood as they banked and circled, spiralling lower. Slough Feg had gathered hundreds upon hundreds of dolmens to the sacred burial grounds of Carnac, souring the land as they leeched the vitality from it. That such a place could exist so close to Murias sent a chill bone-deep.

The Knucker landed amid the barren stones.

Even now it stank of death. Blood had seeped into the stones, sacrificed in battle to the unforgiving aspect of the war Goddess. Sláine slid down from the Knucker's back, grateful to have the ground beneath his feet once more. The draw of the stones on his blood intensified, like lightning coursing through his veins. It was so like – and yet unlike – Carnac. His flesh responded to the lure of the Earth Serpent, but where there it had drained him, weakening him to the point of collapse, here his blood thrilled to it.

He threw his arms wide, moving between the broken dolmens, touching the grey stones, feeling the echoes of suffering, death and battle resonate back through his fingertips. He felt truly alive for the first time he could remember. Myrrdin and Ukko stood on the edge of the stones, as though fearful of violating their sanctity. Sláine harboured no such reservations. He moved from stone to stone, feeding off the residual energy still bound within them. For a moment it felt as though he could absorb even the trace memories of the rock, bringing to life in his mind all the things they had seen. He turned in a full circle, looking out over Magh Tuiredh, imagining it as the battlefield it had been. He savoured the sadness of the place. He saw bodies piled one atop another, guts unravelled, he saw skulls split in two, throats cut, arms clutching at dropped blades. He saw swords driven through ribcages, crows perched on their pommels, the silver blades thrust deep into the belly of the earth. The rancid stench of death rose up out of the ground to fill his nostrils. The wind rose. Sláine knelt, pressing his fingers into the dirt. It was moist with blood.

He shook his head.

The Sidhe had called him Defiler, a word that bordered on evil, the spoiling of innocence, and yet the slaughter of this place, the blood-soaked earth, the death of families and reason, all defiled the innocence of the earth. Still the place remained sanctified, devoted to Danu, albeit in her aspect as the war Goddess. She was not an innocent Goddess. She was as much the mother of war as she was the maiden of flowers or the old hag of the ravens. She was all stages of the sacred feminine, beautiful in all her incarnations. He was no different from these heroes. Myrrdin had said so himself, there was a link between his flesh and Llew Silverhand and all those other heroes of his people. It was the *riastrad*, the warp spasm. He was the earth itself; he felt the insidious sickness of Slough Feg's tainted sour. His flesh answered the call of theirs across the generations. When his musculature warped, the power of the Earth Serpent thundering through his flesh, he was no longer the man, Sláine, he was the champion of his Goddess, eternal: he was Cúchulainn, he was Bran the Blessed, he was Llew Silverhand. He was Sláine Mac Roth.

Sláine looked to the sky, expecting to see the carrion birds circling, so rich was the illusion his mind painted for him.

"Bring her to me, druid."

Myrrdin nodded. "As you wish, champion. What you see and hear may not be pleasant, but it is necessary. I will invoke the pain of this place, stirring memories in the land best left forgotten. She is woven within these memories. She will answer your call. Remember, all that you see is memory, you cannot change anything, you cannot influence what has been, you cannot save lives that have been lost."

"The past does not frighten me, druid, why should it? It cannot reach out to hurt us. The present is full of threats enough. The land is souring. Feg marches north with his damned skull swords, spreading his blight and scheming for Ragnarok. The Crone has been manipulating our every step for centuries, it seems. I would not be surprised to learn Feg himself dances to her piper's tune. So a few ghosts neither interest nor frighten me. I am only interested in the future of my people."

"Good, my friend. There is wisdom in the single-mindedness of that thought, but do not be blinded by it. Our time together runs short; I can feel the truth of that on the aether. There is much that both of us must accomplish from here. And while our destinies cross, they are separate paths we must walk alone." They clasped hands in farewell. "I urge you to remember who it is you are meeting out there between the stones, Sláine. The Morrigan can speak sweetly and can promise she never speaks false. No lies spill from her lips, but seldom does a single word ring true. She has a way of twisting the truth so that it sounds appealing even when it is vile and murderous. Do not blindly offer promises, do not bargain with her, for no matter how good the bargain seems on the surface, no one ever emerges unscathed from negotiations with the Morrigan. We have what she desires, two pieces of her son's prison. She will attempt to lure you with promises of future glories, listen not to those honeyed words. Go with Danu, Sláine."

Too late, Sláine thought to himself, as he watched the druid walk into the centre of the field. With a chalk stone drawn from within the folds of his cloak, Myrrdin paced the battlefield, drawing intricate symbols, some in Ogham, others in a script Sláine did not recognise, on the cracked and broken dolmens. He had lied, he did fear the unknown. Only a fool wouldn't and he was no fool. The druid marked out twelve standing stones and paced out a circle encompassing the six most distant, then uttering the beginnings of a long summoning ritual, moved from point to point within the circle before kneeling in the centre, equidistant from all points on the outer circle, and from all points on the inner circle. He murmured another strain of the invocation, taking a handful of the dirt from the ground and scattering it to each of the cardinal directions of the wind. The wind blew away his words.

Sláine and Ukko stood silent sentry, watching the ritual unfold as slowly the sounds of battle rose around them. Sláine did not trust his senses fully, believing somehow the earth's magic had flooded his mind and the ghosts of the conquered he saw shimmering into existence all across Magh Tuiredh were no more than figments of his imagination or the melancholy of the land's great regret given substance through the strength of his blood.

"What in the seven els?" Ukko muttered, backing away from the stones.

A ghostly warrior, sky-clad, woad-dyed hair streaming wildly behind him, charged straight through the dwarf, stone axe raised high above his head. The ghostly warrior's death-cry was still on his lips as he faded into the aether. Ukko shuddered, knees buckling. He straightened, face pained, and made the sign of the Gallic cross over his chest. A heartbeat later another warrior, face sallow, aquiline, beneath close-cropped raven-black hair, emerged from Ukko's chest, a short stabbing sword in his hand. The memories of blood streamed over the leather strips of his kilt. His stomach was bare where leather armour had been sliced away; the muscles flapped open, lengths of ropy intestine spilling out between the bloody fingers of his left hand. Ukko couldn't look away as the soldier collapsed to his knees, showing the soles of his leather sandals before lurching sideways and collapsing. The mud of Magh Tuiredh swallowed his flesh, to the earth returned.

He watched in mute horror as all across the battlefield more and more warriors rose, recalled to life by the druid's summons, only to fall, reliving their deaths, the battlefield ringing with their cries of death and suffering.

Ukko gripped his own stomach, feeling the lingering pain of the soldier's death bite within his own muscles.

Behind them the Knucker growled, the sound reverberating deep in the drake's throat, as more and more ethereal warriors gathered substance around it.

Surrounded on all sides by the dead reliving their great sacrifice, Myrrdin Emrys threw back his head, calling on the ancient pain of the place. His body convulsed beneath the ecstasy of the invocation. Spasms of pure physical delight tore through his slight frame, his wooden eyes burning. The wind rose and the sky darkened, the elements responding to his demand as over and over he shrieked the Crone's many names, demanding her presence here amongst the dead she had already claimed, calling upon the ties of the blood their sacrifice had forged.

And out of the storm she came, walking among the dead. She carried the third fragment of the Cauldron.

She reached out with her free hand, touching the spirits. As her fingers lingered on the memories of their flesh and the agonies of battle, they shimmered, losing substance, and failed, fading into the aether. She whispered hushed words as she moved between them, her face bereft of its customary hardness as she released the dead from the torments of remembering one at a time.

The Morrigan stood before the druid, tears in her dark eyes as she lashed out, slapping him across the face. "I will not forget this, druid. Neither will I forgive it. Mark my words, Myrrdin. This is my land. I have walked it for thousands of years. I love it in a way you can never hope to comprehend. I am made of the dirt, the hopes of the people flow through my veins. It is all that I am, just as I am all that remains of it. I love this land. I love my children just as I love my sisters and my sisters love this land and her people, druid. Their pain hurts my sisters and I deeply. You crossed a line here, with this. So many innocent souls forced into reliving the agony and folly of mankind when they should be at peace. Your arrogance is too much but I will see you humbled. And one day your soul will be mine, in my darkest aspcct. Never forget that."

"Your threats do not frighten me any longer, old woman," said Myrrdin.

"They should, *old man*. They should," she chittered, the dislike implicit in her tone. "Believe me when I say they are not idle. I have torments in mind that will become legendary amongst the dead, that is my promise to you, Lord of the Trees."

"I have no doubt, witch, but I have nothing to lose now except my life, and this life is not such a good place to be."

"For one who thinks he knows so much your ignorance is staggering, druid. This life is the *only* place to be. Look around you, look at the shades you forced to rise, and tell me you cannot feel their hunger to be back here, in this place where once they loved and lived and died?"

"I feel nothing," said Myrrdin.

"Then you are as good as dead already, and not worthy of my concern." She turned to Sláine, something approaching affection in her face as she smiled and offered up the third piece of the Cauldron to him. Her smile was a physically repugnant thing. His skin crawled. "This is what you want. Return my son to me, warrior."

Sláine took the relic from her, marvelling at the hideous intricacy of the lumpen face embossed in the metal bezel. In places it looked as though the features had melted. There was no nose and part of the creature's left cheek had been eaten away. Huge fangs formed the handle, the distended teeth chipped and broken. This was, he knew, no mere rendition of the face of Avagddu, son of the Goddess, it was the poor demented child, locked in the black iron. He touched the beast's melted face, wondering for a moment if it could feel his fingers.

"This is what it was all for?" Sláine said, without looking up from Avagddu's ravaged visage. "This was why my mother died? Why Wide Mouth died? This was why Finvarra died and all the rest? For this monstrosity?"

The Crone's mask slipped, the affection torn from her face. In its place burned hatred unlike anything Sláine had ever seen, hatred borne of millennia. "Do not goad me, warrior. I did not kill those you loved, nor those you loathed. You did that, you with your stone axe and your damned temper. I did not make you, as much as you would like to excuse your actions, and leave the blame at my feet. You own your actions, *champion*. Those fields of blood are yours. Those broken bodies are yours. Those tattered lives are yours. You would return to your people, to atone for some guilt that no doubt burns within you, I would have my son back, our interests cross for this moment and this moment alone. I did not curse your life, Sláine. You did that all by yourself. I did not make you fall for my pretty sister like a love-sick simpleton. I did not goad you into hurling that gae bolga at Cullen of the Wide Mouth. I did not force you to run with the Red Branch and leave Macha in the care of a drunk. And I most certainly was not the one who rutted with Grufbad's promised maiden. That was your cock you buried in her, your pasty white arse you bared, not mine. You knew what would happen when you were caught, and still you did it, and not once, but again and again, addicted to the danger, wanting to be caught because you were angry at some outrageous sense of betrayal you wanted to believe the old man had done to you, so you cuckolded him. Your exile was your own doing, just as now your return is your own doing. By rights he should have executed you, but the old man had pity. Excuses are easy to find, but a man must own his life, all aspects of it."

Sláine met her hate-filled eyes, unflinching. "You have a clever way of twisting words to suit your need, Morrigan. There is no doubt about that. If I must own *my* actions, I think it is only fair you own yours. It is no coincidence that our 'wants' have crossed. You have fashioned it thus, laying plans that have taken years to come to be."

"Aren't you the clever one, boy? So what if I have served my own purpose? What does it matter to you if my son is returned in the process of you getting what *you* want? You cannot pretend to me that your actions are anything but self-serving, warrior. I have known you and your kind for eternity. Your home was my home long before you were a mote in time's eye, and it will be mine again long after you are dust. I want my son freed; wouldn't any mother want the same? Wouldn't Macha want that for you if the roles were reversed? So save me your self-righteous indignation. Give me my son back and then I will give you the world in return. That is my offer. Take it, champion."

He wanted to say so much, to defend himself, thrust Feg's book in her face until she understood what was at stake, but he forced his anger down, feeling it seethe within his blood. He dropped his sack, opening the drawstring, and put the third fragment inside. When he looked up his face was set, hard.

"Good," the Morrigan said. "There is a cave nearby, where Wayland the Smith shelters. He has the final fragment of the Cauldron, but go lightly, warrior. He is of another time, born of Sidhe blood, last of his kind. He harbours woes of his own that have festered long. In their time, he served as first smith to the Titans, the most skilful of their craftsmen. But he was also a murderous one, tempering his finest blades with the blood of heroes and fashioning gifts for kings from their bones."

"A friendly sort, then," Ukko said, appearing from behind Sláine. "Don't tell me, he's just misunderstood, right? What I want to know is why these ancient relics are never guarded by sweet little old ladies who want to smother you with gummy kisses and bake you a nice cake because they are happy to see you? They're always the fiercest most miserable cusses who want to rip you limb from limb soon as look at you. Frankly, I'm sick and tired of fighting monsters and being heroic. It's dull. I want to bury my face in a big buxom pair of tits and not come up for air for a week."

Ignoring the dwarf, the Morrigan continued: "I do not for a heartbeat believe he will surrender the shard lightly, but I will have my son returned to me, Sláine."

THROUGH THE FADING whispers of the ghosts and the raucous caws of the crows came another sound, slow, rich and rhythmic. Sláine was drawn to the furthest edge of Magh Tuiredh by the ringing of hammer on anvil, though without knowing the great smith was there he would never have discerned the sound amid the chaos of memories and hungry birds.

Sláine was weary, footsore and voraciously hungry. He walked through the path of stones observing the patterns the birds flew in above him and the omens the thick dark cloud promised. *You cannot save Tir-Nan-Og one soul at a time, champion.* The words haunted him still, though in truth he had never heard them spoken. The Morrigan had reached out a feathered hand, her touch lingering on his cheek, and in his mind, a parting gift, the words came unbidden. It was witchery, of that there was no doubt. The Crone had reached into his mind and left the thought like damnation for him to dwell on.

"Is that what I am trying to do?" he said aloud. Ukko looked at him strangely. No, he wasn't looking at him, he was looking *beyond* him. Sláine turned to see seven stone statues, three times his own height, gruesomely ugly in their craftsmanship, brutish gnarled faces overhung by a thick atavistic brow and vacant eye sockets chiselled deep into the stone. Fat cracked lips and tombstone teeth jutted out beneath bulbous noses. The sculptor had worked tangled hanks of hair into the granite, giving each trollish beast an uncomfortably lifelike mien. Sláine moved closer, marvelling at the sheer bulk of the statues and the workmanship of them. The wrist of the first stone troll was thicker than his neck. He moved down the line. Save one they were all turned to face the stones of Magh Tuiredh, merging with the pattern of the rune-carved standing stones. One had a drum at its feet, another had a pile of stones carved like bones. The exception faced due west, towards the steady clangour of the smith's hammer. Sláine moved around the statue. Its face was unlike the others; the troll had no nose. In its place there was a wickedly curved beak, like that of a crow. The statue had a bull-neck, deep crevices weathering into the stone, opening its throat. Malformed arms hung low, knuckles dragging on the grass.

He walked around it again, slowly.

"This is one pig-ugly effigy," Ukko said, staring up into the gaping black of the statue's enormous nostril. He reached out, resting a hand on the stature's pendulous gut, and nodded up at the sagging pectorals. "Kind of reminds me of you, your warpishness. Maybe it's a throwback? What do you think Myrrdin?"

"The Sisters of Magh Tuiredh are quite beautiful, I think," the druid said. "Each in her own way. Not that Sláine doesn't have his moments, of course."

"Sisters?" Ukko said, his face puckering up as though punched. "You mean to say this thing is *female*? You know what I said about burying my face in a big pair of tits? If these are them I take it back."

Myrrdin chuckled indulgently. "You, my lascivious little friend, frequently remind us how much you appreciate the fuller figure. The Sisters are renditions of the divine, raised of the earth just as she is, bountiful and generous in their endowments–"

"Fat," Ukko put in.

"–just as she is. It is fair to say that the sisters were primitive man's attempts to capture the essence of the Earth Mother, to give their faith flesh."

"Ooh, they gave it plenty of flesh all right."

Sláine stopped, realising that the last note of the smith's hammer had faded into silence. He craned his head, listening but slowly, sound by sound, the quiet was distilled. The smith did not take up his hammer again.

"He knows we are here," said Myrrdin. "No doubt the sisters told him."

"They're stone," Ukko said, rolling his eyes, "unlike the bloody great flock of birds circling around our heads. Now, if you'd care to wager: your talking stone against my squawking crows, I'd be more than happy to take your coin off you."

"And here I was thinking you slow-witted, friend Ukko."

"I didn't spend my life herding sheep or mincing around the woods whispering to trees like some people."

"Be that as it may, we shall have to find ourselves another wager on another day. For now, this is where our journey together ends, my friends," said Myrrdin, grasping Sláine's forearm. "The smith's forge lies beyond the crest of this hill, in the shadow of the Sister's beaked nose; it leads the way for the curious. My presence with the smith will only hinder you, and as there is much I must yet do, I think it best we make this our parting of the ways."

Sláine studied Myrrdin's face silently. There was something in the old man's expression that silenced any objection. He drew the druid into an embrace and slapped him on the back. "I will miss your company."

"You have the dwarf to keep you honest."

"As I said, I will miss you."

"The Morrigan did not lie; the smith will not surrender the final piece willingly, and if we are together perhaps not at all. He has reason to hate the Crone and her son, and my hands are far from bloodless in his tragedy. It would not do to provoke his anger, or remind him of her betrayal. The Goddess's speed to you," he turned to Ukko, "and to you, little man."

"Just as I was beginning to like you, you have to go and leave."

"You mean just as you were beginning to delight in the imagined riches my purse had to offer?"

"Like I said," Ukko grinned, "friendship's a funny thing but the best kind of friendship is one where you both get what you want out of it."

"I'm not certain what worries me more," the druid said to Sláine, "that he actually thinks this way, or that we have been together so long the way he thinks is actually beginning to make sense to me?"

"That's the enigma of me," said Ukko, bowing with a flourish.

"I think I might actually miss you, dwarf."

"How about you give me your coin so I have something to remember you by then? I'll take good care of it, I promise."

"I don't doubt it for a moment but I think we should bid our farewells before the ineluctable laws of stupidity and avarice collide, don't you?"

Ukko peered at him, not bothering to hide his confusion. "I have got no idea what you are talking about, druid."

"I believe that was the first law making itself known," Myrrdin said with a grin. "We'd best be quick with our farewells lest the second law take one of us unawares."

"Why do I get the feeling I'm the butt of what passes for mirth around here?" Ukko said.

SLÁINE AND UKKO followed the thin shadow cast by the Sister's beak, scrambling across the ride of shallow mounds, while Myrrdin turned his back on the seven stone Sisters and trudged, bone-weary, back across the battlefield.

They left the Knucker feeding on a goat carcass it had found.

The declivity beyond the last hill was sharp, the bottom of the slope deceptively far below. The shadow was blunted by a ring of stones and charred wood: the remnants of a cooking fire.

There were low bushes and overhanging trees, ash and oak and rowan, hawthorn and sycamore, trees that once would have been at the heart of a great wood now enclosed the fire, giving it the air of seclusion. And while there was no beaten track the ragweed around the fire pit had obviously been tramped flat by huge lumbering feet, as had much of the grasses leading back into the side of the hill almost directly beneath their feet. Sláine assumed they stood above some sort of entrance, which meant that it wasn't a hill they were standing on. The secrets of the earth lay beneath the surface. A mine perhaps, where the smith gathered his ore to fashion miraculous things fit for the demi-gods who he used to serve? On either side of the mound thorns intertwined with briarwood and poison oak to form a natural wall.

There was no sign of the smith.

Sláine stumbled, reaching out for a handful of scree to stall his slide. His boots kicked up chips of stone as he scrambled for purchase, tripping over his own feet as he finally lost his footing and fell, tumbling to the base of the hill. Only it wasn't a hill, or a mine, Sláine realised, it was a burial mound. The entrance was cut deep into the hill, the stonework around the arch carved with the same craftsmanship and eye to detail as the Sisters had been, the lintel deeply scored with Ogham:

"Do not mourn, I am not here," Ukko said, reading the inscription.

The words were vaguely familiar. It took him a moment to place them: the song of mourning the harpist, Siothrún, had played for Caoilfhionn the Weatherwitch. Similar but not the same. Not exactly.

But too close to be coincidental.

There was a link between the harpist and the smith, Finvarra, the dead witch, the druid and the Crone. Myrrdin had said the smith was half-Sidhe; that the blood of the fey folk flowed in his veins. Caoilfhionn had come to him that first night out of Dardun and her words had led him across worlds on his journey home, binding him to the Crone and her quest for her lost child. The Wounded King was Sidhe, his home a palace of glass where death had no dominion. In the eyes of the world he was dead, and had been for centuries, and yet he lived.

"Only a fool would mourn the living," said Sláine, finally beginning to see something of the tangled web they had woven around him. The strands were beginning to work loose, revealing their secrets, and what secrets they were. The harpist's song couldn't have been for the witch, unless... unless... Caoilfhionn was bound to the fallen king, unable to join her love in death for he was not truly dead. The notion sent a thrill of excitement through Sláine. The harpist was not mourning the woman, he was mourning the king they were condemning to death.

That night, when Sláine had dreamed of the Weatherwitch and she had told him hope lay with the Skinless Man, the hope she spoke of was the damnation of her beloved Finvarra, nothing more, nothing less. He knew the dead woman now; Caoilfhionn, the queen of the fey, beloved of Finvarra in this world and the next. Her words set his feet on a journey, but one masked from even his own understanding. She fired his blood with thoughts of going home, manipulating him into the Morrigan's quest as much if not more than the Crone ever had, but this manoeuvring was nothing more than misdirection. Everything had been about Sláine breaking the geas on Ynys Afallach and in doing so ending the curse that kept two lovers apart and a world from mourning.

"What are you talking about?" Ukko said, picking himself up from where he had landed, sprawled in the trampled grass.

"Do not mourn, I am not here. This is Finvarra's tomb, only he was never buried here because of Myrrdin and the Morrigan. He wasn't allowed to die. Who else wouldn't be in their own tomb? The song of mourning we sang with the harpist was for the Wounded King's wife, or rather the king himself, soon to be joined in eternity with Caoilfhionn once again."

"You're a romantic soul, Sláine. Soft in the head, but there's no denying the romance in your soul."

The harpist emerged from the darkness of the tomb, only now he was stripped to the waist and sheened in the sweat of exertion, his muscles hard. He held a ruby-encrusted goblet fashioned from human bone. His hair was pulled back from his face in a neat braid, his brow smeared with the soot of the fire. Half in and half out of the sunlight, the glow gave his skin more colour than the last time they had seen the man, but it was still impossibly pale and pitted with pox scars. He looked different though, more human. His wispish body belied the immense power bound within his rigid muscles.

"You have a passing fair voice for a blacksmith, Siothrún," Sláine said, "or should I call you Weyland?"

The smith inclined his head, accepting the compliment. "There is a difference between a gift and a craft, warrior. You may be an artist with a brush and a butcher with an axe. One tool does not demark the man, rather a man can be many things."

"Indeed."

"You have me at a disadvantage, I must admit. I did not expect to see you again, and yet you have found your way back to me and barely a season has passed. I underestimated you, a mistake I will not make again in a hurry." He set the bone goblet aside. "I assume you know this place?"

"The barrow of kings," said Sláine, nodding. "Or one king, Finvarra."

The smith smiled. "Perhaps my queen was right about you after all, Sláine Mac Roth."

"We all make mistakes, I was sure this dance was the Crone's doing. I did not look past the obvious. Instead I was content to believe this was her tune, the saga all about her child."

"Oh, but it was," the smith said, reaching behind his head to loosen the tie holding his hair back. He shook it loose. "And more to the point, it still is. You have the shards of the old Cú Roi of Goibniu?"

Sláine nodded.

"Which means the geas Myrrdin and the Morrigan placed on the Isle of Glass must have been broken and Finvarra released from his torment. Soon I will journey to what remains of the isle to reclaim his corpse and lay him to rest here, beside his beloved. This place was once the home of the Sidhe, did you know that? Tir-Nan-Og, Land of the Young. Who did you think the 'young' were? It is only fitting that in death absolute, the king is brought home. But you have more pressing needs, no? You want the final part of the Cauldron, and if I am any judge, you're about to go down on your knees and beg me to reforge the relic, are you not?"

"I beg no man," said Sláine.

"A pity, for I am in no mood to be generous. You need it to return home, as my queen foretold, and your bleak Goddess needs it to free her get; without my aid now you are both thwarted. You see, we counted on her arrogance and your ignorance. I look at you now and I see failure and doubt eating away at you. The protector of the Cú Roi must be resolute for the Cauldron is the womb of the Goddess, the source of all things, of life and death and rebirth. It can feed, give drink, heal, nay restore life, soothe raging spears. Its waters contain wisdom – more, it joins the firmament, the primordial soup that was the place of creation. The Cú Roi is more than a mere treasure to be traded; it nurtures the Goddess, it feeds the land."

"If this is so, why deprive us of its magic? You have what you want, Finvarra is released, the Isle of Glass shattered to ten thousand thousand shards."

"No, no, no, warrior. I do not have what I want. I have not had what I *want* for years beyond counting. I *had* what I wanted, but it was wrenched away from me and I was left bereft. It is a world of trades. I helped my queen fulfil her desires so that I might earn back what I lost."

"Explain yourself, smith. You talk in circles."

"Let me show you, warrior. To see is to understand; words are empty."

THEY STOOD BESIDE a small tarn, the water crystal blue, the imperfections of the ripples and the reflected sky adding to its loveliness. A single swan swam in the tarn, its white feathers heavy with water as it glided through the ripples, making more.

"This is what you wanted me to see?"

"Yes," the smith said, melancholy heavy in his voice. He knelt at the water's edge with a handful of seed, trying to entice the bird to him.

"A bird?"

"Sit, let me tell you her story, then perhaps you will understand."

"Tell me, smith. First you say seeing it will make me understand because words are empty, now you want to waste words on me? Which is it?"

"They are rare birds, swans. The female is fiercely loyal to the male. Unlike many species, they are faithful to one another, and mate for life. If the male dies, the female will still resolutely spurn all other loves until she too dies. It is quite remarkable really, one of the beautiful aspects of nature."

"Do you have a point?"

"Besides boring us to death," said Ukko, picking up a flat stone and skimming it across the water. The sudden flurry of movement startled the swan. Its huge wings unfurled, slapping up water as it splashed across the small lake to the other side.

"I do. I do. It is my curse to love the Swan Maiden. She was a gift to me in my loneliness, to be my mate for life."

"She's a bird, you know, flap, flap, flap," Ukko mimed wings, "isn't that a bit sick? I mean I am all for a bit of you know what, but aren't there certain, ah, practicalities, what with her being roughly the same size as your todger?"

"She was made human by Danu so that I might know true love after years of being caught between worlds, neither Sidhe nor human, and she was beautiful, believe me."

"Ahh, well that makes more sense. Even so, she's a bird now, so...?"

"I would have her back, only then am I prepared to help you."

"That is impossible, man. I cannot work magic. Miracles are the realm of the Goddess, not a warrior. I cannot grant such a boon."

"Then you will not leave this place with your treasure, it is as simple as that."

"How can I do it? Tell me? I cannot wave my fingers and make it so," Sláine said bitterly. "Is there an artefact? A quest? What? What can I do?"

The smith shook his head. "There is no treasure that can undo my pain. She is dead to me and dead to this realm."

"Then I don't understand. You hold us to ransom with the impossible?"

A fat crow settled on one of the branches of the briarwood. It craned its neck, beady yellow eyes glaring intently at the smith as it preened its glossy feathers. The intelligence, cold and calculating, betrayed it as the Morrigan's creature long before it spoke. "My sister warned you, smith," the bird cawed, its voice raucous, harsh. "Her gift was pure and heartfelt. You only have yourself to blame for your loneliness now."

Sláine watched as Weyland the Smith clenched his fists, knuckles white, cracking. Anger and guilt tore at the man in equal measure. Sláine understood: he had had happiness and he had thrown it away. The guilt would be impossible to live with.

The bird hopped from branch to branch, mocking the man.

"You would have your vile son released from the hell he is trapped in, Morrigan? Well, I have no love for you, or your damned sisters. What I have is a price: a life for a life. Nature is a constant conflict, a turmoil seeking balance. My price is this: I would have my Swan Maiden returned to me that I might know happiness once more. That is a fair bargain for all: you purchase your son's freedom, the warrior gets his treasure so that he might return home a hero, and I get my wife. Otherwise, let Avagddu rot in a world of rust, let the Sessair return home to face execution, I care not for mortal or immortal concerns."

"You cannot turn back time, smith," the bird cackled, taking momentary flight in a flurry of black wings. It alighted a moment later in the branches of the ash tree. "Burn the feathers, she said. Burn them all. But arrogant mortals don't listen, oh no, they make mirrors of silver to store a single memory, a feather from the bird that was. Mirrors break, bad luck. For you and for your bride, bad luck for the bird."

"How could I know?" the smith pleaded, and Sláine finally understood. Somehow that single feather the man had kept as a token had broken the enchantment, returning the smith's woman to her avian form.

"You were warned. Promises broken, gifts lost."

The bird took flight once more, flitting across the sky before swooping low in a shimmering blur, the twisted form of the Morrigan emerging from the bird's form as it landed amid the flotsam and jetsam of the lakeside. The Crone shuffled towards them, crook-backed, the weight of the years and the tragedy of so many lifetimes upon her shoulders. She thrust a finger towards the smith accusingly. "You want, you want, you want," she heckled, the raucous braying of the bird still present in her voice as she mocked him. "Blodeuwedd is always too loving, her nature to sweet. You took her gift and cast it aside in your arrogance, smith. You refused to listen to the warning. It was no threat – she does not trade in that currency. She loved you and wanted to please you, but all you could think about was your craft – a perfect silver mirror to reflect the beauty of your precious Swan Maiden. Well, mirrors crack, dreams fail and happiness flees. That is the nature of this mortality. That is what galls the most, is it not? Hate festers within you, hate for me, my sister self, the druid, even fate itself, but you cannot own your guilt. You lash out, blaming everyone and everything, yet it is you who is to blame."

"You took her from me, Morrigan. She was my life."

"And now you want her back. She can never be the same again, you understand that?"

"Did you not overhear my conversation with your champion? We are bonded, mates for life. I need her at my side."

"So be it." She turned to Sláine. "Surrender the fragments of the Cauldron to the smith. The bargain has been struck, the price met. I will give him back his pretty one, a life for a life as he so rightly claims, nature will retain her balance *precisely* as it is," and to Weyland the Smith she said, "Now go about your craft. What follows is not for your eyes if you would still love your wife. When you emerge with the Cauldron reforged she will be waiting for you."

WITH THE SOUND of the smith's hammer ringing in the darkness of the barrow, the Morrigan called the bird to her. The Lady of the Feathers had an affinity with the white swan; the bird showed no fear as it glided across the still water to be with her, and appeared quite serene as it laid its head in her callused palm.

"Hush little one, your lover would have you back," the Crone soothed, stroking back the feathers on the swan's head. "It will hurt, it always does," and before Sláine understood what was happening, the Morrigan gripped the bird's neck and wrung it with one brutally sharp twist. The swan's wings flapped on wildly despite the fact that the animal was dead, its nerves crying out as the pain filtered through to its brain for a full minute before they fell still.

Cradling the dead swan in her arms, the Morrigan walked back across to the fire pit, whispered a word and the flames ignited, rising higher and brighter than they reasonably could have from the charred remains that gave them life. The heat emanating from them was intense, fierce enough to drive Sláine and Ukko back a dozen paces to move away from its sting. The Morrigan lifted the dead swan above her head, mouthing a benediction neither of them could hear for the snap and cackle of the flames, and threw the carcass into the hottest part of the fire.

For a moment the fire seemed to wash over the swan without touching it, then the tips of the feathers began to singe, and the dark edge smeared across more of the wings as they charred. Within seconds they were black and shrivelled, the flames eating away at the bird, not merely roasting it. Sláine stared in mute horror as the swan was utterly consumed. It happened so quickly; the carcass succumbed, the meat flensed from the bone, the bones reduced to ash. Within a minute all trace of the swan was eradicated by the fire.

The Morrigan mouthed another word, and as abruptly as it had been born the fire died back to nothing. She knelt amid the ashes, stirring them with her crooked fingers, until she found a single fragment of bone, which she raised to her lips, breathing life onto it. She stepped back, holding the bone chip to her lips. She drew air into her lungs, over the bone. Her breath agitated the ash in the fire pit, causing first one flake to rise, and then another, and two more and more until the air around the bone was full of ash – ash that until a moment before had been the flesh of the swan. The Crone manipulated the bone, stirring the flakes of ash into hypnotic life. And out of the spiral of grey and black, thick and heavy in the air before them, a shape began to take form, limbs gaining substance, face taking on shape.

The intensity of the smith's hammering deepened, the notes of metal on metal taking on a deeper resonance as his task progressed. The barrow dampened the harmonic but there was no mistaking the similarity it bore to the ever-present resonance that had haunted the Wounded King's home. To Sláine it appeared as though the ash danced to the tune of the smith's hammer, not the manipulations of the Crone's fingers.

There was beauty in the ash.

The ash clung to her face, lending it a deathly pallor, the flakes lapping and overlapping like the scales of a lizard to form features: delicate, high cheekbones, the sunken hollows of eyes that could not see, the gentle curve of cracked lips, the cleft dimple of her chin.

The rhythm of Weyland the Smith's hammer blows shifted subtly, matching the movements of the

Swan Maiden as she rose from the ashes of flame, gradually recapturing yesterday's glory.

Sláine could do nothing but stare as the Morrigan crushed the bone beneath her seemingly frail fingers, powdering it. As the fine bone-dust fell through her fingers the heaviest of the scales of ash fell from the risen woman, revealing raw pink skin beneath. She was enchanting, truly a thing of beauty, but then she was not real, not fashioned from sweat and sperm and grunts, she was an ideal, her features shaped by the mind of an immortal. It was no wonder that the smith lamented her loss. She was elemental, raw. The fire that had birthed her still burned in her eyes, the wind that fanned the flames surged through her veins, the earth that gave her flesh substance and the water that was her natural home, all of these combined inside the woman to recreate the love that the smith had so carelessly lost.

But it was not her. Sláine knew that. She was a thing, just as a painting on a cave wall was or a crude image scratched in Ogham on vellum was. She was nothing more than a reproduction. The swan was dead, the Morrigan had banished her soul to the Otherworld with a single sharp twist of the wrist. What had risen in her place was nothing more than a doppelganger raised from the ash of her bones to stand in her place. As the last of the ash fell away the Swan Maiden raised a hand to touch her face. Her mouth moved but no sounds issued forth–but then the dead could not speak.

Sláine held out his hand for her, to lead her from the fire pit.

Her flesh was mortally cold.

He led her towards the mouth of the barrow, the insidious cold creeping up within his flesh. Together, they waited beneath the keystone with its enigmatic inscription until the sound of the hammer blows stopped. And longer still they waited, looking into the heart of the darkness while they waited for the smith to emerge carrying the Cú Roi of Goibniu in his hands, whole once more. He dropped the Cauldron and ran, sweeping the dead maiden up in his arms.

"My love, is it you? Is it truly you? I cannot believe… so long have I longed to hear your voice, to know that you forgive my stupidity." He held her, his hands on either side of her face. "Tell me that you love me."

But no words came to sooth his pain or quell the emptiness, no tenderness from her lips even as her hands mirrored the intimacy of his gesture, cradling his face. And he understood the Morrigan's duplicitous promise: the balance of nature shall be preserved, a life for a life. The Swan Maiden's flesh was here, an empty chalice, her essence lost now wherever Avagddu's had been, while Avagddu was finally released from his prison, able to give voice to his anger and his hungers. The Morrigan had traded the Swan Maiden's spirit, her voice and her mind, in return for the release of her vile offspring. And nature's balance was maintained, a life for a life, a voice for a voice.

Tears stained his cheeks as he turned to face the Morrigan, grief blazing in his eyes.

"It is better than nothing," the smith said. "Now go. Take your damned Cauldron and be gone. I will not wish you well. I do not care what happens to you, only that I never see you again."

Twelve
The King Must Die

THERE WAS NO triumphant homecoming for Sláine, in no short measure because it was no longer his home. He entered the village on foot, leaving the Knucker tethered to a thick-boled oak almost a mile distant. Still the great wyrm's nearness unnerved the empty-eyed cattle. The milkers congregated around the furthest edges of their paddocks, closest to the imagined sanctuary of the village itself. The home he had known had emptied, the life dislodged by change. It didn't matter that the streets were physically the same, whatever it was that had made them feel like home was gone.

A scarecrow pointed the way to Murias's heart.

Sláine walked slowly, keeping his pace even, refusing to hurry even as he saw a young boy running across the path in front of him, turn, stare and bolt. The lad had strawberry-blond hair that reached almost to his waist. It was braided like a man's. The boy's eyes were cornflower blue, startling in their intensity even from a distance. And his grin was infectious. He took off like a jackrabbit, dashing across the dirt track, dropping to his belly and squirming under the paddock fence. A moment later his back was little more than a speck. Sláine watched him go, kicking up dust and dead grass. It could so easily have been himself, or Cullen or any one of the others he had grown up with.

If he closed his eyes he was sure he would have been able to recall the walk to the square; the path that would lead down to the nemeton, the path to the alehouse, and of course, his own home. But Murias had changed in so many subtle ways. Sickness crept into the soil, staining the tips of the tallest grasses as they began to wither against the encroaching cold. He could smell the dirt, the rot that had set into the weeds and scrub, and the dung dried hard on the field. It was a subtle part of the Death Winter that had fallen upon the northern lands, bringing with it despair and the promise of the scourge. It was, Sláine knew, a precursor for Slough Feg's deluge. Everything he saw stood as testimony to the bitter truth: while they had been away questing for the Crone's relic, the Lord Weird's plans for Ragnarok feasted like a canker on the land.

No one greeted him as he walked into the village itself, carrying the Cauldron as he passed the first house. His feet scuffed the dirt into tortured patterns; in the swirls and drags lurked the memories of Macha and Roth, and then more sensual memories of two women, one who had taken his virginity in devotion to a Goddess he hadn't understood, not properly, the other who had cost him his place in the clan.

There was no point in pretending that he had not thought about Niamh; her face blazed brighter than any other memory of this place – save one, and that memory was one he was not prepared to let rise, not yet. But it was there, ever-present. He turned and looked back over his shoulder, to where he had tethered the Knucker, just below the rise where he had stood with the maiden, flowers in her hair, and watched his home burn beneath the wrath of the skull swords.

And he could feel the presence that dwelt within the earth, that fed the spirit of the nemeton and that made him whole. It swirled about through the dust and the dirt, rising into his skin, up through his bones. It sang like some vampiric lover through his veins.

He saw a lone crow in the white of the clouds, climbing, soaring, wings outstretched as it rose only to fold back its wings and plummet like a stone a moment later, swooping down on some unseen vermin.

Sláine shielded his eyes against the sun.

The crow rose into the sky once more, a vole between its sharp claws. Its beak tore at the tiny creature, unpicking its fur and flesh to get at its innards. The naked savagery of the bird on the hunt was as shocking as any kill Sláine had ever witnessed, but there was something comforting to it as well. Nature maintained her own balance. The crow was not evil despite the fact that it fed on the helpless rodent. That was their relationship in the chain of life. The predator fed on the prey.

Sláine saw the vole fall before the crow was halfway over the pasture.

It was peculiar; he could not remember ever seeing a bird eat on the wing before. Normally they landed, devoting themselves to the feast.

He carried on deeper into the village, Ukko walking quietly at his side. The little dwarf's eyes darted everywhere at once.

"You call this civilisation, big man?"

And that was exactly what it was, of course. There was order to Murias, from the common-sense demands that had dictated its layout, the mill beside the river where the currents could turn the millstones, grinding the corn, the silos and barns close to the mill, and so on. Settlements developed a life of their own as they grew from those first few dwellings into villages and towns. Practicalities of distance located the bakers and tanners near the water, and the long house close to the town square, the inn, in turn, close to the long house. The funeral grounds, burial mounds and nemeton lay along sacred geometries, ancient ley lines of power that traversed the Goddess's flesh. One of the duties of Cathbad, the archdruid, was to walk the lines finding favourable locations for the construction of the new buildings, though Sláine had never understood how one piece of dirt could be more blessed than another – they were all a part of Danu, after all. If one piece of earth was sacred, surely all the earth was? That disparity in value had always puzzled the young Sessair. Dian had never managed to explain it in a way that made any sense. Even now, with the draw of the Earth Serpent pulling on his blood, the only difference between Sourland and the good rich soil of the Goddess was how it had been treated by man.

"Just keep out of mischief, dwarf," he said, knowing the chances of that happening were negligible.

"Like I *ever* go looking for trouble," Ukko said, defensively.

"I mean it, Ukko. I must present myself before the Spiral Council, and beg the forgiveness of my king. I do not want to have to be worrying about the Goddess alone knows what you might be up to while my back is turned."

"You can trust me, Sláine."

"There's something ironic about the word trust issuing from your lips, dwarf," said Sláine. He saw a familiar face peering through one of the windows: the daughter of the Goddess, Brighid. He offered her a smile but the curtain fell back covering her face before he could wave. He wanted to believe that the woman did not recognise him but he knew in his heart he had not changed so much no matter how much time had passed since he went away. "Just keep out of trouble. I will find you later. I don't want it to be in the square buckled into the pillory."

"I'll make you proud," Ukko said, his grin saying so much more, before he scurried off.

Sláine stood there a moment longer, taking the opportunity to absorb all of the ghosts this place harboured. He had never thought to return, not in truth. He looked down at the Cauldron, wondering if it truly was enough to stay his execution. And then he remembered the slack-hide cows in the stockade. Sláine took the path that led into the heart of Murias. With each step the reality of his exile became more and more substantial. The last time he had walked these streets he had been a proud warrior, one of the Red Branch, this time he was little more than a wandering vagabond sunk so low his only friend was a backstabbing mealy-mouthed cutpurse with delusions of... well, delusions.

A dozen people milled in the town square. They didn't have an ounce of spare flesh between them. A mongrel pawed at the remains of its own white dung. They had no interest in Sláine. Two of the men, he saw, had been disfigured, their noses carved clean off. From a distance they appeared to have been flayed, but that was a distortion of their weathered skin on desiccating bones. These were not the same proud people he had left. What had only just begun to affect the land afflicted them far worse. Their souls were sour.

All trepidation that he had felt upon entering Murias left then, as he met the eyes of his friend, Dian, leaning on a crude crutch fashioned from a length of rowan. It took the weight from his malformed leg. A latticework of crude scars cut across the sunburnt skin. He almost hadn't recognised him, the man he had become bore so little relation to the boy he had been. There was pain behind his eyes. For a moment there was no recognition, then Dian's face split into a warm – almost desperate – smile, and in that smile Sláine saw the shadow of the boy rise up to overwhelm the pain for just a moment. And then he moved, the crutch dragging in the dirt, and the pain came back with a vengeance.

Sláine wrapped his friend in a fierce embrace, heart-sick when the young druid pulled back, wincing. Sláine held Dian at arm's length, looking from his face to his emaciated chest marked with tribal tattoos akin to Myrrdin's, and finally down at his ruined leg.

"It wasn't so long ago we were running across the fells to Lug's Spike, was it?" Dian said, shaking his head at the memory.

"I am through running, my friend," Sláine said.

"As am I. Damn but it is good to see you, man. Are you back for good?"

"Or ill," said Sláine. "It's good to see a friendly face, Dian. Few others will welcome me home with open arms, even if the king does."

"A lot of water's run under that old bridge, Sláine. Murias isn't the village it was back when Grudnew was king. Few even remember your shame, I am sure."

"You never were a good liar," said Sláine. "Speaking of shame, is she here? I think I need to apologise. Perhaps I can do that before I go in there." He inclined his head towards the thick timbered door of the long house. It had been barely more than a skeleton of wattle framework and half-dug foundations when they had snuck in at night to hide those supposedly ancient texts. He half-smiled at the memory and in that moment he was homesick for the home he had never had.

That ghost of pain flittered behind Dian's eyes again. "It's too late for that. Niamh left months ago." He looked left, and surreptitiously, right, to be sure no one was close enough to eavesdrop. "She was driven out by our *beloved* king's new woman."

"Do you know where she went?"

Dian shrugged his shoulders.

"Away, anywhere but here. She wasn't welcome, Sláine, in no small part because of you. Grudnew didn't want her around to remind him of his cuckolding, and when he was gone Kilian Ragall wanted her, it seemed, to spite the old king. His pursuit was relentless. The man did not like that he could not have what he wanted, but then he fell for Megrim and there was no place for a twice-spurned woman like Niamh. And for obvious reasons

Megrim didn't want her within a hundred leagues of her man."

Kilian Ragall was a name he had not thought about in a long time. "Ragall became king?"

"It was not our finest hour," Dian admitted.

Sláine remembered Ragall's bitterness when Grudnew had taken the oath to be the Sun King, pledging himself as Danu's husband. That promise to be the mountain and the river still rung in Sláine's mind, it summed up so much of what it meant to be Sessair. What made no sense was that somehow a weak and vainglorious man like Kilian Ragall had risen to the kingship. Was he the druids's puppet or was he his own man? Sláine wondered.

"So much has changed, Dian. I hardly recognise the place. It all seems so much... smaller."

"You remember things with the eyes of a child, now you are a man. It is no surprise you see limitations where once you saw possibilities."

"Soth! You've spent too much time with that old faker, Cathbad. You're even starting to sound like him."

"I know you don't believe me, but he's a good man, Sláine. No matter what we thought when we were children, I know the man now. He isn't the sanctimonious prig we delighted in tormenting. Well, he is," Dian conceded, "but he is also a font of wisdom worth drinking from. Believe me, he never does anything without the clan's best interests foremost in mind and deed."

"Perhaps. Come, walk with me, my friend, I would hear stories of my home, but first I must present myself to the Spiral Council and throw myself on the mercy of a damn fool and a charlatan."

They walked to the long house together, Dian recounting years of privation and hardship. The blight stretched deep into the Land of the Young. Over the last six months the farthest fields had begun to sour, the crop lost. He talked of the spate of suicides that had stricken the village as hope gave way to despair as the famine took hold. It pained Sláine to listen. Instinctively he clutched the strap of his sack tighter, as though he could draw assurance from the book inside it. In his daydreams he also returned the conquering hero, triumphant, vanquishing the Drunes and their poisonous skull swords, and reclaiming Tir-Nan-Og for the Tuatha de Dannan. It was a *good* dream. Standing before the doors of the long house the reality was all too apparent.

He hammered three times on the huge timber doors and pushed them open, stepping forwards to stand in the doorway as light streamed into the enormous hall from behind him, bathing him in shadow. More light spilled in through the wide oculus in the centre of the ceiling, an eye onto the sky. Motes of dust twinkled and glittered as they danced their lazy reel in the air. The elders were sat on rows of benches tiered in a circle around the oculus. Kilian Ragall sat sprawled out on a low throne, furs draped over his shoulders, hollow eyes staring at the silhouette in the doorway.

Sláine did not move.

He looked from face to face around the circle, knowing that the shadows masked his identity and enjoying – and at the same time despising – the looks of fear that greeted him. He recognised Cuinn, his brother Ansgar, Orin and Phelan among others. They had stood against Grudnew for the right to rule, and now they bent the knee to Ragall. In another life his father would have been sat amongst them. These men were warriors of the Red Branch. They were fearless, the elite, the heart of the Sessair. They feared nothing – except, it seemed, shadows…

Ragall stiffed. "Who dares enter our council uninvited? Step out of the shadows, coward." It was all bluster, Sláine knew. Fear tinged the man's voice, belittling the power he pretended. It was no surprise that the spine had been ripped out of the Red Branch. Their king had lost the two things he had sworn to uphold; to have the bearing of the mountain and the relentless nature of the stream, carrying the clan forwards into the sea of tomorrow.

Sláine threw down his pack and stepped forwards into the light, standing proud, defiant. "I do. You might remember me, my *king*, I am Sláine son of Roth and Macha. I am son of the Sessair. I am," and he let the word hang in the air, "returned."

"Sláine Mac Roth…" Ragall said slowly, each word rolling off his tongue as though laced with venom.

"Did you think to beg for my mercy? Your father was a drunk, your mother a whore and you, whelp, were never anything more than a freak. As far as I am concerned there is no forgiveness here and there never can be. Your exile stands, as does your punishment. If I remember rightly, boy, Grudnew promised death if you ever dared set foot in our land. That has not changed just because the old man has joined with Danu. I am the Sun King, just as he was, were, are, immortal, eternal, his spirit flows in my veins, his wrath is my wrath, his vengeance will be mine. You will not walk out of this place."

"Quiet, Ragall, your wind smells just as bad coming out of your mouth as it does your arse." That one line spoken from the shadows beyond the oculus was enough to deflate the man who called himself king. Sláine did not recognise the speaker, nor did he need to. The absolute confidence of their tone told him all he needed to know. Ragall was their puppet. Sláine saw the druid Cathbad lurking at the back of the chamber, wringing his hands together as he worried over something. The oddness of the gesture struck Sláine as telling. More peculiar though was the slight smile and the single nod the old man gave him when they made eye contact. The druid had denied his king, Sláine realised, wondering what the significance of it might be.

"I am *king*," Ragall said, though in truth it sounded no more assertive than a petulant whine. "I will not be chastised in my own house."

Another voice spoke up, heavy with irony. "Did you feed us this year, oh great Sun King?"

Another, cold, callous: "Did you nourish the fields with your blood? Wasn't that your promise?"

"No," the man Sláine recognised as Ansgar said, rising to his feet, "you went and begged the skull swords for food, you pleaded, unmanning yourself until they offered you a pax – but what kind of peace was it, oh mighty king? A pax my arse. It's a pox!"

And another: "We were warriors, Ragall. Have you forgotten? Our strength *is* our strength. All around us our children starve, our cattle die and our lands are ravaged by blight brought on by this menace from the south. Yet do we ride out? No. Do we take the fight to this creeping death?"

"No we do not!" several voices chorused. Feet stamped. Palms banged on the wooden rails beside the benches.

"No," the Sessair warrior went on, "instead they mock our hunger with their diseased feeding pits filled to overflowing with rotten carcasses and ruined vegetables claimed as taxes, cut the noses from those too poor to pay their tithe, and still the Red Branch sits impotent. We are warriors, man. We should not bend the knee to anyone."

Still Sláine did not move. He watched Kilian Ragall's face as each barb struck home, and then, like the most fearsome of gae bolga, was wrenched free of his body leaving him to writhe beneath the pain of their accusations.

"And yet you refuse my plea, leaving me to play the king, so I play the king for you," Ragall said, lurching to his feet. The fur fell from his shoulder. "This is your choice, council, though I see no wisdom in it. The king and the land are one, the land is dying, I have begged, I have pleaded, I have humiliated myself at the feet of the enemy, and it makes no difference, so let me die with it. Allow me to merge with the Goddess, leave it to a better man to make the sun shine once more. I am tired of this life. I am beaten, everything you say is true."

It was Cathbad who spoke, the old man's frailty belied by the shadows as he moved through them to stand in the light. "No, Kilian Ragall. Your life is not your own. You are Sun King and as such your life belongs to Danu, the Goddess, mother of the earth. You will serve as husband until the time for your death; a time of *her* choosing not yours. You will honour your oath. You will be the mountain, you will be the river. You will lead us and together we will cut out the canker that grows in our midst. You must show your strength. The man before you is a warrior and, now, more than ever, we need warriors. It is in your power, *king*, to end his exile. Welcome the prodigal son of the Sessair home."

Ragall's face twisted in a brutish sneer as he pushed back his throne, toppling it in his anger. "There is a stench in this place, old man. So be it, you want a king? I will be your king!" his voice rose, his face reddening to match his fury. "Listen to my last command! Let the freak's exile be over! He is a fighter so let him fight! Let the freak become our monster! Let him run at the front of the Red Branch driving those tiny mortals away as his body rips itself apart in its wrath. Let him rain down his vengeance upon the bastards that threaten our land! Isn't that what you want? I hear your whispers; you look at him now and think why can't Kilian Ragall be more like that?" Ragall raged, a failed man aware of his inadequacies. His self-loathing was as real as any malady, lurking deep inside him, eating away at him, unseen, unfathomable. His voice rose once more, in a fervour: "I am worthless, but he, he is blessed by the Goddess! So that is my command, look to the freak for leadership! Let the enemy cower before his monstrosity! Hark! I am greatest amongst you! I am the soul of the Sessair! As your king I have spoken, hear my judgement. The exile of Sláine Mac Roth is over. Welcome the bastard back home! It even looks as though he has brought gifts to buy your forgiveness, perhaps they will sooth your consciences into forgetting about Grudnew's shaming," Ragall stepped down from the first row of tiered seats, his face ugly with bitterness. He pushed past Sláine, leaving the circle of light. In the umbra he turned and said coldly, "just keep him away from your women."

"Trouble, trouble, trouble," Ukko muttered to himself as he stood on tip-toes to peer in through the shutters of one of the larger dwellings. "Never a thanks for saving his skin, oh no, treats me like a child, bossing me around. Sit down, shut up, keep your fingers to yourself..."

Ukko sniffed the air, catching the pungent whiff of the piss wafting up from the trenches out beyond the village's perimeter. The repulsive little runt smiled to himself and scurried off in the direction of the latrine pits. Muck clung to muck as often as not, making the latrines interesting places for a curious dwarf to loiter. People liked to gossip; it was, the dwarf understood, a fundamental flaw in human nature. Secrets got spilled and it was amazing the kind of stuff people shared with their pants down around their ankles.

Lurk around long enough and a diamond would bob up among the turds.

He ducked down, making himself small against the side of the wall, and peered around the corner into a narrow alley crammed between the rows of houses. Ropes had been strung from the rooftops across the alleyway, and wet sheets pegged from them snapped in the breeze. Seeing no one, Ukko ducked beneath the trailing sheets and scuttled forwards, following his nose.

At the first crossroads the little dwarf knelt, stirring the dirt with his fingers and then kissing them with his lips superstitiously. He looked in all three directions, craning his head as he listened to the noises carried across the afternoon. A hooded figure moved between the sheets. It moved with uncommon grace, fleet of foot and light of step. Ukko had watched enough women in his life to know when he was looking at one, even with the heavy cloak and hood drawn up to hide her face. Her body was too slight to pass for masculine.

"How much trouble can a woman be?" Ukko mumbled to himself, and set off after her as she disappeared around a tumbledown section of wall. The answer to his question came soon enough: plenty. She looked furtively over her shoulder five times before she made the next turn; as though she sensed someone was there. She didn't call out or challenge him, and not once did she actually fix her gaze within twenty feet of where Ukko lurked. He couldn't help but grin as the thrill of the chase gripped him. He scuttled forwards, ducking down into a doorway as the woman turned, the right side of her face silhouetted against the white sheet in front of her. There was something vaguely familiar about her profile; it niggled at his mind as he followed her down two more narrow alleyways into the communal latrines. He knew her, and what's more he knew he did, but for all that certainty Ukko couldn't place her face. That disturbed him. It was as though some kind of glamour had been laid across it, one that caused the mind to slip and slide around recognition.

But it would come to him.

She entered the latrine pit. He crouched down beside the doorway and waited, vaguely aware that there was something perverse about listening to a woman relieve herself, but he'd promised no mischief, not that he would sit and stare at the walls while his mind slowly crawled up them. "Besides," he muttered to himself, "a bored Ukko's a bad Ukko and a bad Ukko *always* gets into trouble, so I'm only doing what Sláine told me to do," and with that rationalisation, the dwarf slunk closer to the doorway, pressing his ear to the crack where the woman had left it slightly ajar. Instead of grunts and sighs he heard hushed voices. Ukko edged forwards, straining to overhear, but he was too far away to make any sense of the low whispers.

The latrine pits were open to the elements, to allow the rain to soak the lime and slake the stench. Practicality meant that there was no roof over them, which in turn meant that with a little improvisation Ukko could get a glimpse of whatever skulduggery was going down in the latrines. *It's just a look,* he thought to himself, *no one ever got in trouble just looking.* So he leaned back, craning his neck to check the alley behind him, then both left and right, before boosting himself up and scrambling at the wattle as he struggled to heave himself up the pitted wall until his chin was perched on the top and, straining, he could peer over.

The woman had her back to him, the hood pulled down to mask her completely, but she was not alone. A hideously deformed face looked back at him, eyes milky white, raw pink scars criss-crossing the sunken sockets where the man had been brutalised by knives. He wore ill-fitting sackcloth rags, but strapped across his back were twin blades, wickedly curved and honed so sharp they cut the shadows the blind man wreathed himself in.

Ukko tried to sidle along the wall into a position where he could see at least the side of the woman's face. His toe scraped the wattle causing both woman and warrior to turn instinctively towards the sound. He ducked down, fingertips clinging to the top of the wall and counting to forty in his head before he dared poke his head up above the wall again.

When he did the pair of them had huddled in so close their voices barely carried, but Ukko heard enough to wish he hadn't heard anything at all:

"I must visit with the Lord Weird, Balor," the woman said, drawing the cloak about herself, long white fingers playing over her throat where the edges of the cloak met, "see to the preparations; you know the herbs the enchantment requires, all are indigenous to the forest save this." She held out a small pouch which the warrior took and secreted about his person in one smooth motion that belied his blindness. "I will join you in the forest at sunset. See that the channels are open so that I may communicate with our sovereign."

"It shall be done, mistress," the warrior, Balor, said.

"Good. There is much still that remains to be done, the fool Ragall is in with the council even now, begging to be put out of his misery."

"That is most fortunate, mistress."

"Fortune has nothing to do with it, Balor. Careful schemes bring their own rewards, like any game of strategy, you plan ahead, anticipating your opponent's moves. Kilian Ragall plays like a child. Everything about the man is so utterly predictable, even his death."

"Yes, mistress."

"Predictability is good, Balor, never forget that. Better an opponent whose every move you can presuppose than one who is going to surprise you at every turn."

"Yes, mistress, predictability is good, as is fortune, but neither are a match for skill."

"Spoken like a true man."

"I do not deny my sex, mistress." The blind man reached out, his fingertips caressing the woman's face. Her hood fell back, revealing lush long locks of dark hair. "Just as I do not deny yours."

The woman took his hand in hers and lifted it to her lips, kissing each callused fingertip lovingly, then she pushed him away with surprising force. "Do not presume to touch me again, warrior, unless you want your fingers chewed off next time."

Balor laughed, a chillingly mirthless sound coming from the blind man's mouth. Ukko winced. His grip slipped and a heartbeat later he lost his balance, his foot scraping down the wattle before he caught himself, cursing. Balor turned slightly, inclining his head so that his scarred eyes bore into the wall three feet below Ukko's hiding place – level, precisely, with his traitorous feet.

The dwarf held his breath, not daring to move a muscle even though his arms began to burn from the exertion of holding himself up for so long.

"We are not alone," Balor said, his white-blind eyes eerie in the half-sun half-shadow.

"Who is there?" the woman said, turning to follow the direction of his blind stare, and Ukko saw her face full in the light. There was something repulsively familiar about her beauty – and she was beautiful, the lines of her face, the curves and shallows, but she was ugly too, through her eyes into her core – and it was so, so familiar, but after years of drunken whoring she could have been any lover spurned, wench plucked, barmaid seduced and abandoned, cherry plucked, widow entertained or maiden deflowered.

Ukko bit his lip, closed his eyes and slunk lower, inch by inch until his feet were dangling no more than six inches above the dirt. He dropped to the ground, grunting as he landed, and took off on his heels, running even as her shrieks of: "*Kill him, Balor! Gut him on your swords! Rip out his tongue! He cannot be allowed to talk!*" hounded him out of the latrines and back into the warren of alleyways and damp laundry.

Feet slapping harshly against the dusty earth, Ukko threw himself over fences and under hedges, pulled down sheets and knocked over barrels of rainwater to muddy the trail, desperate to put as much distance between himself and the trouble he had found.

And despite the fear coursing through his veins, Ukko grinned fiercely every terrified step of the way; he couldn't help it, he was having fun.

"I BRING TOKENS of appeasement," Sláine said, gesturing to the black metal Cauldron and the oilskin-wrapped book stolen from the Lord Weird.

"So you did hope to buy our forgiveness?" Cathbad said, "Tell us, Sláine son of Roth, how cheap did you think it would be?"

"You offer us a pot to cook in, or is it a pot to piss in?" Ansgar said, chuckling bleakly at his own humour. "There's no food, lad, didn't you look around the fields on your way in? The harvest was blighted. Our bellies are empty, boy."

"Then I would say I am buying your welcome for precisely the right price, Ansgar, and yours druid, all of yours."

"Are you touched, lad? Wandering alone addled your brain? It's understandable, I suppose," Raif of the Bloody Axe told the council.

"Most likely drunk like his old man," Anrai Ardal said gruffly. The man had little liking for Roth, Sláine remembered – and he remembered the cause. Old Anrai had been sweet on his mother, Macha, and had never forgiven her for choosing Bellyshaker over him at the Feis Samain dance twenty-some years ago. It was a jealousy Sláine could understand. He didn't rise to the bait.

"Let the boy speak." A familiar voice cut across the rabble. "Not that he's a boy any longer." Gorian, warlord of the Red Branch, rose to his feet. He looked every inch the king where Kilian Ragall had appeared a pretender dressed up in a better man's furs. Beside him, red-headed Murdo grinned approvingly. "So, young Sláine, it only seems like yesterday I was interceding with Grudnew on your behalf. Do you remember the vow you made when you took the Red Branch?"

Sláine nodded. "It is writ on my soul."

"Then remind us all of it."

"We are Sessair. We are proud. Unbreakable."

"And tell me, Sláine, when you look around this chamber do you see proud unbreakable men?"

"No," Sláine said.

"Neither do I, lad. Now, tell us of the gifts that you believe worthy enough of our embrace, let's see if they're silver or coal."

"You do not recognise it, warlord?"

"Other than as a grand cooking pot? No, lad. Should I?"

"Light a fire, warm the pit, and see if the miracle of the Cú Roi is enough to remind the hungry of the bounty our Goddess offers the faithful."

A flicker of understanding lit up behind the druid Cathbad's eyes; the old man had an inkling of the treasure Sláine had returned. *Indeed, he is long-lived enough to have seen it before the sundering shattered the Cú Roi of Goibniu into pieces and scattered it to the four winds*, Sláine thought to himself.

"Light the fire," Gorian said, coming down to embrace Sláine wrist to wrist. "Soth! But it is good to see you again, boy. I had no liking for the way you were driven out," the warlord said, his voice pitched low enough that his words were for Sláine's ears only.

"Thank you, Gorian. May Danu reward your faith," said Sláine. He turned to face the remainder of the Spiral Council and slowly unwrapped oilskin to reveal the bark-covered book of vellum that the Lord Weird had poured his darkest desires into. "With this book we win our freedom from the yoke of oppression, my people."

"With a book? Do we read fairy tales to the skull swords until they fall asleep from boredom?" Madad the Quarrelsome heckled, shaking his head in disbelief at the gullibility of his own people, so desperate to believe that salvation had walked in out of the Death Winter. The gristle of the warrior's nose had been sliced off to reveal a huge cavity in the centre of his face. The maiming left the once fearsome warrior looking comical with his shaved scalp and his single tuft of flame-red hair like a unicorn's horn hanging down over the centre of his forehead.

"You are quick to judge, Madad," said Sláine, holding the precious Ragnarok book in his hands and lifting it so that all could see precisely what it was. "Dian, my friend," Sláine looked around for the young druid who stood still in the doorway to the chamber, out of the light from the oculus. "Come, I would ask you to read the first line of Ogham to the doubters. Perhaps your words will silence them."

"No need, I can read the scripts," Cathbad said, reaching out for the book.

"No, druid. I would have my friend read them, you can confirm his translation if need be, but Dian will address the council."

Dian, uncomfortable between the two men, friend and master, looked to Cathbad for instruction. The older man inclined his head in acquiescence. "Read to us, young Dian. I believe I speak for everyone assembled when I say that we are most eager to hear the secrets of this most secretive tome."

Dian took the book from Sláine, his hands trembling as he cracked open the bark cover and scanned the first few words. He looked to Sláine: "Is this true?"

The young warrior nodded. "Every word, my friend."

"How on earth did you come by such a thing?"

"That is a long story, one for another day."

"What is it?" Gorian asked, "What does it say?"

Dian cleared his throat and raised his eyes from the page. "I, Slough Feg, servant of Carnun, Horned God of the Forests, speak, hear my words that they may sour the earth and bring on the deluge, for this land is corrupt, pustulant, putrescent. This world is vile, the bitch Goddess has turned her back on her people but the great wyrm knows, yes the great Crom-Cruach knows and feels the wounding of the soil. Only the cleansing of the filth will do. The rotten must be purged. The filth of humanity, the pox of blood and shit and piss must be driven from the land, to the dirt returned..." his words had a distressingly hypnotic rhythm to them, the poetry of insanity drawing the listener deeper and deeper into the nightmare woven by the words.

"Nothing more than the ravings of a madman, surely," said Gorian.

"Read on, Dian," said Sláine said, knowing full well the promises to come, and the impact they would have upon the Spiral Council.

"The darkness of the world, the winter of mankind, is upon us, but soon the winter will be glorious spring, the souring will cease and the deluge from the heavens will bring deliverance, the scourge of the living cleansed, the canker of flesh scoured from the hills and the fields. There shall be no relief, no salvation, no testament to the will of the bitch Goddess because I am great, my reach long, my loyalty unflinching, my drive relentless. I loved her once, was faithful and pure, the purest and most faithful, but no more, no, no more. I know my master's mind, the voice of his reason, the reason of his voice. I, Slough Feg, the Lord Weird, servant of Crom, speak, and all of Albion, forests and field, sea and stream, will listen to my words and know fear for I bring the end of her reign with the rain. The seas shall rise up and swallow the land whole, the skies shall break and the unbelievers drown. Only then shall the Death Winter's grip on the land slacken, only then shall the will of Crom relent, only then shall the bitch Goddess suffer as she made me and mine suffer. Vengeance shall be me, sayeth the Horned Man, Lord of the Forests, Haunter of the Trees, Bringer of the Flood."

"Can it be?" Dian looked up, his face blanched white with fear at the insidious lure of the words he spoke.

"Who is this monster?" Gorian asked, shaking his head to be free of the vision the words of madness had conjured in his mind.

"He is the demon who, with his skull swords, killed my mother and so many of the wives and children of Murias," said Sláine. "The book is the darkness of his mind, the perversions of his spirit, laid down. If the druid Myrrdin Emrys–"

"The Lord of the Trees? Impossible!" Cathbad interrupted.

"– is to be believed the book holds his schemes to bring on the end of the world as we know it. With it, I believe we can thwart him."

"And we're supposed to listen to a vagabond son of a drunkard?" Madad's sudden outburst earned him scowls from Murdo and several other Red Branch warriors close to him.

"Silence!" Gorian bellowed, wheeling round on Madad, "unless you want to lose another piece of your face?"

"Couldn't make him any uglier," Murdo chuckled. Despite being poor, the joke broke the spell Dian's reading had placed upon the chamber. A hubbub of urgent chatter spread from seat to seat as the warriors leaned over to whisper with their neighbours. Few bar Cathbad and Dian knew who the Lord of the Trees was, or how impossible it was for Sláine to have spent his exile in the company of what to them was little more than a myth.

Gorian turned to Sláine. "The council would know more of your travels, and what you know of the threat that gathers at our door. I suspect you know far more of this menace than we do as you have walked among them, and no doubt fought them hand to hand, while Ragall has scraped his knees so desperate to please them."

Before he could say more Cathbad grabbed Sláine by the shoulder and twisted him around. "You met the Lord of the Trees? How is that possible? How? He has been lost to us for centuries."

"Not merely met; serving the Morrigan I delivered Myrrdin from his prison and returned him from the El Worlds, Cathbad."

"He walks among us, even now? I… I…"

"You can thank me later," Sláine said, and to Gorian, "Much of the land south of here has soured. No crops ripen, no herds fatten, but that is not the worst of it. Feg uses ancient lines of power to drain the earth itself of its power, leeching the life out of Danu. In Carnac thousands of standing stones act as foci for his evil. He uses the might of the Earth Serpent to raise great sky chariots kept aloft by blood magic."

"No, surely... no... blood magic taints the land... defiles it."

"The Lord Weird has no care for Danu, druid. You heard his thoughts, she is the bitch Goddess he once loved, nothing more, and like any lover spurned he would hurt the one who hurt him."

"Talk of lovers spurned is ironic, is it not?" Mongan Flint said, "You come before us, exiled, yourself a lover spurned, banished for your infidelity. Why should we believe you?"

"Because," Sláine said, slowly, "to disbelieve is to damn all of Tir-Nan-Og with your stupidity." The condemnation hung in the air with the dust motes.

"What should we do, warlord?" Ansgar asked, clearly torn by all that he had heard.

"We are Sessair!" Gorian answered, his cry swelling to fill the long house, the power of his words venting up through the oculus and into the coming dusk, daring the Death Winter to answer. "We will not be humbled by a madman!"

The Red Branch warriors stamped their feet in appreciation, faster and faster until the sound fused into a thunderous warcry. It took two full minutes before the tumult died down and a lone voice questioned: "But how do we fight with no food in our bellies? We are as weak of body as Kilian Ragall is of spirit!"

"When the fire is ready, you shall see, Phelan Oxbow," Sláine assured the man.

"I have no love for what you did to old Grudnew, Warped One, that was lower than low and you got what you deserved," Phelan said, "but if you silence the hunger in my belly with thin air and water I will follow you anywhere for truly you are a magician to be feared!"

"Me too," Cuinn agreed, beside him.

"How about you Orin? And you Madad? Mongan? Murdo? If I can fill your bellies will you remember what it means to be Sessair?"

"Aye, lad, we will, and we'll thank you for it."

"Then fetch your stone axes as well as your feeding forks, for the Cú Roi of Goibniu shall put an end to the ache in your guts."

"Can it truly be the Cauldron of Plenty?" Gorian said, kneeling to look at the bezel and the intricate rendering of Avagddu hammered into it. "Such a treasure," he breathed, marvelling at the relic. "You are a man of surprises, Sláine Mac Roth."

"I am Sessair, Gorian."

"Indeed you are, indeed you are."

"The treasure was lost, forfeit, sundered as a testament to our shame. Now you return it to us whole. If this truly is the Cú Roi you could not have brought a more precious gift. With our ancestors' shame laid finally to rest we shall rise up and remind the world what it means to be a Celt. We shall grovel and scrape in the dirt no more."

"Set it on the fire, Gorian," Sláine told him. "Every warrior shall eat his fill tonight. None with pure hearts shall go hungry. Come the morrow the Red Branch shall march, bringing death and destruction to the evils that infest our glorious land!"

A roar of agreement went up, the cheers reaching out through the oculus to drown the whole of Murias in its fervour.

Sláine drank in the acceptance of the warriors.

He was home among his people where he belonged.

UKKO HEARD THE sudden roar and ran towards it, thinking only to find Sláine and warn him that His Weirdness had spies inside Murias, pretty spies that they knew from somewhere... the woman's identity plagued him. Ukko chased it even as the woman's blind thug, Balor, chased him.

But all thoughts of dire warning spilled from his head as he stumbled to a stop, staring at the woman, her hood pulled back to reveal a single long braid and the blue-inked tribal tattoos of Sláine's people across the ridge of her brow and cut into the coarse hairs of her eyebrows. He dropped to a crouch, trying to make himself small. She hadn't seen him. A man wearing only a colourful kilt of coarse wool caught her by the shoulders, talking earnestly, hurriedly, desperate for her to understand the import of his words.

Ukko couldn't hear a word of it.

He cast a nervous glance over his shoulder but there was no sign of Balor; though the blind man probably tracked by scent like a dog and would prove as relentless as a damned bloodhound on his trail. Ukko risked scuffling a few feet closer, close enough to make out the gist of their argument:

"I could have been a goddess once, Kilian Ragall! Wife of the most powerful god of all! And you crawl around on your hands and knees expecting me to be grateful for the scraps you feed me? I am of the Babd, you fool! I am more that you could ever be or dream of being."

The man, Ragall, let his hand fall from her shoulder. "I don't... ? Goddess? Wife of Lug the Sun? Hu the Mighty? Women do not marry the sky gods... Megrim, what are you saying? I do not understand."

"No you pathetic fool, the god who feeds on war, disease and disaster. The god who will save us by putting an end to the misery of life on this plane of the els, the Wyrm God, Crom-Cruach! How I have longed to smell his foetid breath on my face, to taste the slime of his flagellum around me, entering me, to hear the screams of his victims as he sucks at their souls, freeing them from the pain of living!"

"I don't know you at all, wife," Kilian Ragall said.

"No," the woman agreed, turning to stare directly at Ukko. "But he does, don't you, dwarf?"

Ukko didn't say a word. He looked at the dirt wishing fervently it would open up to swallow him whole – and then remembering the fate of Slough Throt, fervently wished he hadn't wished any such thing. He shook his head vigorously. "Never seen you before in my life, woman. I'd remember a She Devil like you, believe me."

The woman, Megrim, laughed. "Oh you know me, dwarf, as does your damned companion Sláine. You may not recognise me, but *you* I will never forget."

She stepped closer to Kilian Ragall, her arms encircling him in an embrace as she kissed him on the left cheek. "Goodbye, King Ragall," she said, stepping back. Ukko stared in horror at the blade buried deep in the man's gut and the thick black blood spilling out around his fingers. He fell to his knees.

"The king is dead!" Megrim shouted, and again: "The king is dead! He has taken his own life! The coward has fallen on his own sword! My husband the Coward King!"

Her cries brought people running. Kilian Ragall crawled forwards towards the warriors emerging from the long house, drawn by the woman's cries. Ukko didn't move, didn't say a word. Something was happening here that he didn't understand. All he needed to know was what he had seen – the woman, Megrim, had murdered the king of the Sessair with one brutal thrust of the king's own blade.

The fallen king reached out, imploring, his mouth working over and over, but only forming gurgles, no words. He did not decry his murderer. In the eyes of his people gathered around to watch his last breaths, he was what she claimed, the Coward King who had taken his own life. No one moved to help him.

As the blood flowed out of the dying man, Cathbad stepped forwards, his shadow looming over Ragall. "The blood! The blood is a sign!" And for a heartbeat, no more, Ukko believed by some arcane chicanery the druid knew of the woman's treachery. He didn't. With the next breath Cathbad declared: "It flows towards the true successor of the coward!"

Weeping, men and women followed the blood from where Megrim had plunged the sword into her husband's gut all the way back to the dying man. The idiocy of them amazed Ukko; surely it didn't take a genius to fathom it out. The blood was no omen, it was damning evidence of her betrayal.

"No," a red-headed warrior gasped. "It cannot be so! A woman has never led the Sessair!"

"And yet you worship one," Megrim said confidently. "Let me make amends for my husband's shame! Let me bring honour back to our people! Let me be your queen!"

But before the druid could declare it so, the shadow-wreathed figure of a powerful warrior emerged from the long house, a crippled man hobbling on a crutch at his side. An awed hush fell over the crowd as Sláine stepped out of the shadows.

"Why is no one helping him?" Sláine bellowed, striding to the fallen king's side. He knelt, gathering Ragall's limp body into his arms and cradling the man in his lap as he took his final breaths.

"The blood!" Someone cried, pointing. The trail of Kilian Ragall's lifeblood had curled away from the woman who would be queen soaking into the stone as it gathered at the knees of Sláine Mac Roth.

"It is as the druid claimed! A sign from the earth Goddess!"

"The king is dead!" Another cried.

And the last voice: "Long live the king!" declared Cathbad.

Ukko looked from face to face, Sláine to Megrim, amused by their mutual expressions of abject and absolute horror as the reality of what was happening to them sank in. There was something wonderfully perverse and capricious about the whims of deities.

"I AM DONE, Sláine."

"You are, Kilian," Sláine agreed.

"I have failed my people."

"You have."

"But you came back."

"I did."

"They need you. You must... make... the sun shine... again."

"I will."

"She–" but Kilian Ragall's eyes rolled back in his skull before he could finish and then the death rattle escaped the old king's lips and his body fell limp in Sláine's arms. The warrior set him gently aside. The woman was gone; there had been something naggingly familiar about her but he put it out of his mind. The time for understanding would come and with it whatever truths needed to be understood. But now it was the time for mourning.

Sláine turned to the druid.

"The king is dead."

And the cry went up again: "Long live the king!"

Thirteen
Sláine the King

COME DAWN THE new king was crowned.

"Water heat and water boil," Cathbad intoned, stirring the mighty Cú Roi with a wand of ash, "make the wheel of heaven toil! Fire flame and fire burn! Make the wheel of heaven turn!"

Sláine's hair had been dyed three colours, brown at the roots using the dung of a white horse, yellow with lime to spike it until it resembled the rays of the sun, and red on the tips, in blood. His body was covered blue with woad, the tattoos depicting the sacred symbols of his people, inked in by Ukko's painstaking brush strokes: the winged birds of the Morrigan rose up each muscular leg, the life tree dominated his chest, and beneath it the bestial face of Lug, burning like the sun. And all around these huge icons, smaller, more intricate patterns, endless knots scaled the ripples of his abdominals like a serpent's scales, and on his rear a chuckling Ukko rendered his enemies so that he might defecate on them.

Mixed with the woad were other tribal intoxicants meant to ease the pain of the boiling water on his skin. He felt their hallucinogenic touch as they seeped beneath his skin to fill his blood. His vision swam. Sláine stood straight backed, proudly naked before his people. Kilian's death played over and over in his mind, remembering the look of abhorrence in the woman, Megrim's eyes as he emerged from the long house. The capricious ribbon of blood that had fated him from falling on the mercy of the Spiral Council to presiding over them as liege had been used to dye his hair. The druid, Cathbad, had explained that by doing so his blood might absorb the qualities of the dead man, blood to blood.

The people of the tribe gathered, hundreds of them carrying blazing torches despite the burgeoning sunlight. Like so much of the ceremony it was symbolic. He saw friends in the crowd, faces he hadn't seen since childhood, men now, but so familiar: Dian, Núada, thickset and muscled now, and the brothers Cormac and Niall. And for a moment, bathed in a blue haze, he fancied he saw another face, so much younger, starting with open dislike, jealousy in his eyes: Cullen of the Wide Mouth, but then the haze shivered and it was just another wide-eyed boy watching his new king.

Cathbad raised a cadaverous hand, urging quiet. A reverent hush descended, its silence contagious.

"Oh Goddess of the Earth Maiden, woman and hag, be with us here in your fullness of limb, as green as the Daughter of Spring, the fair

Blodeuwedd who brings joy and new life to the Land of the Young," the druid intoned, his eyes closed, hands outstretched over the broiling Cú Roi. "Earth Goddess and Sun King, we are gathered here that through earthly union the cows will give milk, the corn will grow high and the fish fill the rivers once more. That you will lighten our darkness, banish the sour from our land and free us from the yoke of fear, from the encroaching Winter of Death."

The waters of the Cauldron roiled, far more than the mere heat of flame could have inspired. As the curls of steam rose the shape of beauty itself began to gather substance and form within them, coalescing into the ethereal face of the Goddess, Danu. The steam swirled about her form, clothing her in wisps of translucent pearl. She wore blossoms in her hair. As Blodeuwedd emerged from the waters, reaching out a hand for Sláine to help her down, the men of the Sessair fell to their knees, their eyes averted from the glory of the divine feminine.

"Sláine Mac Roth, do you as Sun King of the Sessair, pledge yourself as consort to the maiden, to love, know and serve for the span of seven years?"

Sláine looked into the face of the Goddess, recalling with vivid clarity the first time he had seen her, at the funeral of Calum mac Cathair, leading the spirit of the old king by the hand into the depths of the forest, and through the trees into the Summerland. Of all things, he remembered the sensation of the rain running down his neck in the silence of the ceremony. That simplest of things had proved he was alive. Now, as her fingers twined with his, another simple sensation, of skin on skin, validated that simple proof. She wore the same garlands in her hair now that she had then. He breathed in deeply of their scent, losing himself in her eyes.

She smiled at him, her lips moving silently to say into his heart: *it was you, it was always you.*

And in that smile she was more than beautiful; she was once again the innocent daughter of spring that had swept away his childhood heart.

"I do and shall," he said, and meant it with all his being.

Cathbad held a wand of mistletoe between them, in his other hand he held a golden torc, the ends gathered into the trinity of symbols; crow, skull and blossom, representing each aspect of the living Goddess. "With this torc I seal your union, you are husband to the stars, to the earth below, to the stones and like the mistletoe you are suspended between them," the old druid smiled. "And as time passes remember, like a star your love should be constant, like the mountain should your love be strong, like the river should your love be relentless, carrying you forwards into tomorrow."

The fragrance of the flowers was heady, overpowering. Sláine felt it swimming through his thoughts, the druid's voice seeming to drift further and further away even as he stepped near to fasten the marriage torc about his throat.

His sense of self shifted. He soared within himself, releasing his totem, his spirit creature, the phoenix, the golden eagle of the sun. It flew, chasing the white horse until at last his totem plunged into the heart of the sun and erupted into flame and he heard music, singing, and he felt himself being reborn from its ashes. The light filled his mind and he knew the ceremony was no mere ritual, but a recognition that life was the ultimate of treasures, a way of ensuring that the Sun King, no matter what wars his tribal duty forged, would never harm his wife, the earth. And somewhere in the distance of his swimming conscious, he could hear the druid Cathbad chanting over and over: "Sun King and Earth Mother merry meet and merry part."

Sláine opened his eyes and saw the Goddess dissipating, her flesh returned to the steam that gave it substance. She held out a hand for him to follow her into the boiling waters of the Cú Roi.

Sláine followed her into the Cauldron.

He felt nothing as its searing waters closed around him.

"Do you swear as the sun is above the clouds of the earth so your soul shall be above the clouds of fear?"

"I swear fear shall roll dark beneath me."

"Do you swear to nurture the land, to care for her crop and feed your people?"

"I so swear," Sláine said, reaching into the water and raising his hand again, his fist clenched around a succulent slab of broiled meat. "Come to me, my people, eat the flesh of the Goddess so that her strength may be your strength! Eat!"

And one by one his people came to pay homage at the Cauldron's rim, as the heat boiled the Sun King's flesh raw, each receiving, chewing and swallowing a mouthful of the meat Sláine offered them. When the last had taken their fill, he sank beneath the rim into the still-boiling water. The heat brought out the internal engravings on the Cú Roi's walls. He had thought to see Avagddu or the faces of the Goddess; he had not thought to see the leering antlered visage of Carnun surrounded by his menagerie of animals. The sight of the Lord of the Beasts did not fill him with dread or foreboding, rather it reassured him for Carnun held in one hand the Earth Serpent, and no more potent symbol of the Goddess was there.

And her voice came to him: *only when you have overcome your fears will you be ready for what lies beyond them, my love, my husband, my king. I will be waiting for you beyond the water, but for now your people need you. Arise my love, arise.*

Coming up from beneath the water, Sláine knew with a certainty that just because his enemies worshipped the Horned God, their benediction did not make Carnun evil. There was an important distinction between the deity and his followers.

Sláine opened his eyes, hot water rolling down his cheeks and into his mouth as he gasped for breath.

"Arise," Cathbad echoed, holding out the feathered cloak of beams for Sláine to step into. The scolding water had cleansed his body of the woad tattoos. He held his arms wide, like wings as the druid laid the cloak about the warrior's shoulders, and with it a geas: "You are forbidden to listen to the swallows of Loch Swilly when the sun sets, drink the waters of Bo Nemridh between dawn and dark, eat the flesh of a hound or wear a cloak of many colours on the Heath of Lonrad; should any of these come to pass your geas will break and disaster will befall those you are sworn to protect, mark well your geas, Sun King of the Sessair!"

And his people greeted him with rapture: "Behold the raging storm! Behold the crimson blade! Behold the king!"

Above them the Morrigan's crows circled, thousands of black winged birds gathering to dispel the lowering clouds to reveal the sun in all of its glory, their caws louder than ten thousand men.

"He has brought the sun back to us!"

Fourteen
The Umasking

"SUN KING, EH? And there was me thinking they were going to boil you alive, gut you like a fish and stick your head on a spike. If I'd known they were going to fall at your feet and *worship* you I'd have insisted we came up here years ago."

"What do you want, dwarf?" Sláine sighed wearily. Already the events of the ritual had become a distant blur, buried beneath the fug of the tribal intoxicants and their heady narcotic rush. His brain throbbed. He lay on the bed he had once shared with Niamh, wondering where in the world she was now; and how he could bring her home to Murias, if she would even come. It felt like a betrayal, thinking of his earthly yearnings, but he knew somehow that it wasn't, that a man could love both spiritually and physically.

"We need to talk."

"Do we have to? Really?"

"It's important."

And so Sláine listened as Ukko confessed everything from his wanderings; what he overheard from outside the latrine pits; Megrim's killing of the old king; and his flight from the disquieting blind Balor with his twin blades so sharp they seemed to cut through both sun and shadow alike.

"But I just want to say it isn't as though I deliberately went looking for trouble, like you said I was quite happily keeping myself to myself, and then I saw the woman. It wasn't like I went looking for a traitor, oh no, not Ukko. You can rely on old Ukko to keep his head down, keep out of trouble."

"What *are* you blathering on about, dwarf?"

"It's her, Sláine, I saw her."

"Who?"

"Her. I don't know who but I *know* her, if that makes sense?"

"None whatsoever." But it did, because Sláine had recognised her without knowing who she was. He had looked into her face, seeing beneath the glamour of her skin, and known who she was without knowing her name. And then he realised the truth of her deception: "A glamour," he said, shaking his head slowly. "A simple lie cast upon her flesh by some hedge wizard. How can the man have been so blind?"

"Lust, love, need?" A voice came from behind them. It was a voice from the past, risen up like a welcome ghost. Sláine turned in his seat to see the grinning face of Fionn as his friend came into the old king's roundhouse. Tall Iesin stood in the doorway behind him. His friend had changed. Time on the road had worn the softness from his muscles and the innocent wonder from his face. The man he had grown into was handsome where the boy had been pretty like his mother. "We are happy to blind ourselves to the truth, my friend, especially when it suits our needs. Kilian Ragall lived in the shadows of so many great men, but never emerged from them, even when crowned Sun King. He was always second, behind Grudnew and Gorian and Calum and so many others. He was never his own man and always their shadow. Come on, for truth, tell me who would have ever imagined the child Sláine draped in the cloak of beams, wedded to the earth herself? Not I."

"Well met, Sláine," Tall Iesin bowed low. The storyteller had not aged a day since the last time Sláine had seen him almost a decade ago. It was uncanny. "There is wisdom in my apprentice's words, I feel. To be second always can be worse in many ways than being last. Few can bear to be so close to greatness yet never achieve it."

And here, with memories of childhood all around him, Sláine could not argue with either man. The grave of Cullen of the Wide Mouth was too close to home for that.

He rose from the bed and gripped Fionn in a fierce embrace. "I have missed you, my friend. The day seven became six still aches in my memory."

"And mine," Fionn agreed. "But for now at least we are home so let us enjoy that small miracle, shall we?"

"Leave us, Ukko. We will talk more about the traitor, but for now I would live in the past a while longer. Ask around for Dian, Núada, Cormac and Niall. People will remember our bonds, send them to join us. Tonight is for old friends to drink and reminisce."

"Fine well, whatever, Megrim's going off into the forests to contact His Weirdness. I shall *try* to keep out of mischief."

BUT HE DIDN'T try particularly hard.

Ukko left the long house with a scowl on his face. He sniffed the air as though able to scent the woman, Megrim, on it – and then he recalled Balor's blind eyes and sniffed his own fragrant armpits. If a hunter was going to be smelling anyone on the air it was him. He had tried to tell Sláine that the woman was a traitor, but the big dumb ox wouldn't listen. That was so typical of the man, wrapped up in his own sense of immortality. A knife in the gut had seen to Kilian Ragall, ending his life then and there, no glory, no ceremony. He wasn't welcomed back into the earth womb of his Goddess. His guts spilling out around his fists, his blood, his limbs convulsing even as he tried to crawl for help, unable to talk for the blinding agony of death, and from that agony the druid had foretold the next seven years of the Sessair. The dead man's blood fated Sláine to be their king. Well, Sláine's blood could just as easily fate some other fool stupid enough to be standing close-by as he died out.

He stalked off, looking up at the moon, a warrior's heart hanging with so much promise in the sky.

Just like he knew who she was but not *who* she was, he knew where she was going but not *where.* Drawing his rag-cloak furtively about his shoulders and his leather skull cap down to cover most of his protruding ears, the dwarf turned his back on the dubious comfort of the village lights and crept along the waterline of the river, the rush of the whitecaps in his ears. Sláine had filled his head with stories of Murias, so much so he felt almost comfortable with the geography of the place, seeing it now. The cold waters of the River Dôn with its whirling rapids and further from the source, its enormous waterfall, the thunderous crash, the foaming mist and the rainbows in the summer sky, all of them were things Sláine had waxed lyrical about as he meandered down memory lane. Beyond lay the plains of Airghialla, the great cairn itself, and in the other direction the shelter of the forest.

Ukko scanned the lie of the land, but saw no sign of the hooded Megrim, or her friend Balor. No telltale thickening of shadows or furtive moments of clumsy stealth. They were out there, though, of that the wily old dwarf was in no doubt.

He could smell the bitter and acrid tangs of the weave-and-dye houses, the heady yeast of the ale room, the reek of burning straw and tar from the torches shoved into the ground to light the way between houses and worn-out tracks, and hear the distant clang and bustle of the market coming down for the night. The men of the Sessair were out in numbers, the festivities wild as they celebrated the coming of the new king. At some point Sláine would emerge from the long house to walk among them, pressing the flesh, kissing wives and locking arms with the warriors. The celebrations would run deep into the night, making it perfect for Megrim's purposes. Who would miss the wife of the shamed king on a night like this? Indeed, they would almost certainly expect the widow to hide herself away with her grief so her absence was something they would expect.

Unlike so many of the Celtic settlements there was no defending wall, no ditch or ramparts, making it easy for Ukko to sneak along the curve of the riverbank and out of reach of the torchlight. It was arrogance on the Sessair's behalf, of course. If a city needed a wall to keep it safe it deserved to fall, so said Sláine. Sometimes the barbarian's reasoning beggared understanding.

The dwarf tried to recall any stories Sláine had told of sacred groves hidden in the trees, but all he could think of was his tale of endurance in the nemeton, which was not the kind of place Megrim would seek out to perform her ritual. No, it needed to be somewhere remote, and while dedicated to

Danu still serve as a receptacle for communion with Carnun. For a moment he considered Lug's Spike but it was too exposed, too remote. Nothing Sláine had ever spoken of struck the dwarf as suitable.

A part of him just wanted to turn around and go back into the settlement; some big-titted beauty would help him forget all about the sinister Megrim. Indeed the whole world could disappear to the els in a handcart – if his head was buried in a fulsome breast suckling away at a pair of ripe nipples he would neither notice nor care. And for a moment it was tempting, but for once the dwarf turned his back on temptation and went in search of trouble.

There was nothing for it, with one backward glance at the straw torches still burning brightly in the heart of Murias, promising so much on a night of festivities and drunken revelry, Ukko scurried off into the darker heart of the forest.

No more than one hundred nervous paces in, and the nameless wood was unnervingly like Dardun, the skeletal limbs of the trees denuded, moss clinging to the bark, eating away into it like the same sour canker that had undone the home of Myrrdin. He listened; there were no sounds, none of the usual nocturnal hints of life he expected from a wood, not the flit and leathery flutter of bat wings or the scratching of badgers rustling through the deadfall. All around the wood not a single creature stirred.

Ukko slumped down against a rotting tree trunk, his back to the moonlit side of the tree's bole, and closed his eyes.

And heard voices; as out of place in the silence of the forest as a maiden in a brothel.

Ukko scrambled to his feet, muttering about curiosity killing the rat, and moved closer, struggling to make out words where there were none. As he neared, the quality of the voices shifted; one separating from the other, taking on a deep, rich resonance while the other grew softer, more obviously feminine, two people deep in conversation. They drew him like a fly to dung, an ant to honey. He crept closer, edging through the undergrowth, ever-mindful of the deadfall and the mulch of fallen leaves, placing each foot with care until he could see her through the trees.

The moonlight smothered her nakedness as the woman slipped out of her hooded cloak and pulled her shift up over her head. Her body was lithe, muscular, almost boyish for its flatness, but definitely feminine around the swell of hips and thighs. He could not see Balor, but the blind warrior was almost certainly the second voice he had heard. Ukko craned forwards, trying to see past more of the trees, but his eyes were drawn back again and again to her nakedness as she began dancing in the moonlight, her voice rising in shrill ululations as she beseeched the moon and the dirt and the wood, calling forth Carnun, Lord of the Beasts. He lost sight of her through the trees as her dance propelled her to the far side of the grove. Ukko shuffled forwards, barely stifling a sharp intake of breath at sight of the moon-bathed silhouette of a crumbling ruin as it was gradually revealed by the forest.

It wasn't the presence of the temple, for temple it most assuredly was, that unnerved the dwarf; it was the repellent masonry, the hammer and chisels of so long ago crafting the likeness of the Wyrm God Crom-Cruach in the stone where he had expected the Earth Serpent, and alone on a crumbling section of wall, the antlered visage of the Horned God himself, Carnun. The sight of the emaciated deity engraved in stones so close to Murias sent a thrill of fear coursing through Ukko.

And then he saw the blind warrior, Balor, stripped also, hard, joined in the same dance; in the centre of his chest where his heart ought to have been was a huge poisoned eye, its lids thick with pus and fester. This demon was not Balor the Blind but Balor of the One Eye. And where the gaze of that one eye fell the deadfall withered, its decay accelerated by Balor's vile sight, corruption spreading out through the defiled glade like a contagion.

Megrim's dance took on a wild, primal quality, her limbs flailing in and out of the shadows, her voice shrieking, all coherence of word and movement banished as she opened the conduit between the Lord Weird and this unholy place. The total abandonment of the flesh was intensely erotic;

despite the thrill of fear coursing through his veins, Ukko found himself aroused, responding to the primal nature of her dance, his eyes drawn again and again to the thinness of her waist and the moonlight's ladder of shadows tracing the curvature of her spine to the thickness of her rump and the darkness between as she twisted and turned, giving herself utterly to the invocation.

Ukko fell to his knees, pressing his chest and chin close to the dead leaves, desperate to make himself invisible as the engraving of Carnun began to move, detaching itself from the stonework of the defiled temple.

"My Mebd, sweet sweet Mebd," the voice of Feg came from the stone, naming the naked woman, and though she wore the face of another, Ukko knew her, knew her eyes. The Bride of Crom, Mebd, the grateful sow Sláine had rescued from the inferno of the wickerman. "You called, daughter of the Babd? Are our schemes bountiful? I hunger for word of the Sun King's demise and the ruin of these damnable people."

The woman, Megrim, Mebd, fell to her knees, devotion writ bright across her moonlit face as she pulled at her hair, crawling forwards to kneel at the feet of the stone effigy come to life like some great colossus.

"Kilian Ragall is dead," she said, unable to look the statue in its mad eyes, "but our schemes are in ruins, my Lord Weird."

"I hear your words but they make no sense to my ears, the king is dead and yet our schemes have failed? How can this be so? The sour encroaches, their bellies are thin, their courage moreso. This place is ripe for plundering, no? Their fabled warriors have proved cowards, certainly no match for the viciousness of the skull swords, so how could you have failed me, daughter of the Babd? Tell me, Mebd, how could you have failed Him? How could you have disappointed your betrothed? How could you have failed Crom-Cruach, Mebd? Tell me, for I should know before I reach into you and tear your withered heart from your breast. Tell me!" the Lord Weird demanded, vitriol and insanity pouring out of his translocated mouth.

"It was Sláine," she whispered, barely daring to voice the name. "He emerged from the long house even as the enchantment drew the fool's blood to my feet, assuring my ascendancy. Ragall crawled on his belly, his own blade in his gut, but before their precious druid could proclaim the blood magic fate and secure me as queen, that wretched moron rushed to Ragall's side, his pity breaking my draw on the blood. We were undone by our own cleverness, my lord. The superstitious fools saw the blood twist towards Sláine and proclaimed him immediately their saviour."

"Oh how I loathe that name." Slough Feg's mellifluous sigh soured the grove, withering Ukko's resolve to hear more. The sudden urge to flee gripped him. He fought it stubbornly, his fingers digging into the dirt. "Who will rid me of this meddlesome wretch? You were so sure his own would turn on him, so sure."

"I was wrong, Lord Weird," the woman admitted, gaze downcast.

"I do not accept weakness nor failure lightly, Mebd. There must be retribution, a levelling. You have failed me in this, I have no use for those who fail."

"It will not happen again, my lord," she promised.

"It will not," Feg agreed, "for you would have to be breathing for it to repeat."

"No, please, Lord Weird, have mercy!"

"There is no place in the world for mercy, Mebd, you of all my faithful should be aware of that truth."

The woman lifted her head defiantly, rising from her knees slowly. The strength of will it must have required to go against the Slough priest was phenomenal, but muster it she did, meeting his vile stone eyes squarely. "So be it, I submit to your will, Lord Feg."

"Better," the Lord Weird crooned, savouring the dankness of the word in his stone mouth. "Tell me, daughter of the Babd, do they suspect your presence?"

Mebd shook her head, "No, to them I am the weeping widow of a weak man."

"Better still. Here is what I would have you do;seduce the warrior, you have ample charms. Do not allow him to resist. When he is yours, slit his throat in the marital bed, leave nothing to chance this time. Twice widowed to two kings, the tribesmen will welcome you as their queen. They are so desperate to worship the feminine, ignoring the strength of the masculine. That blindness shall be their undoing."

"There is another face I could wear, Lord Weird, one that would surely guarantee his seduction."

"Is that so, daughter of the Babd?"

"The woman, Niamh, stole his heart when they were young. His lust for her led to his banishment by the old king. I know her skin well enough to shape the glamour, that fool Ragall was obsessed with her so-called beauty. It would be no great feat to wrap the Warped One around my finger dressed in the guise of his childhood love."

"Then make it so, Mebd. I will brook no more disappointment. This land will fall, Mebd, for I am death's artist. I shall guide the living across the waters of oblivion, I shall stand in a field of corpses, staring down at eyes without life, plundered heads and sundered flesh. I shall revel in the death I have wrought, for I am tired, Mebd, so tired of this life. I would have release from twenty thousand years of torment at the bitch Goddess's whim, throwing her vengeance back in her face by destroying the one thing she truly loves – herself."

"It will be so, my Lord Weird, you have my word. Sláine Mac Roth will perish in my arms. It will be a slow and painful demise, one worthy of his perfidy."

Ukko had been so wrapped up in eavesdropping he had lost sight of Balor, allowing the warrior to work his way around behind him, skyclad, his vile eye wide open and blazing with hate. The sharp snap of a broken branch betrayed Balor's prowling. The blind warrior had worked his way through the trees and was already too close to Ukko's hiding place for comfort.

"Cowardice always was the better part of valour," Ukko mumbled, scrambling to his feet and taking off like a startled deer.

He had to warn Sláine.

The young king's life depended upon it – which meant, in turn, that *his* life depended upon it, and that was much more important to the ugly little dwarf.

Ukko didn't stop running until he was surrounded on all sides by drunks and burning straw beacons, the celebrations in full swing. Drunken hands mauled him, lifting him up, spinning him around in joyful dances frighteningly similar to Mebd's invocation, and equally uninhibited. On another night he would have enjoyed the stray hands, making a point of feeling his way through the women of Murias, but shame of shames, he only had eyes for Sláine.

He saw the king, deep in his cups, dancing a clumsy reel with a flaxen-haired matron, her face flushed and his ruddy. He saw the dwarf and grinned, obviously enjoying himself. Ukko wormed his way between the press of dancers, pushing between kicking legs and linked arms to Sláine's side. He tugged at Sláine's wrist urgently but the new king brushed him off. Having none of it, Ukko hit him, hard, in the side, then ducked beneath Sláine's swinging fist.

"The Bride of Crom is here," the dwarf hissed even as Sláine cuffed him around the side of the head and knocked him off his feet. "So much for regal gratitude," Ukko muttered bleakly, rubbing at his jaw, the purple bruise already rising to the surface. "But you know, maybe they got all this Defiler stuff wrong. Maybe it has something to do with virgins, or better yet, sheep."

On the fringe of the crowd, Ukko saw Mebd watching him intently. Beside her stood the blind warrior, Balor, his evil eye hidden once more by clothing.

Unable to leave the safety of the dance, Ukko linked hands with the first woman he saw and threw himself into the reel, working his way, wench to matron to maiden, through the press of bodies until he came out on the other side.

He had warned Sláine, now he had to look after himself, and the best place to hide was right here in plain sight for the time being. Mebd couldn't touch him when he was surrounded by people. When Sláine had drunk and danced his fill he would drive the witch out of Murias. For now all Ukko could do was try to enjoy himself.

A giggling daughter of Danu blew him a playful kiss across the heads of the revellers. She cupped her ample breasts suggestively, and inclined her head.

Perhaps, he thought to himself, catching it, *I won't have to try too hard.*

Epilogue
The Morrigan's Promise

SLÁINE DID NOT sleep well during his first night as king.

The Morrigan came to him in his dreams.

"Greetings, Sun King."

"Is this real?" Sláine asked, staring into her feathered face.

"As much as anything ever is, Sessair."

"What are you doing inside my head, Crone?"

"Oh how short the memories of mortals are. I have come to collect my promise, Sun King. Walk with me through the dreams of your people, Sun King."

"This is the promise you would have me keep?"

"No, this is something you must do."

He took her feathered hand and followed as she led him through the deserted streets of Murias to the dying trees of the forest, and into the defiled temple of Crom-Cruach. As he stood before the ruin, the quality of the light shifted and gradually the dissolution was reversed, the temple returning to its lost glory. The carvings of the Wyrm God sank back into the stone, replaced by images of Danu.

"Behold the great Sun King," the Crone cawed, a feathered talon thrust towards the antlered figure pacing back and forth through the sacred grove. Sláine knew the man instinctively; it was Slough Feg, crowned in the antlered headdress of Carnun, Horned God, the cloak of beams wrapped around his powerful shoulders. This Feg is not the withered caricature of humanity that so defiled the body of Danu. He is a tall vibrant man, a great Sun King, noble and proud, not unlike Sláine himself. "Yes," the Crone said, as though reading his mind, "he was once like you, wed to my sister Goddess, leader of men, but he loved life more than he ever loved Blodeuwedd. That was his vanity and vanity was his failing."

"What is this promise, Morrigan? Would you have me return to this time to slay him before he becomes the evil he is today? I can do that. I can deliver wounds that will not whiten if that is what you desire."

"Oh, no, Sláine," the Crone came around to stand before him, "I would have you promise something far more difficult. I would have you return him to his one true love, your wife, my sister. I would have this once great man whole again. And more, I would have you rise up in his stead to replace him. That is the promise you gave me, Sláine, that you shall take on the antlers of the Horned God and save this wretched soul!"

"You would have me become my enemy?" said Sláine, knowing even as he said it that he was bound by his blind promise. "That is no promise, Crone, that is a curse."

Glossary

CARNUN – The Horned God, Lord of the Beasts.

CROM-CRUACH – The Worm God, Lord of the Mounds. Worshipped by the Southern tribes.

DANU – The Earth Goddess.

DRUIDS – Priests of the Northern tribes.

DRUNE LORDS – Evil Priest-Kings of the Southern tribes.

EARTH POWER – The spiral force that runs through the Weird Stones (Megaliths). It can be used for good or evil. Also known as The Earth Serpent.

HALF-DEAD – Warriors killed but trapped between the worlds.

HERO-HARNESS – Worn by warped warriors, so their clothes don't rip during the spasm.

LUG – The Sun God. The Sun and Earth are worshipped by the Northern tribes.

OGHAMS – Early form of writing. Also a sign language.

RED BRANCH – Sláine's tribe's greatest warriors.

SALMON-LEAP – Jumping your own height. A Sessair battle-skill – like shield-jumping and spear-catching.

SKULL SWORDS – Drune soldiers.

SLOUGH – Drune leader who has shed (sloughed) his skin.

SOURLAND – Land warped by sorcery.

THE LORD WEIRD SLOUGH FEG – Supreme Drune, thousands of years old.

TIR-NAN-OG – The Land of the Young.

TRIBES OF THE EARTH GODDESS – The legendary Northern tribes, including the Sessair.

WARP-SPASM – A strange and terrifying battle-frenzy, much worse than a berserker fury. Caused by Earth Power, which some warriors can warp through their bodies.

ABOUT THE AUTHOR

British author **Steven Savile** is an expert in cult fiction, having written a wide variety of SF (including *Star Wars* and *Jurassic Park*), fantasy and horror stories, as well as a slew of editorial work on anthologies in the UK and USA. He won the L Ron Hubbard Writers of the Future award in 2002, was runner-up in the British Fantasy Award in 2000 and has been nominated three times for the Bram Stoker Award. He currently lives in Stockholm, Sweden.